[redacted]

my LITTLE PONY

Friendship is Magic

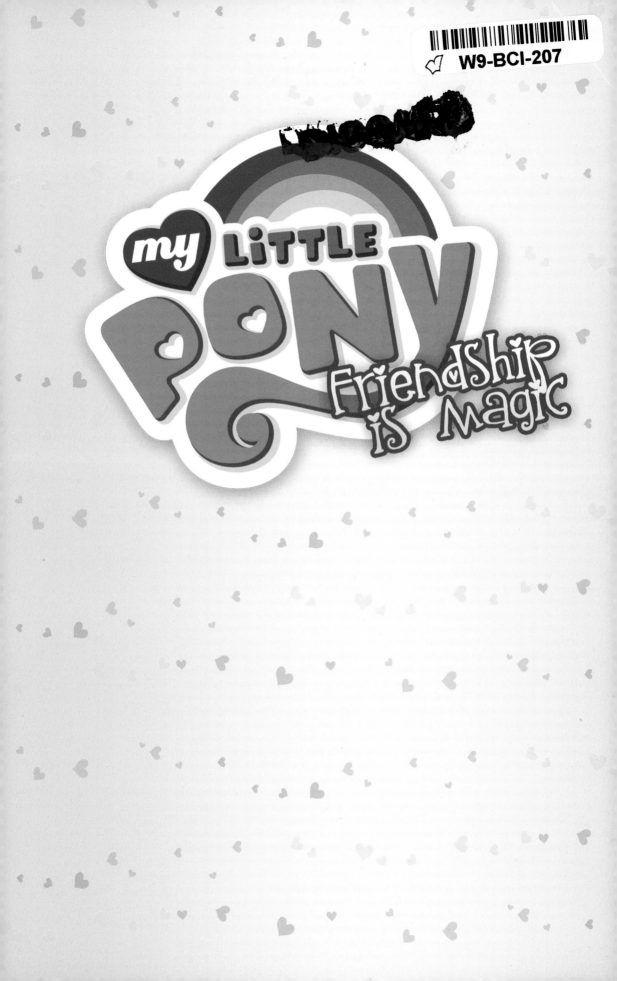

MY LITTLE PONY
FRIENDSHIP IS MAGIC

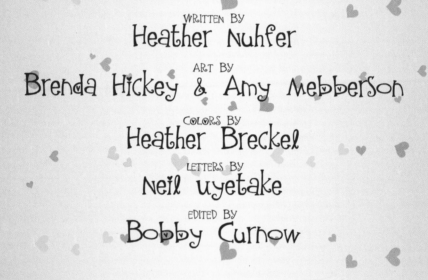

WRITTEN BY
Heather Nuhfer

ART BY
Brenda Hickey & Amy Mebberson

COLORS BY
Heather Breckel

LETTERS BY
Neil Uyetake

EDITED BY
Bobby Curnow

COVER BY
Brenda Hickey

COLLECTION EDITS BY
Justin Eisinger & Alonzo Simon

COLLECTION DESIGN BY
Neil Uyetake

For international rights, contact **licensing@idwpublishing.com**

Special thanks to Erin Comella, Robert Fewkes, Joe Furfaro, Heather Hopkins, Pat Jarret, Ed Lane, Brian Lenard, Marissa Mansolillo, Donna Tobin, Michael Vogel, and Michael Kelly for their invaluable assistance.

ISBN: 978-1-61377-960-6

20 19 18 17 5 6 7 8

IDW

www.IDWPUBLISHING.com

Licensed By: Hasbro

Ted Adams, CEO & Publisher • **Greg Goldstein**, President & COO • **Robbie Robbins**, EVP/Sr. Graphic Artist • **Chris Ryall**, Chief Creative Officer • **David Hedgecock**, Editor-in-Chief • **Laurie Windrow**, Senior Vice President of Sales & Marketing • **Matthew Ruzicka**, CPA, Chief Financial Officer • **Lorelei Bunjes**, VP of Digital Services • **Jerry Bennington**, VP of New Product Development

Facebook: **facebook.com/idwpublishing** • Twitter: **@idwpublishing** • YouTube: **youtube.com/idwpublishing**
Tumblr: **tumblr.idwpublishing.com** • Instagram: **instagram.com/idwpublishing**

Originally published as MY LITTLE PONY: FRIENDSHIP IS MAGIC issues #13–16.

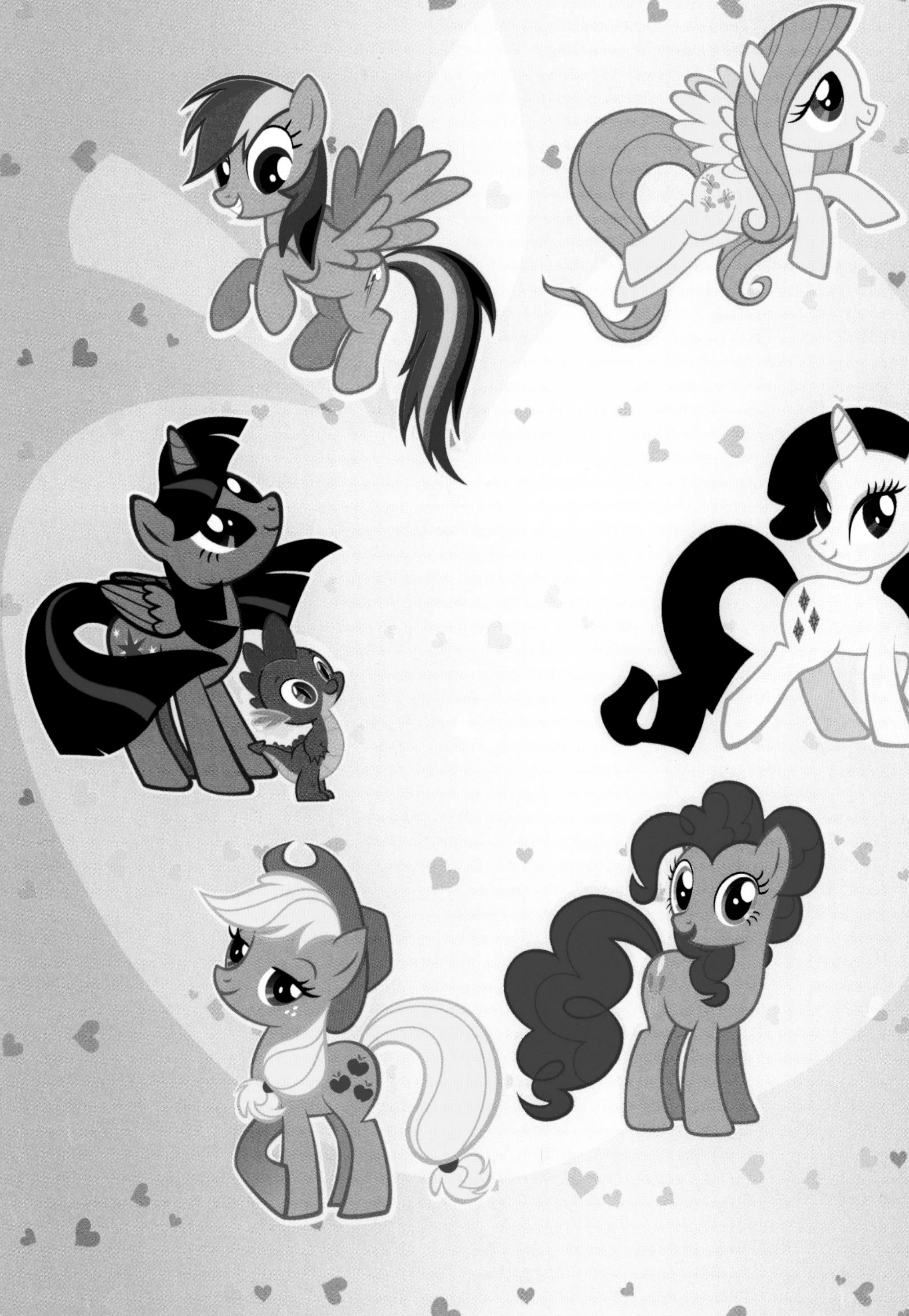

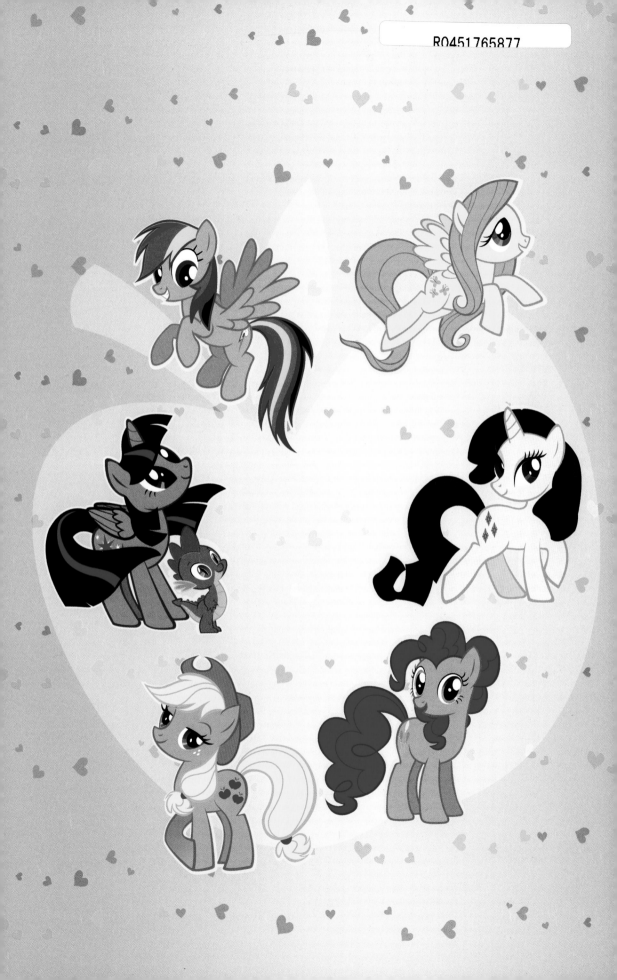

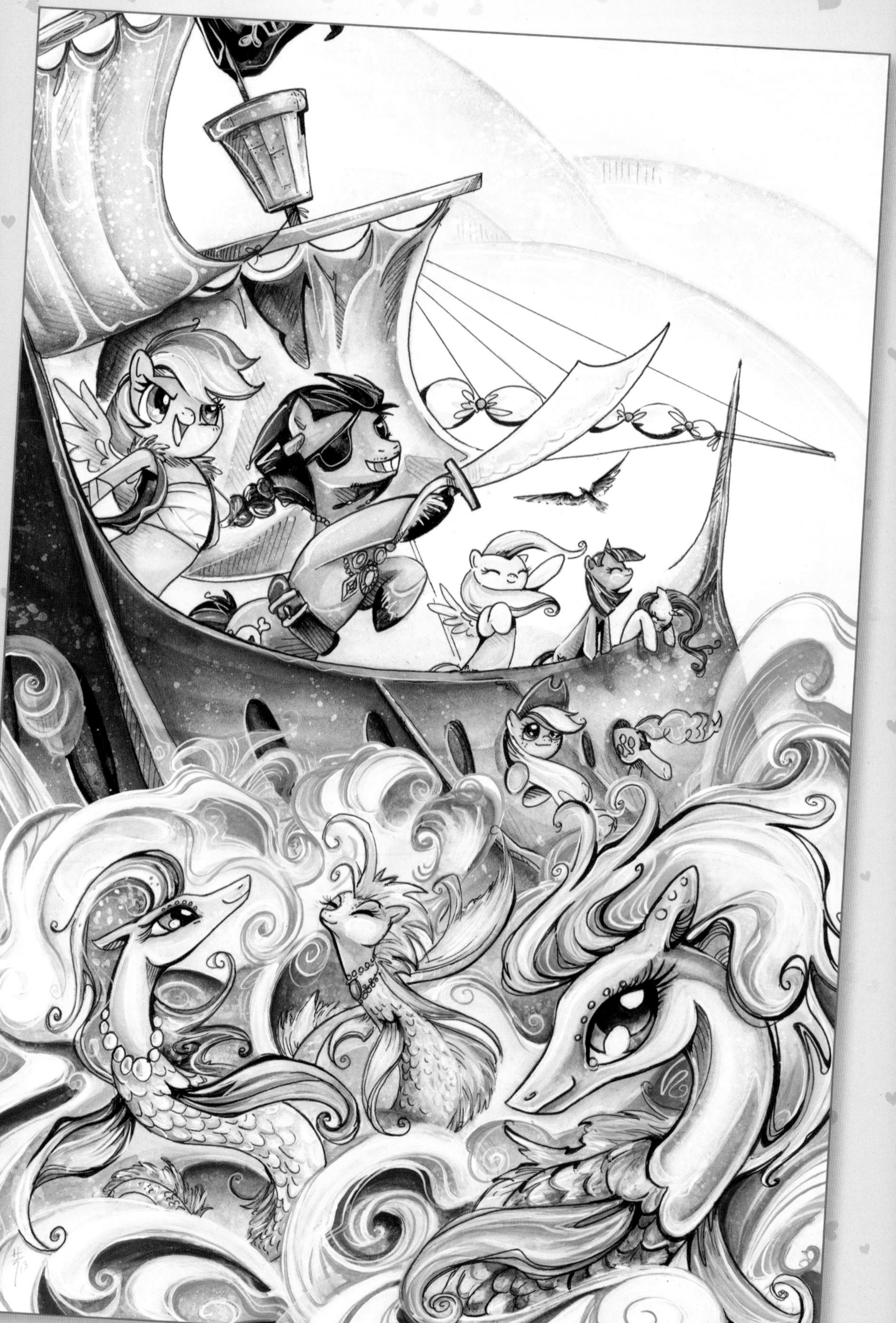

art BY Sara Richard

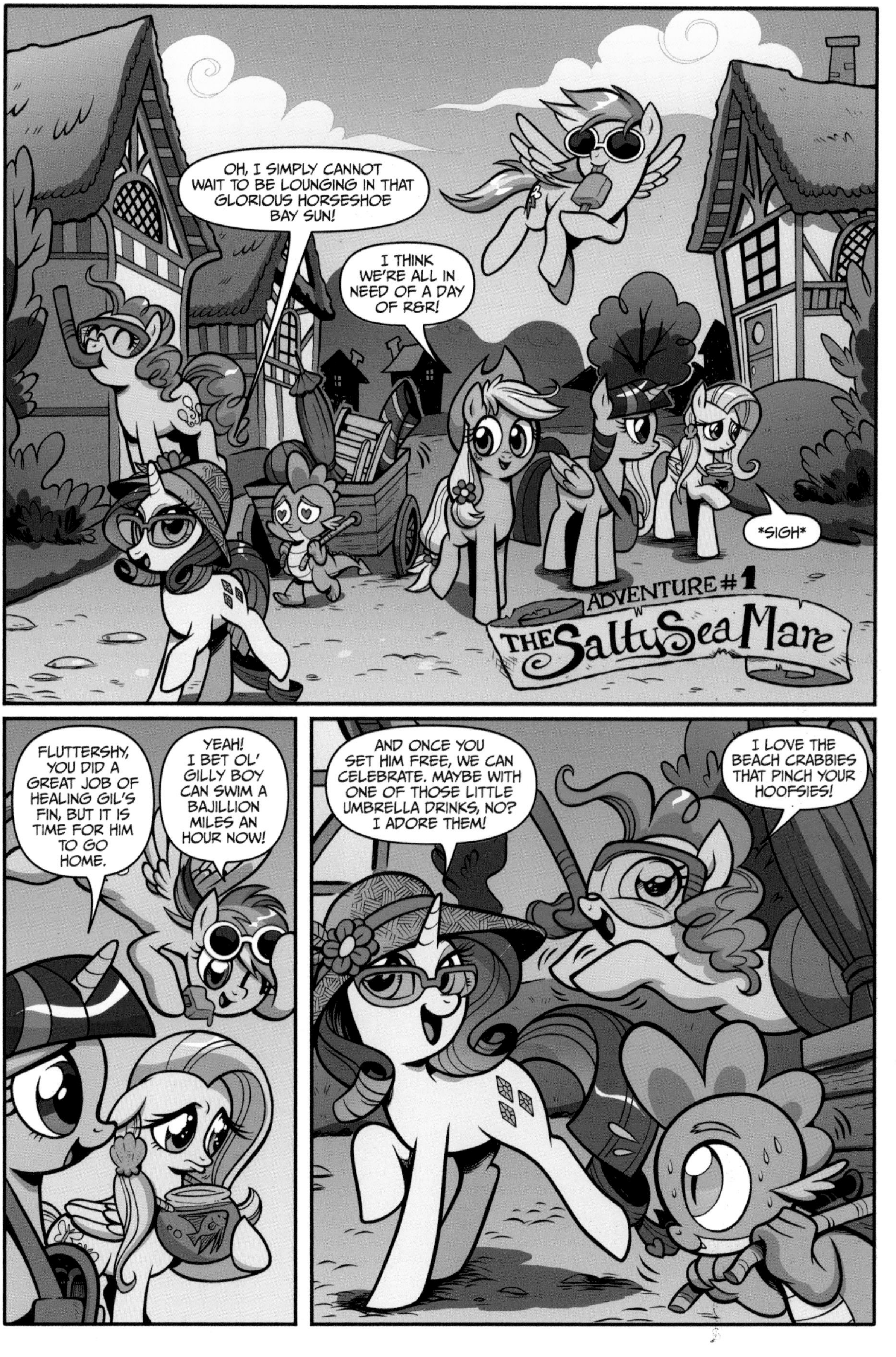
OH, I SIMPLY CANNOT WAIT TO BE LOUNGING IN THAT GLORIOUS HORSESHOE BAY SUN!
I THINK WE'RE ALL IN NEED OF A DAY OF R&R!
SIGH
ADVENTURE #1
THE Salty Sea Mare
FLUTTERSHY, YOU DID A GREAT JOB OF HEALING GIL'S FIN, BUT IT IS TIME FOR HIM TO GO HOME.
YEAH! I BET OL' GILLY BOY CAN SWIM A BAJILLION MILES AN HOUR NOW!
AND ONCE YOU SET HIM FREE, WE CAN CELEBRATE. MAYBE WITH ONE OF THOSE LITTLE UMBRELLA DRINKS, NO? I ADORE THEM!
I LOVE THE BEACH CRABBIES THAT PINCH YOUR HOOFSIES!

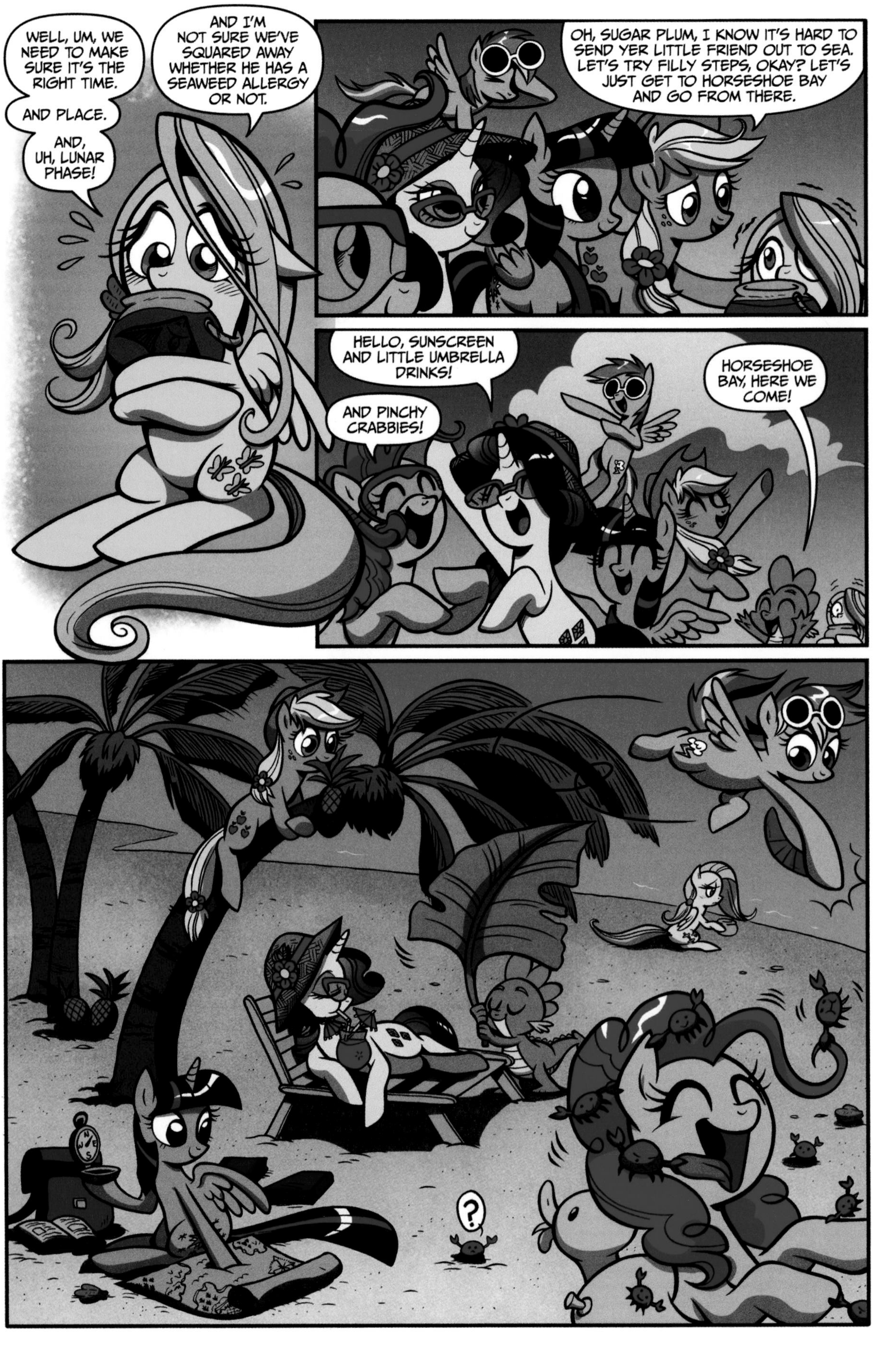

WELL, UM, WE NEED TO MAKE SURE IT'S THE RIGHT TIME.
AND PLACE.
AND, UH, LUNAR PHASE!
AND I'M NOT SURE WE'VE SQUARED AWAY WHETHER HE HAS A SEAWEED ALLERGY OR NOT.
OH, SUGAR PLUM, I KNOW IT'S HARD TO SEND YER LITTLE FRIEND OUT TO SEA. LET'S TRY FILLY STEPS, OKAY? LET'S JUST GET TO HORSESHOE BAY AND GO FROM THERE.
HELLO, SUNSCREEN AND LITTLE UMBRELLA DRINKS!
AND PINCHY CRABBIES!
HORSESHOE BAY, HERE WE COME!
?

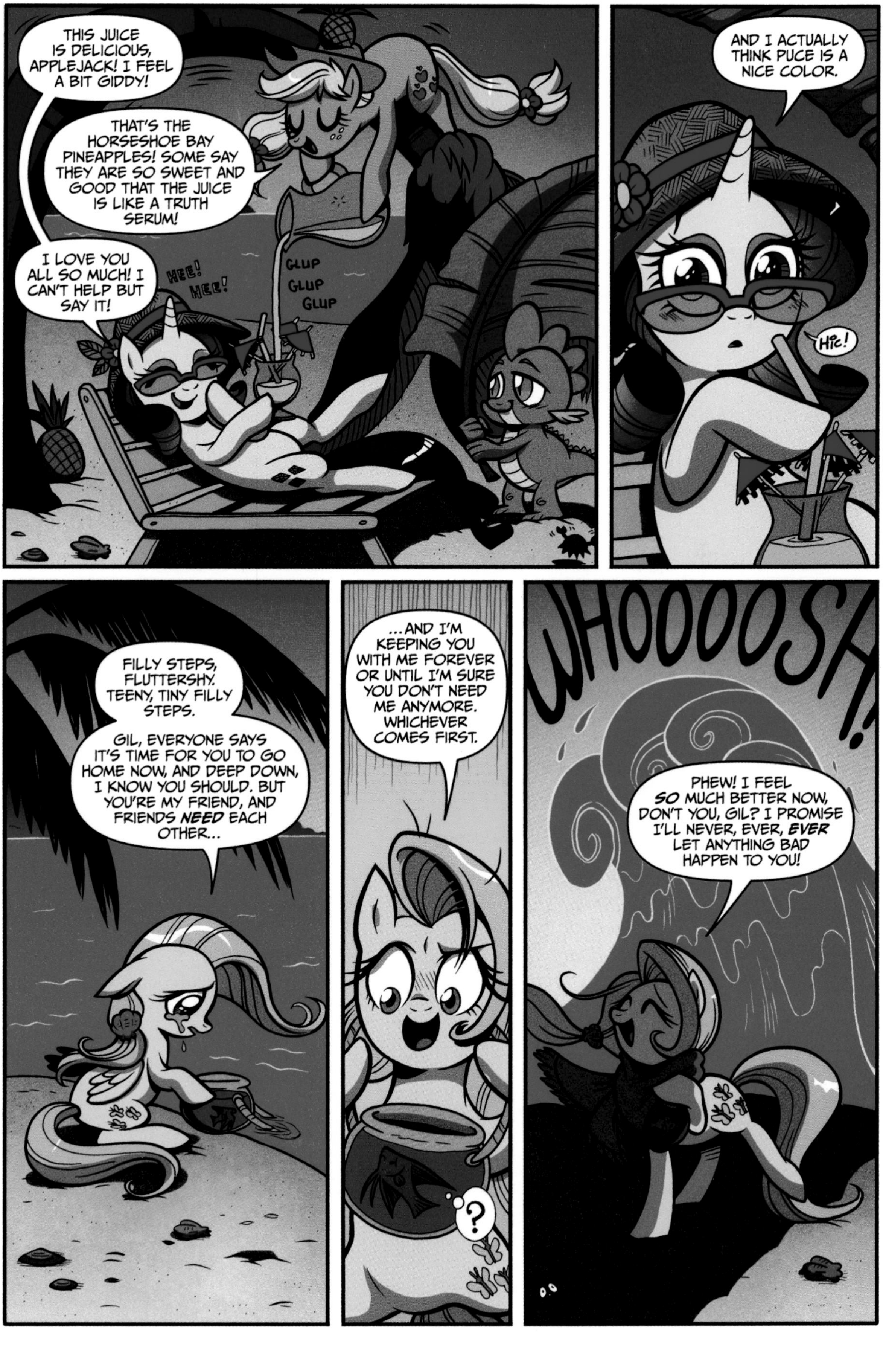
THIS JUICE IS DELICIOUS, APPLEJACK! I FEEL A BIT GIDDY!
THAT'S THE HORSESHOE BAY PINEAPPLES! SOME SAY THEY ARE SO SWEET AND GOOD THAT THE JUICE IS LIKE A TRUTH SERUM!
I LOVE YOU ALL SO MUCH! I CAN'T HELP BUT SAY IT!
HEE! HEE!
GLUP GLUP GLUP
AND I ACTUALLY THINK PUCE IS A NICE COLOR.
Hic!
FILLY STEPS, FLUTTERSHY. TEENY, TINY FILLY STEPS.
GIL, EVERYONE SAYS IT'S TIME FOR YOU TO GO HOME NOW, AND DEEP DOWN, I KNOW YOU SHOULD. BUT YOU'RE MY FRIEND, AND FRIENDS ***NEED*** EACH OTHER...
...AND I'M KEEPING YOU WITH ME FOREVER OR UNTIL I'M SURE YOU DON'T NEED ME ANYMORE. WHICHEVER COMES FIRST.
?
WHOOOOSH!!
PHEW! I FEEL ***SO*** MUCH BETTER NOW, DON'T YOU, GIL? I PROMISE I'LL NEVER, EVER, ***EVER*** LET ANYTHING BAD HAPPEN TO YOU!

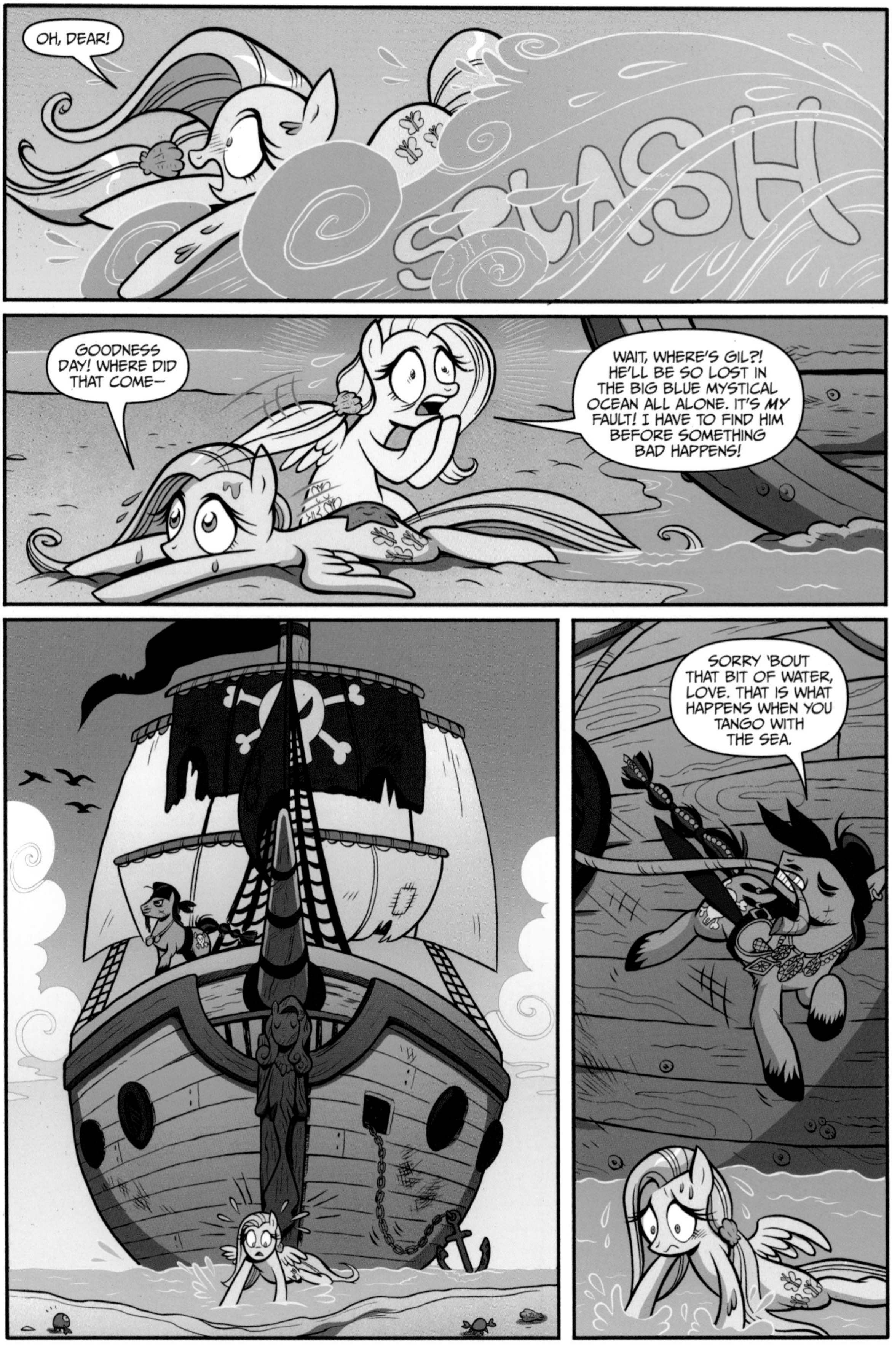
OH, DEAR!
SPLASH
GOODNESS DAY! WHERE DID THAT COME—
WAIT, WHERE'S GIL?! HE'LL BE SO LOST IN THE BIG BLUE MYSTICAL OCEAN ALL ALONE. IT'S *MY* FAULT! I HAVE TO FIND HIM BEFORE SOMETHING BAD HAPPENS!
SORRY 'BOUT THAT BIT OF WATER, LOVE. THAT IS WHAT HAPPENS WHEN YOU TANGO WITH THE SEA.

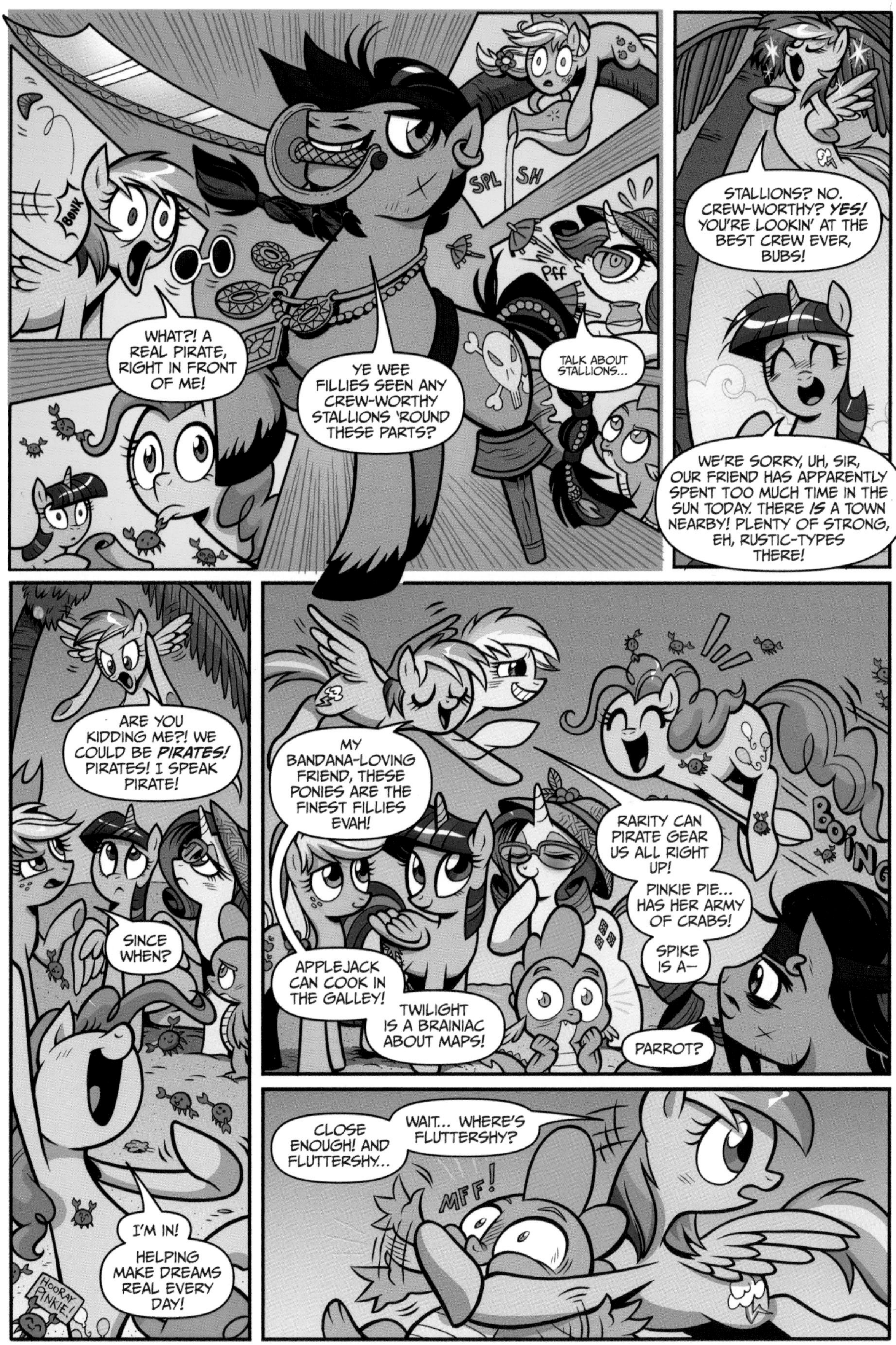

BONK
WHAT?! A REAL PIRATE, RIGHT IN FRONT OF ME!
YE WEE FILLIES SEEN ANY CREW-WORTHY STALLIONS 'ROUND THESE PARTS?
SPLSH
Pff
TALK ABOUT STALLIONS...
STALLIONS? NO. CREW-WORTHY? YES! YOU'RE LOOKIN' AT THE BEST CREW EVER, BUBS!
WE'RE SORRY, UH, SIR, OUR FRIEND HAS APPARENTLY SPENT TOO MUCH TIME IN THE SUN TODAY. THERE IS A TOWN NEARBY! PLENTY OF STRONG, EH, RUSTIC-TYPES THERE!
ARE YOU KIDDING ME?! WE COULD BE PIRATES! PIRATES! I SPEAK PIRATE!
SINCE WHEN?
I'M IN!
HELPING MAKE DREAMS REAL EVERY DAY!
HOORAY PINKIE!
MY BANDANA-LOVING FRIEND, THESE PONIES ARE THE FINEST FILLIES EVAH!
RARITY CAN PIRATE GEAR US ALL RIGHT UP!
PINKIE PIE... HAS HER ARMY OF CRABS!
BOING
SPIKE IS A—
APPLEJACK CAN COOK IN THE GALLEY!
TWILIGHT IS A BRAINIAC ABOUT MAPS!
PARROT?
CLOSE ENOUGH! AND FLUTTERSHY...
WAIT... WHERE'S FLUTTERSHY?
MFF!

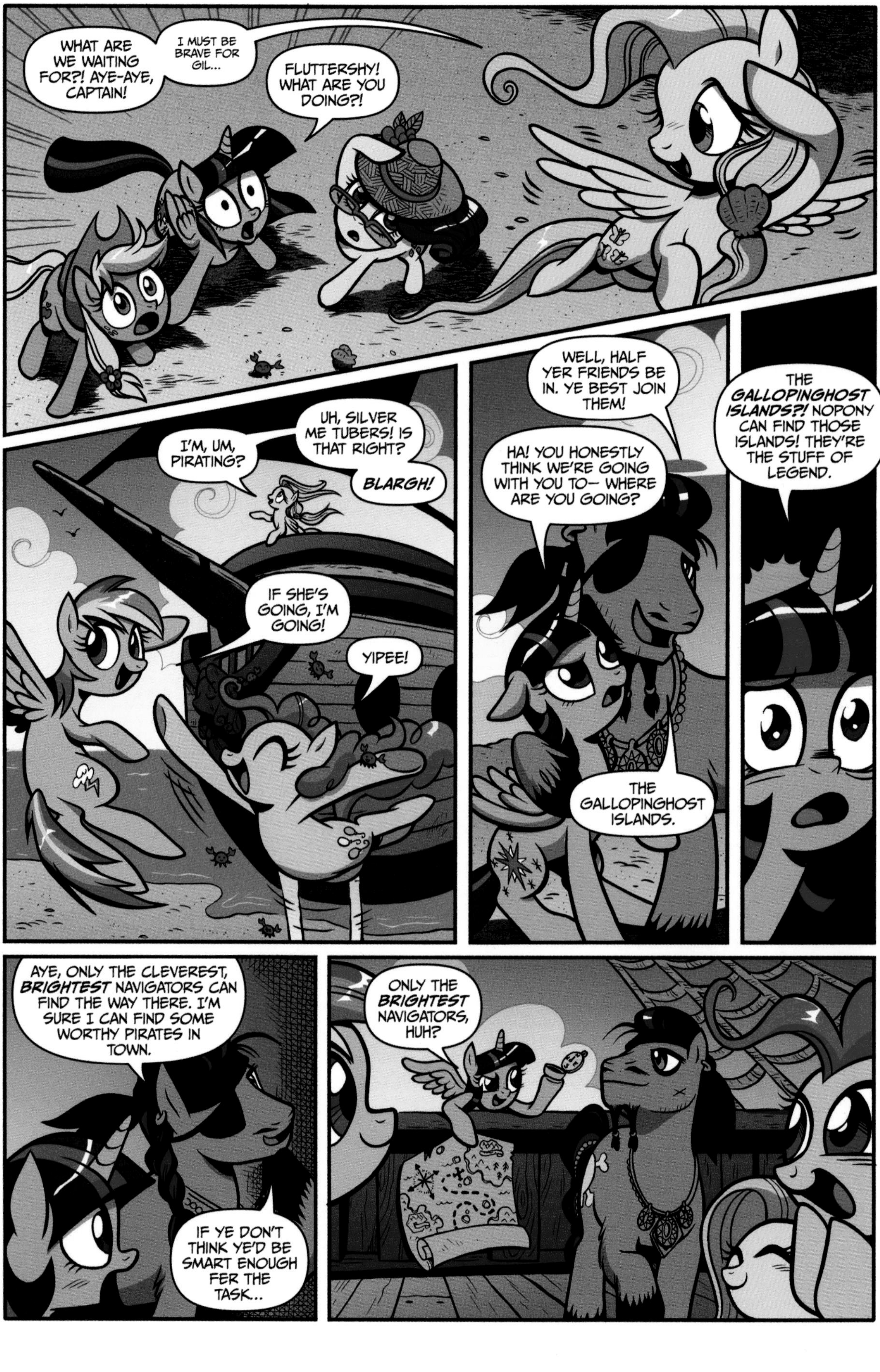
WHAT ARE WE WAITING FOR?! AYE-AYE, CAPTAIN!
I MUST BE BRAVE FOR GIL...
FLUTTERSHY! WHAT ARE YOU DOING?!
I'M, UM, PIRATING?
UH, SILVER ME TUBERS! IS THAT RIGHT?
BLARGH!
IF SHE'S GOING, I'M GOING!
YIPEE!
WELL, HALF YER FRIENDS BE IN. YE BEST JOIN THEM!
HA! YOU HONESTLY THINK WE'RE GOING WITH YOU TO— WHERE ARE YOU GOING?
THE GALLOPINGHOST ISLANDS.
THE GALLOPINGHOST ISLANDS?! NOPONY CAN FIND THOSE ISLANDS! THEY'RE THE STUFF OF LEGEND.
AYE, ONLY THE CLEVEREST, BRIGHTEST NAVIGATORS CAN FIND THE WAY THERE. I'M SURE I CAN FIND SOME WORTHY PIRATES IN TOWN.
IF YE DON'T THINK YE'D BE SMART ENOUGH FER THE TASK...
ONLY THE BRIGHTEST NAVIGATORS, HUH?

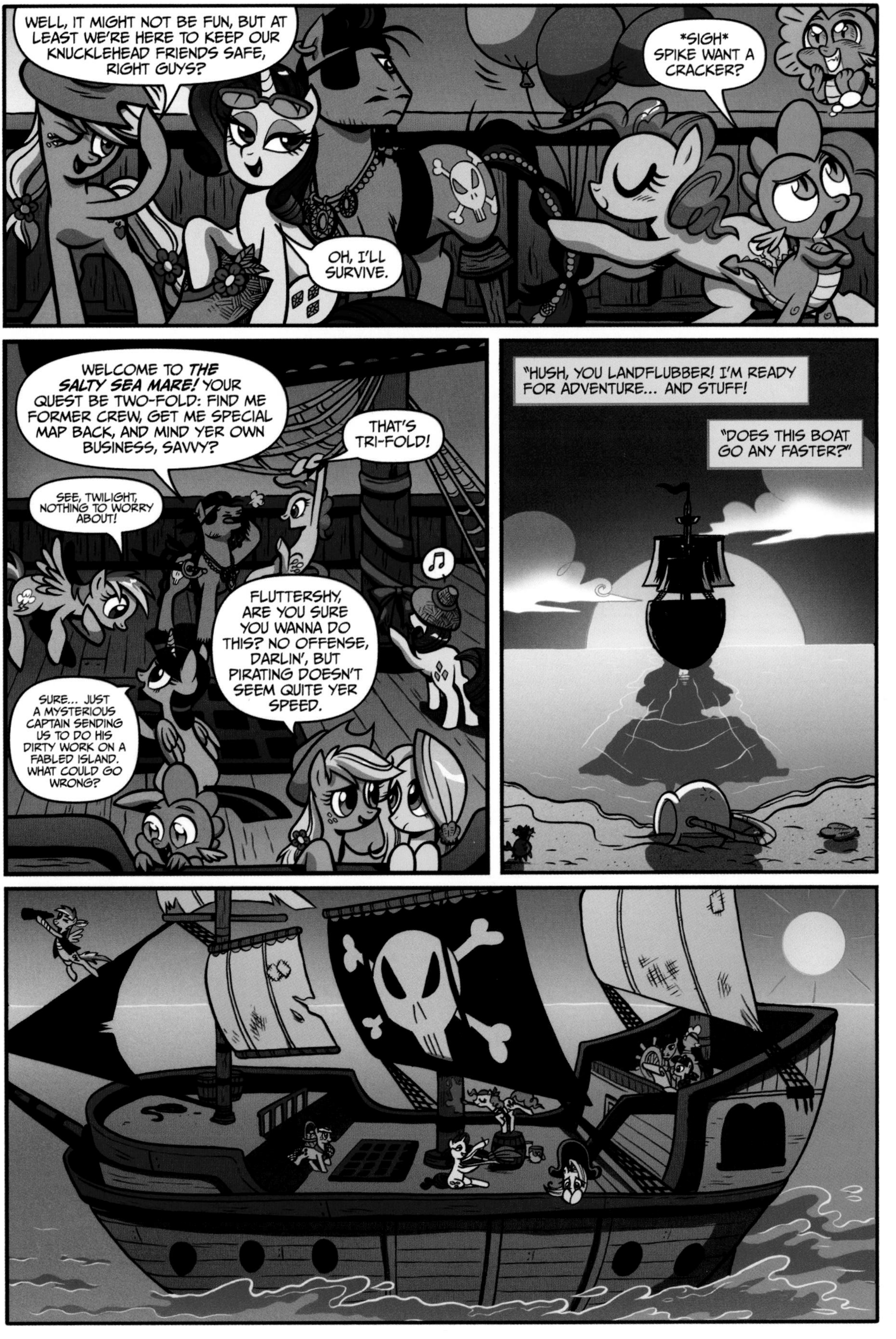
WELL, IT MIGHT NOT BE FUN, BUT AT LEAST WE'RE HERE TO KEEP OUR KNUCKLEHEAD FRIENDS SAFE, RIGHT GUYS?
OH, I'LL SURVIVE.
SIGH SPIKE WANT A CRACKER?
WELCOME TO THE SALTY SEA MARE! YOUR QUEST BE TWO-FOLD: FIND ME FORMER CREW, GET ME SPECIAL MAP BACK, AND MIND YER OWN BUSINESS, SAVVY?
THAT'S TRI-FOLD!
SEE, TWILIGHT, NOTHING TO WORRY ABOUT!
FLUTTERSHY, ARE YOU SURE YOU WANNA DO THIS? NO OFFENSE, DARLIN', BUT PIRATING DOESN'T SEEM QUITE YER SPEED.
SURE... JUST A MYSTERIOUS CAPTAIN SENDING US TO DO HIS DIRTY WORK ON A FABLED ISLAND. WHAT COULD GO WRONG?
"HUSH, YOU LANDFLUBBER! I'M READY FOR ADVENTURE... AND STUFF!
"DOES THIS BOAT GO ANY FASTER?"

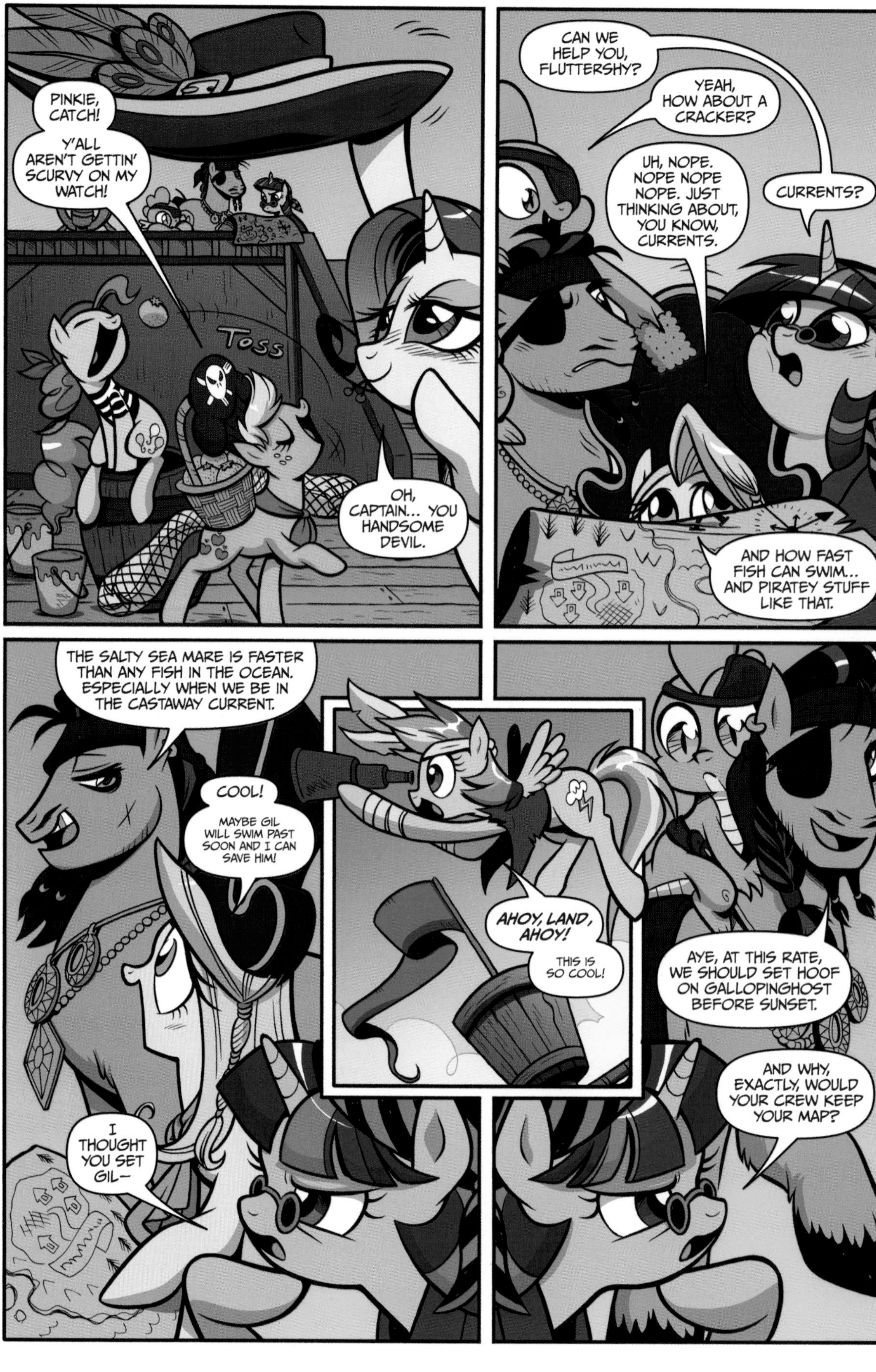
PINKIE, CATCH!
Y'ALL AREN'T GETTIN' SCURVY ON MY WATCH!
TOSS
OH, CAPTAIN... YOU HANDSOME DEVIL.
CAN WE HELP YOU, FLUTTERSHY?
YEAH, HOW ABOUT A CRACKER?
UH, NOPE. NOPE NOPE NOPE. JUST THINKING ABOUT, YOU KNOW, CURRENTS.
CURRENTS?
AND HOW FAST FISH CAN SWIM... AND PIRATEY STUFF LIKE THAT.
THE SALTY SEA MARE IS FASTER THAN ANY FISH IN THE OCEAN. ESPECIALLY WHEN WE BE IN THE CASTAWAY CURRENT.
COOL!
MAYBE GIL WILL SWIM PAST SOON AND I CAN SAVE HIM!
I THOUGHT YOU SET GIL—
AHOY, LAND, AHOY!
THIS IS SO COOL!
AYE, AT THIS RATE, WE SHOULD SET HOOF ON GALLOPINGHOST BEFORE SUNSET.
AND WHY, EXACTLY, WOULD YOUR CREW KEEP YOUR MAP?

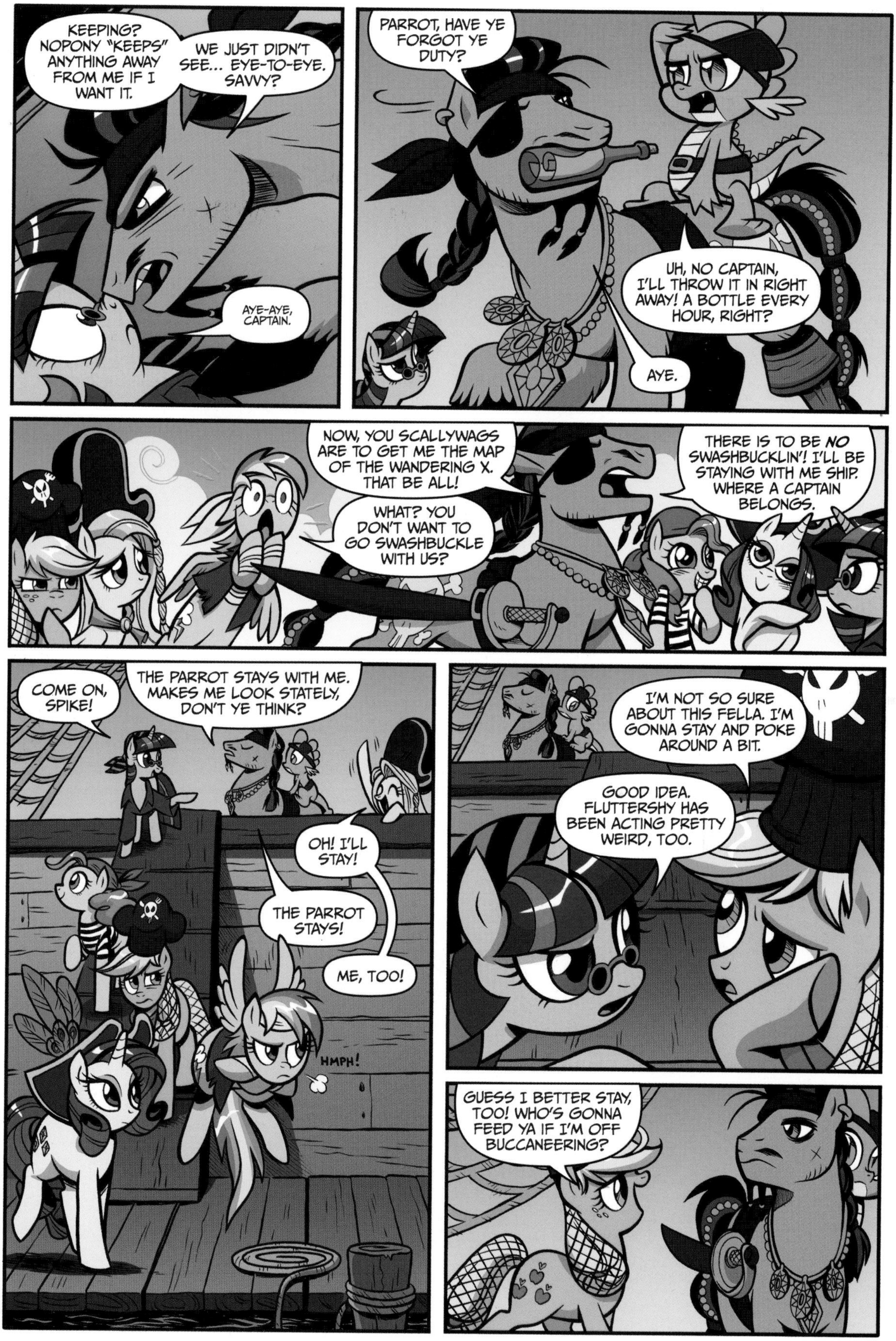
KEEPING? NOPONY "KEEPS" ANYTHING AWAY FROM ME IF I WANT IT.
WE JUST DIDN'T SEE... EYE-TO-EYE. SAVVY?
AYE-AYE, CAPTAIN.
PARROT, HAVE YE FORGOT YE DUTY?
UH, NO CAPTAIN, I'LL THROW IT IN RIGHT AWAY! A BOTTLE EVERY HOUR, RIGHT?
AYE.
NOW, YOU SCALLYWAGS ARE TO GET ME THE MAP OF THE WANDERING X. THAT BE ALL!
WHAT? YOU DON'T WANT TO GO SWASHBUCKLE WITH US?
THERE IS TO BE NO SWASHBUCKLIN'! I'LL BE STAYING WITH ME SHIP. WHERE A CAPTAIN BELONGS.
COME ON, SPIKE!
THE PARROT STAYS WITH ME. MAKES ME LOOK STATELY, DON'T YE THINK?
OH! I'LL STAY!
THE PARROT STAYS!
ME, TOO!
HMPH!
I'M NOT SO SURE ABOUT THIS FELLA. I'M GONNA STAY AND POKE AROUND A BIT.
GOOD IDEA. FLUTTERSHY HAS BEEN ACTING PRETTY WEIRD, TOO.
GUESS I BETTER STAY, TOO! WHO'S GONNA FEED YA IF I'M OFF BUCCANEERING?

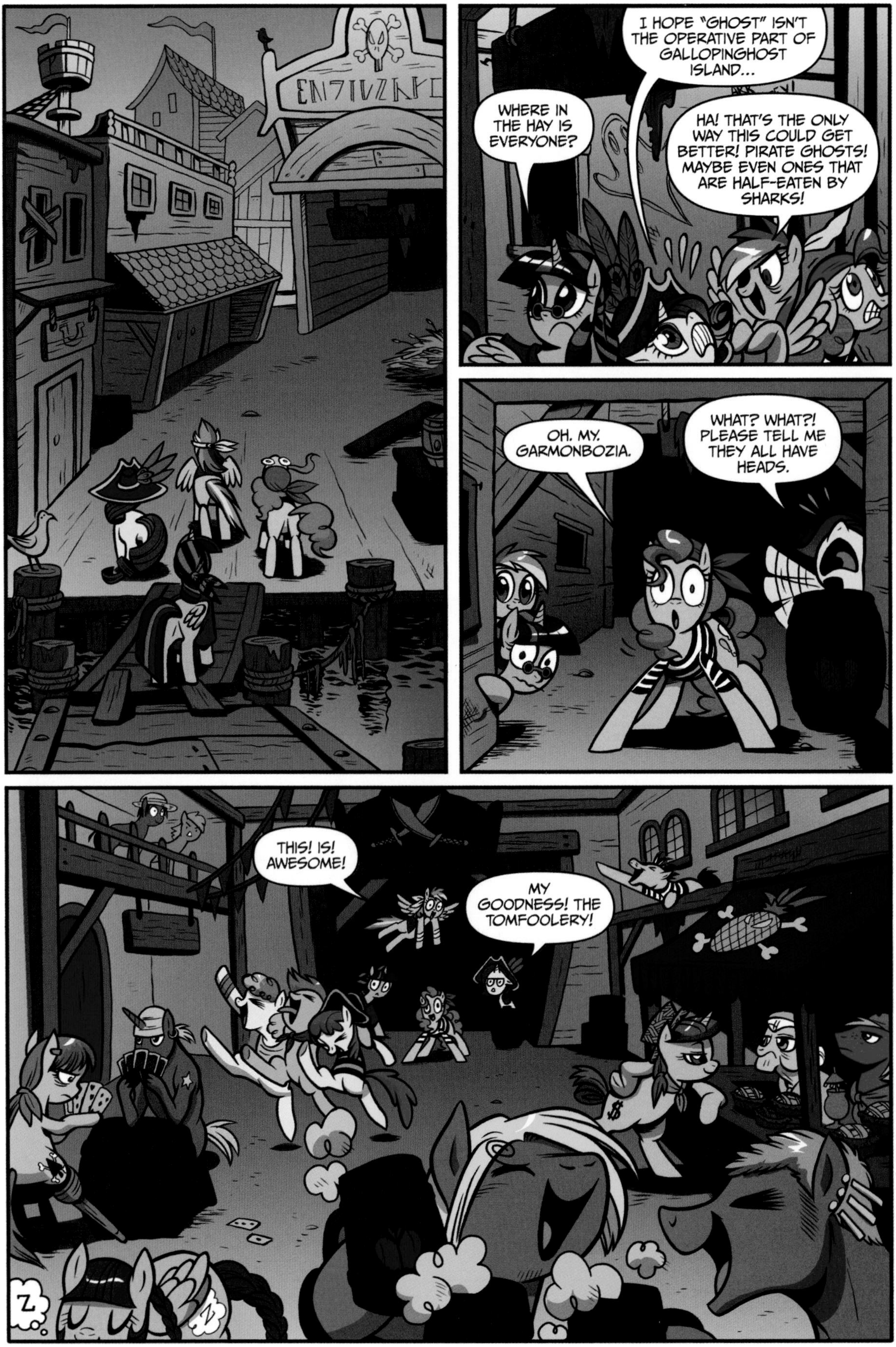

WHERE IN THE HAY IS EVERYONE?
I HOPE "GHOST" ISN'T THE OPERATIVE PART OF GALLOPINGHOST ISLAND...
HA! THAT'S THE ONLY WAY THIS COULD GET BETTER! PIRATE GHOSTS! MAYBE EVEN ONES THAT ARE HALF-EATEN BY SHARKS!
OH. MY. GARMONBOZIA.
WHAT? WHAT?! PLEASE TELL ME THEY ALL HAVE HEADS.
THIS! IS! AWESOME!
MY GOODNESS! THE TOMFOOLERY!
Z

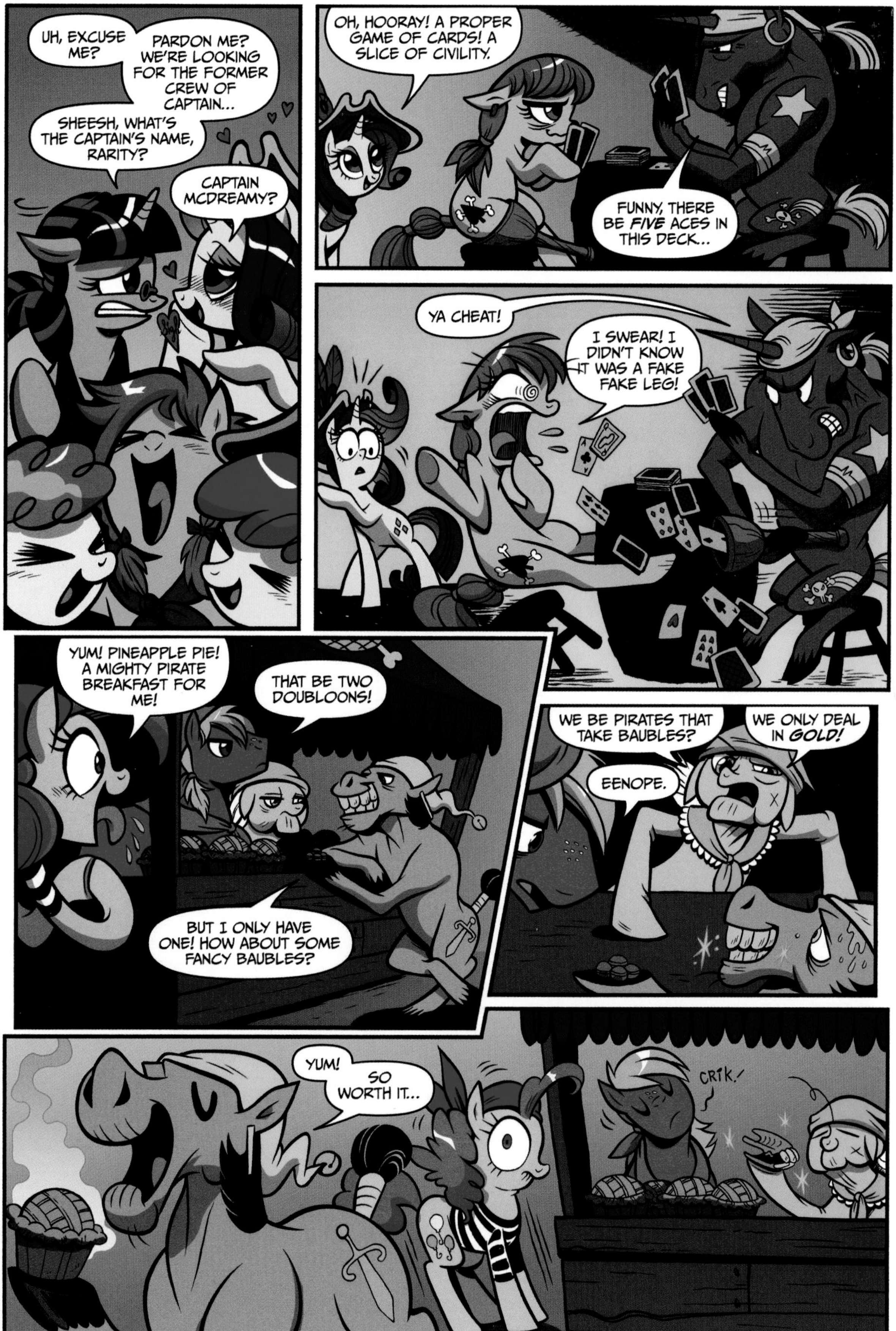
UH, EXCUSE ME?
PARDON ME? WE'RE LOOKING FOR THE FORMER CREW OF CAPTAIN...
SHEESH, WHAT'S THE CAPTAIN'S NAME, RARITY?
CAPTAIN MCDREAMY?
OH, HOORAY! A PROPER GAME OF CARDS! A SLICE OF CIVILITY.
FUNNY, THERE BE *FIVE* ACES IN THIS DECK...
YA CHEAT!
I SWEAR! I DIDN'T KNOW IT WAS A FAKE FAKE LEG!
YUM! PINEAPPLE PIE! A MIGHTY PIRATE BREAKFAST FOR ME!
THAT BE TWO DOUBLOONS!
BUT I ONLY HAVE ONE! HOW ABOUT SOME FANCY BAUBLES?
WE BE PIRATES THAT TAKE BAUBLES?
WE ONLY DEAL IN *GOLD!*
EENOPE.
YUM! SO WORTH IT...
CRIK!

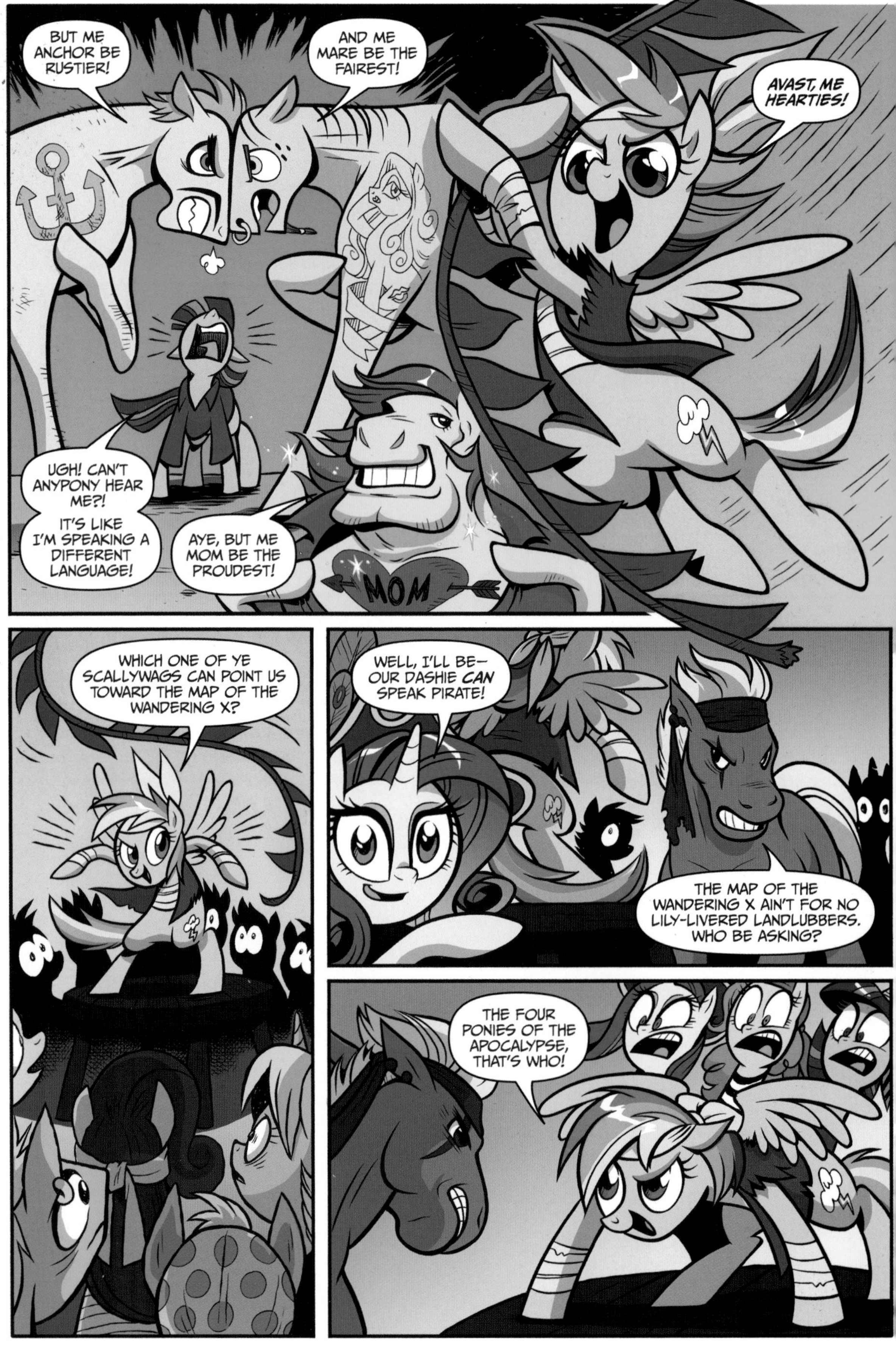
BUT ME ANCHOR BE RUSTIER!
AND ME MARE BE THE FAIREST!
AVAST, ME HEARTIES!
UGH! CAN'T ANYPONY HEAR ME?!
IT'S LIKE I'M SPEAKING A DIFFERENT LANGUAGE!
AYE, BUT ME MOM BE THE PROUDEST!
MOM
WHICH ONE OF YE SCALLYWAGS CAN POINT US TOWARD THE MAP OF THE WANDERING X?
WELL, I'LL BE— OUR DASHIE CAN SPEAK PIRATE!
THE MAP OF THE WANDERING X AIN'T FOR NO LILY-LIVERED LANDLUBBERS. WHO BE ASKING?
THE FOUR PONIES OF THE APOCALYPSE, THAT'S WHO!

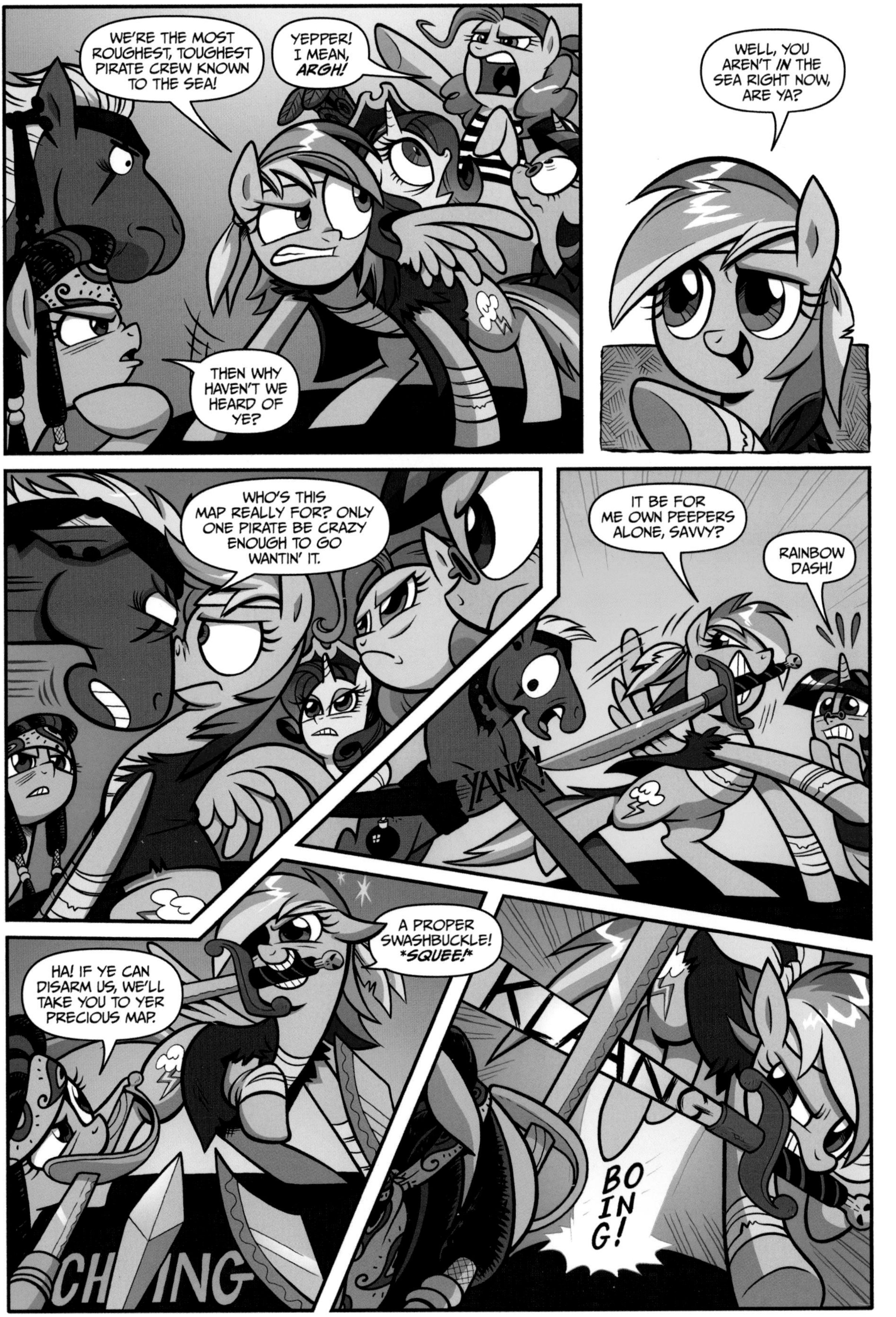
WE'RE THE MOST ROUGHEST, TOUGHEST PIRATE CREW KNOWN TO THE SEA!
YEPPER! I MEAN, ARGH!
THEN WHY HAVEN'T WE HEARD OF YE?
WELL, YOU AREN'T IN THE SEA RIGHT NOW, ARE YA?
WHO'S THIS MAP REALLY FOR? ONLY ONE PIRATE BE CRAZY ENOUGH TO GO WANTIN' IT.
IT BE FOR ME OWN PEEPERS ALONE, SAVVY?
RAINBOW DASH!
YANK!
HA! IF YE CAN DISARM US, WE'LL TAKE YOU TO YER PRECIOUS MAP.
A PROPER SWASHBUCKLE! *SQUEE!*
CHING
BOING!

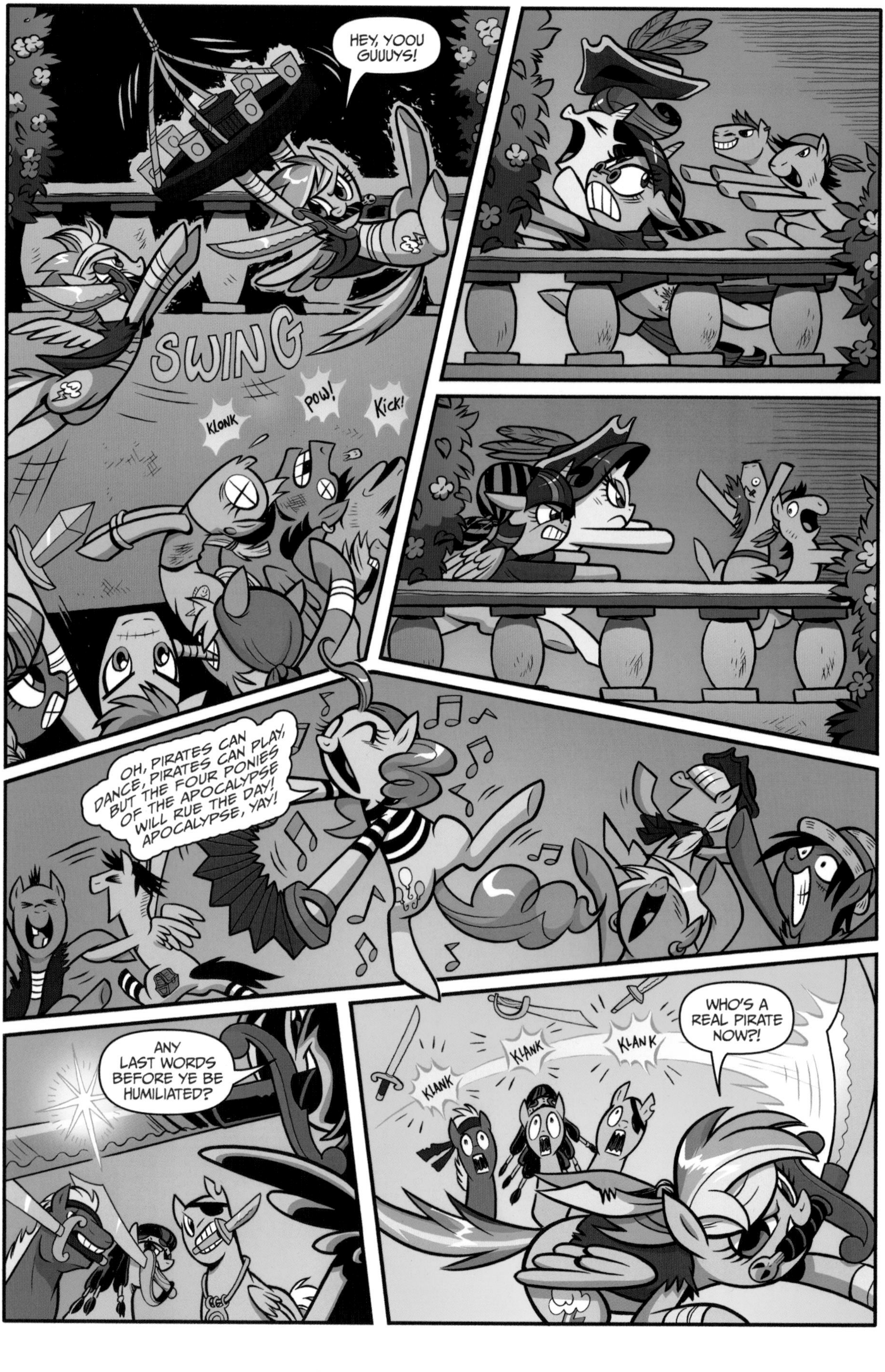
HEY, YOOU GUUUYS!
SWING
KLONK
POW!
KICK!
OH, PIRATES CAN DANCE, PIRATES CAN PLAY, BUT THE FOUR PONIES OF THE APOCALYPSE WILL RUE THE DAY! APOCALYPSE, YAY!
ANY LAST WORDS BEFORE YE BE HUMILIATED?
KLANK
KLANK
KLANK
WHO'S A REAL PIRATE NOW?!

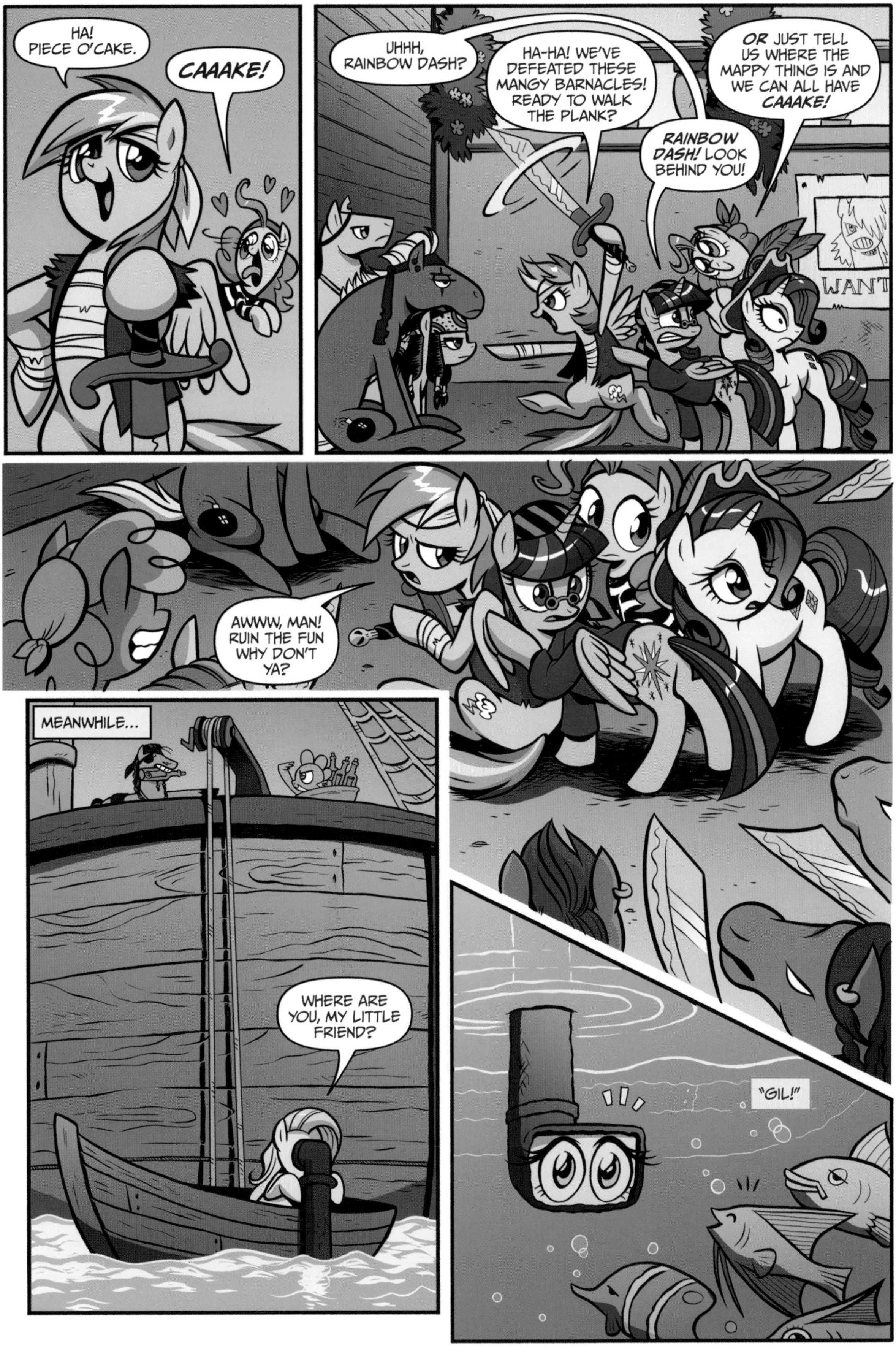
HA! PIECE O'CAKE.
CAAAKE!
UHHH, RAINBOW DASH?
HA-HA! WE'VE DEFEATED THESE MANGY BARNACLES! READY TO WALK THE PLANK?
RAINBOW DASH! LOOK BEHIND YOU!
OR JUST TELL US WHERE THE MAPPY THING IS AND WE CAN ALL HAVE CAAAKE!
WANT
AWWW, MAN! RUIN THE FUN WHY DON'T YA?
MEANWHILE...
WHERE ARE YOU, MY LITTLE FRIEND?
"GIL!"

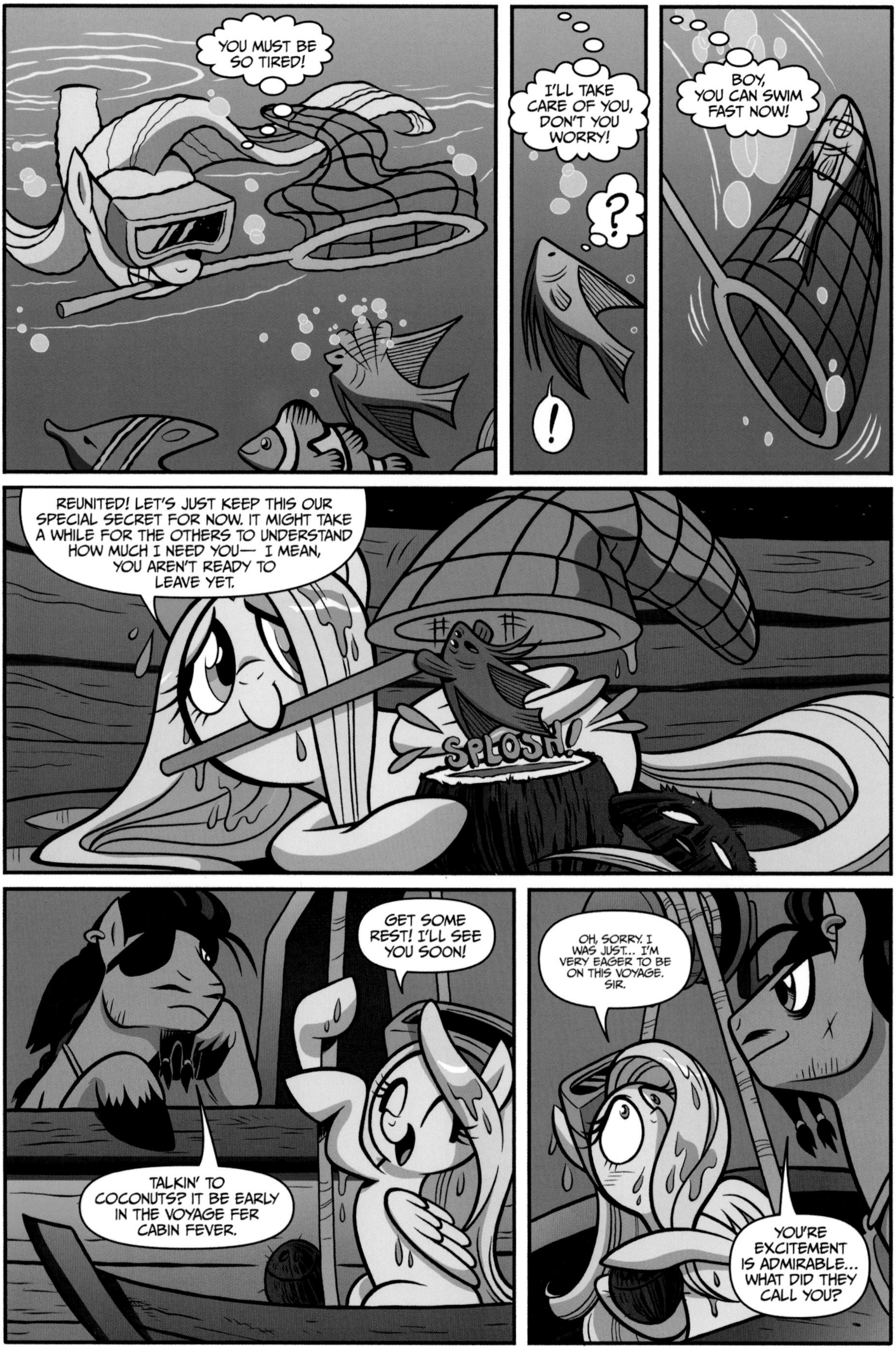
YOU MUST BE SO TIRED!
I'LL TAKE CARE OF YOU, DON'T YOU WORRY!
?
!
BOY, YOU CAN SWIM FAST NOW!
REUNITED! LET'S JUST KEEP THIS OUR SPECIAL SECRET FOR NOW. IT MIGHT TAKE A WHILE FOR THE OTHERS TO UNDERSTAND HOW MUCH I NEED YOU— I MEAN, YOU AREN'T READY TO LEAVE YET.
SPLOSH!
GET SOME REST! I'LL SEE YOU SOON!
TALKIN' TO COCONUTS? IT BE EARLY IN THE VOYAGE FER CABIN FEVER.
OH, SORRY. I WAS JUST... I'M VERY EAGER TO BE ON THIS VOYAGE. SIR.
YOU'RE EXCITEMENT IS ADMIRABLE... WHAT DID THEY CALL YOU?

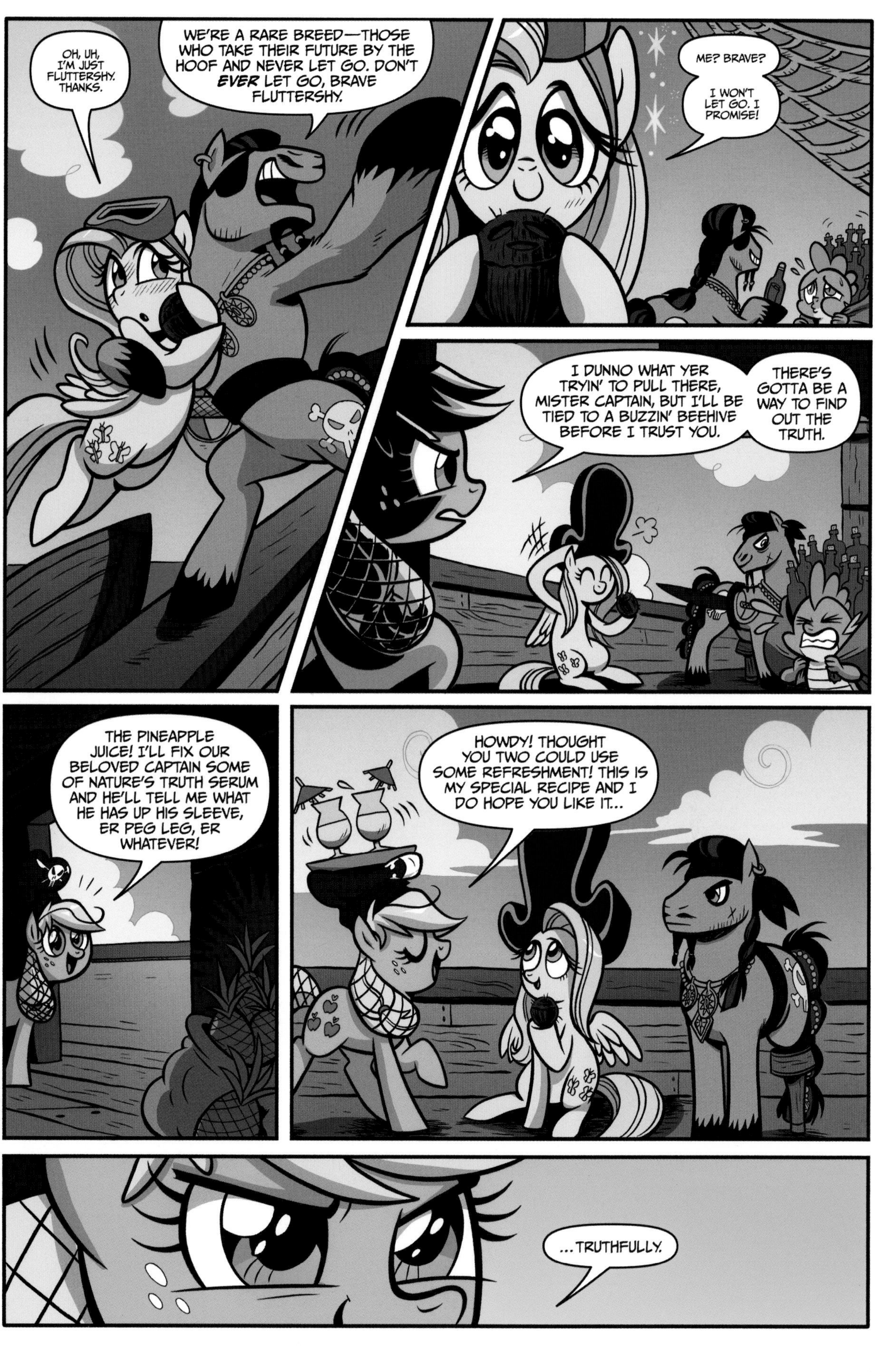
OH, UH, I'M JUST FLUTTERSHY. THANKS.
WE'RE A RARE BREED—THOSE WHO TAKE THEIR FUTURE BY THE HOOF AND NEVER LET GO. DON'T **EVER** LET GO, BRAVE FLUTTERSHY.
ME? BRAVE?
I WON'T LET GO. I PROMISE!
I DUNNO WHAT YER TRYIN' TO PULL THERE, MISTER CAPTAIN, BUT I'LL BE TIED TO A BUZZIN' BEEHIVE BEFORE I TRUST YOU.
THERE'S GOTTA BE A WAY TO FIND OUT THE TRUTH.
THE PINEAPPLE JUICE! I'LL FIX OUR BELOVED CAPTAIN SOME OF NATURE'S TRUTH SERUM AND HE'LL TELL ME WHAT HE HAS UP HIS SLEEVE, ER PEG LEG, ER WHATEVER!
HOWDY! THOUGHT YOU TWO COULD USE SOME REFRESHMENT! THIS IS MY SPECIAL RECIPE AND I DO HOPE YOU LIKE IT...
...TRUTHFULLY.

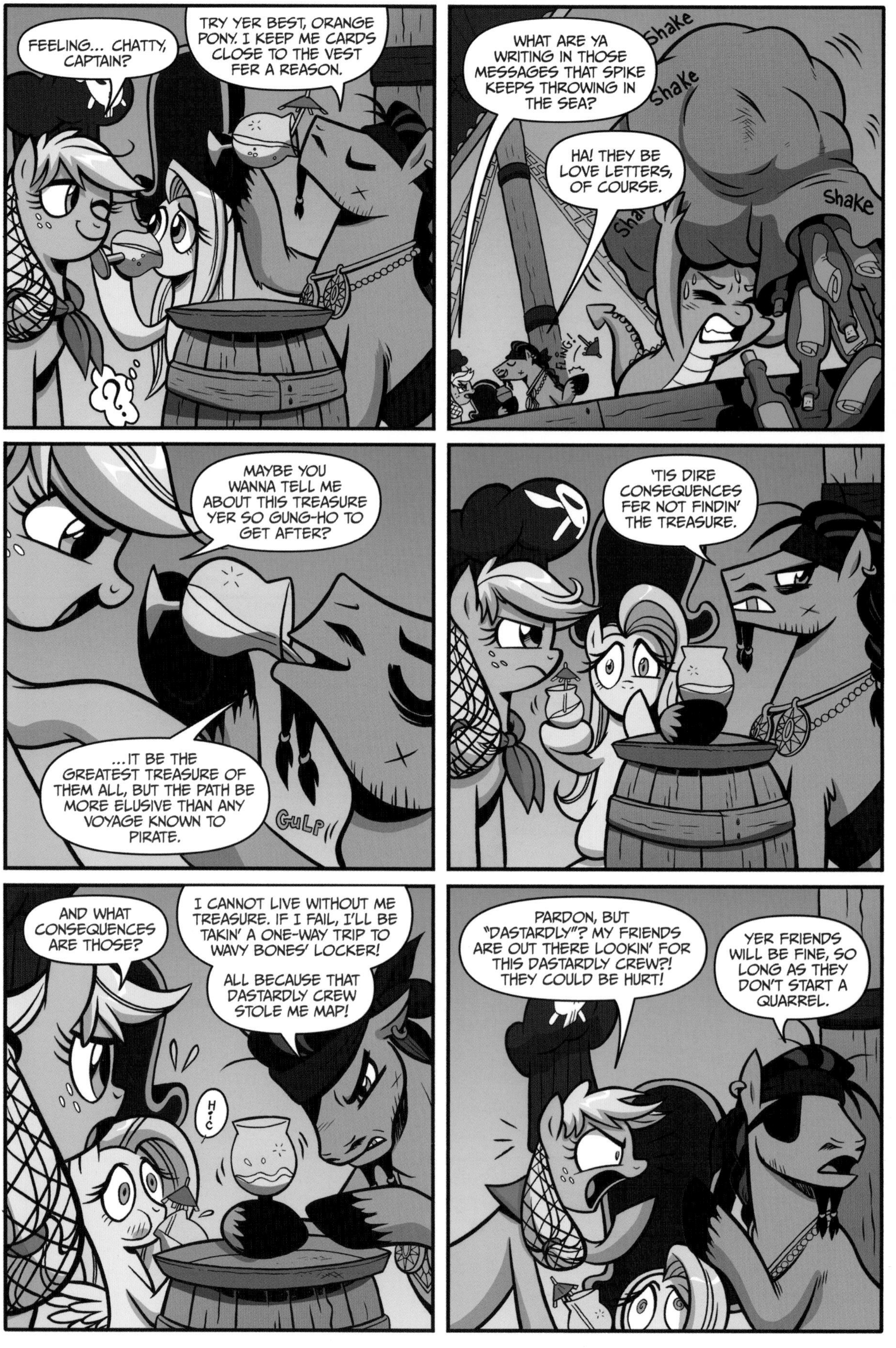
FEELING... CHATTY, CAPTAIN?
TRY YER BEST, ORANGE PONY. I KEEP ME CARDS CLOSE TO THE VEST FER A REASON.
?
WHAT ARE YA WRITING IN THOSE MESSAGES THAT SPIKE KEEPS THROWING IN THE SEA?
Shake
Shake
HA! THEY BE LOVE LETTERS, OF COURSE.
Shake
FLING!
MAYBE YOU WANNA TELL ME ABOUT THIS TREASURE YER SO GUNG-HO TO GET AFTER?
...IT BE THE GREATEST TREASURE OF THEM ALL, BUT THE PATH BE MORE ELUSIVE THAN ANY VOYAGE KNOWN TO PIRATE.
GULP
'TIS DIRE CONSEQUENCES FER NOT FINDIN' THE TREASURE.
AND WHAT CONSEQUENCES ARE THOSE?
I CANNOT LIVE WITHOUT ME TREASURE. IF I FAIL, I'LL BE TAKIN' A ONE-WAY TRIP TO WAVY BONES' LOCKER!
ALL BECAUSE THAT DASTARDLY CREW STOLE ME MAP!
HIC
PARDON, BUT "DASTARDLY"? MY FRIENDS ARE OUT THERE LOOKIN' FOR THIS DASTARDLY CREW?! THEY COULD BE HURT!
YER FRIENDS WILL BE FINE, SO LONG AS THEY DON'T START A QUARREL.

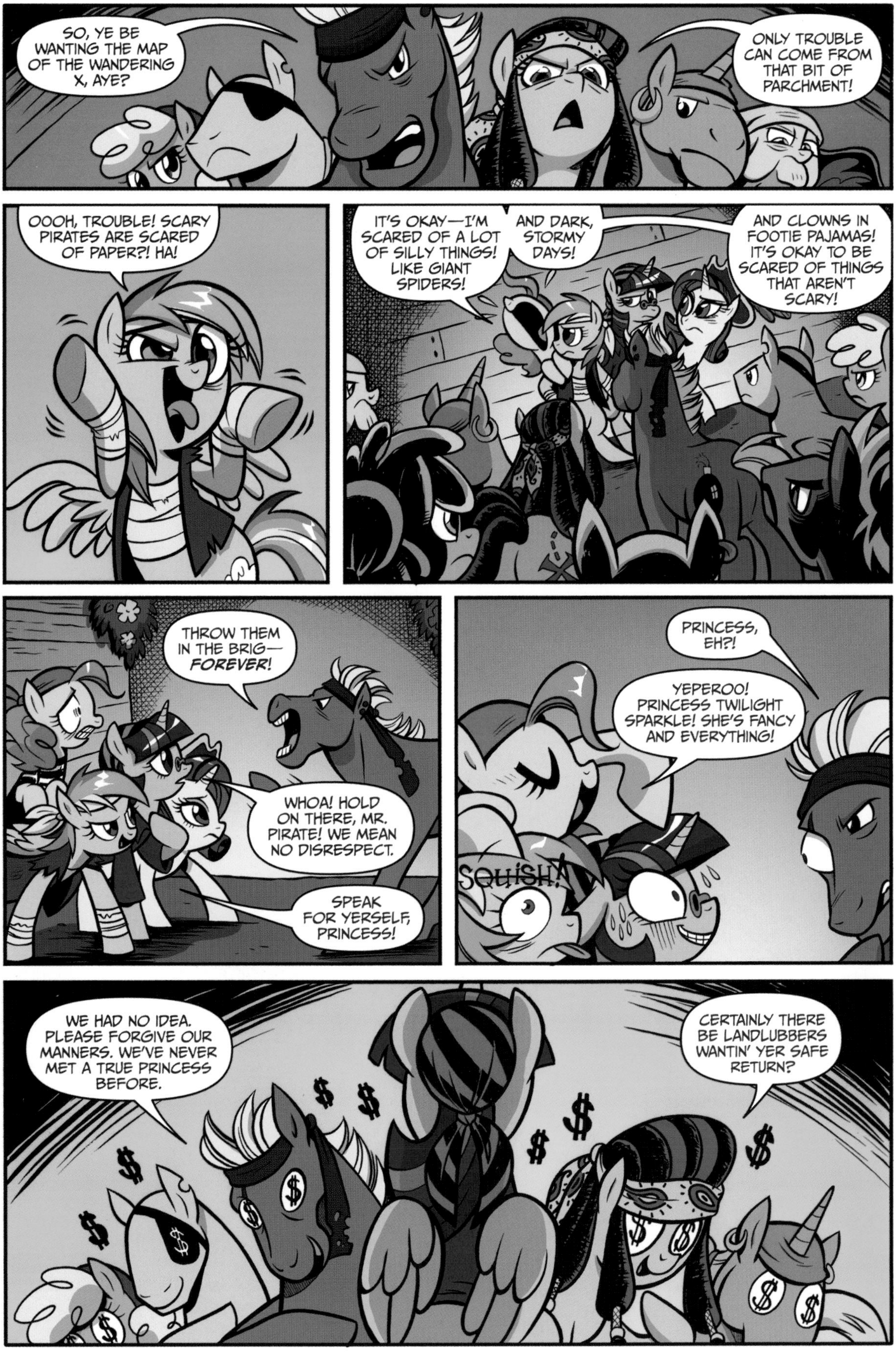
SO, YE BE WANTING THE MAP OF THE WANDERING X, AYE?
ONLY TROUBLE CAN COME FROM THAT BIT OF PARCHMENT!
OOOH, TROUBLE! SCARY PIRATES ARE SCARED OF PAPER?! HA!
IT'S OKAY—I'M SCARED OF A LOT OF SILLY THINGS! LIKE GIANT SPIDERS!
AND DARK, STORMY DAYS!
AND CLOWNS IN FOOTIE PAJAMAS! IT'S OKAY TO BE SCARED OF THINGS THAT AREN'T SCARY!
THROW THEM IN THE BRIG—FOREVER!
WHOA! HOLD ON THERE, MR. PIRATE! WE MEAN NO DISRESPECT.
SPEAK FOR YERSELF, PRINCESS!
PRINCESS, EH?!
YEPEROO! PRINCESS TWILIGHT SPARKLE! SHE'S FANCY AND EVERYTHING!
SQUISH!
WE HAD NO IDEA. PLEASE FORGIVE OUR MANNERS. WE'VE NEVER MET A TRUE PRINCESS BEFORE.
CERTAINLY THERE BE LANDLUBBERS WANTIN' YER SAFE RETURN?

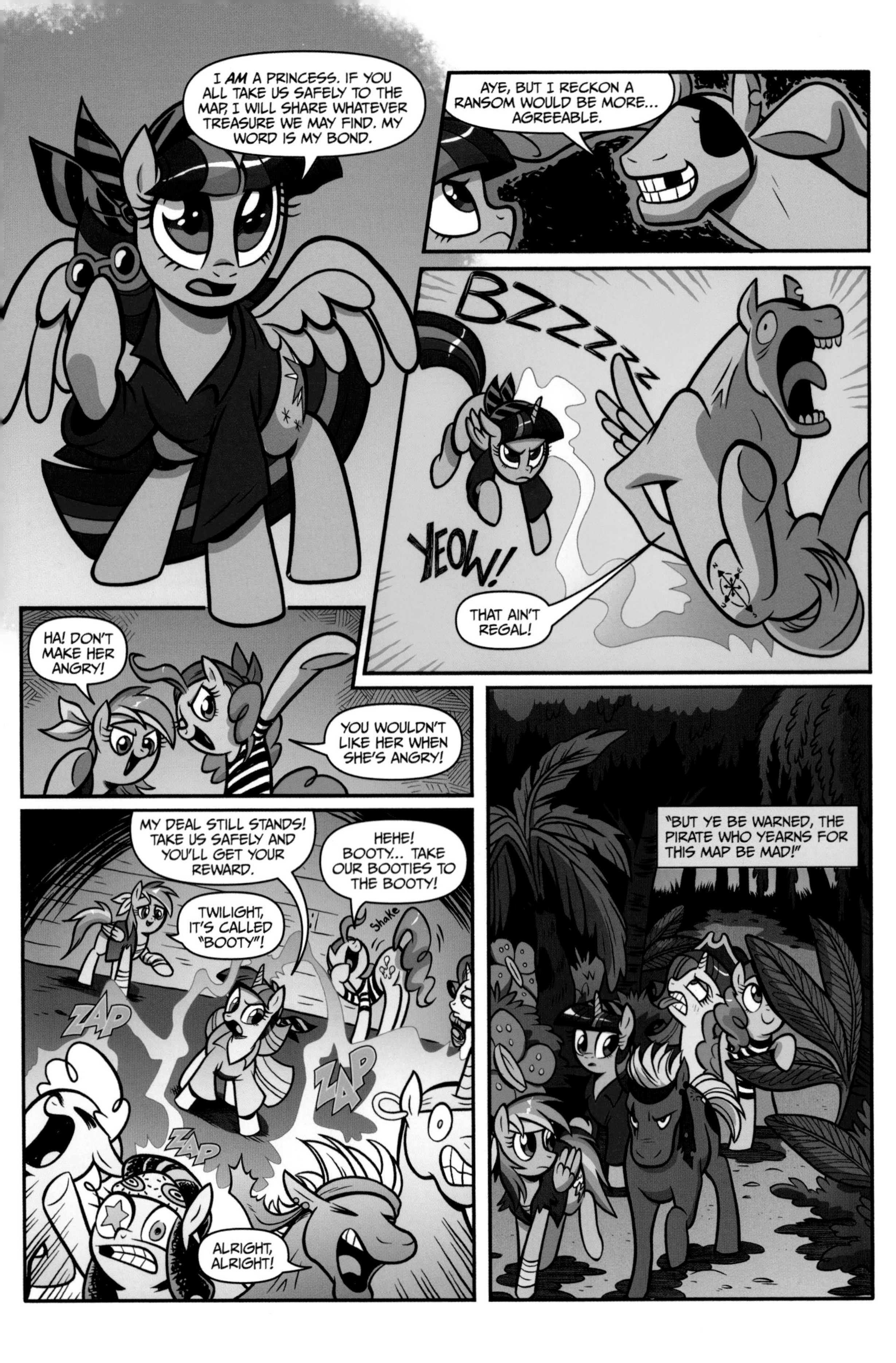
I AM A PRINCESS. IF YOU ALL TAKE US SAFELY TO THE MAP, I WILL SHARE WHATEVER TREASURE WE MAY FIND. MY WORD IS MY BOND.
AYE, BUT I RECKON A RANSOM WOULD BE MORE... AGREEABLE.
BZZZZZZ
YEOW!
THAT AIN'T REGAL!
HA! DON'T MAKE HER ANGRY!
YOU WOULDN'T LIKE HER WHEN SHE'S ANGRY!
MY DEAL STILL STANDS! TAKE US SAFELY AND YOU'LL GET YOUR REWARD.
TWILIGHT, IT'S CALLED "BOOTY"!
HEHE! BOOTY... TAKE OUR BOOTIES TO THE BOOTY!
Shake
ZAP
ZAP
ZAP
ALRIGHT, ALRIGHT!
"BUT YE BE WARNED, THE PIRATE WHO YEARNS FOR THIS MAP BE MAD!"

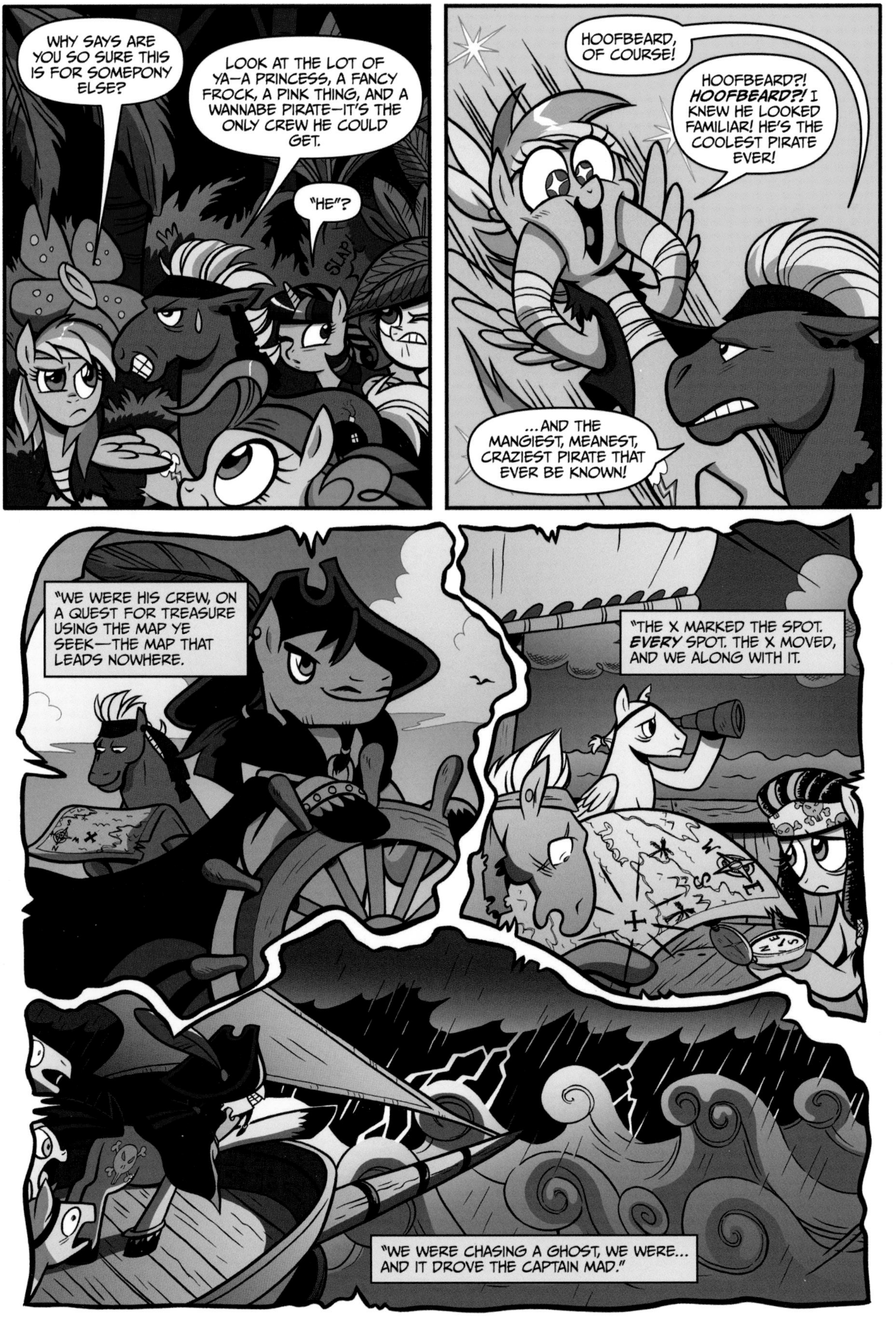
WHY SAYS ARE YOU SO SURE THIS IS FOR SOMEPONY ELSE?
LOOK AT THE LOT OF YA—A PRINCESS, A FANCY FROCK, A PINK THING, AND A WANNABE PIRATE—IT'S THE ONLY CREW HE COULD GET.
"HE"?
SLAP!
HOOFBEARD, OF COURSE!
HOOFBEARD?! **HOOFBEARD?!** I KNEW HE LOOKED FAMILIAR! HE'S THE COOLEST PIRATE EVER!
...AND THE MANGIEST, MEANEST, CRAZIEST PIRATE THAT EVER BE KNOWN!
"WE WERE HIS CREW, ON A QUEST FOR TREASURE USING THE MAP YE SEEK—THE MAP THAT LEADS NOWHERE.
"THE X MARKED THE SPOT. **EVERY** SPOT. THE X MOVED, AND WE ALONG WITH IT.
"WE WERE CHASING A GHOST, WE WERE... AND IT DROVE THE CAPTAIN MAD."

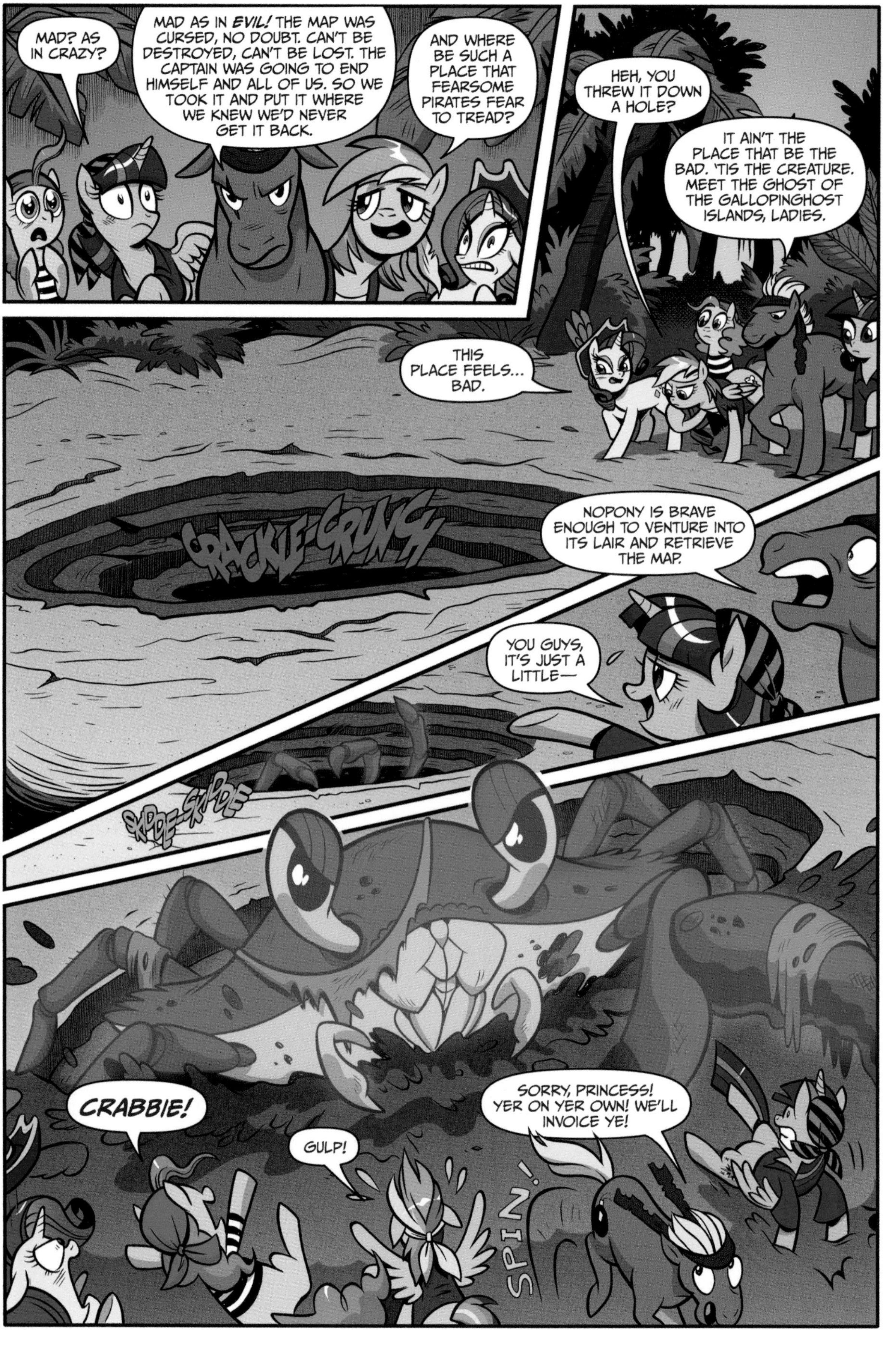
MAD? AS IN CRAZY?
MAD AS IN EVIL! THE MAP WAS CURSED, NO DOUBT. CAN'T BE DESTROYED, CAN'T BE LOST. THE CAPTAIN WAS GOING TO END HIMSELF AND ALL OF US. SO WE TOOK IT AND PUT IT WHERE WE KNEW WE'D NEVER GET IT BACK.
AND WHERE BE SUCH A PLACE THAT FEARSOME PIRATES FEAR TO TREAD?
HEH, YOU THREW IT DOWN A HOLE?
IT AIN'T THE PLACE THAT BE THE BAD. 'TIS THE CREATURE. MEET THE GHOST OF THE GALLOPINGHOST ISLANDS, LADIES.
THIS PLACE FEELS... BAD.
CRACKLE-CRUNCH
NOPONY IS BRAVE ENOUGH TO VENTURE INTO ITS LAIR AND RETRIEVE THE MAP.
YOU GUYS, IT'S JUST A LITTLE—
SKIDDLE-SKIDDLE
CRABBIE!
GULP!
SORRY, PRINCESS! YER ON YER OWN! WE'LL INVOICE YE!
SPIN!

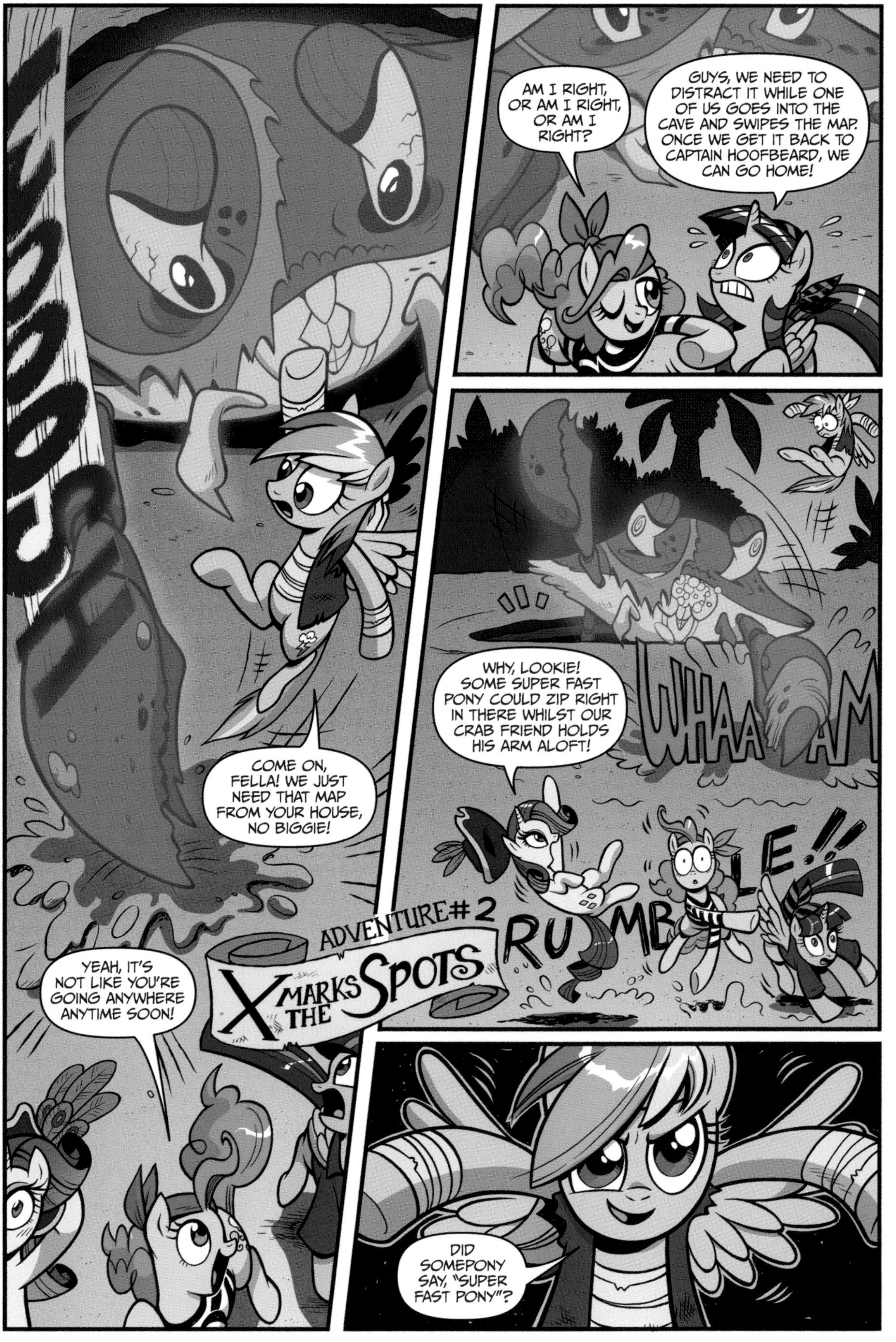

THOOOOP
AM I RIGHT, OR AM I RIGHT, OR AM I RIGHT?
GUYS, WE NEED TO DISTRACT IT WHILE ONE OF US GOES INTO THE CAVE AND SWIPES THE MAP. ONCE WE GET IT BACK TO CAPTAIN HOOFBEARD, WE CAN GO HOME!
COME ON, FELLA! WE JUST NEED THAT MAP FROM YOUR HOUSE, NO BIGGIE!
WHAAAAM
WHY, LOOKIE! SOME SUPER FAST PONY COULD ZIP RIGHT IN THERE WHILST OUR CRAB FRIEND HOLDS HIS ARM ALOFT!
RUMBLE!!
ADVENTURE #2
X MARKS THE SPOTS
YEAH, IT'S NOT LIKE YOU'RE GOING ANYWHERE ANYTIME SOON!
DID SOMEPONY SAY, "SUPER FAST PONY"?

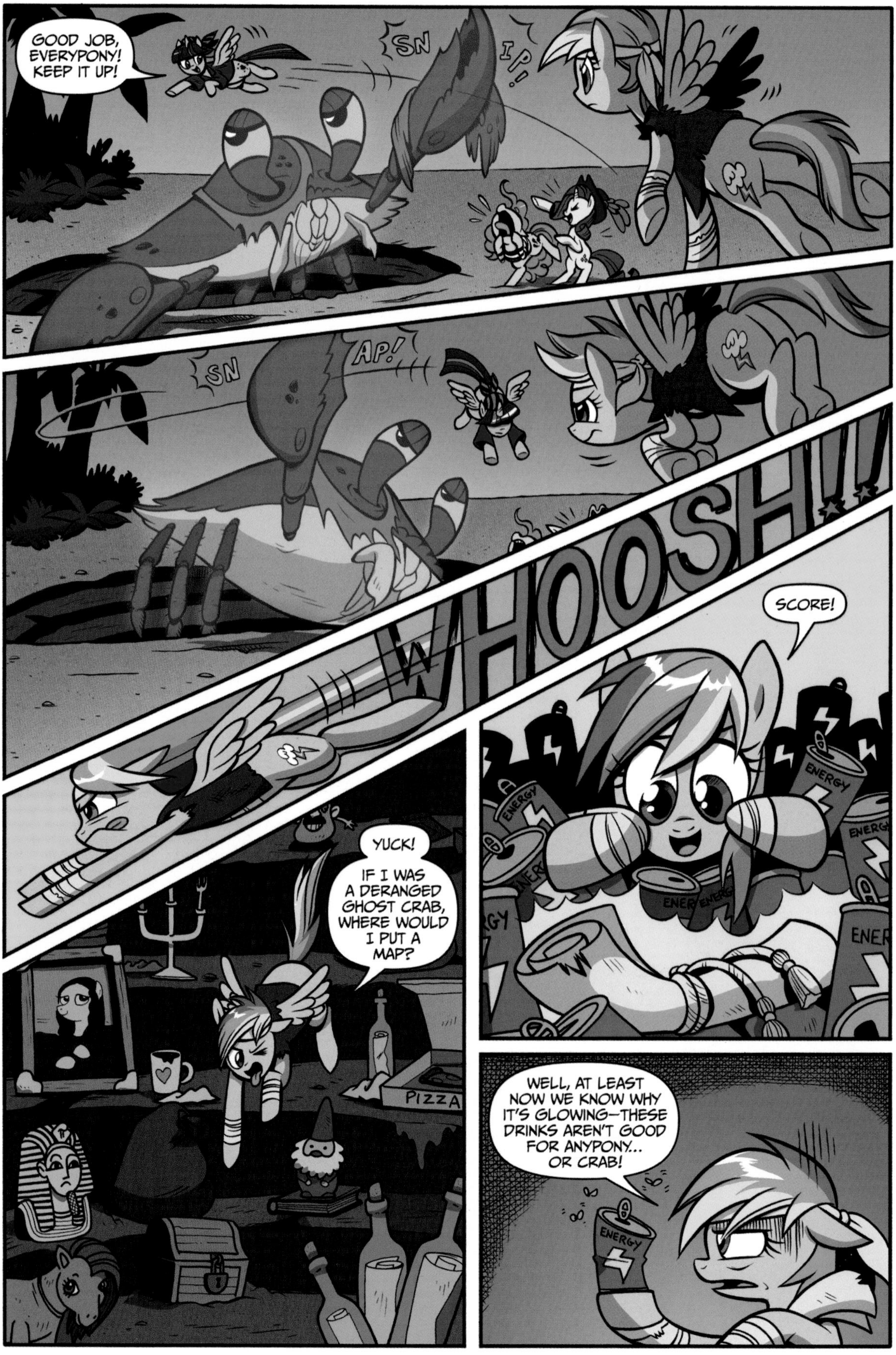
GOOD JOB, EVERYPONY! KEEP IT UP!
SN
IP!
SN
AP!
WHOOSH!!!
SCORE!
YUCK!
IF I WAS A DERANGED GHOST CRAB, WHERE WOULD I PUT A MAP?
PIZZA
ENERGY
WELL, AT LEAST NOW WE KNOW WHY IT'S GLOWING—THESE DRINKS AREN'T GOOD FOR ANYPONY... OR CRAB!
ENERGY

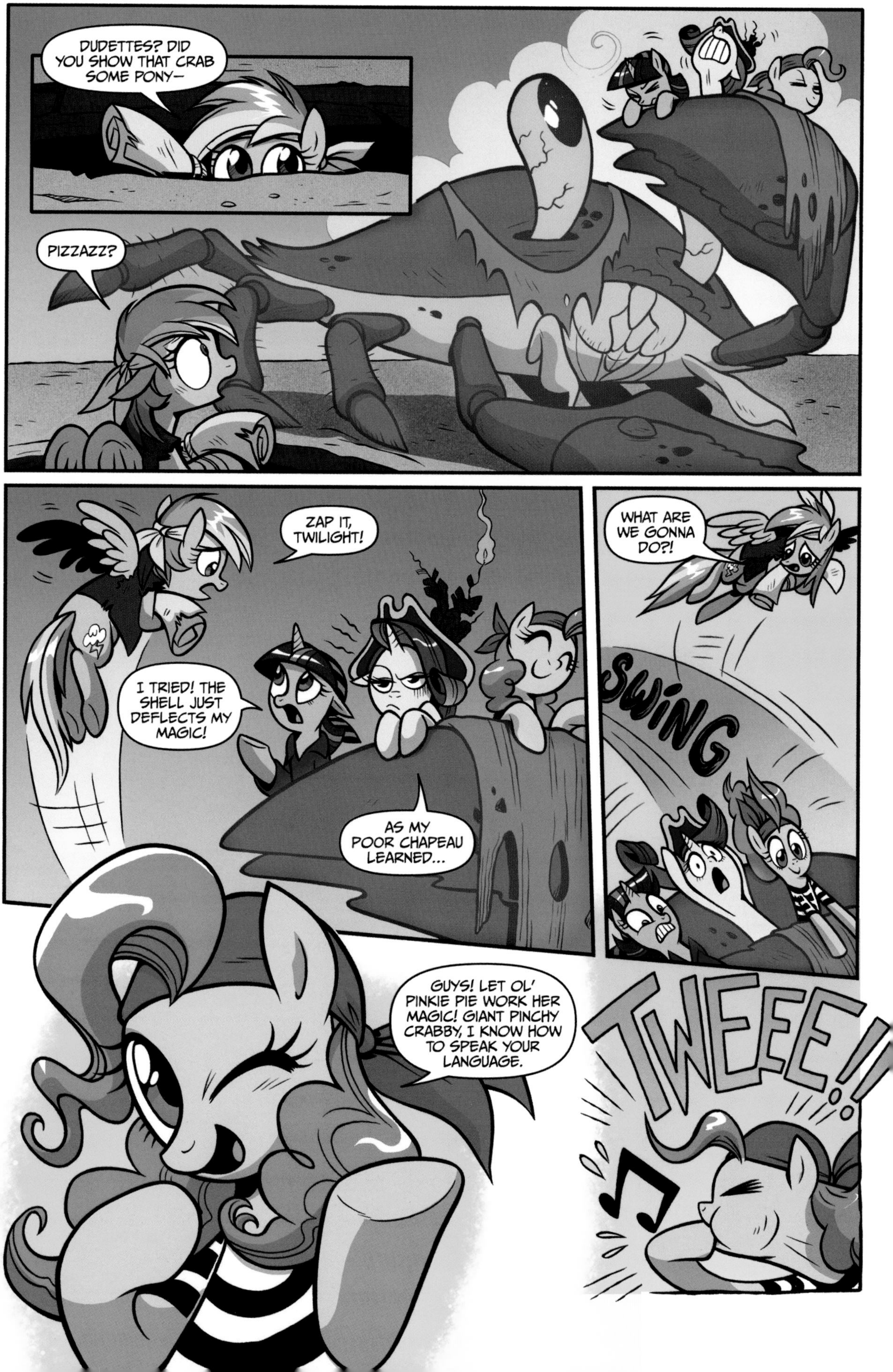
DUDETTES? DID YOU SHOW THAT CRAB SOME PONY—
PIZZAZZ?
ZAP IT, TWILIGHT!
I TRIED! THE SHELL JUST DEFLECTS MY MAGIC!
AS MY POOR CHAPEAU LEARNED...
WHAT ARE WE GONNA DO?!
SWING
GUYS! LET OL' PINKIE PIE WORK HER MAGIC! GIANT PINCHY CRABBY, I KNOW HOW TO SPEAK YOUR LANGUAGE.
TWEEE!!

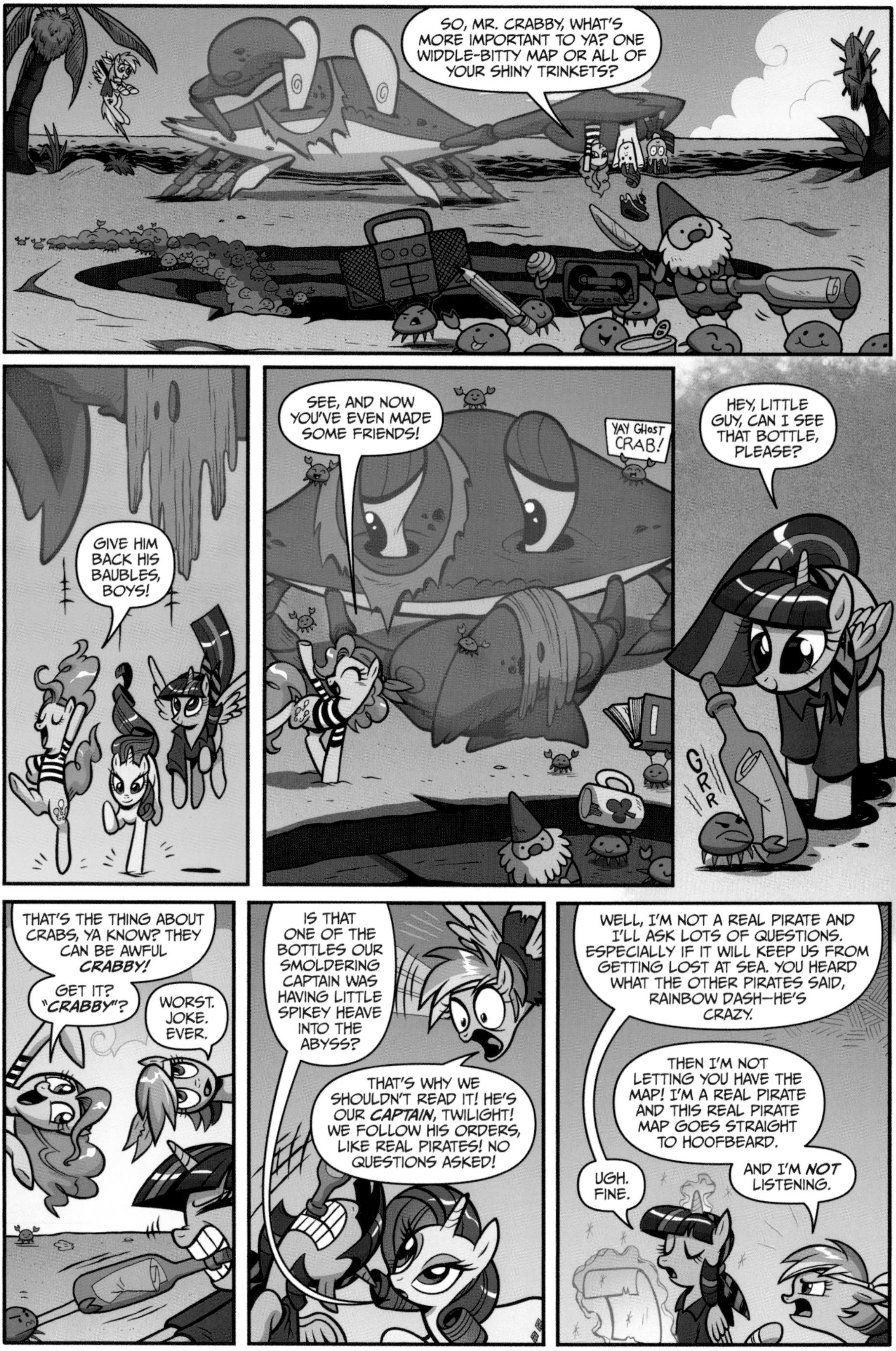
SO, MR. CRABBY, WHAT'S MORE IMPORTANT TO YA? ONE WIDDLE-BITTY MAP OR ALL OF YOUR SHINY TRINKETS?
GIVE HIM BACK HIS BAUBLES, BOYS!
SEE, AND NOW YOU'VE EVEN MADE SOME FRIENDS!
YAY GHOST CRAB!
HEY, LITTLE GUY, CAN I SEE THAT BOTTLE, PLEASE?
GRRR
THAT'S THE THING ABOUT CRABS, YA KNOW? THEY CAN BE AWFUL *CRABBY!*
GET IT? "*CRABBY*"?
WORST. JOKE. EVER.
IS THAT ONE OF THE BOTTLES OUR SMOLDERING CAPTAIN WAS HAVING LITTLE SPIKEY HEAVE INTO THE ABYSS?
THAT'S WHY WE SHOULDN'T READ IT! HE'S OUR *CAPTAIN*, TWILIGHT! WE FOLLOW HIS ORDERS, LIKE REAL PIRATES! NO QUESTIONS ASKED!
WELL, I'M NOT A REAL PIRATE AND I'LL ASK LOTS OF QUESTIONS. ESPECIALLY IF IT WILL KEEP US FROM GETTING LOST AT SEA. YOU HEARD WHAT THE OTHER PIRATES SAID, RAINBOW DASH—HE'S CRAZY.
THEN I'M NOT LETTING YOU HAVE THE MAP! I'M A REAL PIRATE AND THIS REAL PIRATE MAP GOES STRAIGHT TO HOOFBEARD.
UGH. FINE.
AND I'M *NOT* LISTENING.

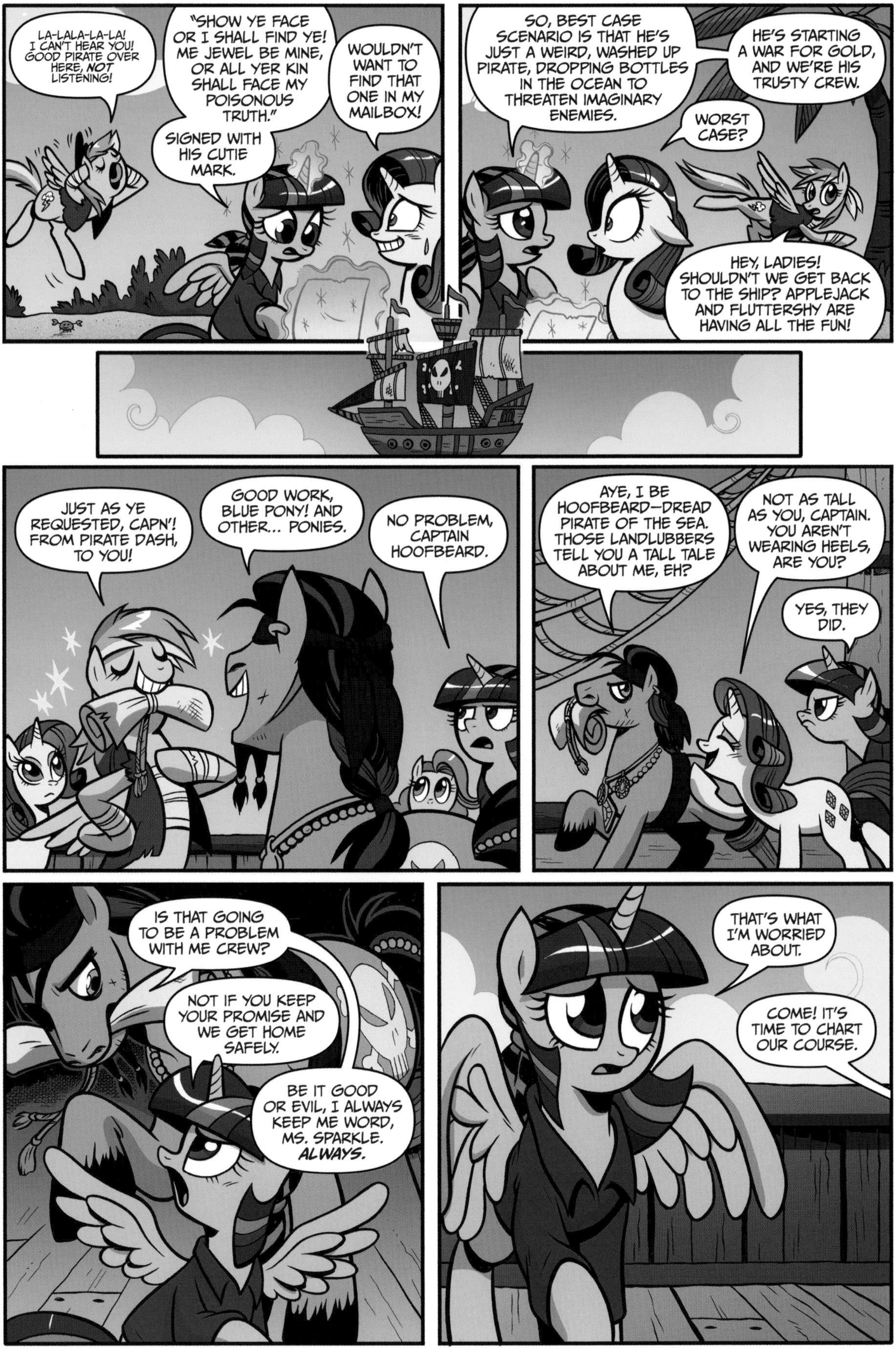
LA-LALA-LA-LA! I CAN'T HEAR YOU! GOOD PIRATE OVER HERE, *NOT* LISTENING!
"SHOW YE FACE OR I SHALL FIND YE! ME JEWEL BE MINE, OR ALL YER KIN SHALL FACE MY POISONOUS TRUTH."
SIGNED WITH HIS CUTIE MARK.
WOULDN'T WANT TO FIND THAT ONE IN MY MAILBOX!
SO, BEST CASE SCENARIO IS THAT HE'S JUST A WEIRD, WASHED UP PIRATE, DROPPING BOTTLES IN THE OCEAN TO THREATEN IMAGINARY ENEMIES.
WORST CASE?
HE'S STARTING A WAR FOR GOLD, AND WE'RE HIS TRUSTY CREW.
HEY, LADIES! SHOULDN'T WE GET BACK TO THE SHIP? APPLEJACK AND FLUTTERSHY ARE HAVING ALL THE FUN!
JUST AS YE REQUESTED, CAPN'! FROM PIRATE DASH, TO YOU!
GOOD WORK, BLUE PONY! AND OTHER... PONIES.
NO PROBLEM, CAPTAIN HOOFBEARD.
AYE, I BE HOOFBEARD—DREAD PIRATE OF THE SEA. THOSE LANDLUBBERS TELL YOU A TALL TALE ABOUT ME, EH?
NOT AS TALL AS YOU, CAPTAIN. YOU AREN'T WEARING HEELS, ARE YOU?
YES, THEY DID.
IS THAT GOING TO BE A PROBLEM WITH ME CREW?
NOT IF YOU KEEP YOUR PROMISE AND WE GET HOME SAFELY.
BE IT GOOD OR EVIL, I ALWAYS KEEP ME WORD, MS. SPARKLE. ***ALWAYS.***
THAT'S WHAT I'M WORRIED ABOUT.
COME! IT'S TIME TO CHART OUR COURSE.

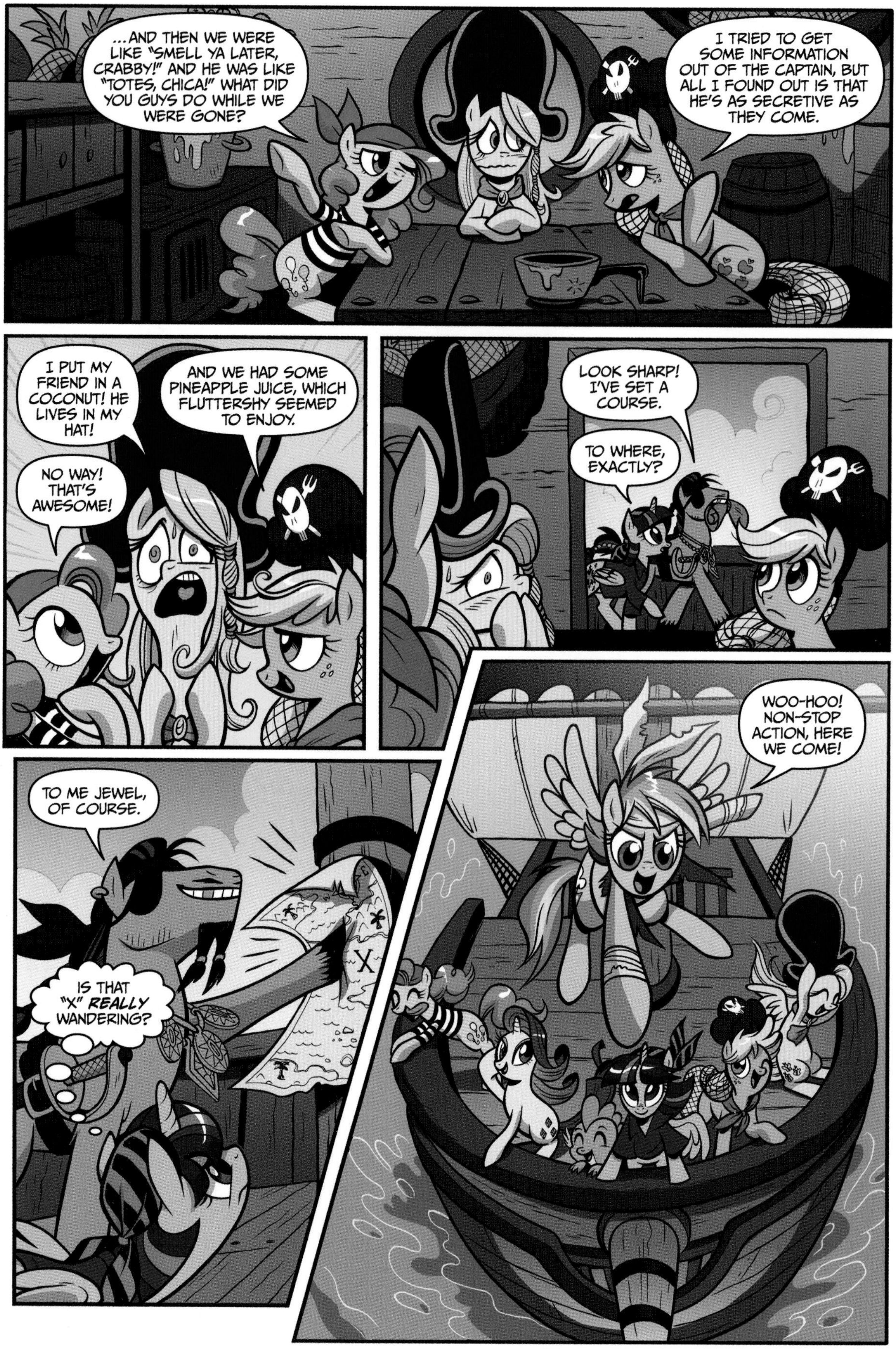
...AND THEN WE WERE LIKE "SMELL YA LATER, CRABBY!" AND HE WAS LIKE "TOTES, CHICA!" WHAT DID YOU GUYS DO WHILE WE WERE GONE?
I TRIED TO GET SOME INFORMATION OUT OF THE CAPTAIN, BUT ALL I FOUND OUT IS THAT HE'S AS SECRETIVE AS THEY COME.
I PUT MY FRIEND IN A COCONUT! HE LIVES IN MY HAT!
AND WE HAD SOME PINEAPPLE JUICE, WHICH FLUTTERSHY SEEMED TO ENJOY.
NO WAY! THAT'S AWESOME!
LOOK SHARP! I'VE SET A COURSE.
TO WHERE, EXACTLY?
TO ME JEWEL, OF COURSE.
IS THAT "X" REALLY WANDERING?
WOO-HOO! NON-STOP ACTION, HERE WE COME!

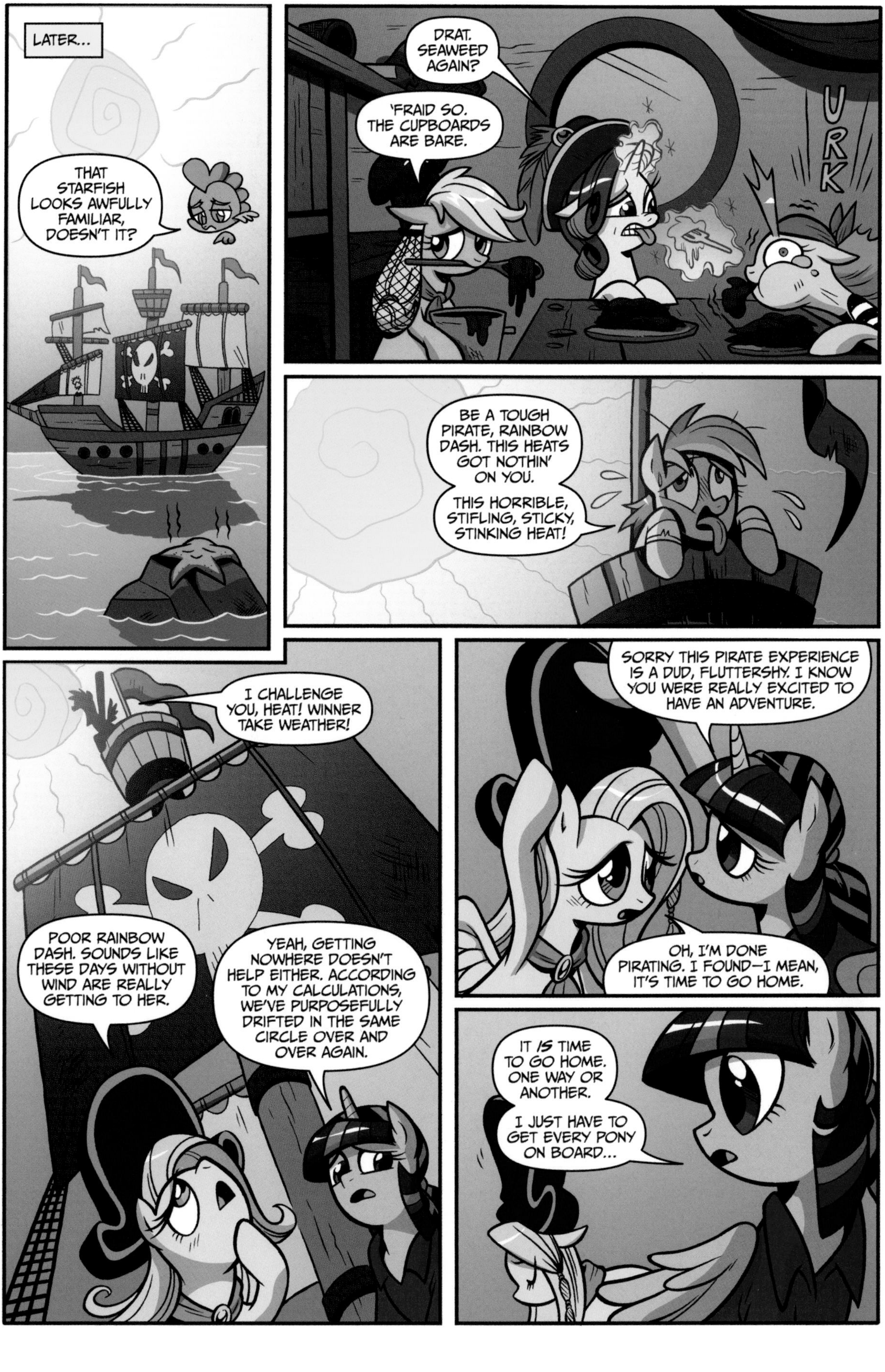
LATER...
THAT STARFISH LOOKS AWFULLY FAMILIAR, DOESN'T IT?
DRAT. SEAWEED AGAIN?
'FRAID SO. THE CUPBOARDS ARE BARE.
URK
BE A TOUGH PIRATE, RAINBOW DASH. THIS HEATS GOT NOTHIN' ON YOU.
THIS HORRIBLE, STIFLING, STICKY, STINKING HEAT!
I CHALLENGE YOU, HEAT! WINNER TAKE WEATHER!
POOR RAINBOW DASH. SOUNDS LIKE THESE DAYS WITHOUT WIND ARE REALLY GETTING TO HER.
YEAH, GETTING NOWHERE DOESN'T HELP EITHER. ACCORDING TO MY CALCULATIONS, WE'VE PURPOSEFULLY DRIFTED IN THE SAME CIRCLE OVER AND OVER AGAIN.
SORRY THIS PIRATE EXPERIENCE IS A DUD, FLUTTERSHY. I KNOW YOU WERE REALLY EXCITED TO HAVE AN ADVENTURE.
OH, I'M DONE PIRATING. I FOUND—I MEAN, IT'S TIME TO GO HOME.
IT *IS* TIME TO GO HOME. ONE WAY OR ANOTHER.
I JUST HAVE TO GET EVERY PONY ON BOARD...

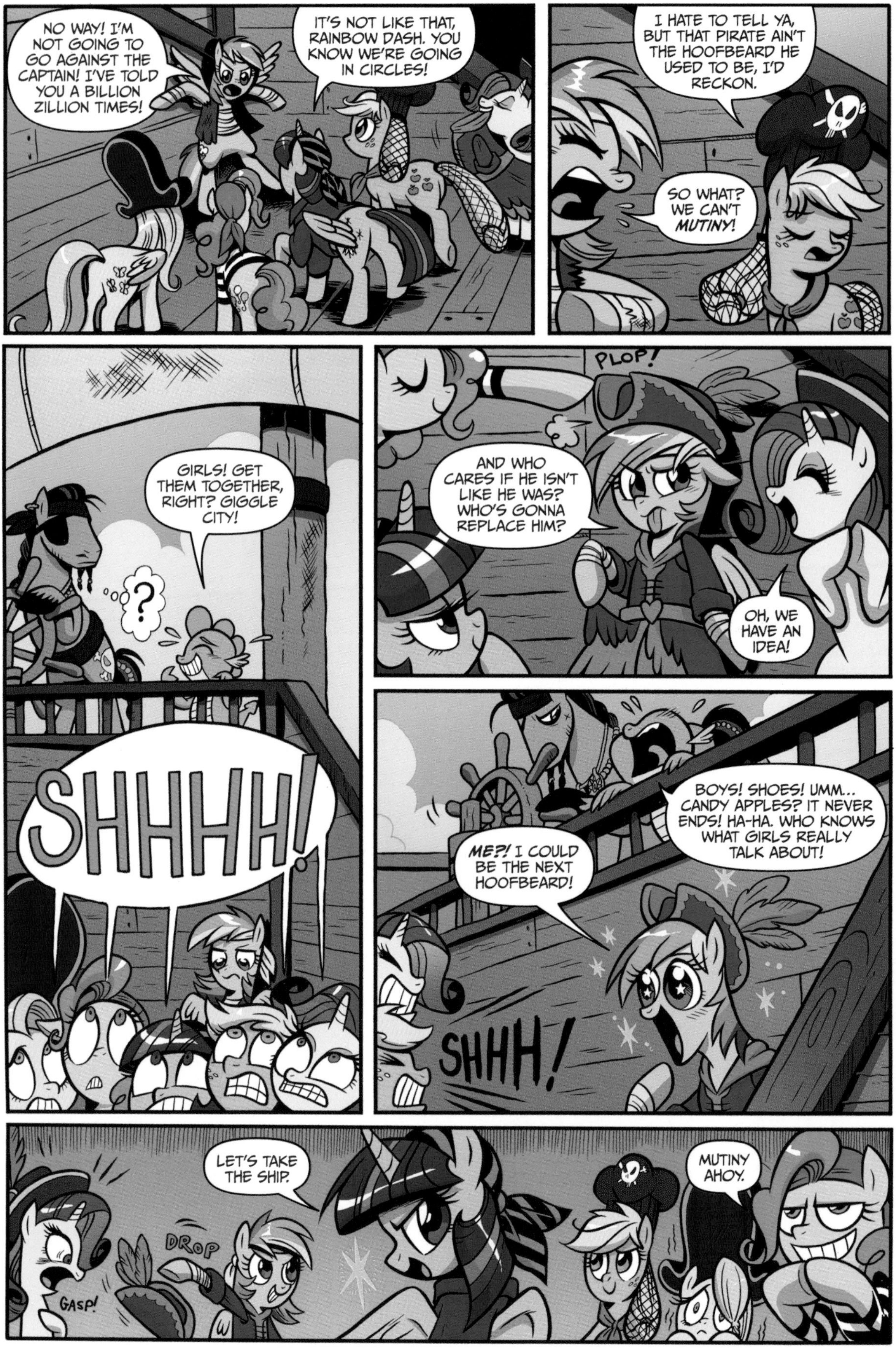
NO WAY! I'M NOT GOING TO GO AGAINST THE CAPTAIN! I'VE TOLD YOU A BILLION ZILLION TIMES!
IT'S NOT LIKE THAT, RAINBOW DASH. YOU KNOW WE'RE GOING IN CIRCLES!
I HATE TO TELL YA, BUT THAT PIRATE AIN'T THE HOOFBEARD HE USED TO BE, I'D RECKON.
SO WHAT? WE CAN'T *MUTINY*!
GIRLS! GET THEM TOGETHER, RIGHT? GIGGLE CITY!
?
SHHHH!
PLOP!
AND WHO CARES IF HE ISN'T LIKE HE WAS? WHO'S GONNA REPLACE HIM?
OH, WE HAVE AN IDEA!
BOYS! SHOES! UMM... CANDY APPLES? IT NEVER ENDS! HA-HA. WHO KNOWS WHAT GIRLS REALLY TALK ABOUT!
ME?! I COULD BE THE NEXT HOOFBEARD!
SHHH!
LET'S TAKE THE SHIP.
MUTINY AHOY.
DROP
GASP!

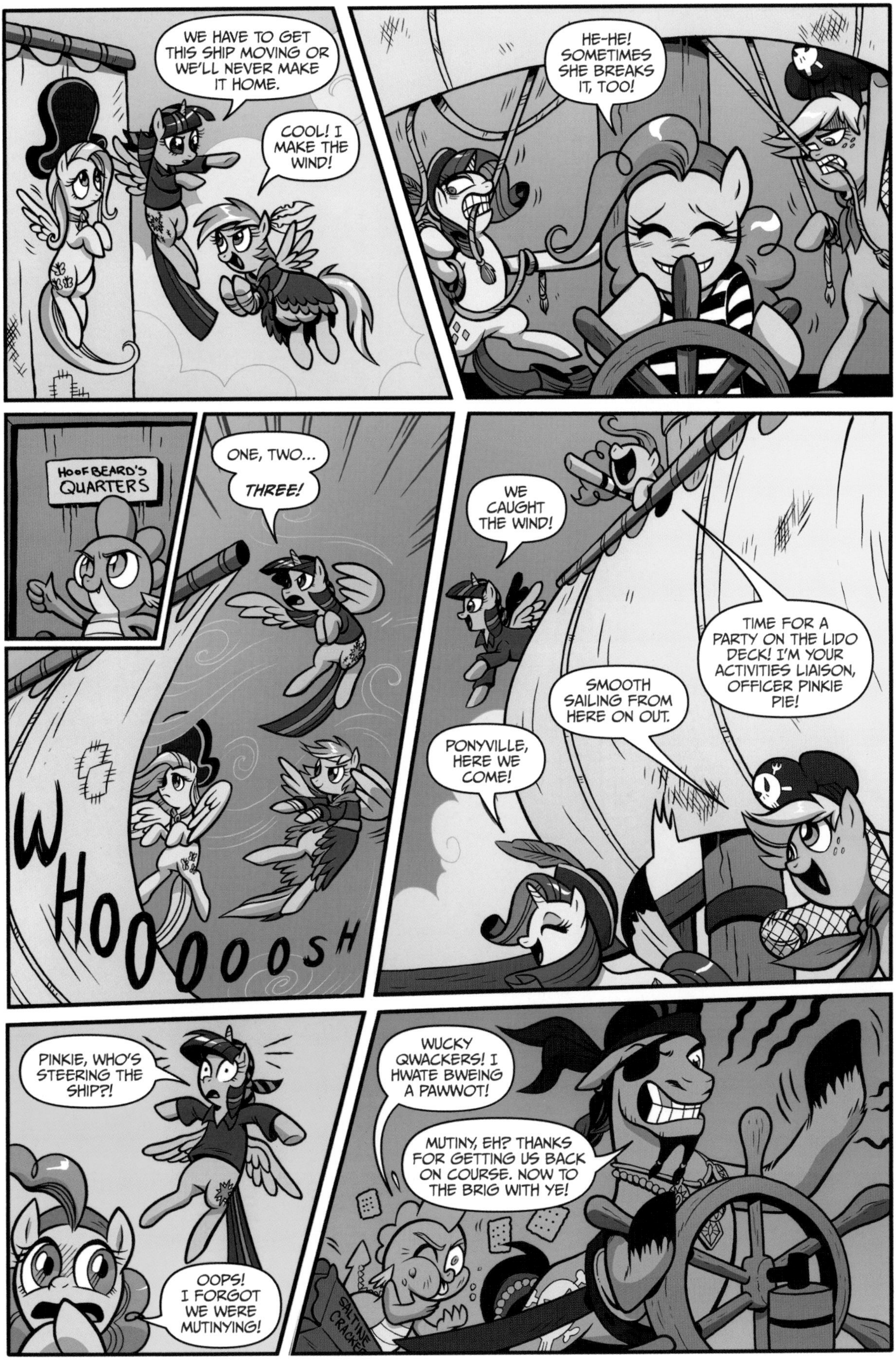
WE HAVE TO GET THIS SHIP MOVING OR WE'LL NEVER MAKE IT HOME.
COOL! I MAKE THE WIND!
HE-HE! SOMETIMES SHE BREAKS IT, TOO!
HOOFBEARD'S QUARTERS
ONE, TWO...
THREE!
WHOOOOOOSH
WE CAUGHT THE WIND!
TIME FOR A PARTY ON THE LIDO DECK! I'M YOUR ACTIVITIES LIAISON, OFFICER PINKIE PIE!
SMOOTH SAILING FROM HERE ON OUT.
PONYVILLE, HERE WE COME!
PINKIE, WHO'S STEERING THE SHIP?!
OOPS! I FORGOT WE WERE MUTINYING!
WUCKY QWACKERS! I HWATE BWEING A PAWWOT!
MUTINY, EH? THANKS FOR GETTING US BACK ON COURSE. NOW TO THE BRIG WITH YE!

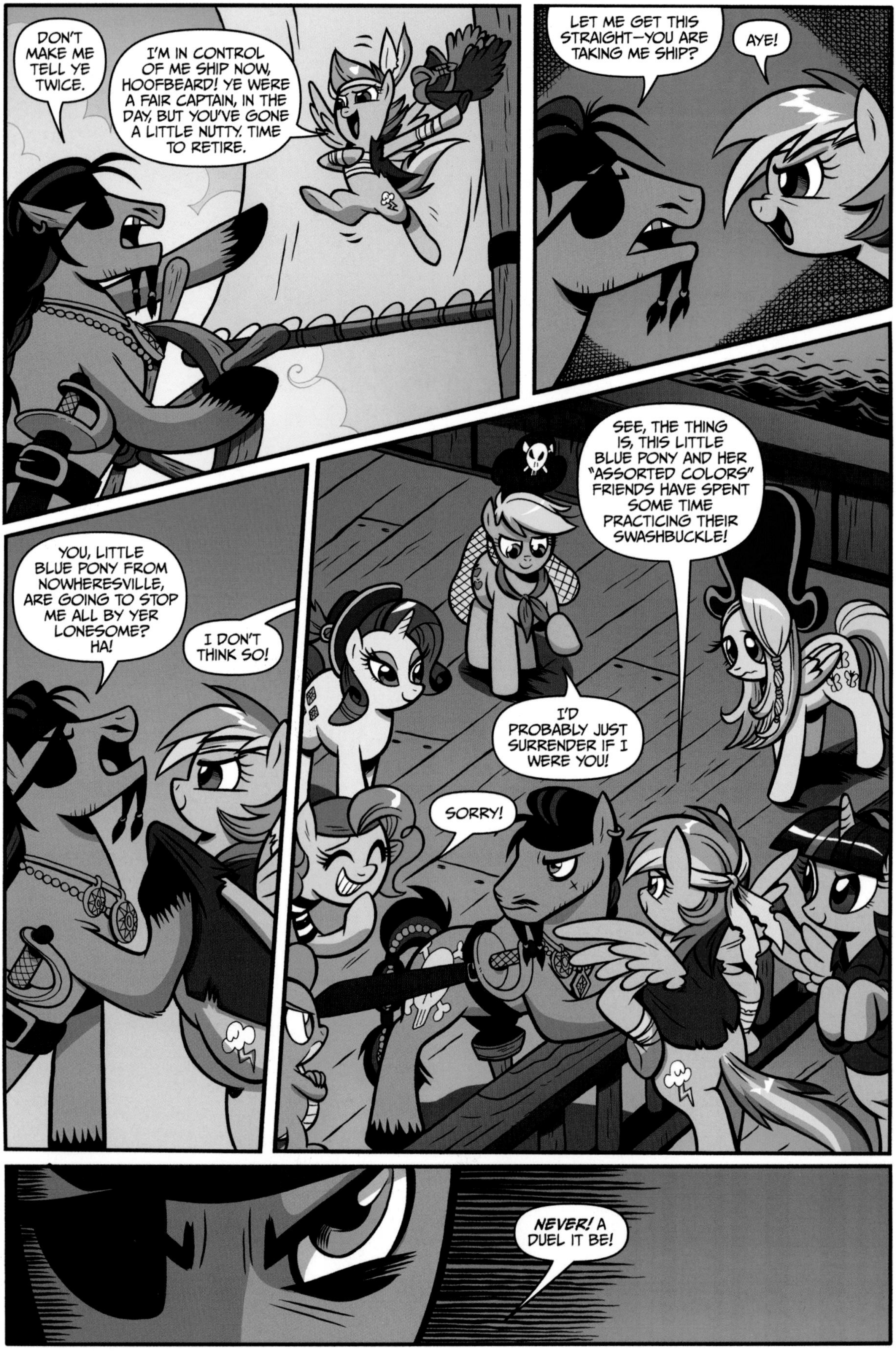
DON'T MAKE ME TELL YE TWICE.
I'M IN CONTROL OF ME SHIP NOW, HOOFBEARD! YE WERE A FAIR CAPTAIN, IN THE DAY, BUT YOU'VE GONE A LITTLE NUTTY. TIME TO RETIRE.
LET ME GET THIS STRAIGHT—YOU ARE TAKING ME SHIP?
AYE!
YOU, LITTLE BLUE PONY FROM NOWHERESVILLE, ARE GOING TO STOP ME ALL BY YER LONESOME? HA!
I DON'T THINK SO!
SEE, THE THING IS, THIS LITTLE BLUE PONY AND HER "ASSORTED COLORS" FRIENDS HAVE SPENT SOME TIME PRACTICING THEIR SWASHBUCKLE!
I'D PROBABLY JUST SURRENDER IF I WERE YOU!
SORRY!
NEVER! A DUEL IT BE!

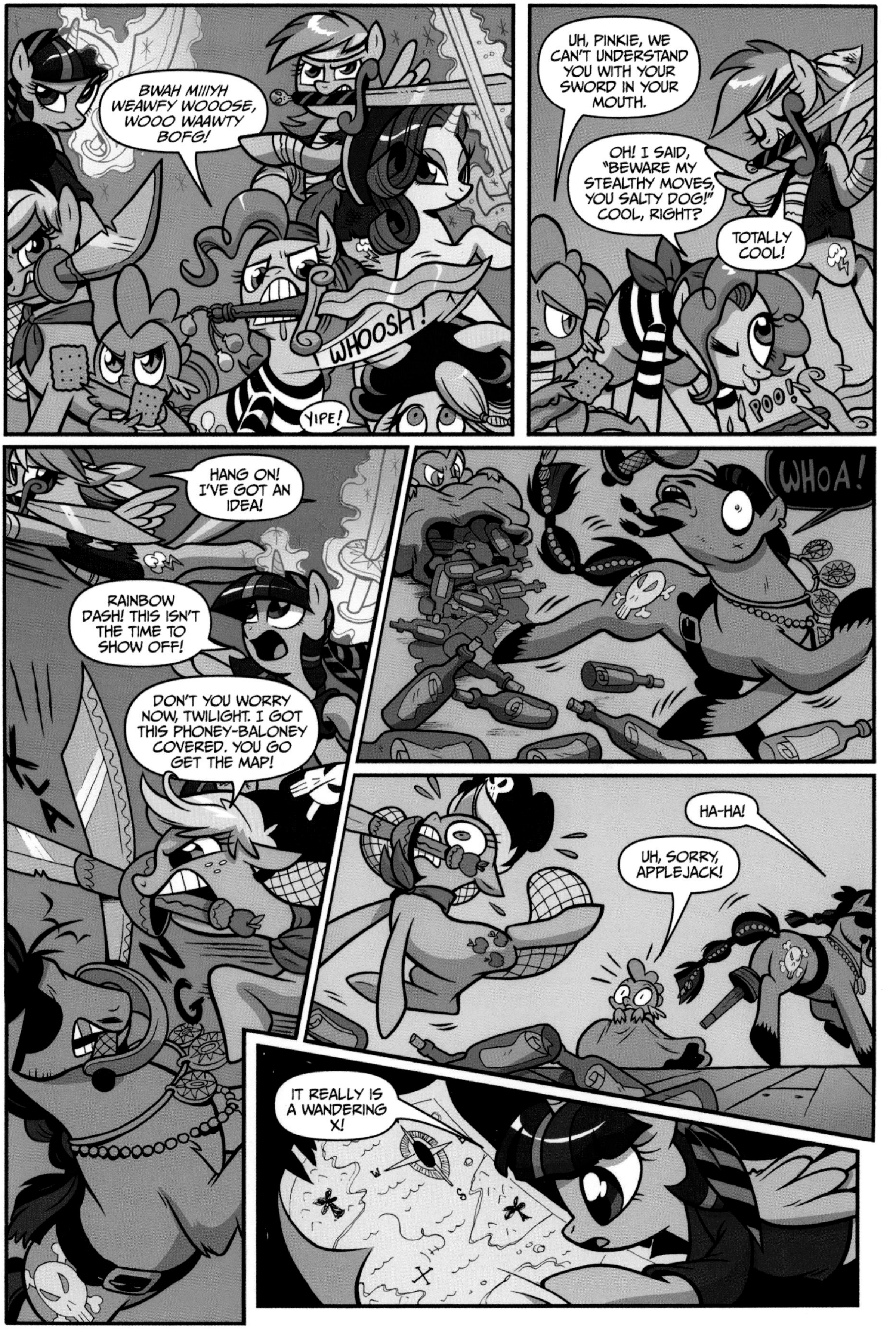
BWAH MIIIYH WEAWFY WOOOSE, WOOO WAAWTY BOFG!
WHOOSH!
YIPE!
UH, PINKIE, WE CAN'T UNDERSTAND YOU WITH YOUR SWORD IN YOUR MOUTH.
OH! I SAID, "BEWARE MY STEALTHY MOVES, YOU SALTY DOG!" COOL, RIGHT?
TOTALLY COOL!
POO!
HANG ON! I'VE GOT AN IDEA!
RAINBOW DASH! THIS ISN'T THE TIME TO SHOW OFF!
DON'T YOU WORRY NOW, TWILIGHT. I GOT THIS PHONEY-BALONEY COVERED. YOU GO GET THE MAP!
WHOA!
HA-HA!
UH, SORRY, APPLEJACK!
IT REALLY IS A WANDERING X!

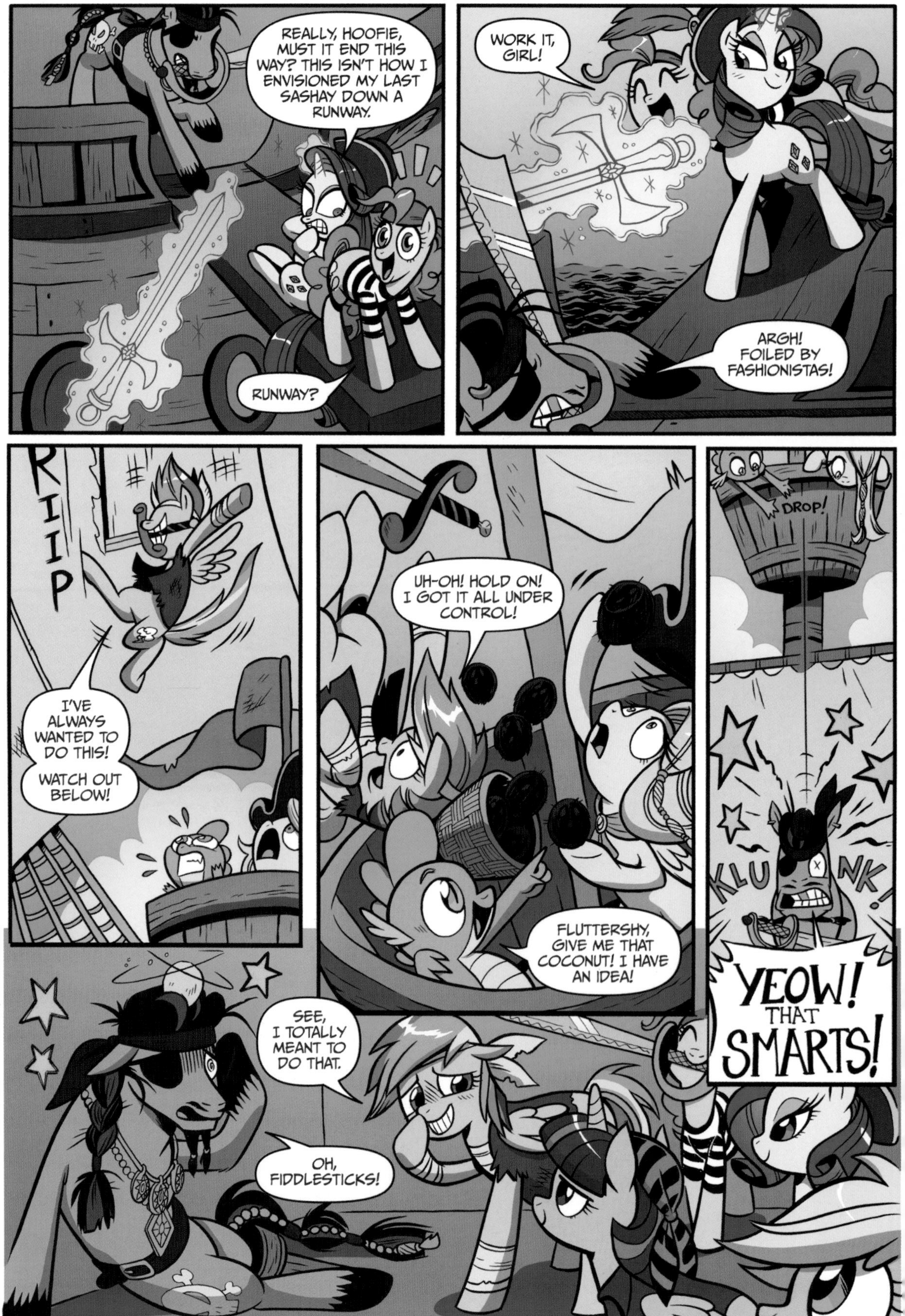
REALLY, HOOFIE, MUST IT END THIS WAY? THIS ISN'T HOW I ENVISIONED MY LAST SASHAY DOWN A RUNWAY.
RUNWAY?
WORK IT, GIRL!
ARGH! FOILED BY FASHIONISTAS!
RIIP
I'VE ALWAYS WANTED TO DO THIS!
WATCH OUT BELOW!
UH-OH! HOLD ON! I GOT IT ALL UNDER CONTROL!
FLUTTERSHY, GIVE ME THAT COCONUT! I HAVE AN IDEA!
DROP!
KLUNK!
YEOW! THAT SMARTS!
SEE, I TOTALLY MEANT TO DO THAT.
OH, FIDDLESTICKS!

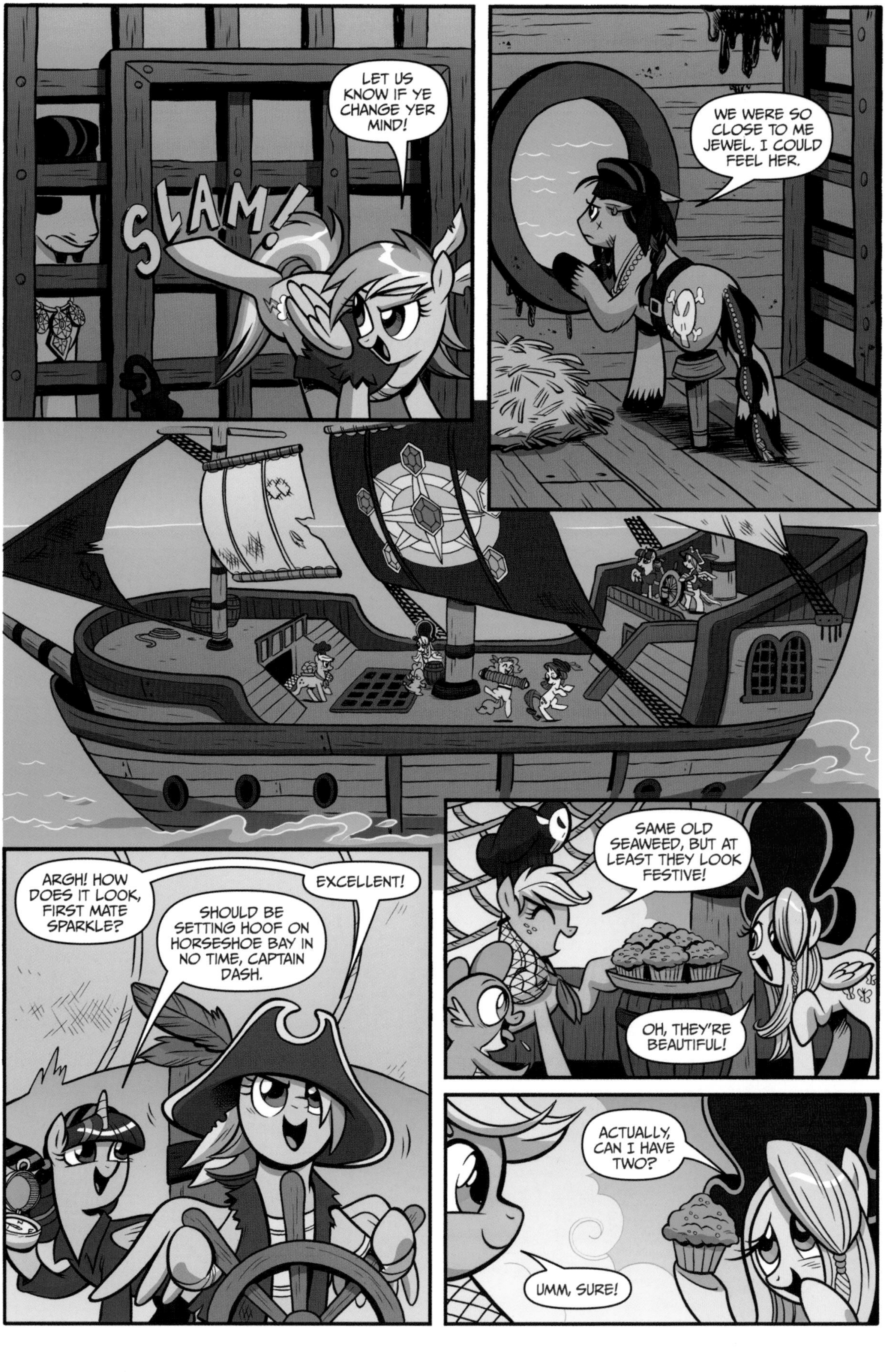
LET US KNOW IF YE CHANGE YER MIND!
SLAM!
WE WERE SO CLOSE TO ME JEWEL. I COULD FEEL HER.
ARGH! HOW DOES IT LOOK, FIRST MATE SPARKLE?
EXCELLENT!
SHOULD BE SETTING HOOF ON HORSESHOE BAY IN NO TIME, CAPTAIN DASH.
SAME OLD SEAWEED, BUT AT LEAST THEY LOOK FESTIVE!
OH, THEY'RE BEAUTIFUL!
ACTUALLY, CAN I HAVE TWO?
UMM, SURE!

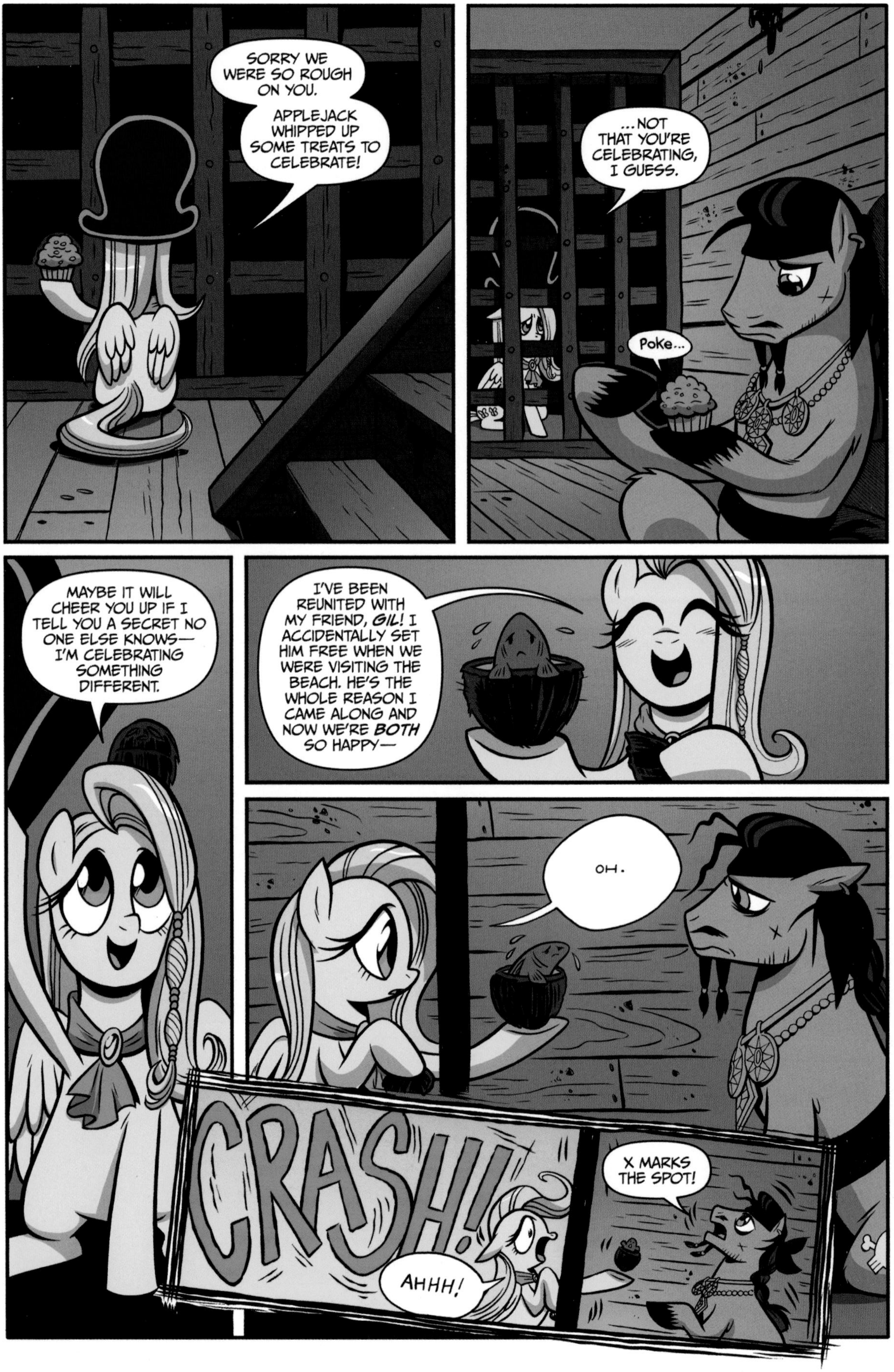
SORRY WE WERE SO ROUGH ON YOU.
APPLEJACK WHIPPED UP SOME TREATS TO CELEBRATE!
...NOT THAT YOU'RE CELEBRATING, I GUESS.
Poke...
MAYBE IT WILL CHEER YOU UP IF I TELL YOU A SECRET NO ONE ELSE KNOWS— I'M CELEBRATING SOMETHING DIFFERENT.
I'VE BEEN REUNITED WITH MY FRIEND, *GIL!* I ACCIDENTALLY SET HIM FREE WHEN WE WERE VISITING THE BEACH. HE'S THE WHOLE REASON I CAME ALONG AND NOW WE'RE *BOTH* SO HAPPY—
OH.
CRASH!!
AHHH!
X MARKS THE SPOT!

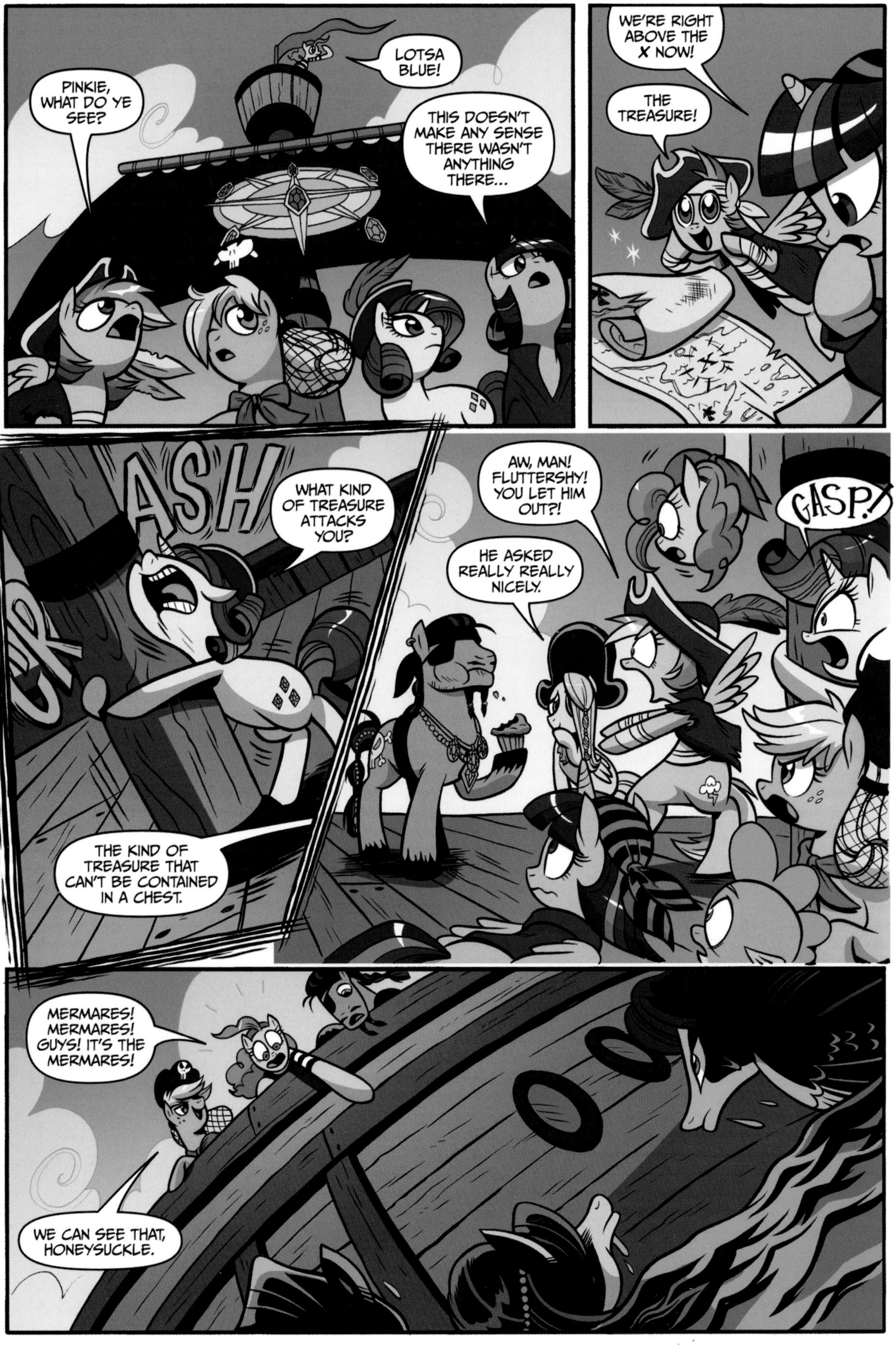
PINKIE, WHAT DO YE SEE?
LOTSA BLUE!
THIS DOESN'T MAKE ANY SENSE THERE WASN'T ANYTHING THERE...
WE'RE RIGHT ABOVE THE X NOW!
THE TREASURE!
ASH
WHAT KIND OF TREASURE ATTACKS YOU?
THE KIND OF TREASURE THAT CAN'T BE CONTAINED IN A CHEST.
AW, MAN! FLUTTERSHY! YOU LET HIM OUT?!
HE ASKED REALLY REALLY NICELY.
GASP!
MERMARES! MERMARES! GUYS! IT'S THE MERMARES!
WE CAN SEE THAT, HONEYSUCKLE.

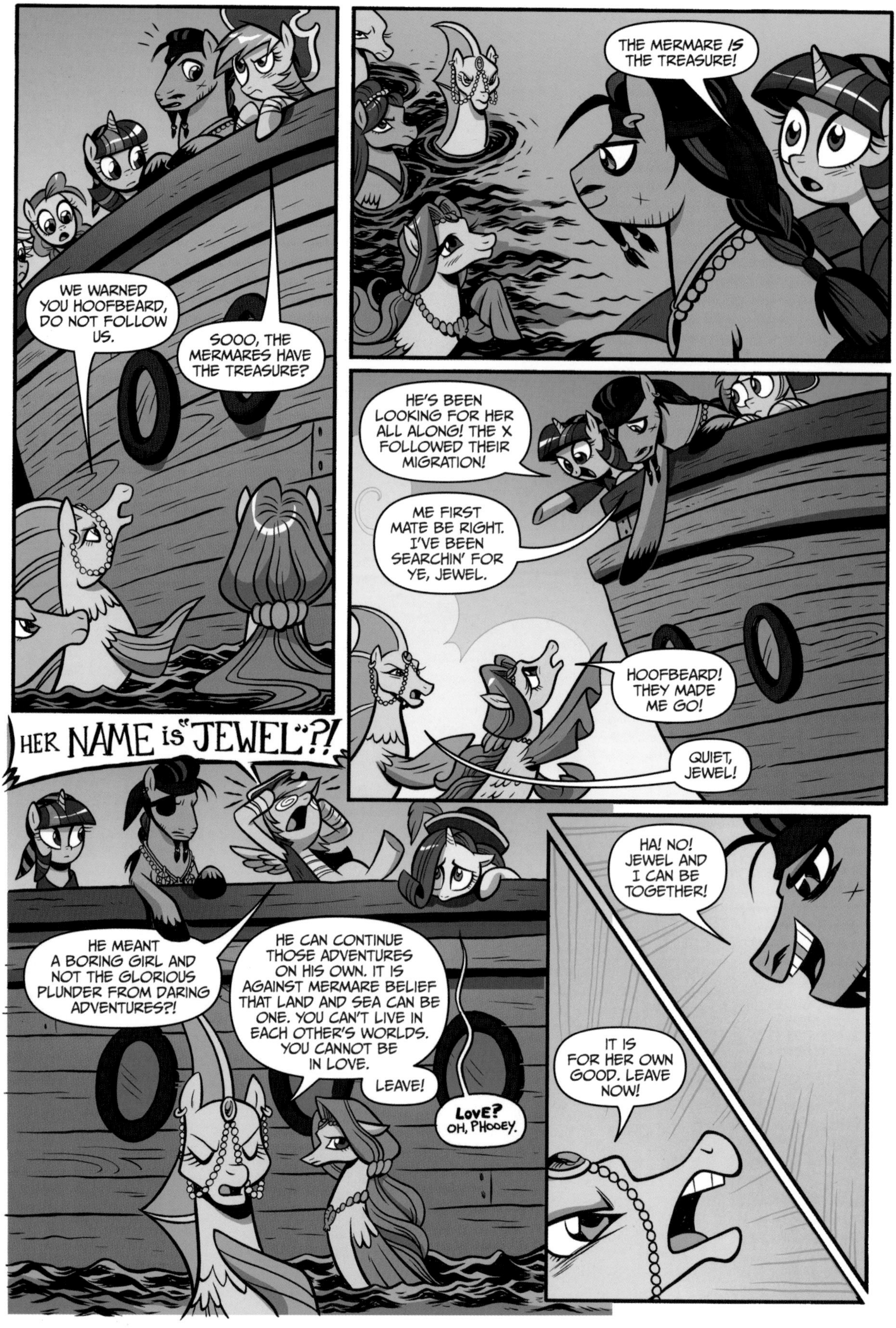
WE WARNED YOU HOOFBEARD, DO NOT FOLLOW US.
SOOO, THE MERMARES HAVE THE TREASURE?
THE MERMARE *IS* THE TREASURE!
HE'S BEEN LOOKING FOR HER ALL ALONG! THE X FOLLOWED THEIR MIGRATION!
ME FIRST MATE BE RIGHT. I'VE BEEN SEARCHIN' FOR YE, JEWEL.
HOOFBEARD! THEY MADE ME GO!
QUIET, JEWEL!
HER NAME is "JEWEL"?!
HE MEANT A BORING GIRL AND NOT THE GLORIOUS PLUNDER FROM DARING ADVENTURES?!
HE CAN CONTINUE THOSE ADVENTURES ON HIS OWN. IT IS AGAINST MERMARE BELIEF THAT LAND AND SEA CAN BE ONE. YOU CAN'T LIVE IN EACH OTHER'S WORLDS. YOU CANNOT BE IN LOVE.
LEAVE!
LOVE? OH, PHOOEY.
HA! NO! JEWEL AND I CAN BE TOGETHER!
IT IS FOR HER OWN GOOD. LEAVE NOW!

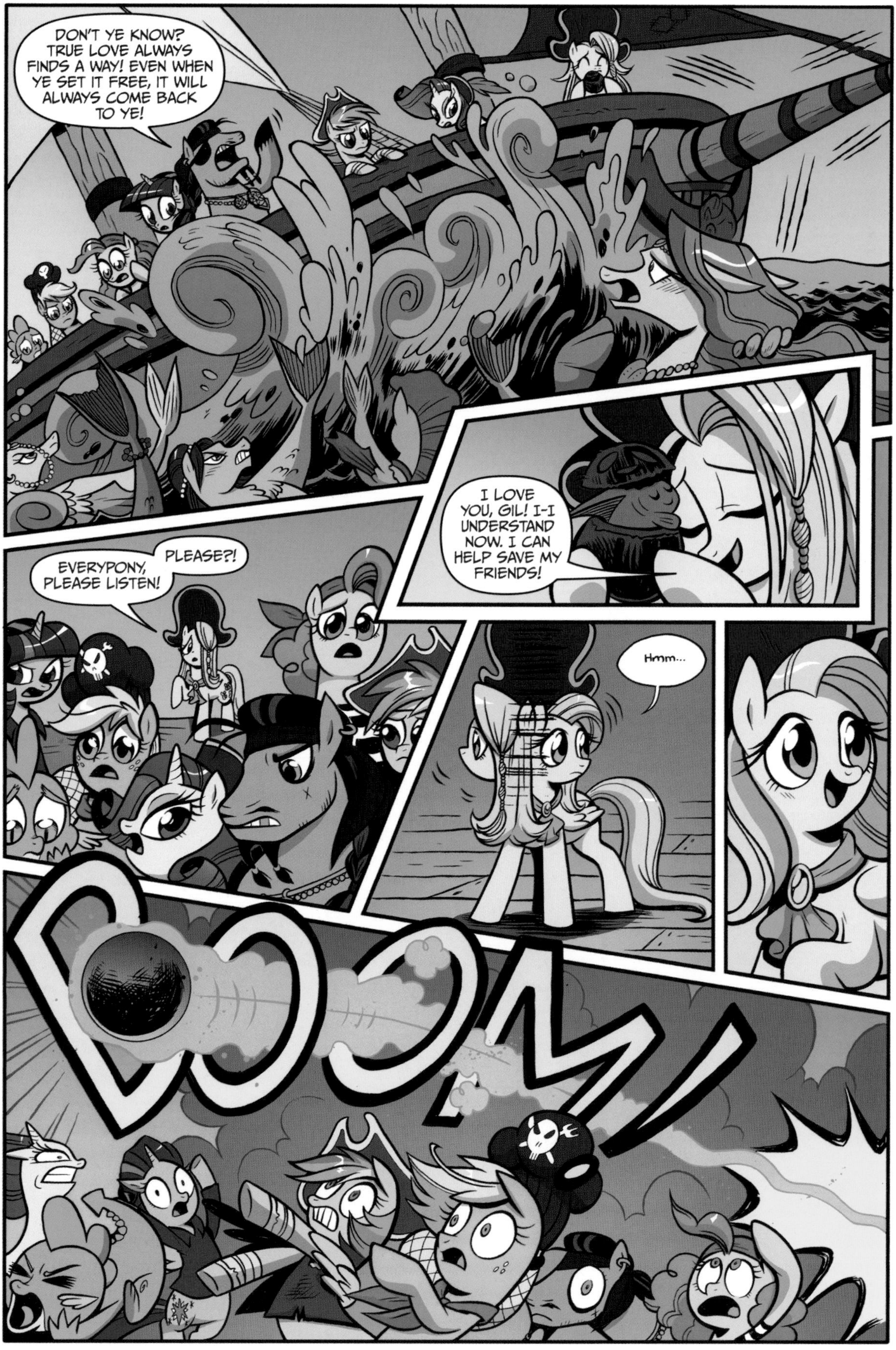
DON'T YE KNOW? TRUE LOVE ALWAYS FINDS A WAY! EVEN WHEN YE SET IT FREE, IT WILL ALWAYS COME BACK TO YE!
I LOVE YOU, GIL! I-I UNDERSTAND NOW. I CAN HELP SAVE MY FRIENDS!
EVERYPONY, PLEASE LISTEN!
PLEASE?!
Hmm...
BOOM!

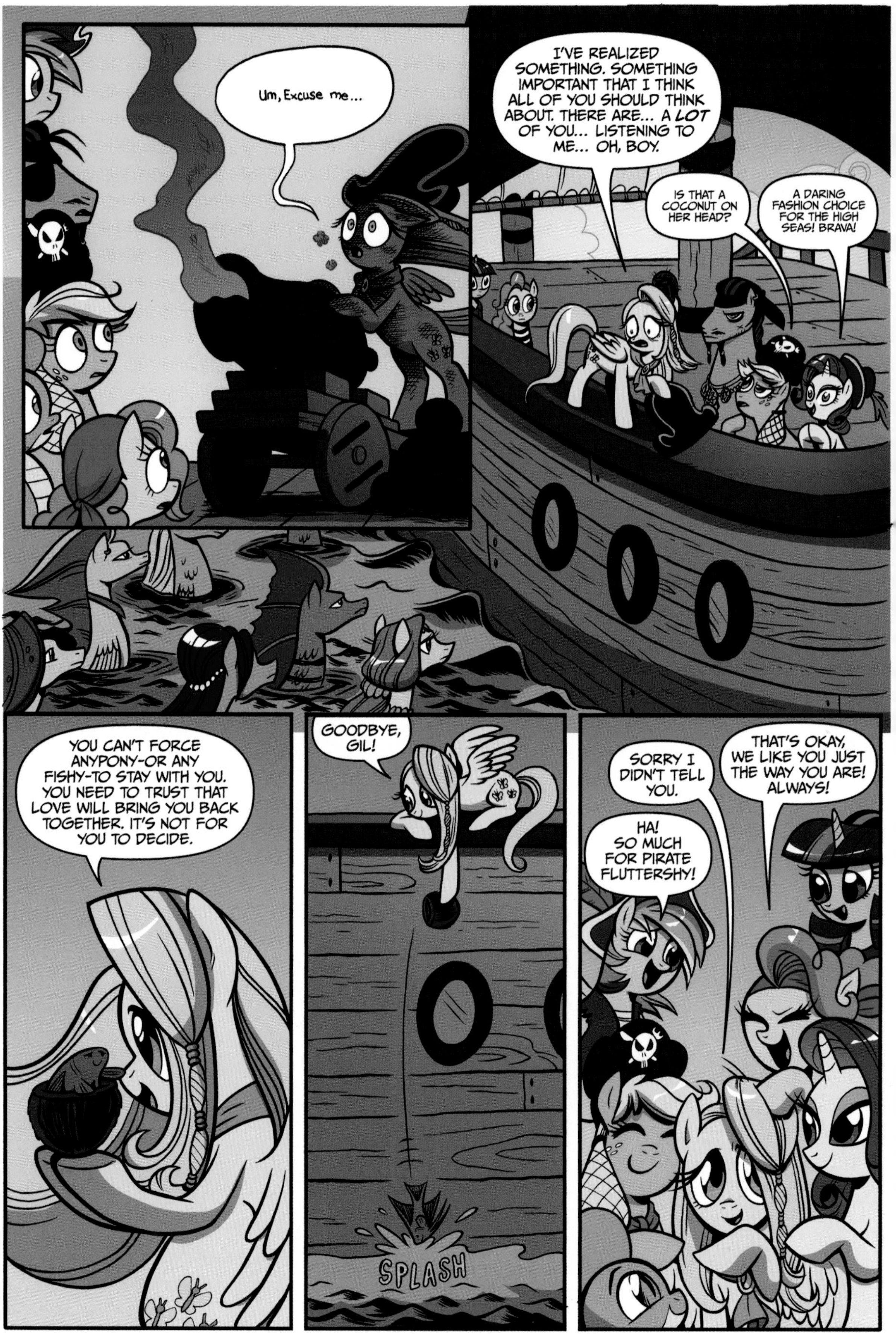
Um, Excuse me...
I'VE REALIZED SOMETHING. SOMETHING IMPORTANT THAT I THINK ALL OF YOU SHOULD THINK ABOUT. THERE ARE... A *LOT* OF YOU... LISTENING TO ME... OH, BOY.
IS THAT A COCONUT ON HER HEAD?
A DARING FASHION CHOICE FOR THE HIGH SEAS! BRAVA!
YOU CAN'T FORCE ANYPONY-OR ANY FISHY-TO STAY WITH YOU. YOU NEED TO TRUST THAT LOVE WILL BRING YOU BACK TOGETHER. IT'S NOT FOR YOU TO DECIDE.
GOODBYE, GIL!
SPLASH
SORRY I DIDN'T TELL YOU.
THAT'S OKAY, WE LIKE YOU JUST THE WAY YOU ARE! ALWAYS!
HA! SO MUCH FOR PIRATE FLUTTERSHY!

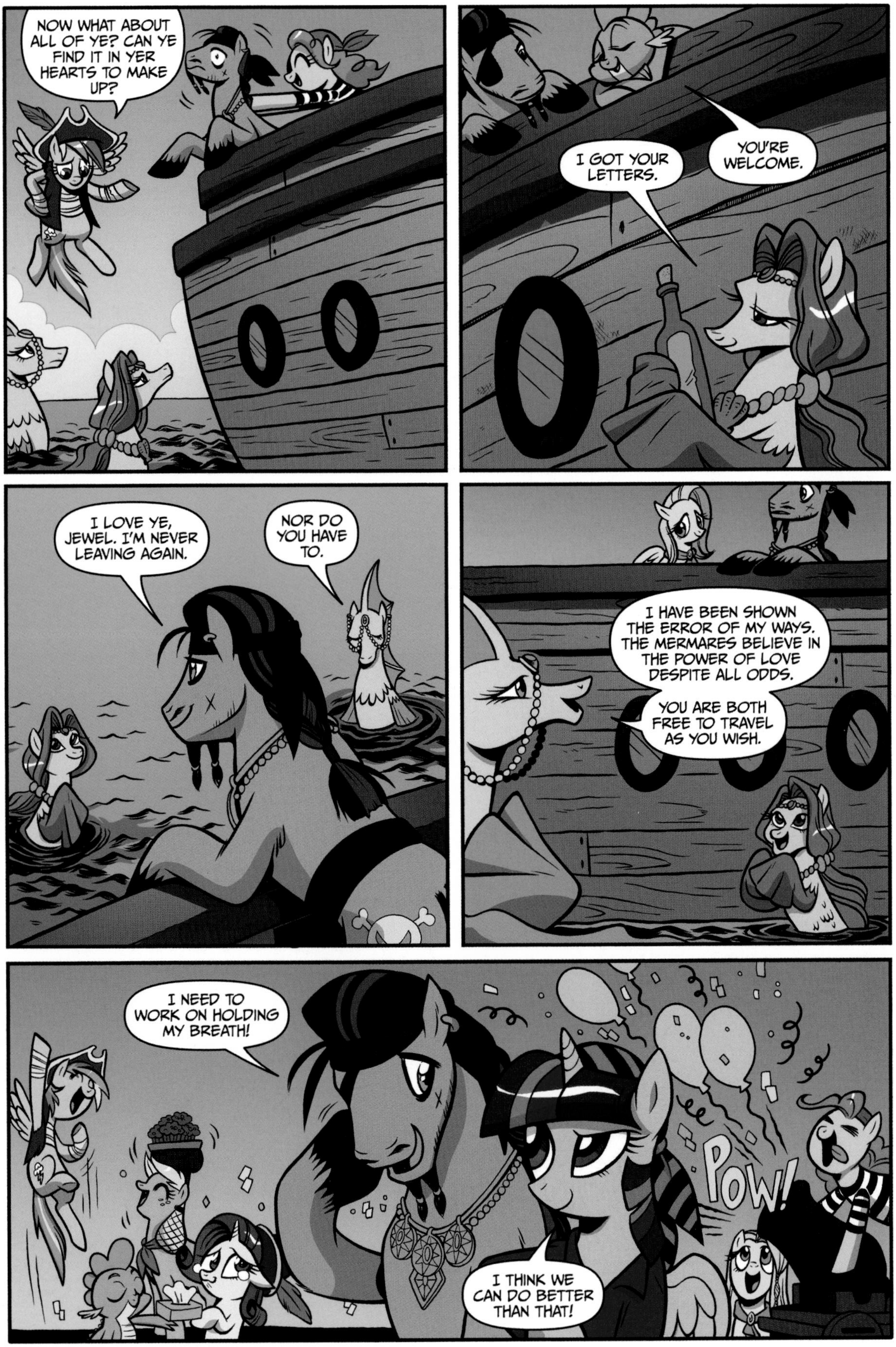
NOW WHAT ABOUT ALL OF YE? CAN YE FIND IT IN YER HEARTS TO MAKE UP?
I GOT YOUR LETTERS.
YOU'RE WELCOME.
I LOVE YE, JEWEL. I'M NEVER LEAVING AGAIN.
NOR DO YOU HAVE TO.
I HAVE BEEN SHOWN THE ERROR OF MY WAYS. THE MERMARES BELIEVE IN THE POWER OF LOVE DESPITE ALL ODDS.
YOU ARE BOTH FREE TO TRAVEL AS YOU WISH.
I NEED TO WORK ON HOLDING MY BREATH!
I THINK WE CAN DO BETTER THAN THAT!
POW!

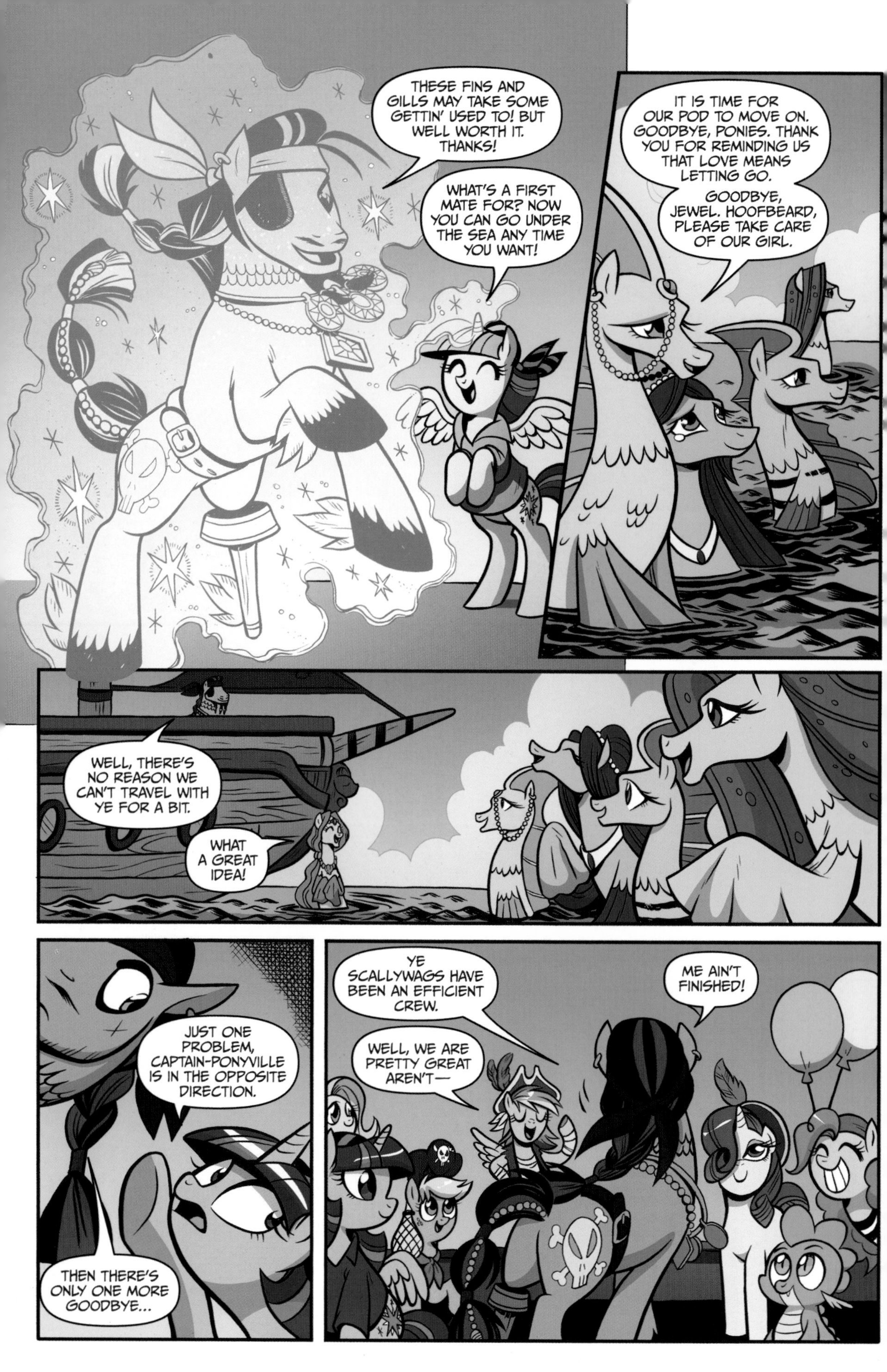
THESE FINS AND GILLS MAY TAKE SOME GETTIN' USED TO! BUT WELL WORTH IT. THANKS!
WHAT'S A FIRST MATE FOR? NOW YOU CAN GO UNDER THE SEA ANY TIME YOU WANT!
IT IS TIME FOR OUR POD TO MOVE ON. GOODBYE, PONIES. THANK YOU FOR REMINDING US THAT LOVE MEANS LETTING GO.
GOODBYE, JEWEL. HOOFBEARD, PLEASE TAKE CARE OF OUR GIRL.
WELL, THERE'S NO REASON WE CAN'T TRAVEL WITH YE FOR A BIT.
WHAT A GREAT IDEA!
JUST ONE PROBLEM, CAPTAIN-PONYVILLE IS IN THE OPPOSITE DIRECTION.
THEN THERE'S ONLY ONE MORE GOODBYE...
YE SCALLYWAGS HAVE BEEN AN EFFICIENT CREW.
WELL, WE ARE PRETTY GREAT AREN'T—
ME AIN'T FINISHED!

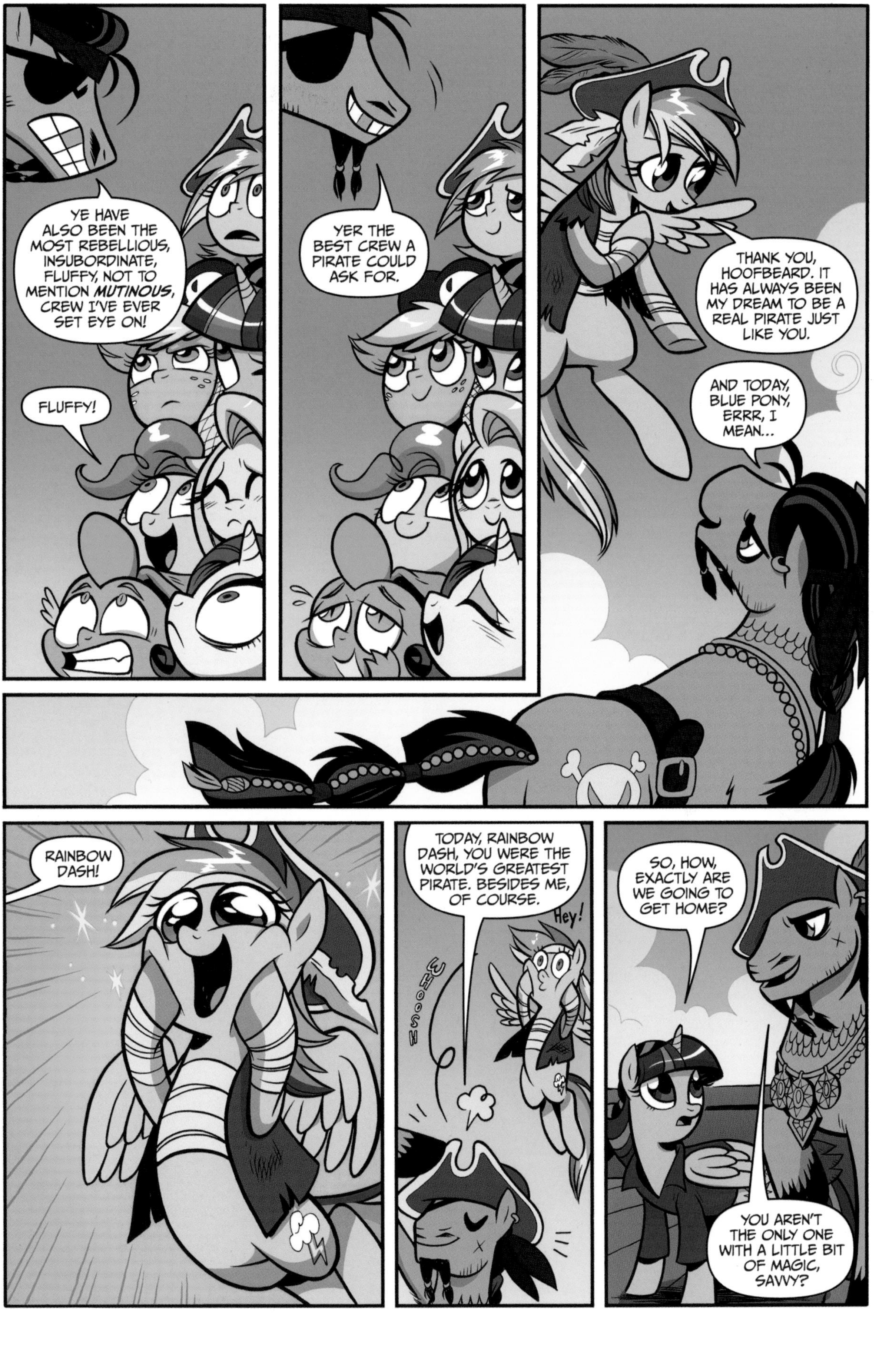
YE HAVE ALSO BEEN THE MOST REBELLIOUS, INSUBORDINATE, FLUFFY, NOT TO MENTION MUTINOUS, CREW I'VE EVER SET EYE ON!
FLUFFY!
YER THE BEST CREW A PIRATE COULD ASK FOR.
THANK YOU, HOOFBEARD. IT HAS ALWAYS BEEN MY DREAM TO BE A REAL PIRATE JUST LIKE YOU.
AND TODAY, BLUE PONY, ERRR, I MEAN...
RAINBOW DASH!
TODAY, RAINBOW DASH, YOU WERE THE WORLD'S GREATEST PIRATE. BESIDES ME, OF COURSE.
Hey!
WHOOOSH
SO, HOW, EXACTLY ARE WE GOING TO GET HOME?
YOU AREN'T THE ONLY ONE WITH A LITTLE BIT OF MAGIC, SAVVY?

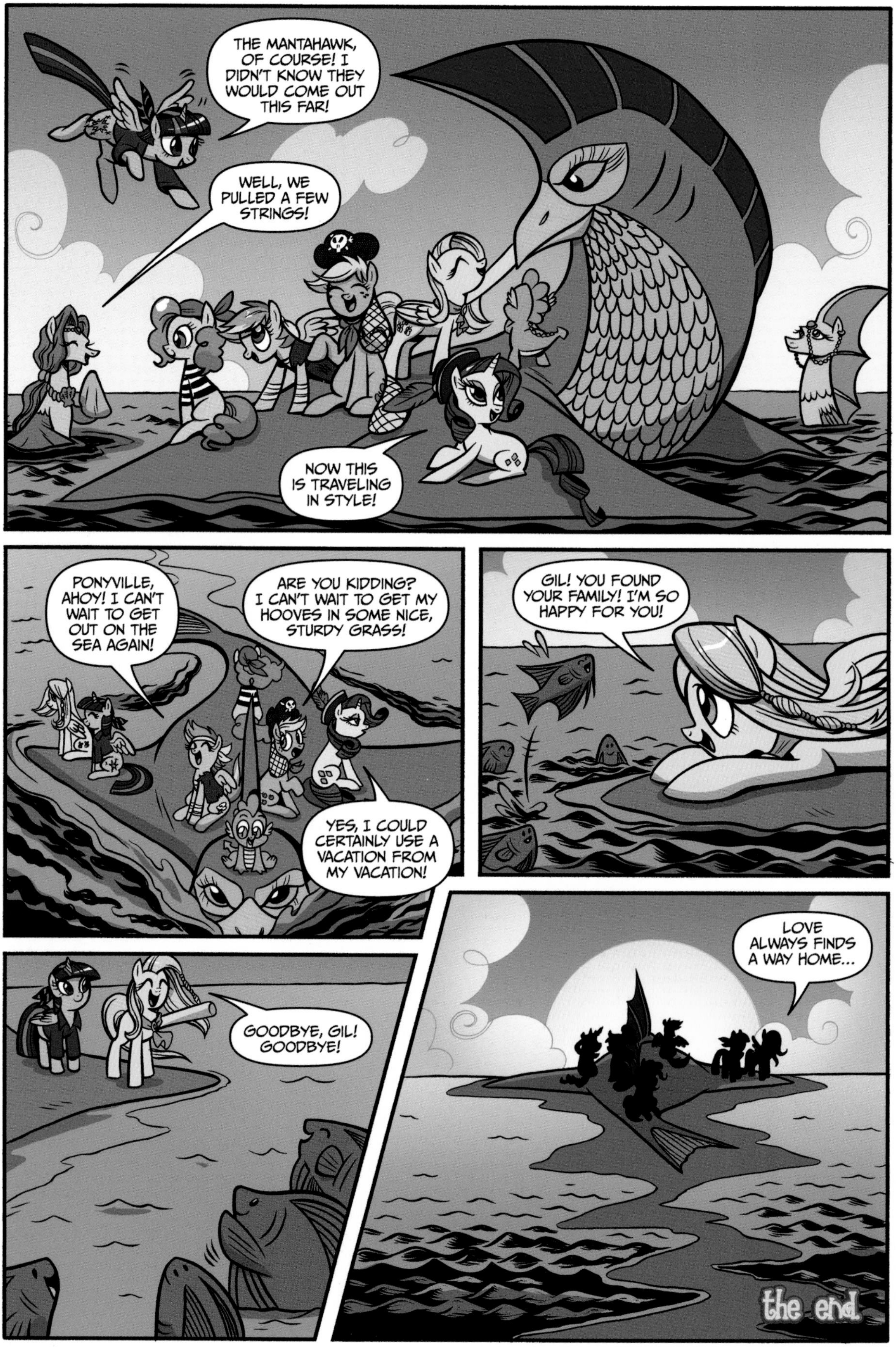
THE MANTAHAWK, OF COURSE! I DIDN'T KNOW THEY WOULD COME OUT THIS FAR!
WELL, WE PULLED A FEW STRINGS!
NOW THIS IS TRAVELING IN STYLE!
PONYVILLE, AHOY! I CAN'T WAIT TO GET OUT ON THE SEA AGAIN!
ARE YOU KIDDING? I CAN'T WAIT TO GET MY HOOVES IN SOME NICE, STURDY GRASS!
YES, I COULD CERTAINLY USE A VACATION FROM MY VACATION!
GIL! YOU FOUND YOUR FAMILY! I'M SO HAPPY FOR YOU!
GOODBYE, GIL! GOODBYE!
LOVE ALWAYS FINDS A WAY HOME...
the end.

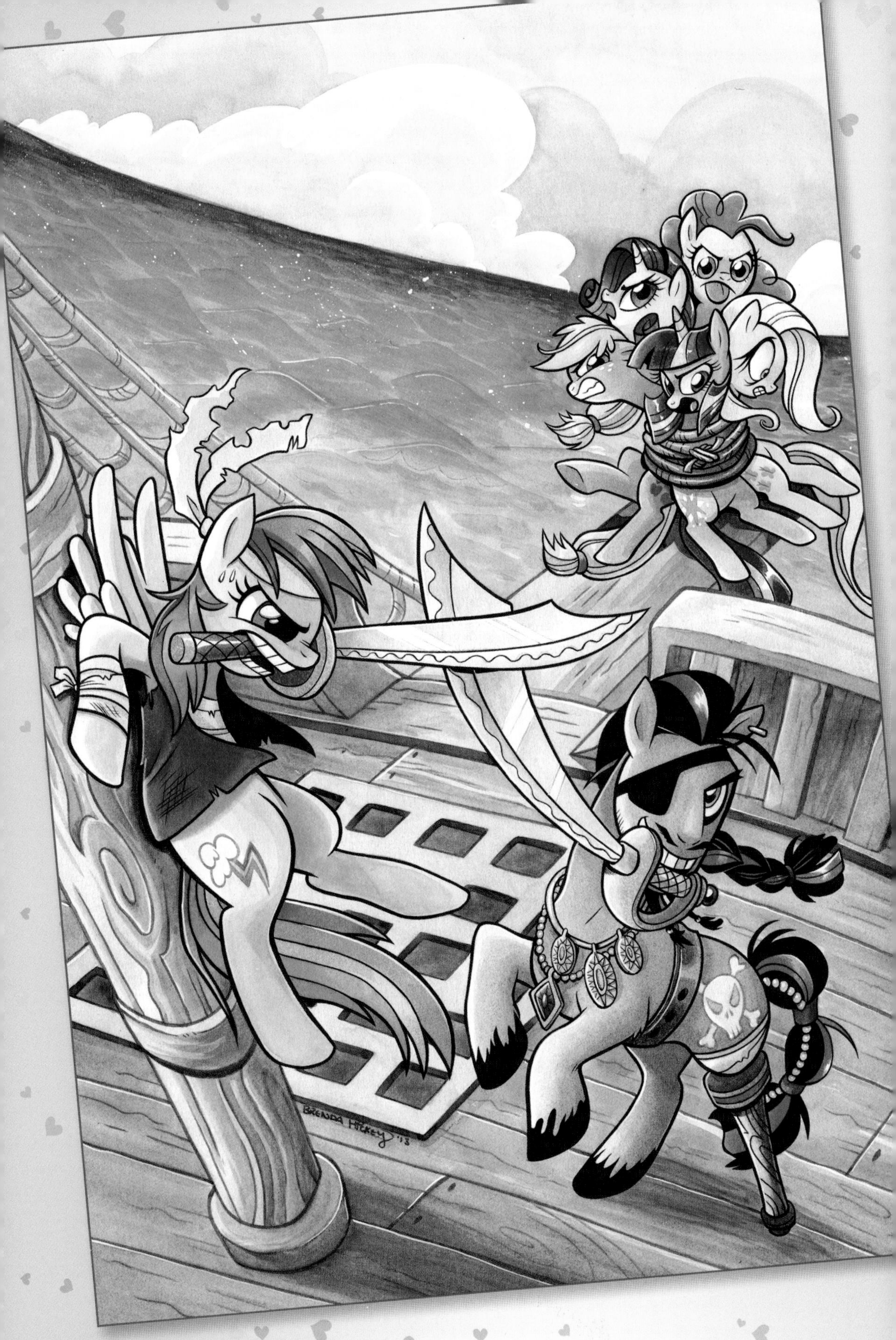
BRENDA HICKEY '13

art BY Brenda Hickey

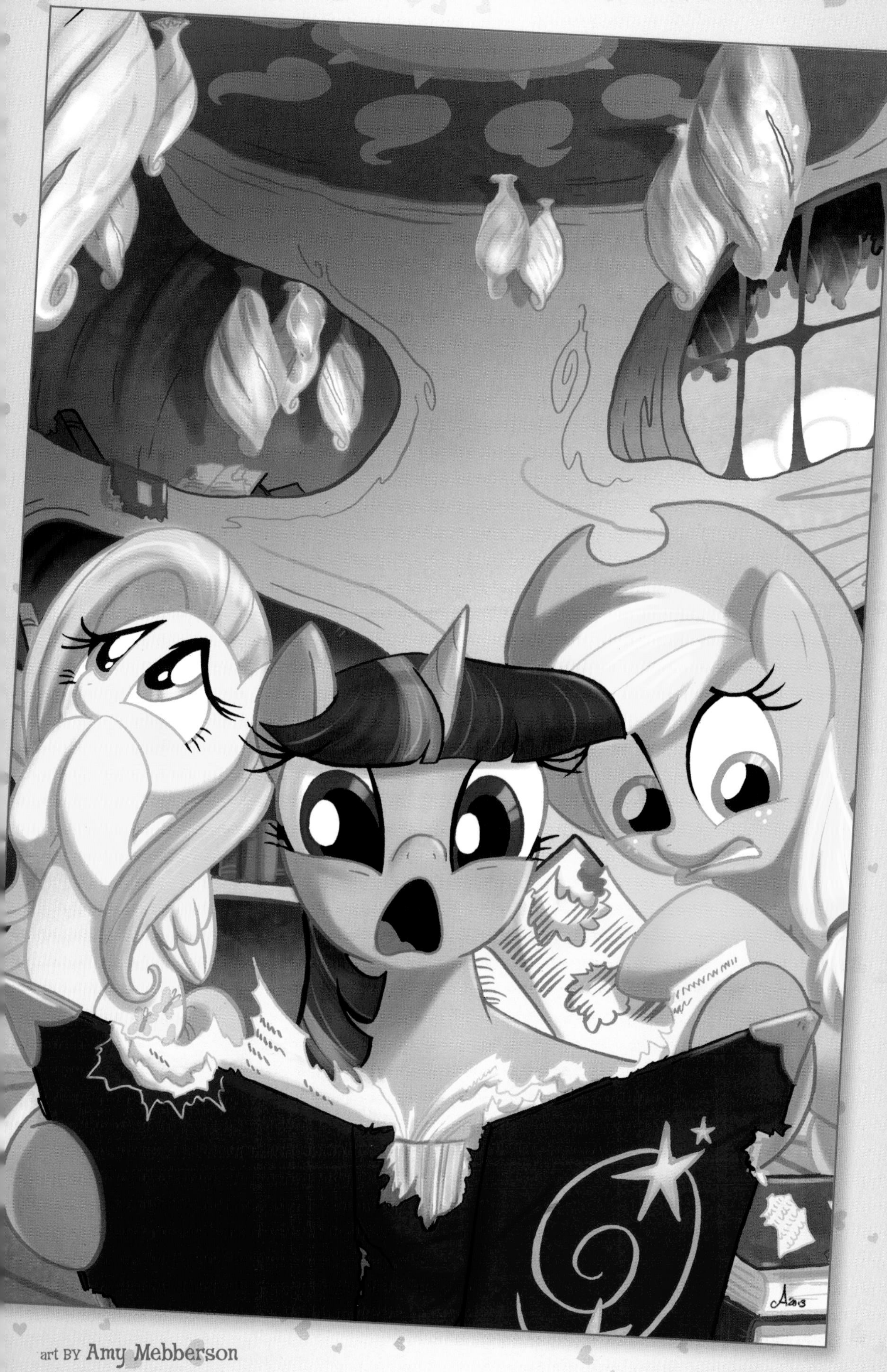

art BY Amy Mebberson

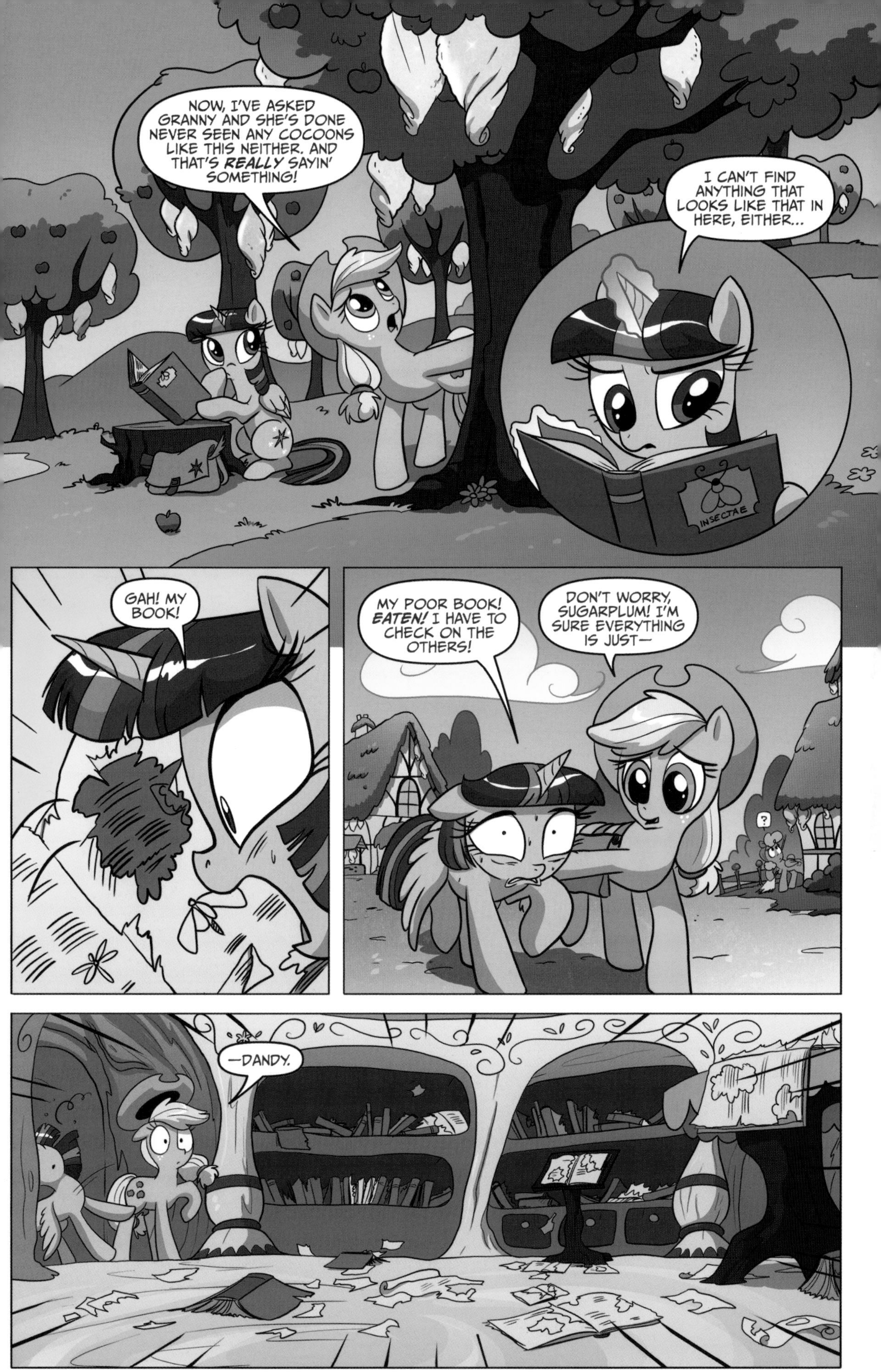
NOW, I'VE ASKED GRANNY AND SHE'S DONE NEVER SEEN ANY COCOONS LIKE THIS NEITHER. AND THAT'S **REALLY** SAYIN' SOMETHING!
I CAN'T FIND ANYTHING THAT LOOKS LIKE THAT IN HERE, EITHER...
INSECTAE
GAH! MY BOOK!
MY POOR BOOK! **EATEN!** I HAVE TO CHECK ON THE OTHERS!
DON'T WORRY, SUGARPLUM! I'M SURE EVERYTHING IS JUST—
?
—DANDY.

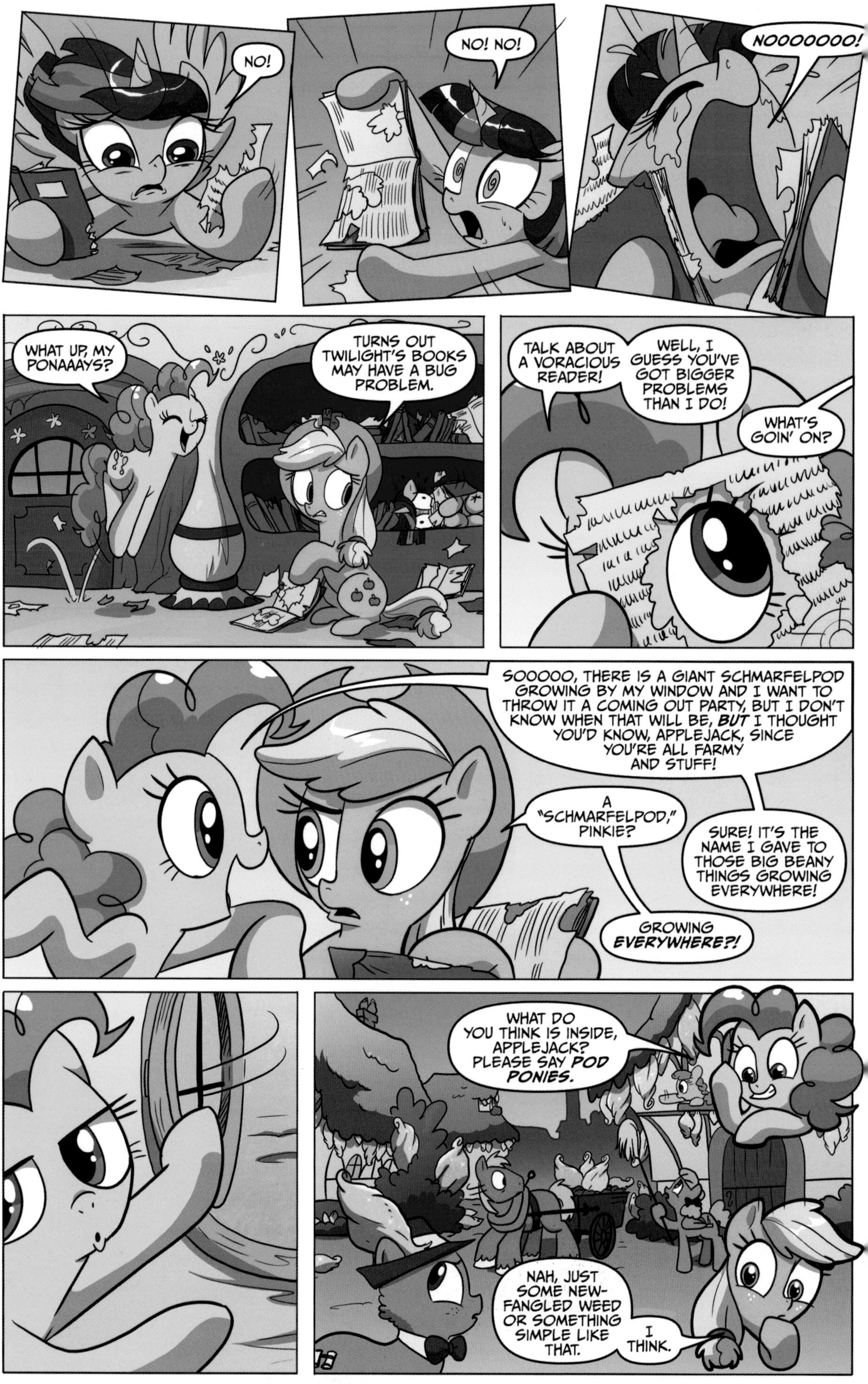
NO!
NO! NO!
NOOOOOOO!
WHAT UP, MY PONAAAYS?
TURNS OUT TWILIGHT'S BOOKS MAY HAVE A BUG PROBLEM.
TALK ABOUT A VORACIOUS READER!
WELL, I GUESS YOU'VE GOT BIGGER PROBLEMS THAN I DO!
WHAT'S GOIN' ON?
SOOOOO, THERE IS A GIANT SCHMARFELPOD GROWING BY MY WINDOW AND I WANT TO THROW IT A COMING OUT PARTY, BUT I DON'T KNOW WHEN THAT WILL BE, BUT I THOUGHT YOU'D KNOW, APPLEJACK, SINCE YOU'RE ALL FARMY AND STUFF!
A "SCHMARFELPOD," PINKIE?
SURE! IT'S THE NAME I GAVE TO THOSE BIG BEANY THINGS GROWING EVERYWHERE!
GROWING EVERYWHERE?!
WHAT DO YOU THINK IS INSIDE, APPLEJACK? PLEASE SAY POD PONIES.
NAH, JUST SOME NEW-FANGLED WEED OR SOMETHING SIMPLE LIKE THAT.
I THINK.

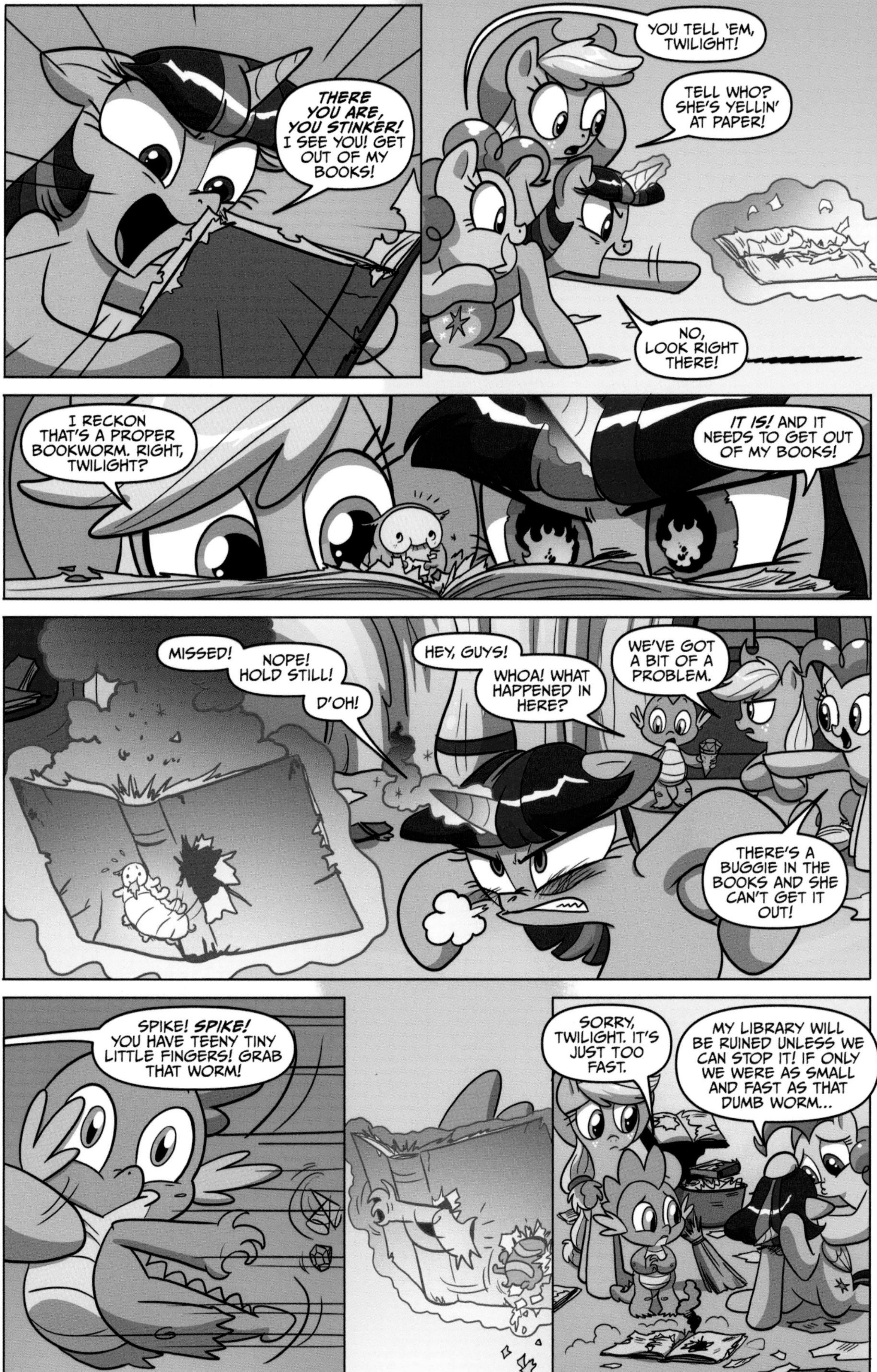

THERE YOU ARE, YOU STINKER! I SEE YOU! GET OUT OF MY BOOKS!
YOU TELL 'EM, TWILIGHT!
TELL WHO? SHE'S YELLIN' AT PAPER!
NO, LOOK RIGHT THERE!
I RECKON THAT'S A PROPER BOOKWORM. RIGHT, TWILIGHT?
IT IS! AND IT NEEDS TO GET OUT OF MY BOOKS!
MISSED!
NOPE! HOLD STILL!
D'OH!
HEY, GUYS!
WHOA! WHAT HAPPENED IN HERE?
WE'VE GOT A BIT OF A PROBLEM.
THERE'S A BUGGIE IN THE BOOKS AND SHE CAN'T GET IT OUT!
SPIKE! SPIKE! YOU HAVE TEENY TINY LITTLE FINGERS! GRAB THAT WORM!
SORRY, TWILIGHT. IT'S JUST TOO FAST.
MY LIBRARY WILL BE RUINED UNLESS WE CAN STOP IT! IF ONLY WE WERE AS SMALL AND FAST AS THAT DUMB WORM...

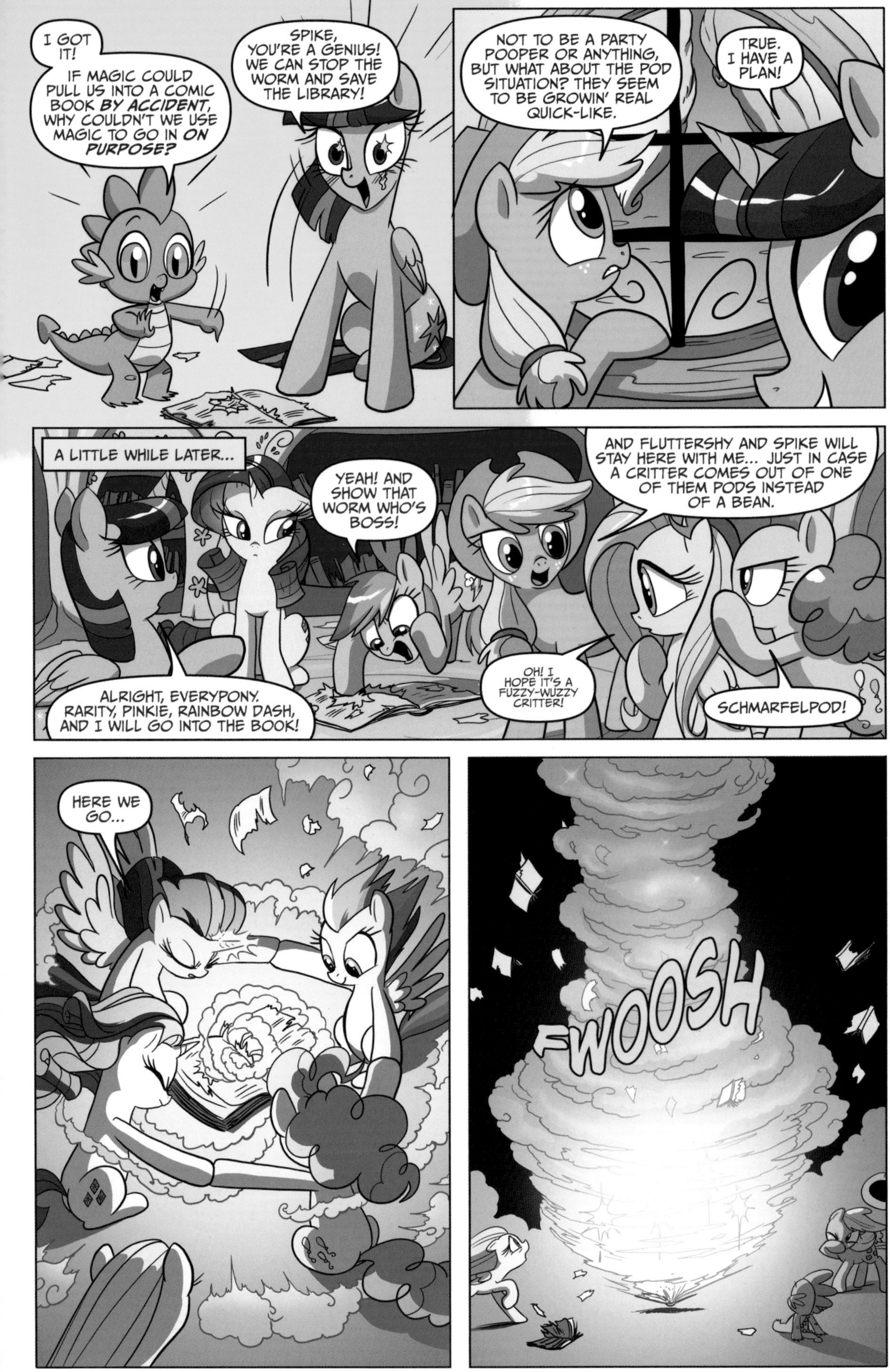
I GOT IT!
IF MAGIC COULD PULL US INTO A COMIC BOOK ***BY ACCIDENT***, WHY COULDN'T WE USE MAGIC TO GO IN ***ON PURPOSE?***
SPIKE, YOU'RE A GENIUS! WE CAN STOP THE WORM AND SAVE THE LIBRARY!
NOT TO BE A PARTY POOPER OR ANYTHING, BUT WHAT ABOUT THE POD SITUATION? THEY SEEM TO BE GROWIN' REAL QUICK-LIKE.
TRUE. I HAVE A PLAN!
A LITTLE WHILE LATER...
ALRIGHT, EVERYPONY. RARITY, PINKIE, RAINBOW DASH, AND I WILL GO INTO THE BOOK!
YEAH! AND SHOW THAT WORM WHO'S BOSS!
AND FLUTTERSHY AND SPIKE WILL STAY HERE WITH ME... JUST IN CASE A CRITTER COMES OUT OF ONE OF THEM PODS INSTEAD OF A BEAN.
OH! I HOPE IT'S A FUZZY-WUZZY CRITTER!
SCHMARFELPOD!
HERE WE GO...
FWOOSH

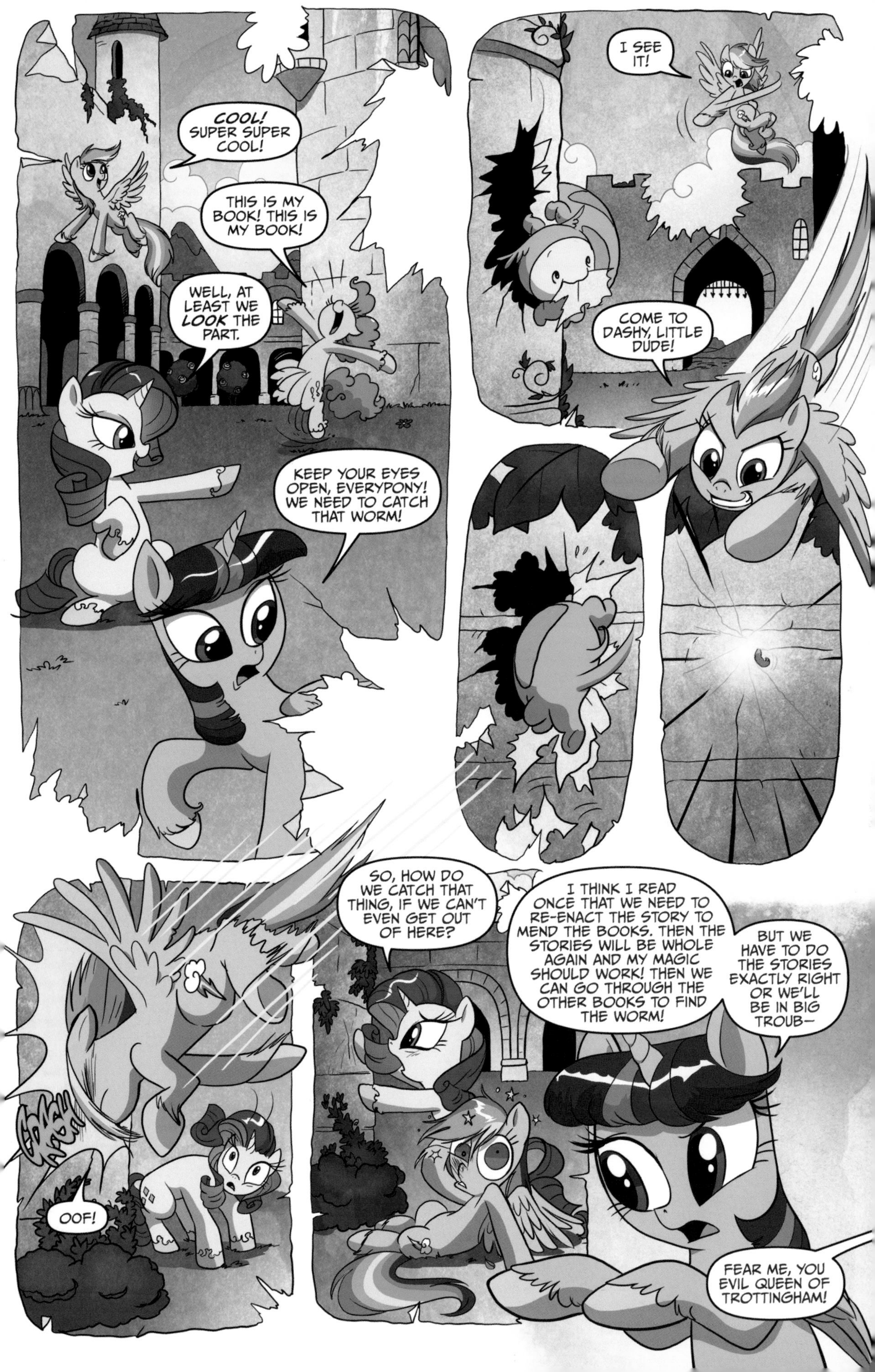
COOL! SUPER SUPER COOL!
THIS IS MY BOOK! THIS IS MY BOOK!
WELL, AT LEAST WE LOOK THE PART.
KEEP YOUR EYES OPEN, EVERYPONY! WE NEED TO CATCH THAT WORM!
I SEE IT!
COME TO DASHY, LITTLE DUDE!
OOF!
SO, HOW DO WE CATCH THAT THING, IF WE CAN'T EVEN GET OUT OF HERE?
I THINK I READ ONCE THAT WE NEED TO RE-ENACT THE STORY TO MEND THE BOOKS. THEN THE STORIES WILL BE WHOLE AGAIN AND MY MAGIC SHOULD WORK! THEN WE CAN GO THROUGH THE OTHER BOOKS TO FIND THE WORM!
BUT WE HAVE TO DO THE STORIES EXACTLY RIGHT OR WE'LL BE IN BIG TROUB—
FEAR ME, YOU EVIL QUEEN OF TROTTINGHAM!

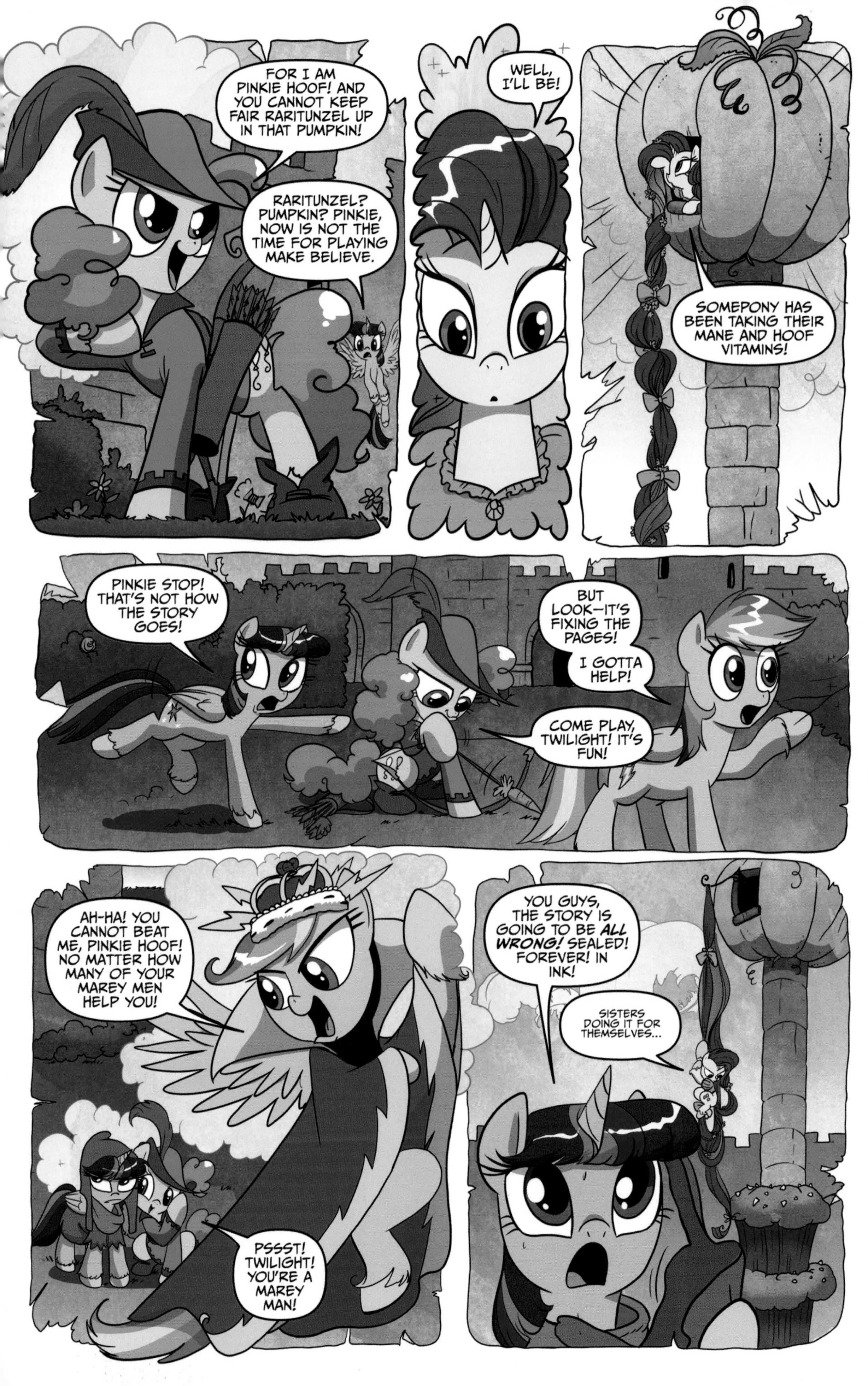
FOR I AM PINKIE HOOF! AND YOU CANNOT KEEP FAIR RARITUNZEL UP IN THAT PUMPKIN!
RARITUNZEL? PUMPKIN? PINKIE, NOW IS NOT THE TIME FOR PLAYING MAKE BELIEVE.
WELL, I'LL BE!
SOMEPONY HAS BEEN TAKING THEIR MANE AND HOOF VITAMINS!
PINKIE STOP! THAT'S NOT HOW THE STORY GOES!
BUT LOOK—IT'S FIXING THE PAGES!
I GOTTA HELP!
COME PLAY, TWILIGHT! IT'S FUN!
AH-HA! YOU CANNOT BEAT ME, PINKIE HOOF! NO MATTER HOW MANY OF YOUR MAREY MEN HELP YOU!
PSSST! TWILIGHT! YOU'RE A MAREY MAN!
YOU GUYS, THE STORY IS GOING TO BE ***ALL WRONG!*** SEALED! FOREVER! IN INK!
SISTERS DOING IT FOR THEMSELVES...

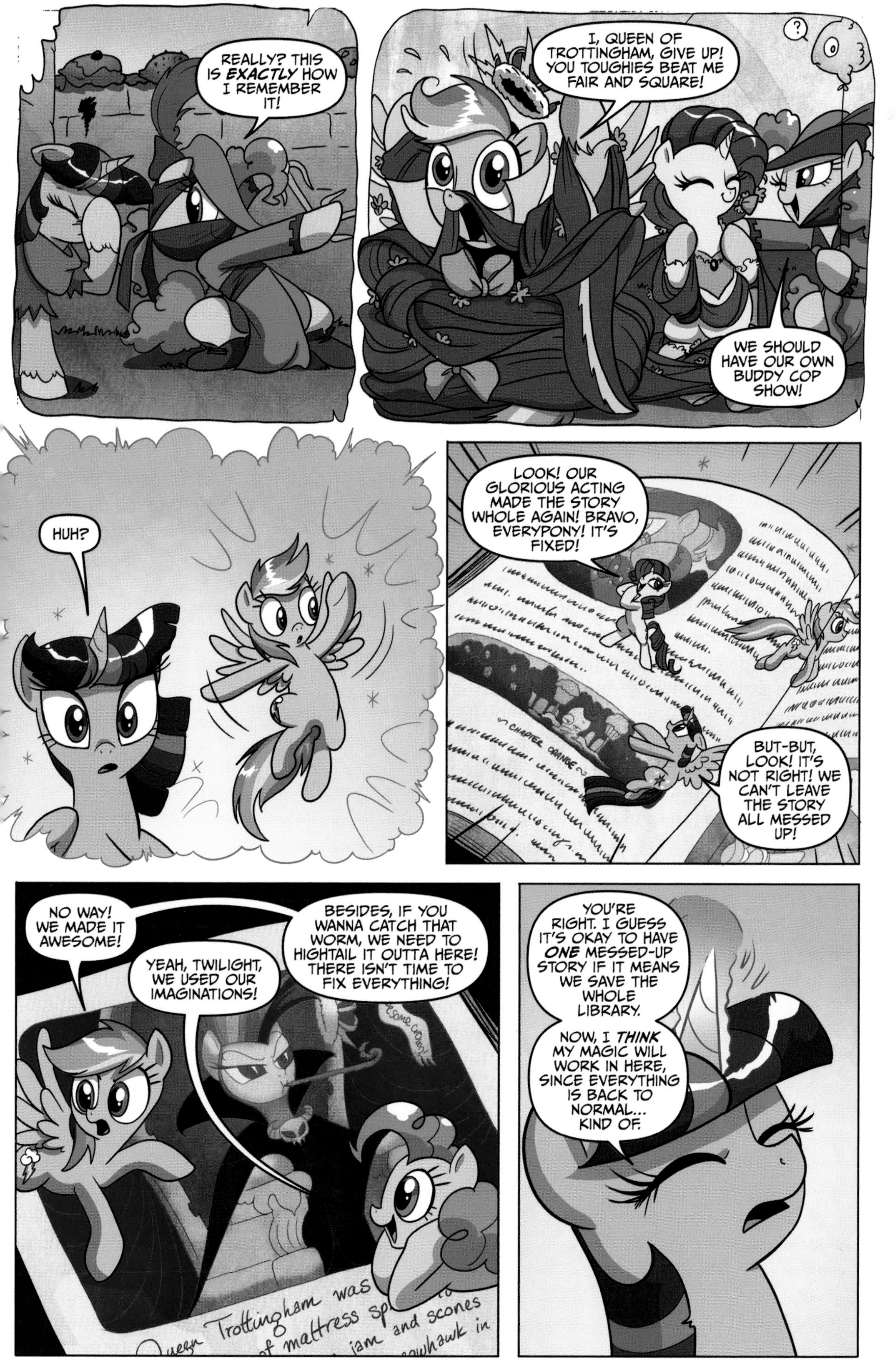

REALLY? THIS IS EXACTLY HOW I REMEMBER IT!
I, QUEEN OF TROTTINGHAM, GIVE UP! YOU TOUGHIES BEAT ME FAIR AND SQUARE!
?
WE SHOULD HAVE OUR OWN BUDDY COP SHOW!
HUH?
LOOK! OUR GLORIOUS ACTING MADE THE STORY WHOLE AGAIN! BRAVO, EVERYPONY! IT'S FIXED!
CHAPTER ORANGE
BUT-BUT, LOOK! IT'S NOT RIGHT! WE CAN'T LEAVE THE STORY ALL MESSED UP!
NO WAY! WE MADE IT AWESOME!
YEAH, TWILIGHT, WE USED OUR IMAGINATIONS!
BESIDES, IF YOU WANNA CATCH THAT WORM, WE NEED TO HIGHTAIL IT OUTTA HERE! THERE ISN'T TIME TO FIX EVERYTHING!
Queen Trottingham was
of mattress
jam and scones
YOU'RE RIGHT. I GUESS IT'S OKAY TO HAVE ONE MESSED-UP STORY IF IT MEANS WE SAVE THE WHOLE LIBRARY.
NOW, I THINK MY MAGIC WILL WORK IN HERE, SINCE EVERYTHING IS BACK TO NORMAL... KIND OF.

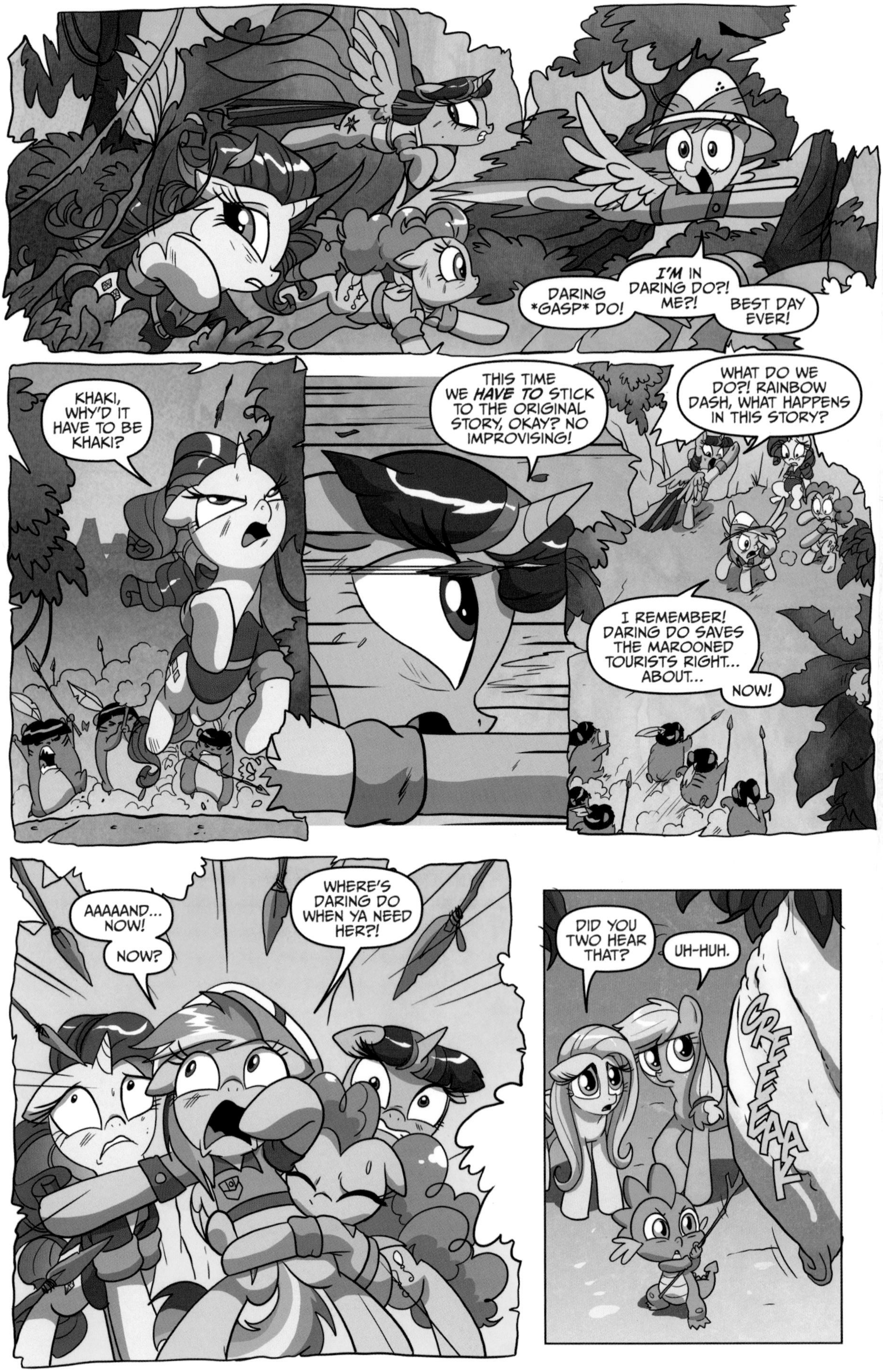
DARING *GASP* DO!
I'M IN DARING DO?! ME?!
BEST DAY EVER!
KHAKI, WHY'D IT HAVE TO BE KHAKI?
THIS TIME WE HAVE TO STICK TO THE ORIGINAL STORY, OKAY? NO IMPROVISING!
WHAT DO WE DO?! RAINBOW DASH, WHAT HAPPENS IN THIS STORY?
I REMEMBER! DARING DO SAVES THE MAROONED TOURISTS RIGHT... ABOUT...
NOW!
AAAAAND... NOW!
NOW?
WHERE'S DARING DO WHEN YA NEED HER?!
DID YOU TWO HEAR THAT?
UH-HUH.
CREEEAAK

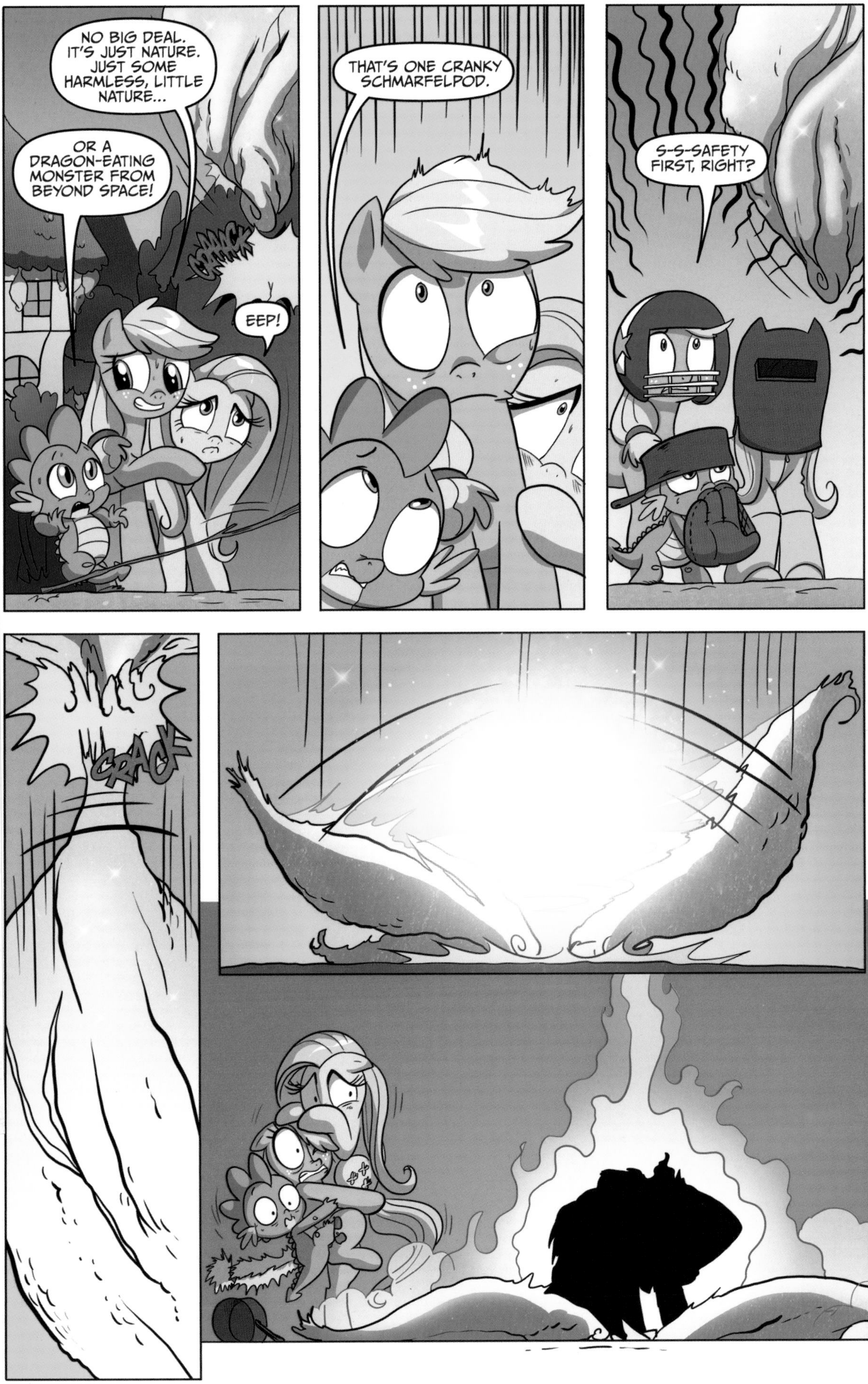
NO BIG DEAL. IT'S JUST NATURE. JUST SOME HARMLESS, LITTLE NATURE...
OR A DRAGON-EATING MONSTER FROM BEYOND SPACE!
CRACK
EEP!
THAT'S ONE CRANKY SCHMARFELPOD.
S-S-SAFETY FIRST, RIGHT?
CRACK

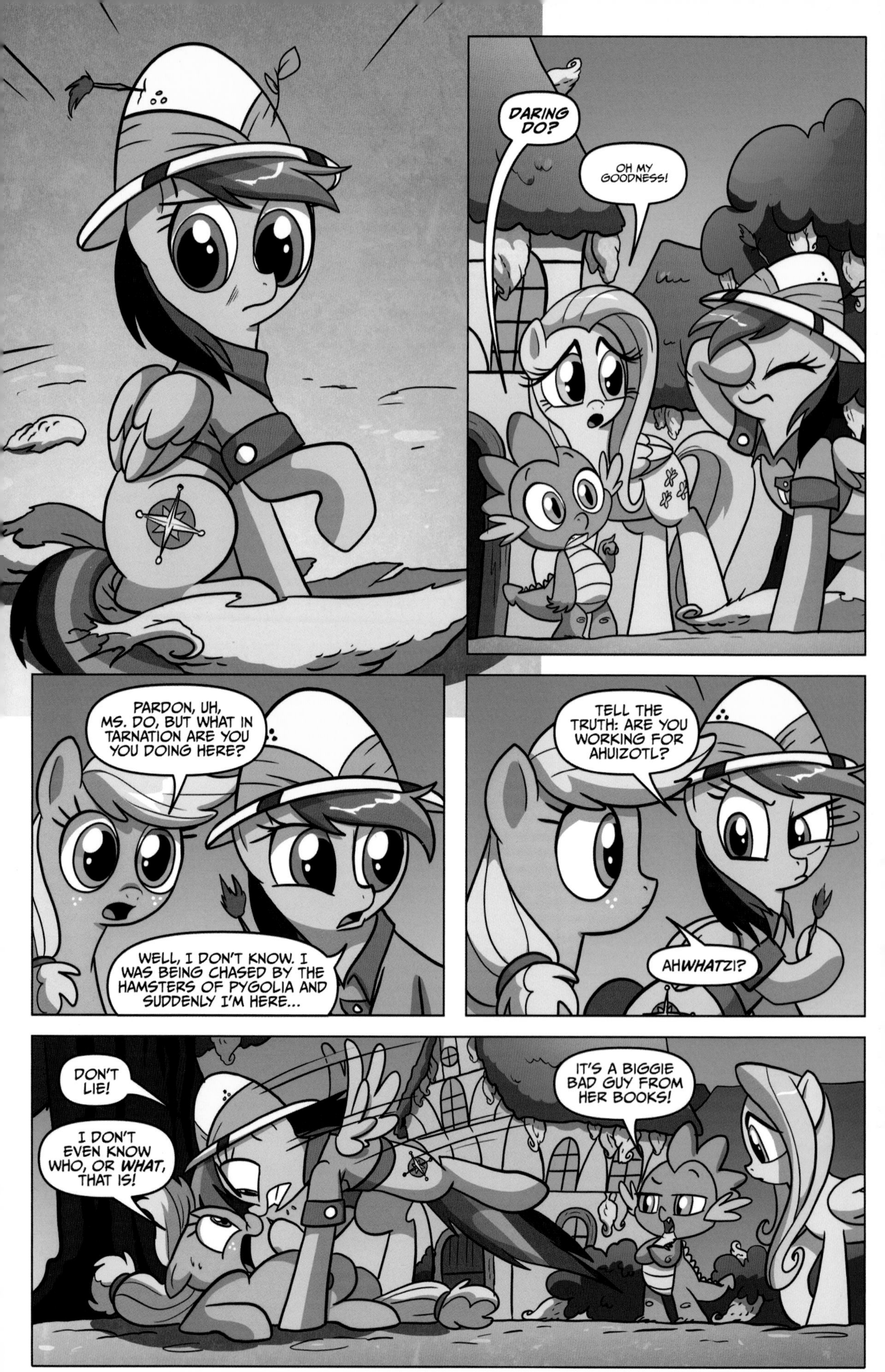
DARING DO?
OH MY GOODNESS!
PARDON, UH, MS. DO, BUT WHAT IN TARNATION ARE YOU YOU DOING HERE?
WELL, I DON'T KNOW. I WAS BEING CHASED BY THE HAMSTERS OF PYGOLIA AND SUDDENLY I'M HERE...
TELL THE TRUTH: ARE YOU WORKING FOR AHUIZOTL?
AHWHATZI?
DON'T LIE!
I DON'T EVEN KNOW WHO, OR WHAT, THAT IS!
IT'S A BIGGIE BAD GUY FROM HER BOOKS!

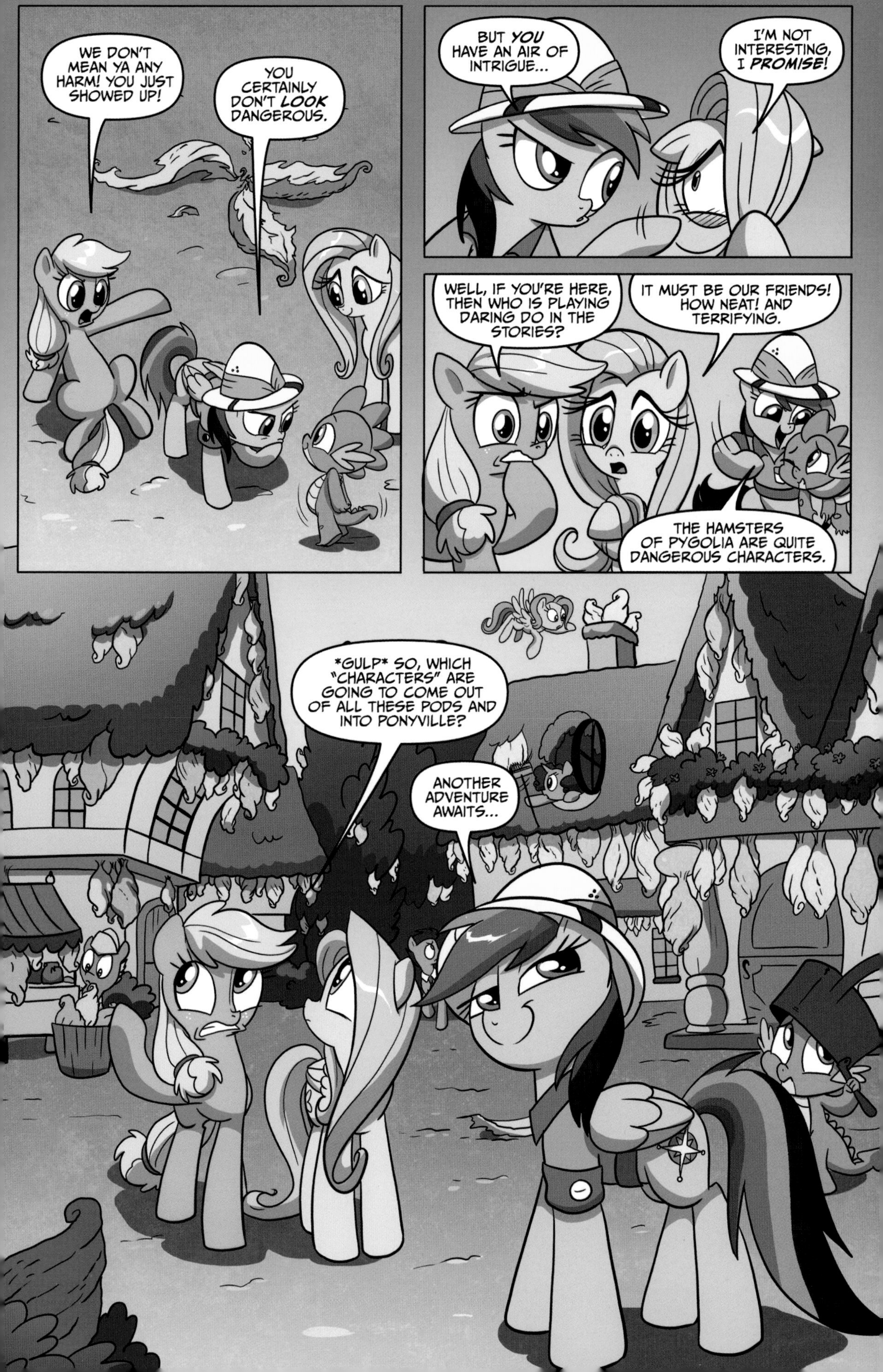
WE DON'T MEAN YA ANY HARM! YOU JUST SHOWED UP!
YOU CERTAINLY DON'T LOOK DANGEROUS.
BUT YOU HAVE AN AIR OF INTRIGUE...
I'M NOT INTERESTING, I PROMISE!
WELL, IF YOU'RE HERE, THEN WHO IS PLAYING DARING DO IN THE STORIES?
IT MUST BE OUR FRIENDS! HOW NEAT! AND TERRIFYING.
THE HAMSTERS OF PYGOLIA ARE QUITE DANGEROUS CHARACTERS.
GULP SO, WHICH "CHARACTERS" ARE GOING TO COME OUT OF ALL THESE PODS AND INTO PONYVILLE?
ANOTHER ADVENTURE AWAITS...

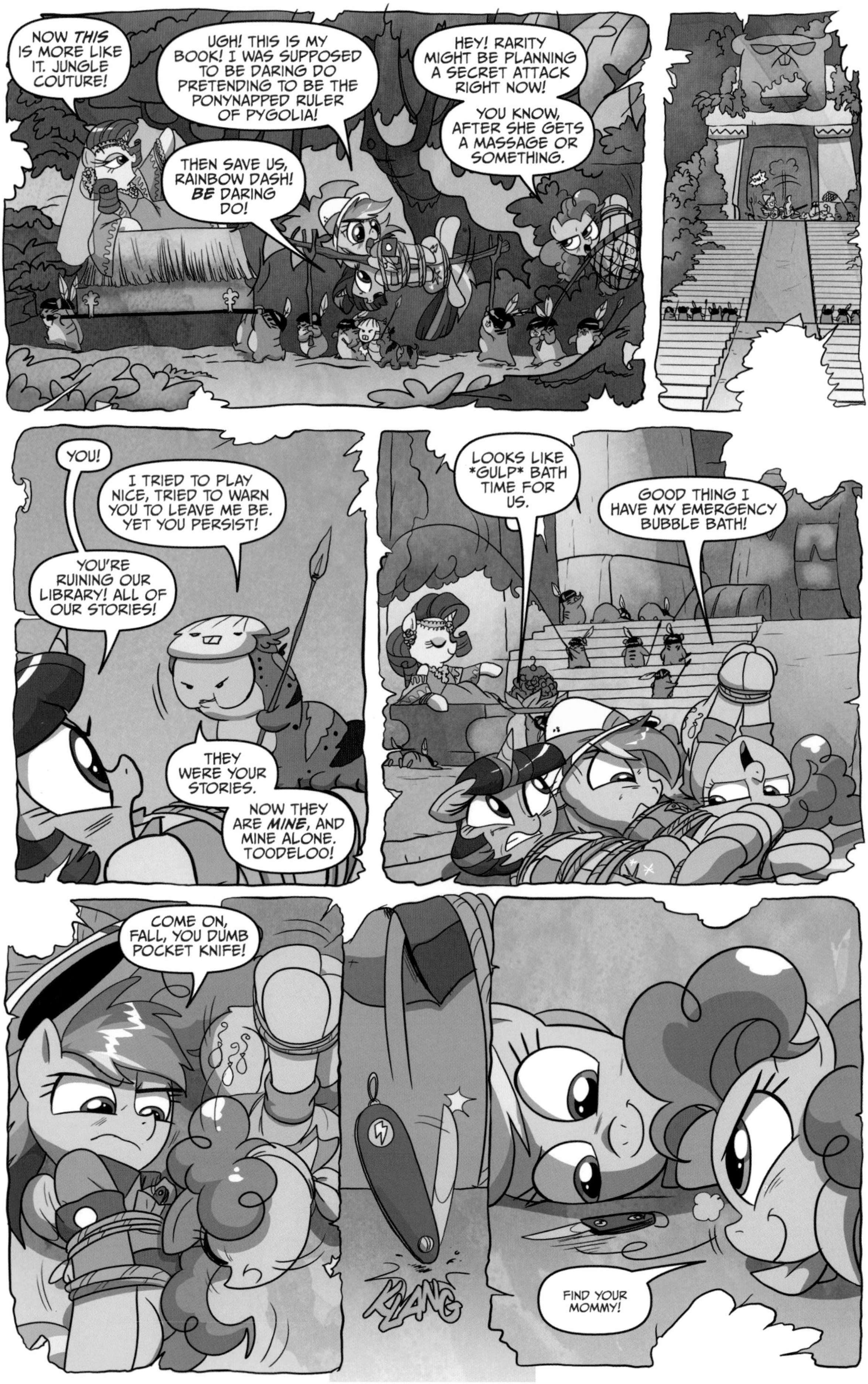
NOW *THIS* IS MORE LIKE IT. JUNGLE COUTURE!
UGH! THIS IS MY BOOK! I WAS SUPPOSED TO BE DARING DO PRETENDING TO BE THE PONYNAPPED RULER OF PYGOLIA!
THEN SAVE US, RAINBOW DASH! *BE* DARING DO!
HEY! RARITY MIGHT BE PLANNING A SECRET ATTACK RIGHT NOW!
YOU KNOW, AFTER SHE GETS A MASSAGE OR SOMETHING.
YOU!
I TRIED TO PLAY NICE, TRIED TO WARN YOU TO LEAVE ME BE. YET YOU PERSIST!
YOU'RE RUINING OUR LIBRARY! ALL OF OUR STORIES!
THEY WERE YOUR STORIES.
NOW THEY ARE *MINE*, AND MINE ALONE. TOODELOO!
LOOKS LIKE *GULP* BATH TIME FOR US.
GOOD THING I HAVE MY EMERGENCY BUBBLE BATH!
COME ON, FALL, YOU DUMB POCKET KNIFE!
KLANG
FIND YOUR MOMMY!

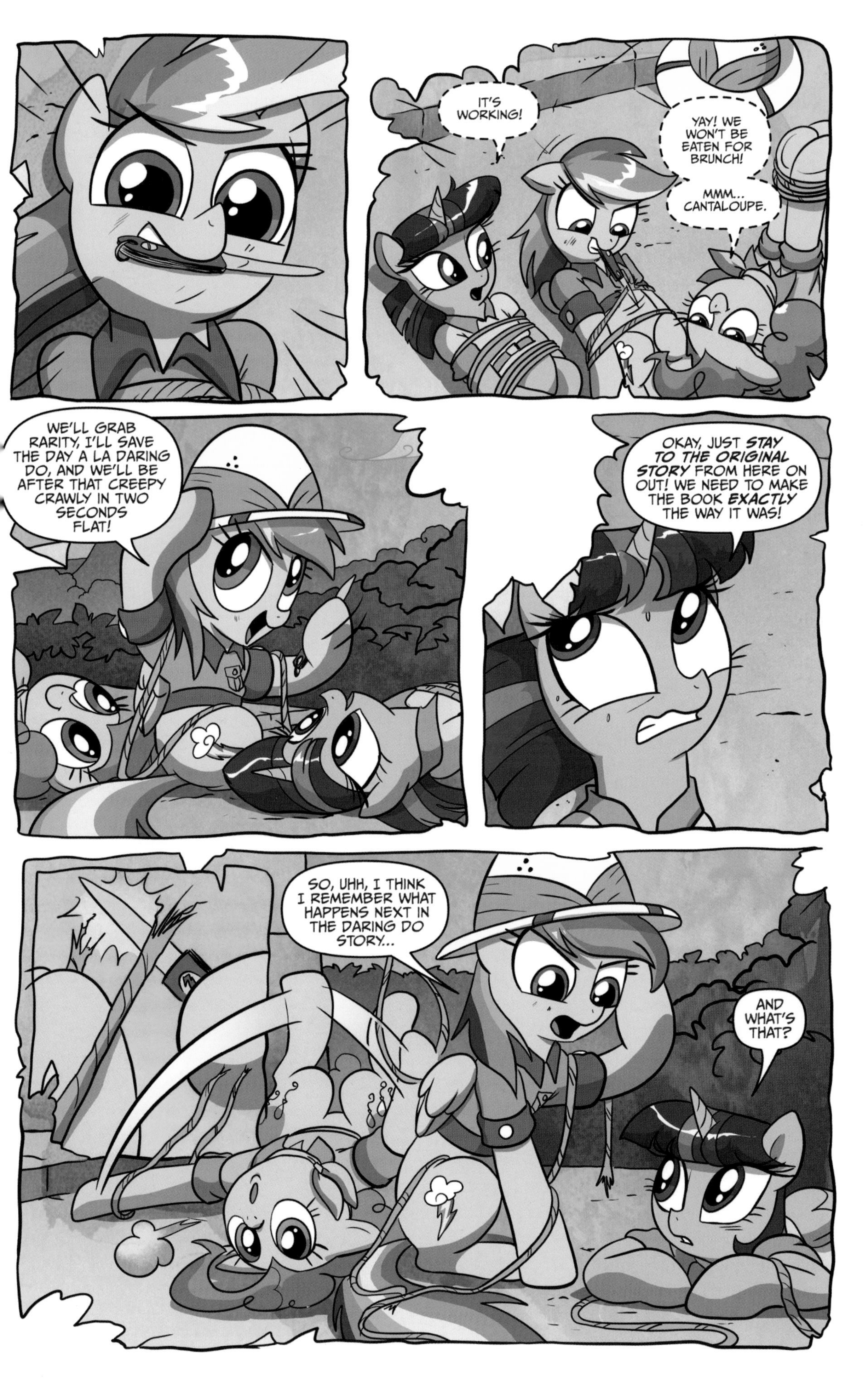
IT'S WORKING!
YAY! WE WON'T BE EATEN FOR BRUNCH!
MMM... CANTALOUPE.
WE'LL GRAB RARITY, I'LL SAVE THE DAY A LA DARING DO, AND WE'LL BE AFTER THAT CREEPY CRAWLY IN TWO SECONDS FLAT!
OKAY, JUST **STAY TO THE ORIGINAL STORY** FROM HERE ON OUT! WE NEED TO MAKE THE BOOK **EXACTLY** THE WAY IT WAS!
SO, UHH, I THINK I REMEMBER WHAT HAPPENS NEXT IN THE DARING DO STORY...
AND WHAT'S THAT?

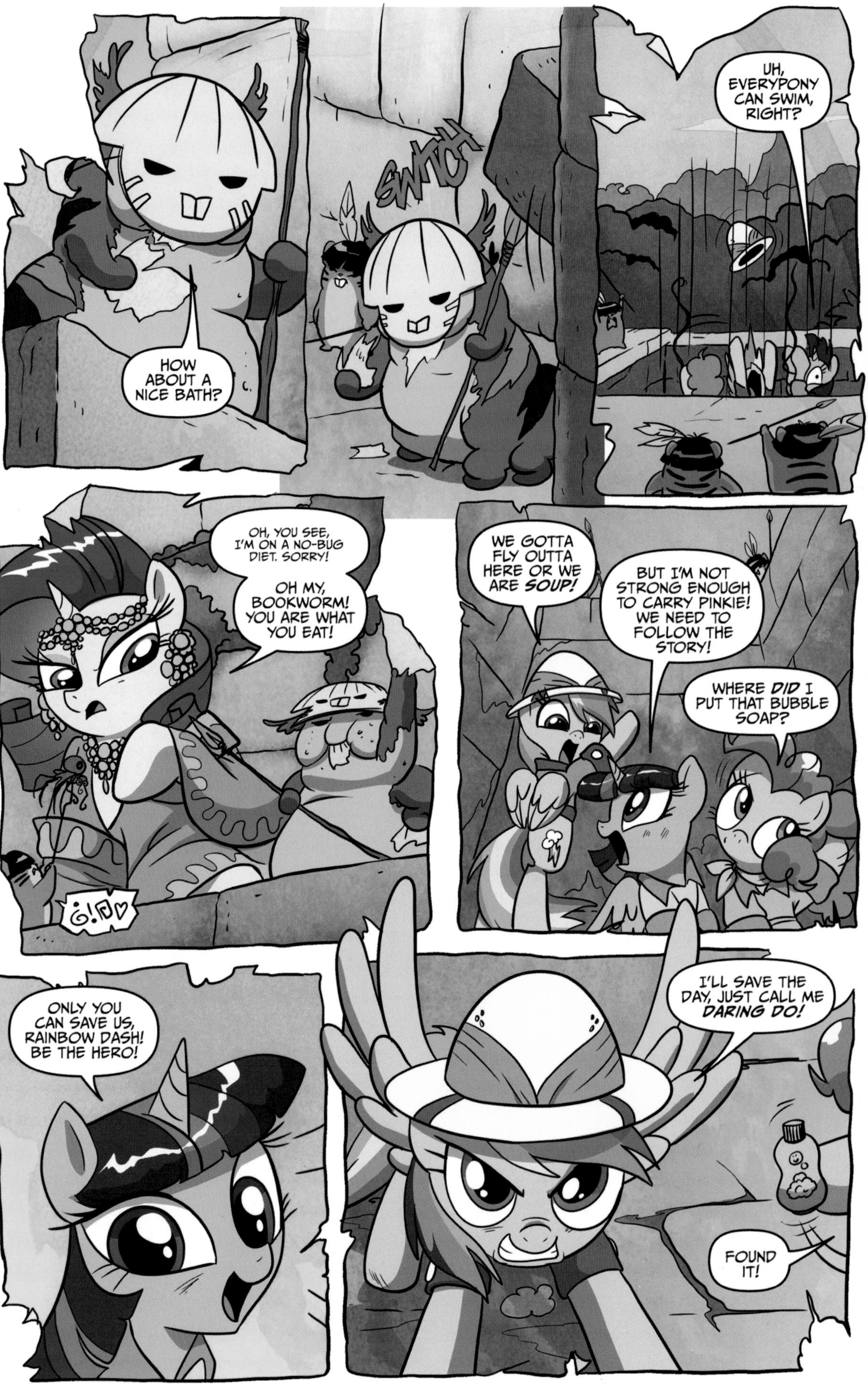
HOW ABOUT A NICE BATH?
SWTCH
UH, EVERYPONY CAN SWIM, RIGHT?
OH, YOU SEE, I'M ON A NO-BUG DIET. SORRY!
OH MY, BOOKWORM! YOU ARE WHAT YOU EAT!
WE GOTTA FLY OUTTA HERE OR WE ARE *SOUP!*
BUT I'M NOT STRONG ENOUGH TO CARRY PINKIE! WE NEED TO FOLLOW THE STORY!
WHERE *DID* I PUT THAT BUBBLE SOAP?
ONLY YOU CAN SAVE US, RAINBOW DASH! BE THE HERO!
I'LL SAVE THE DAY, JUST CALL ME *DARING DO!*
FOUND IT!

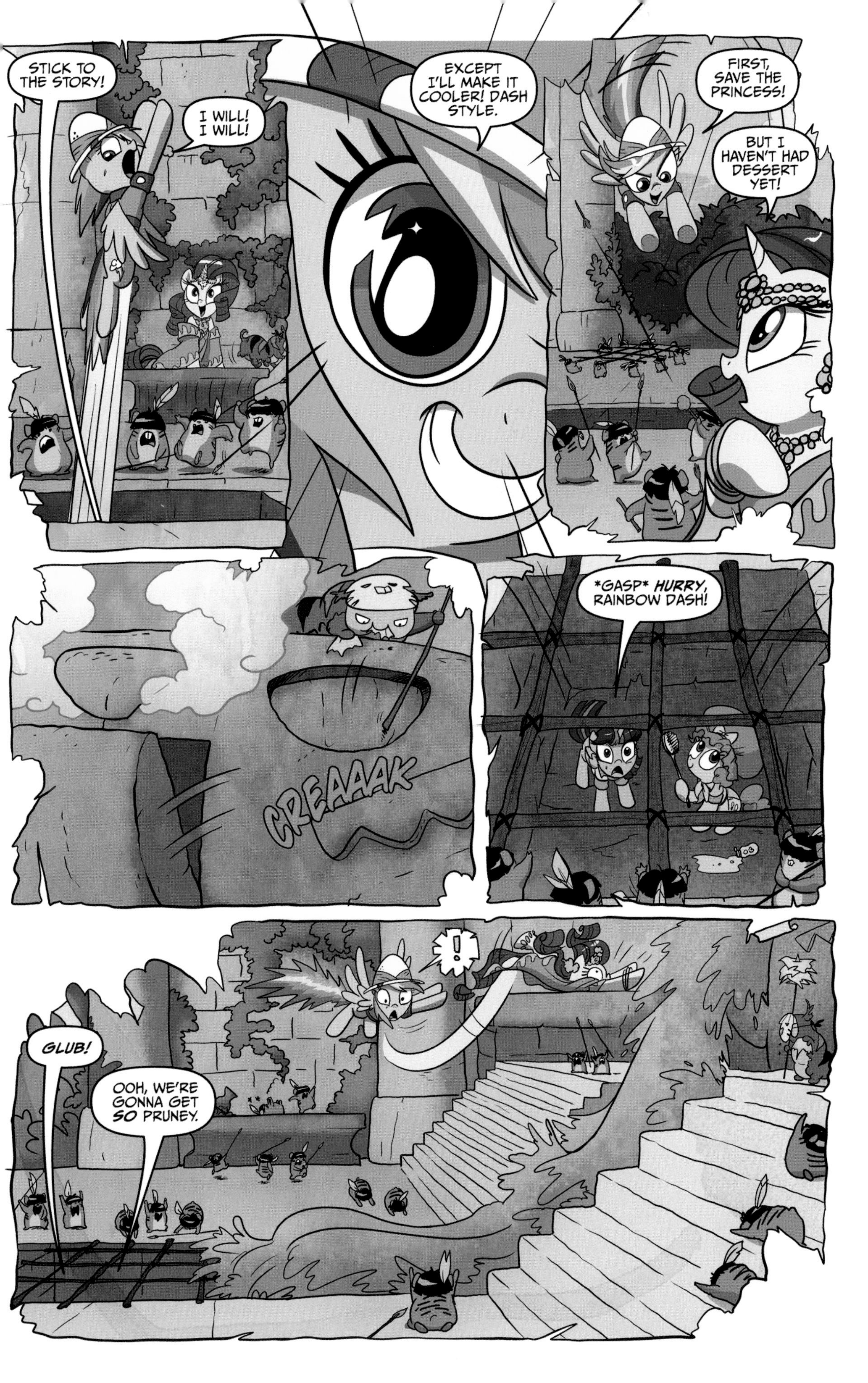
STICK TO THE STORY!
I WILL! I WILL!
EXCEPT I'LL MAKE IT COOLER! DASH STYLE.
FIRST, SAVE THE PRINCESS!
BUT I HAVEN'T HAD DESSERT YET!
CREAAAK
GASP HURRY, RAINBOW DASH!
!
GLUB!
OOH, WE'RE GONNA GET SO PRUNEY.

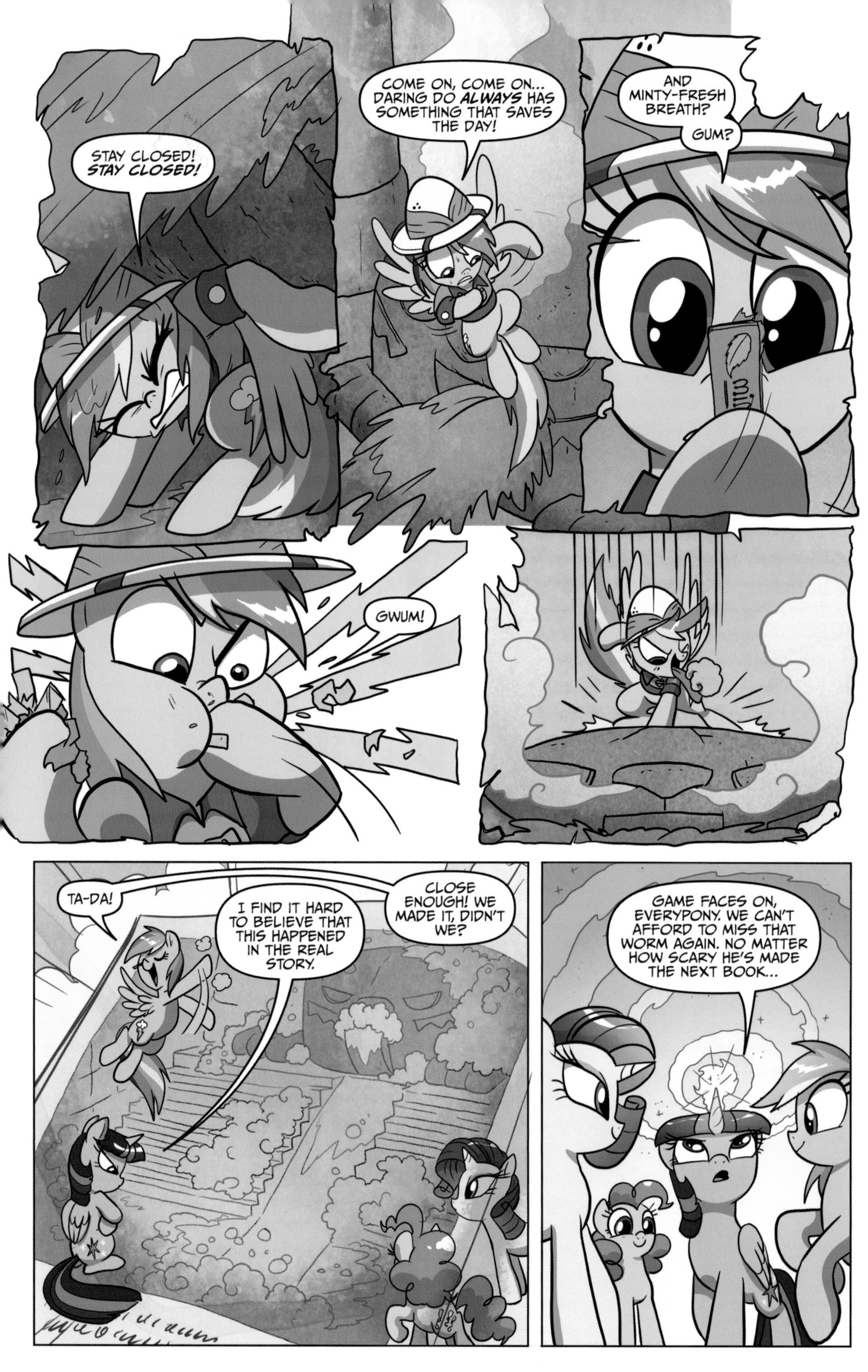
STAY CLOSED! STAY CLOSED!
COME ON, COME ON... DARING DO ALWAYS HAS SOMETHING THAT SAVES THE DAY!
AND MINTY-FRESH BREATH?
GUM?
GWUM!
TA-DA!
I FIND IT HARD TO BELIEVE THAT THIS HAPPENED IN THE REAL STORY.
CLOSE ENOUGH! WE MADE IT, DIDN'T WE?
GAME FACES ON, EVERYPONY. WE CAN'T AFFORD TO MISS THAT WORM AGAIN. NO MATTER HOW SCARY HE'S MADE THE NEXT BOOK...

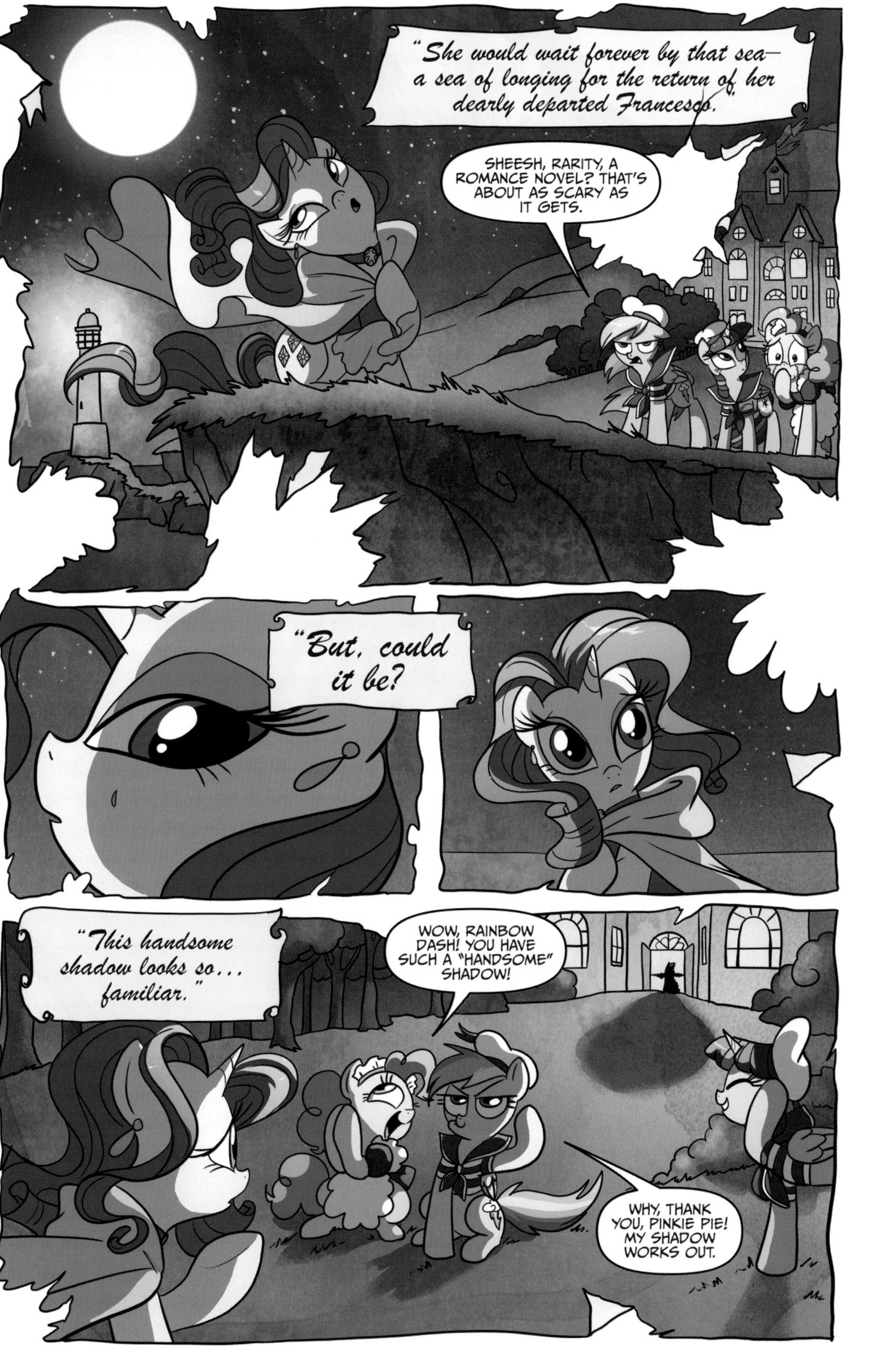
"She would wait forever by that sea— a sea of longing for the return of her dearly departed Francesco."
SHEESH, RARITY, A ROMANCE NOVEL? THAT'S ABOUT AS SCARY AS IT GETS.
"But, could it be?
"This handsome shadow looks so... familiar."
WOW, RAINBOW DASH! YOU HAVE SUCH A "HANDSOME" SHADOW!
WHY, THANK YOU, PINKIE PIE! MY SHADOW WORKS OUT.

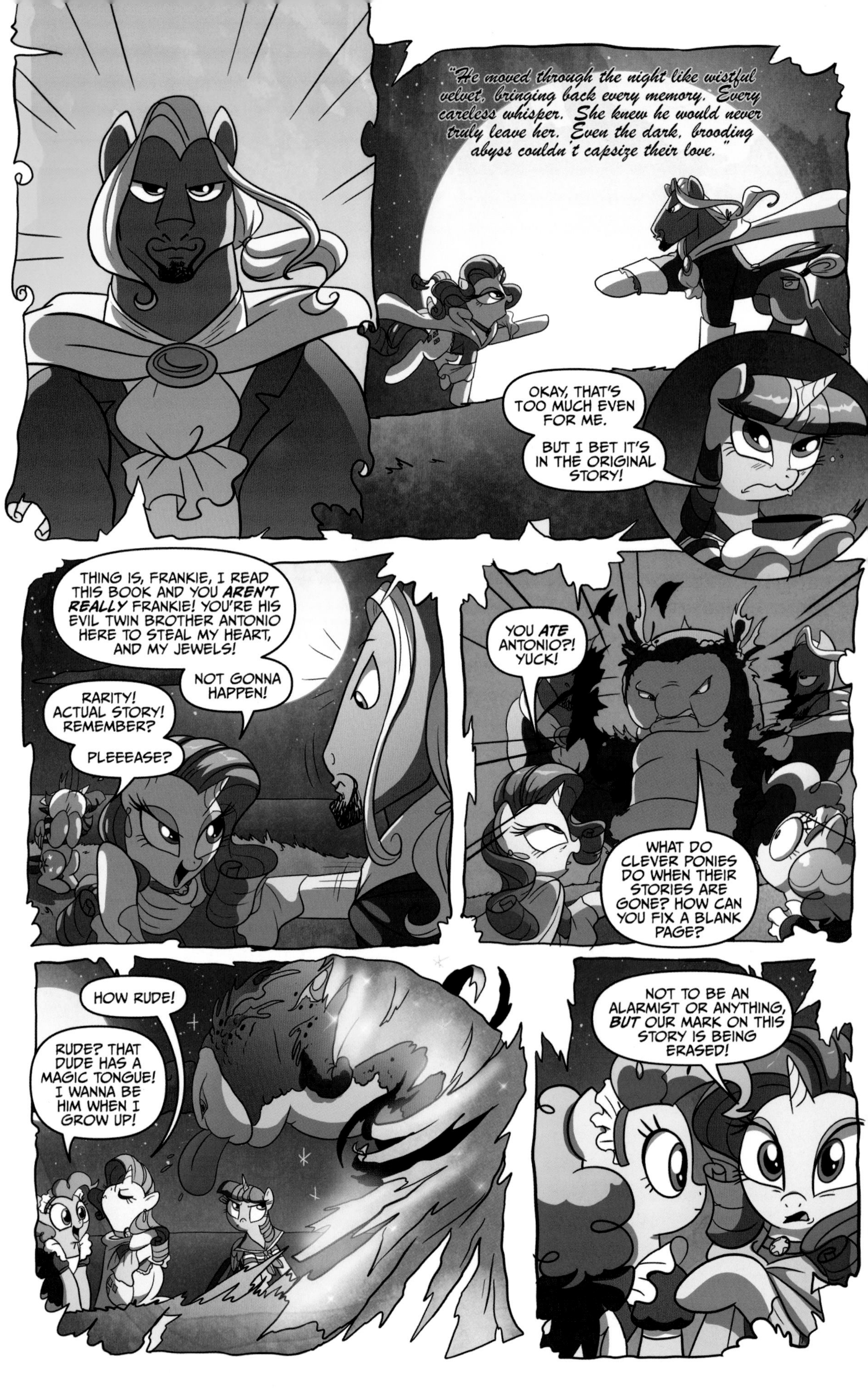

"He moved through the night like wistful velvet, bringing back every memory. Every careless whisper. She knew he would never truly leave her. Even the dark, brooding abyss couldn't capsize their love."
OKAY, THAT'S TOO MUCH EVEN FOR ME.
BUT I BET IT'S IN THE ORIGINAL STORY!
THING IS, FRANKIE, I READ THIS BOOK AND YOU AREN'T REALLY FRANKIE! YOU'RE HIS EVIL TWIN BROTHER ANTONIO HERE TO STEAL MY HEART, AND MY JEWELS!
NOT GONNA HAPPEN!
RARITY! ACTUAL STORY! REMEMBER?
PLEEEASE?
YOU ATE ANTONIO?! YUCK!
WHAT DO CLEVER PONIES DO WHEN THEIR STORIES ARE GONE? HOW CAN YOU FIX A BLANK PAGE?
HOW RUDE!
RUDE? THAT DUDE HAS A MAGIC TONGUE! I WANNA BE HIM WHEN I GROW UP!
NOT TO BE AN ALARMIST OR ANYTHING, BUT OUR MARK ON THIS STORY IS BEING ERASED!

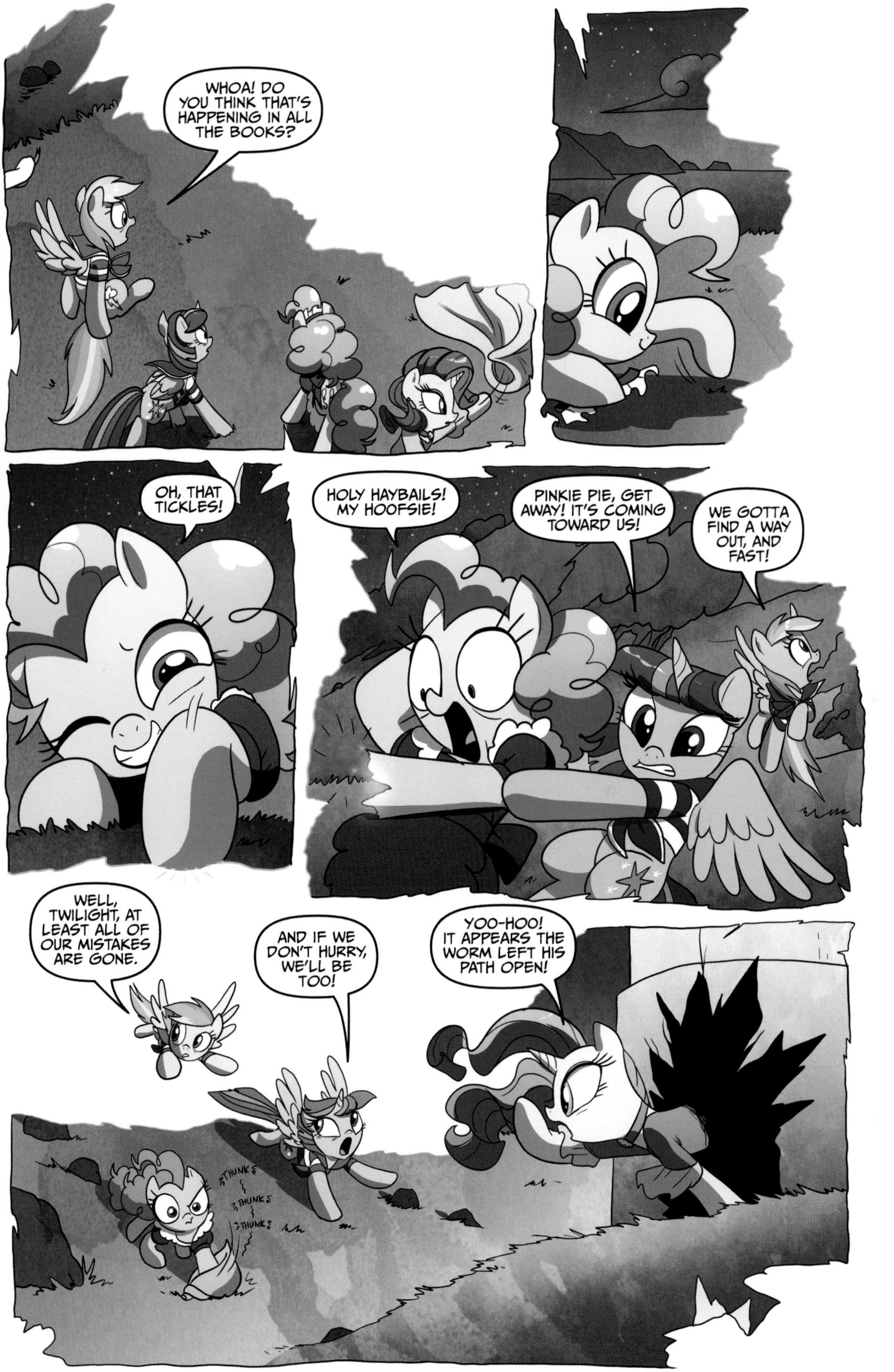
WHOA! DO YOU THINK THAT'S HAPPENING IN ALL THE BOOKS?
OH, THAT TICKLES!
HOLY HAYBAILS! MY HOOFSIE!
PINKIE PIE, GET AWAY! IT'S COMING TOWARD US!
WE GOTTA FIND A WAY OUT, AND FAST!
WELL, TWILIGHT, AT LEAST ALL OF OUR MISTAKES ARE GONE.
AND IF WE DON'T HURRY, WE'LL BE TOO!
YOO-HOO! IT APPEARS THE WORM LEFT HIS PATH OPEN!
THUNK
THUNK
THUNK

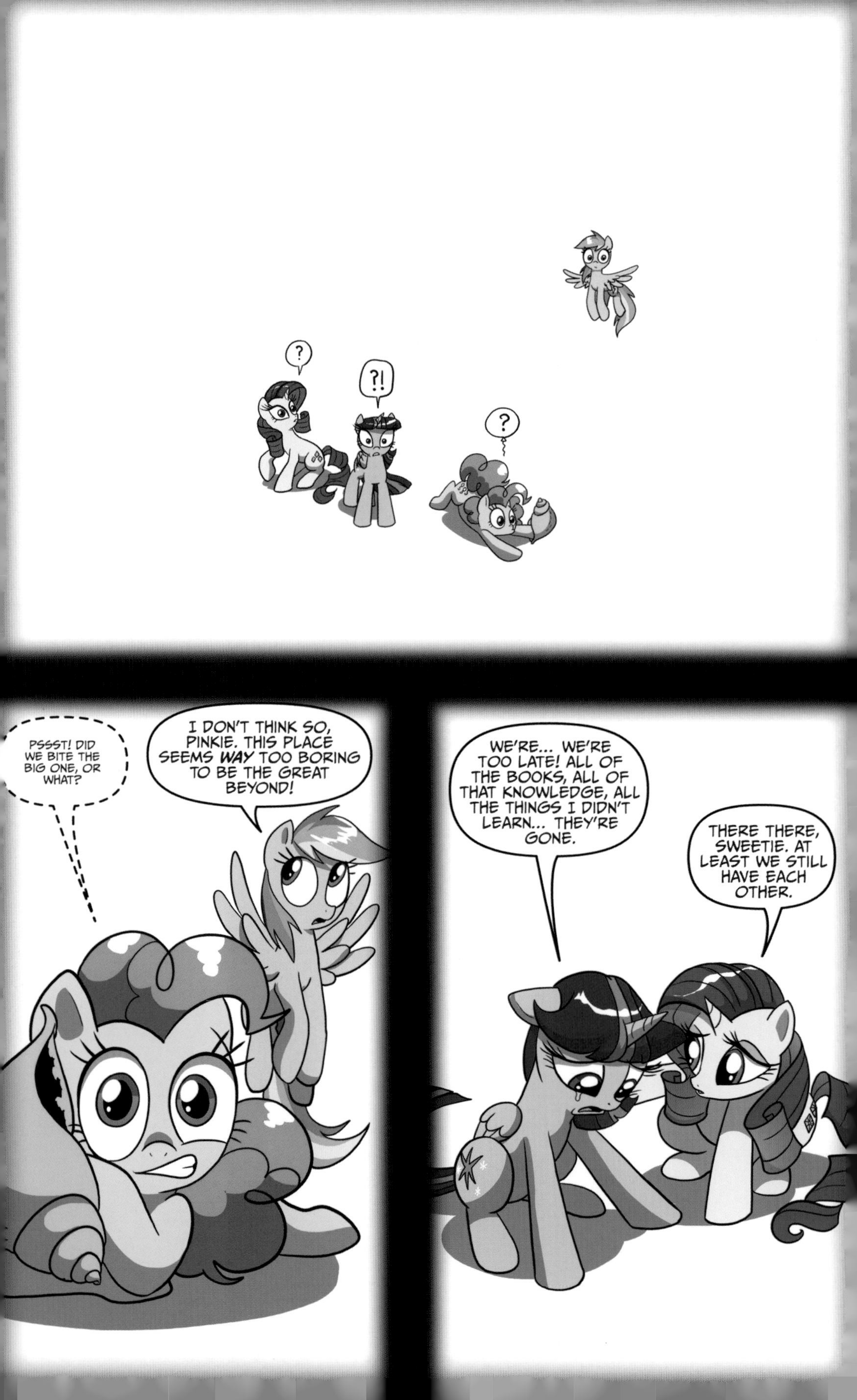
?
?!
?
PSSST! DID WE BITE THE BIG ONE, OR WHAT?
I DON'T THINK SO, PINKIE. THIS PLACE SEEMS WAY TOO BORING TO BE THE GREAT BEYOND!
WE'RE... WE'RE TOO LATE! ALL OF THE BOOKS, ALL OF THAT KNOWLEDGE, ALL THE THINGS I DIDN'T LEARN... THEY'RE GONE.
THERE THERE, SWEETIE. AT LEAST WE STILL HAVE EACH OTHER.

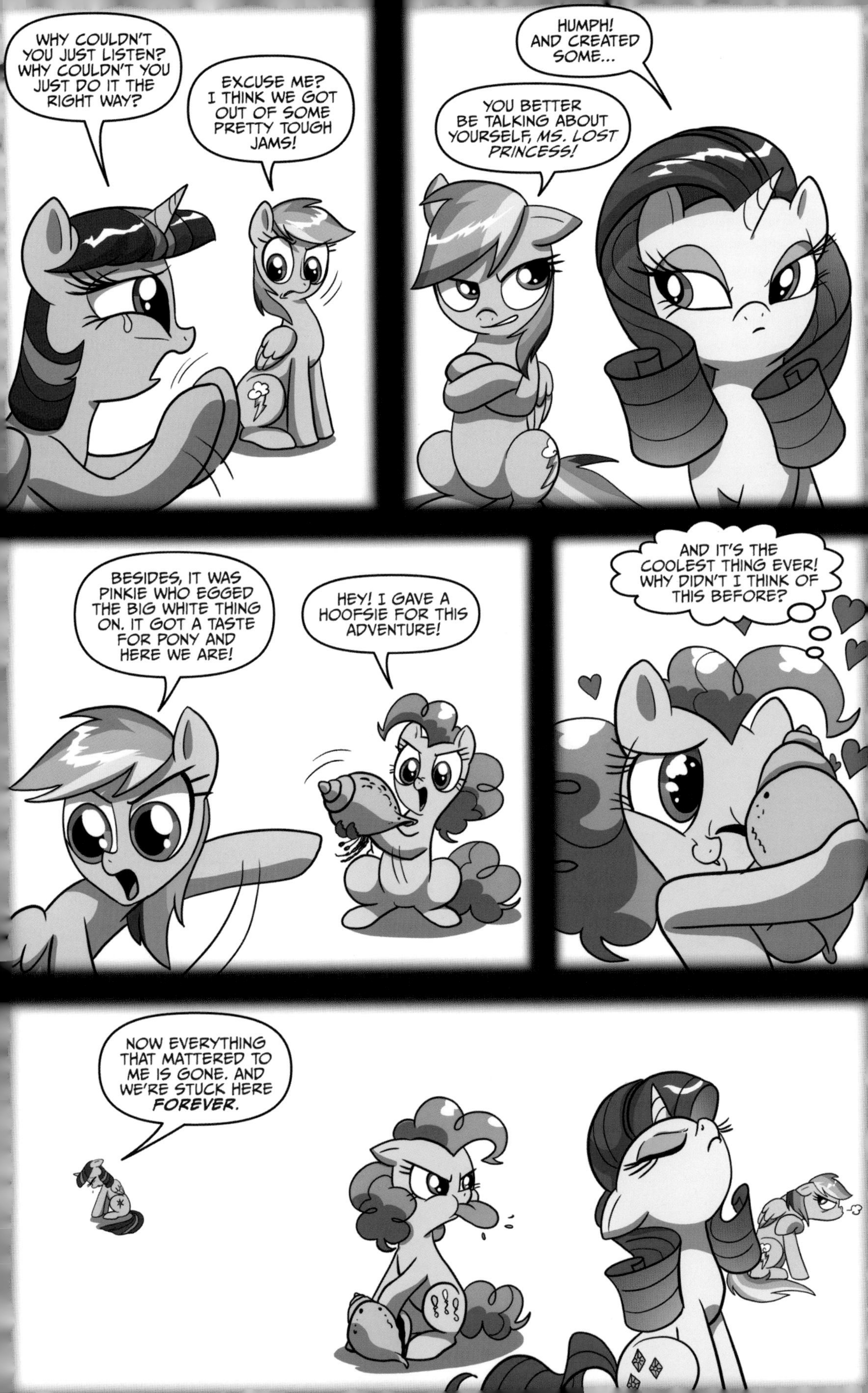
WHY COULDN'T YOU JUST LISTEN? WHY COULDN'T YOU JUST DO IT THE RIGHT WAY?
EXCUSE ME? I THINK WE GOT OUT OF SOME PRETTY TOUGH JAMS!
HUMPH! AND CREATED SOME...
YOU BETTER BE TALKING ABOUT YOURSELF, MS. LOST PRINCESS!
BESIDES, IT WAS PINKIE WHO EGGED THE BIG WHITE THING ON. IT GOT A TASTE FOR PONY AND HERE WE ARE!
HEY! I GAVE A HOOFSIE FOR THIS ADVENTURE!
AND IT'S THE COOLEST THING EVER! WHY DIDN'T I THINK OF THIS BEFORE?
NOW EVERYTHING THAT MATTERED TO ME IS GONE. AND WE'RE STUCK HERE *FOREVER*.

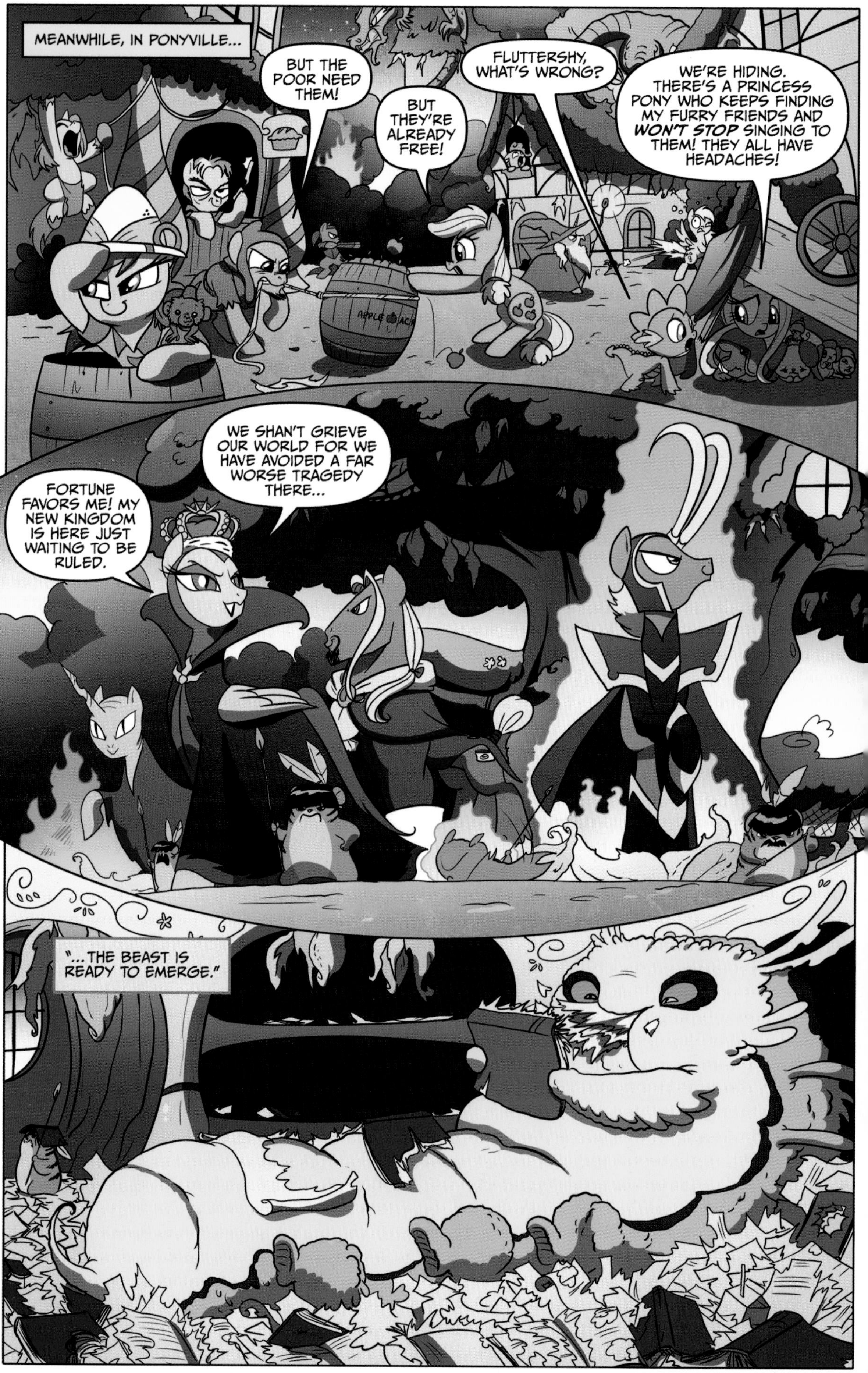
MEANWHILE, IN PONYVILLE...
BUT THE POOR NEED THEM!
BUT THEY'RE ALREADY FREE!
FLUTTERSHY, WHAT'S WRONG?
WE'RE HIDING. THERE'S A PRINCESS PONY WHO KEEPS FINDING MY FURRY FRIENDS AND WON'T STOP SINGING TO THEM! THEY ALL HAVE HEADACHES!
APPLE ACK
FORTUNE FAVORS ME! MY NEW KINGDOM IS HERE JUST WAITING TO BE RULED.
WE SHAN'T GRIEVE OUR WORLD FOR WE HAVE AVOIDED A FAR WORSE TRAGEDY THERE...
"...THE BEAST IS READY TO EMERGE."

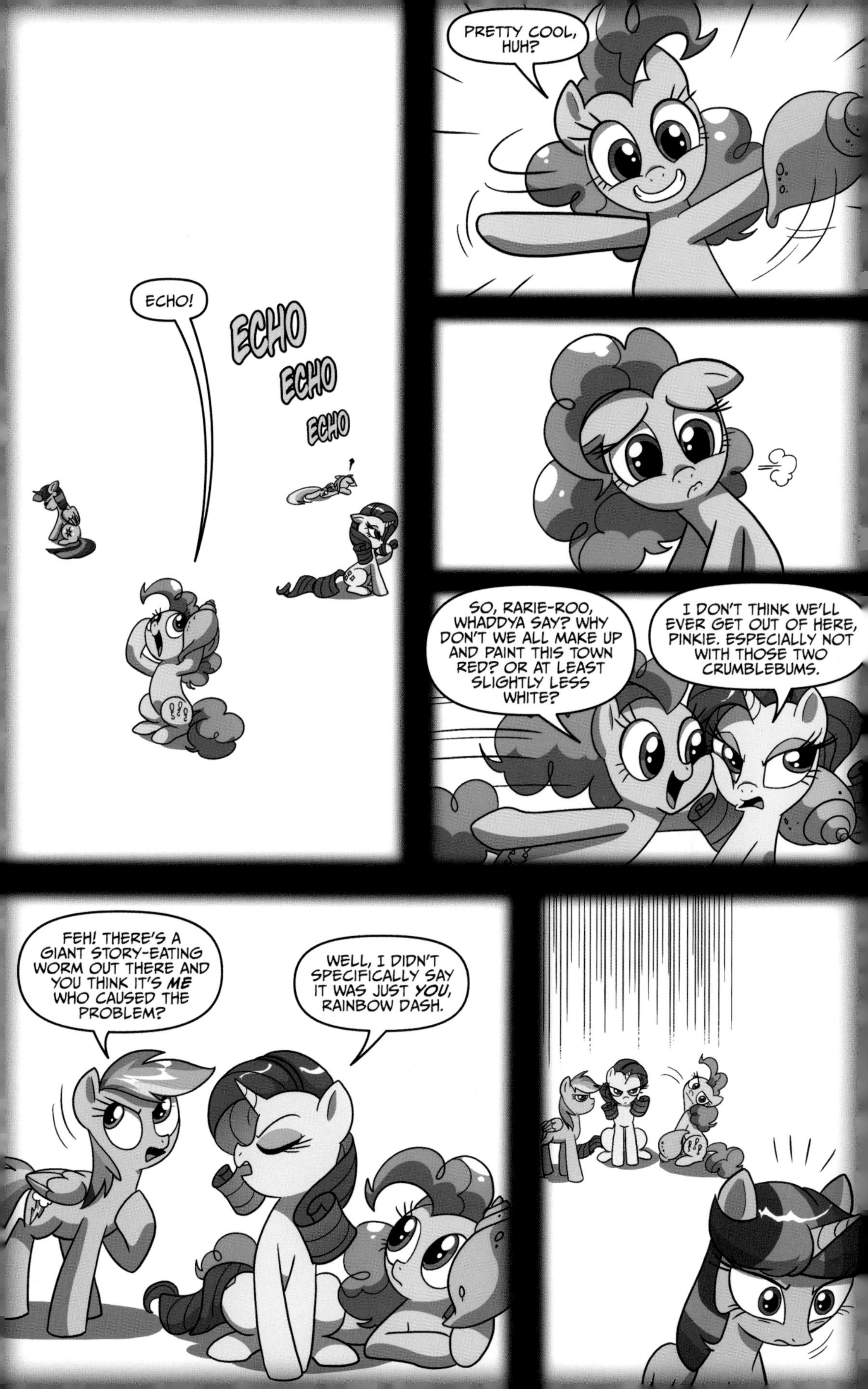
ECHO!
ECHO
ECHO
ECHO
PRETTY COOL, HUH?
SO, RARIE-ROO, WHADDYA SAY? WHY DON'T WE ALL MAKE UP AND PAINT THIS TOWN RED? OR AT LEAST SLIGHTLY LESS WHITE?
I DON'T THINK WE'LL EVER GET OUT OF HERE, PINKIE. ESPECIALLY NOT WITH THOSE TWO CRUMBLEBUMS.
FEH! THERE'S A GIANT STORY-EATING WORM OUT THERE AND YOU THINK IT'S *ME* WHO CAUSED THE PROBLEM?
WELL, I DIDN'T SPECIFICALLY SAY IT WAS JUST *YOU*, RAINBOW DASH.

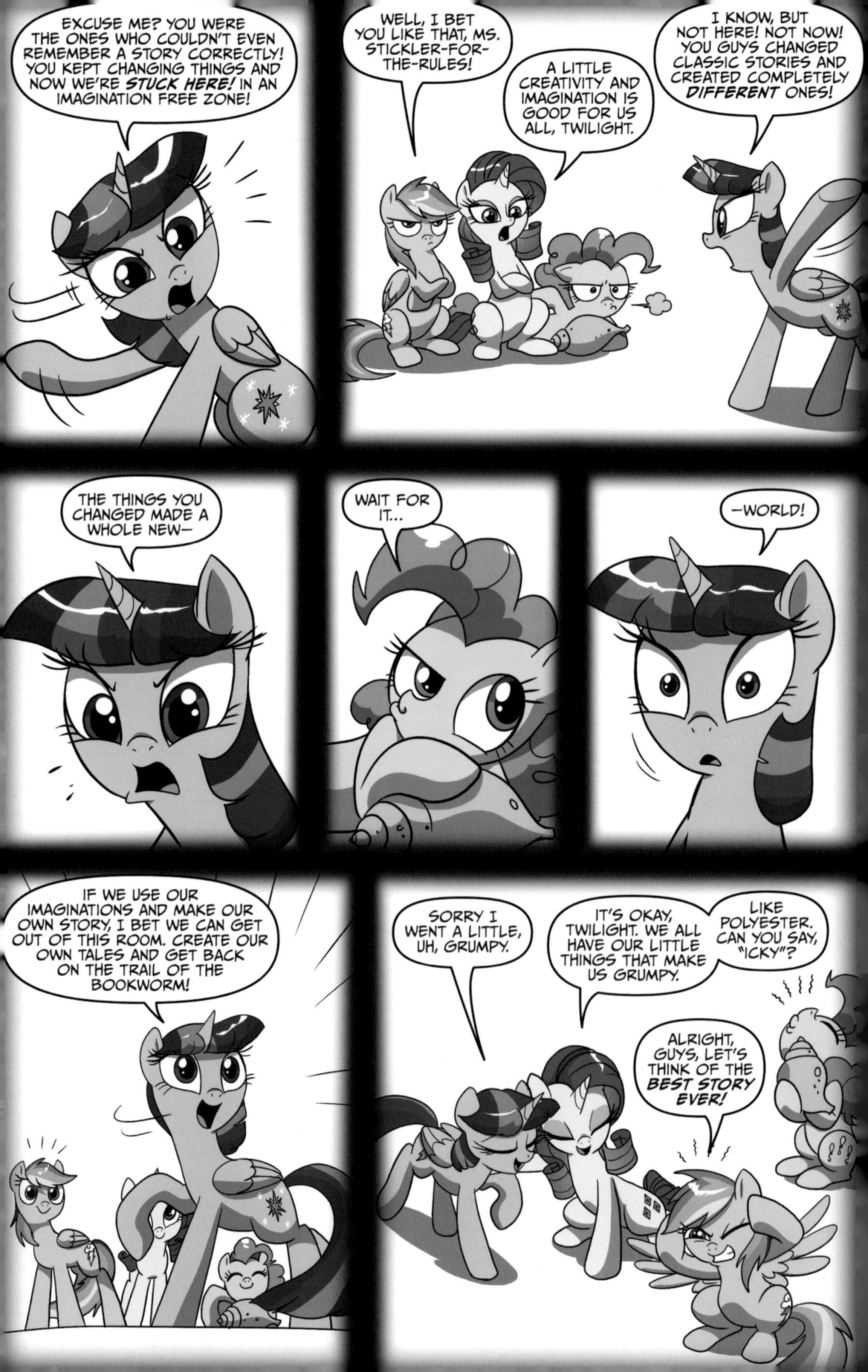
EXCUSE ME? YOU WERE THE ONES WHO COULDN'T EVEN REMEMBER A STORY CORRECTLY! YOU KEPT CHANGING THINGS AND NOW WE'RE STUCK HERE! IN AN IMAGINATION FREE ZONE!
WELL, I BET YOU LIKE THAT, MS. STICKLER-FOR-THE-RULES!
A LITTLE CREATIVITY AND IMAGINATION IS GOOD FOR US ALL, TWILIGHT.
I KNOW, BUT NOT HERE! NOT NOW! YOU GUYS CHANGED CLASSIC STORIES AND CREATED COMPLETELY DIFFERENT ONES!
THE THINGS YOU CHANGED MADE A WHOLE NEW—
WAIT FOR IT...
—WORLD!
IF WE USE OUR IMAGINATIONS AND MAKE OUR OWN STORY, I BET WE CAN GET OUT OF THIS ROOM. CREATE OUR OWN TALES AND GET BACK ON THE TRAIL OF THE BOOKWORM!
SORRY I WENT A LITTLE, UH, GRUMPY.
IT'S OKAY, TWILIGHT. WE ALL HAVE OUR LITTLE THINGS THAT MAKE US GRUMPY.
LIKE POLYESTER. CAN YOU SAY, "ICKY"?
ALRIGHT, GUYS, LET'S THINK OF THE BEST STORY EVER!

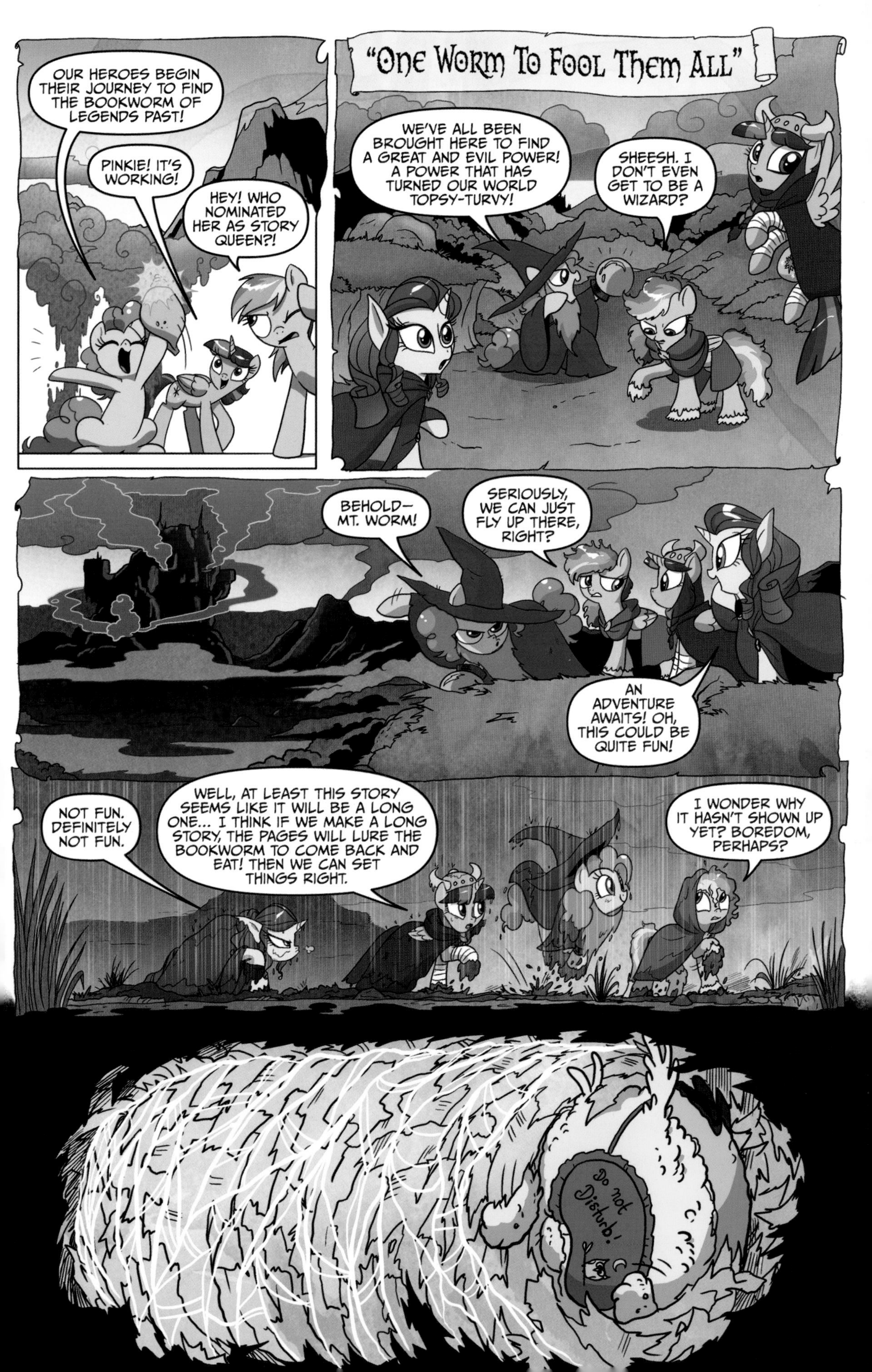
OUR HEROES BEGIN THEIR JOURNEY TO FIND THE BOOKWORM OF LEGENDS PAST!
PINKIE! IT'S WORKING!
HEY! WHO NOMINATED HER AS STORY QUEEN?!
"One Worm To Fool Them All"
WE'VE ALL BEEN BROUGHT HERE TO FIND A GREAT AND EVIL POWER! A POWER THAT HAS TURNED OUR WORLD TOPSY-TURVY!
SHEESH. I DON'T EVEN GET TO BE A WIZARD?
BEHOLD— MT. WORM!
SERIOUSLY, WE CAN JUST FLY UP THERE, RIGHT?
AN ADVENTURE AWAITS! OH, THIS COULD BE QUITE FUN!
NOT FUN. DEFINITELY NOT FUN.
WELL, AT LEAST THIS STORY SEEMS LIKE IT WILL BE A LONG ONE... I THINK IF WE MAKE A LONG STORY, THE PAGES WILL LURE THE BOOKWORM TO COME BACK AND EAT! THEN WE CAN SET THINGS RIGHT.
I WONDER WHY IT HASN'T SHOWN UP YET? BOREDOM, PERHAPS?
Do not Disturb!

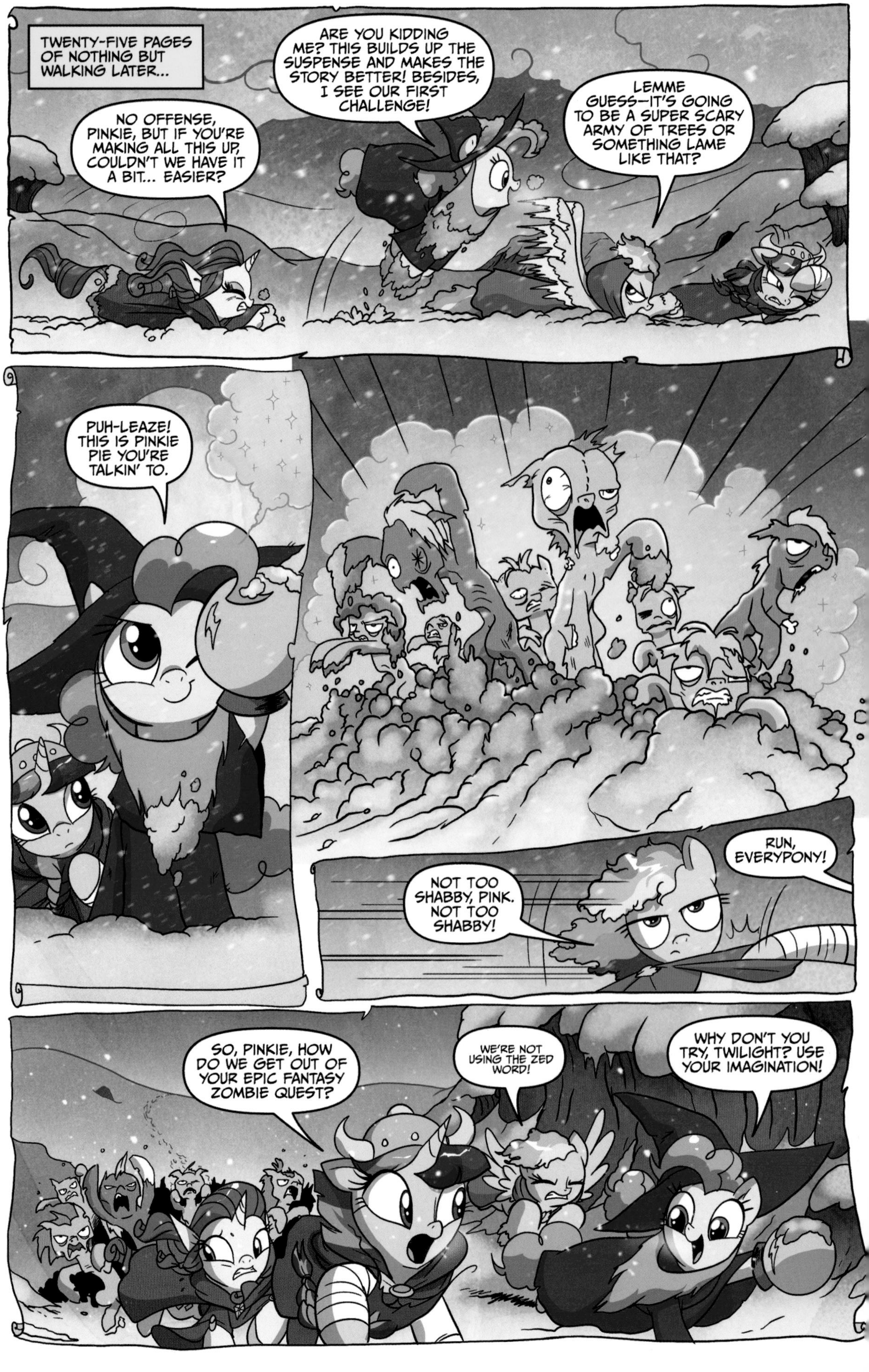
TWENTY-FIVE PAGES OF NOTHING BUT WALKING LATER...
NO OFFENSE, PINKIE, BUT IF YOU'RE MAKING ALL THIS UP, COULDN'T WE HAVE IT A BIT... EASIER?
ARE YOU KIDDING ME? THIS BUILDS UP THE SUSPENSE AND MAKES THE STORY BETTER! BESIDES, I SEE OUR FIRST CHALLENGE!
LEMME GUESS—IT'S GOING TO BE A SUPER SCARY ARMY OF TREES OR SOMETHING LAME LIKE THAT?
PUH-LEAZE! THIS IS PINKIE PIE YOU'RE TALKIN' TO.
RUN, EVERYPONY!
NOT TOO SHABBY, PINK. NOT TOO SHABBY!
SO, PINKIE, HOW DO WE GET OUT OF YOUR EPIC FANTASY ZOMBIE QUEST?
WE'RE NOT USING THE ZED WORD!
WHY DON'T YOU TRY, TWILIGHT? USE YOUR IMAGINATION!

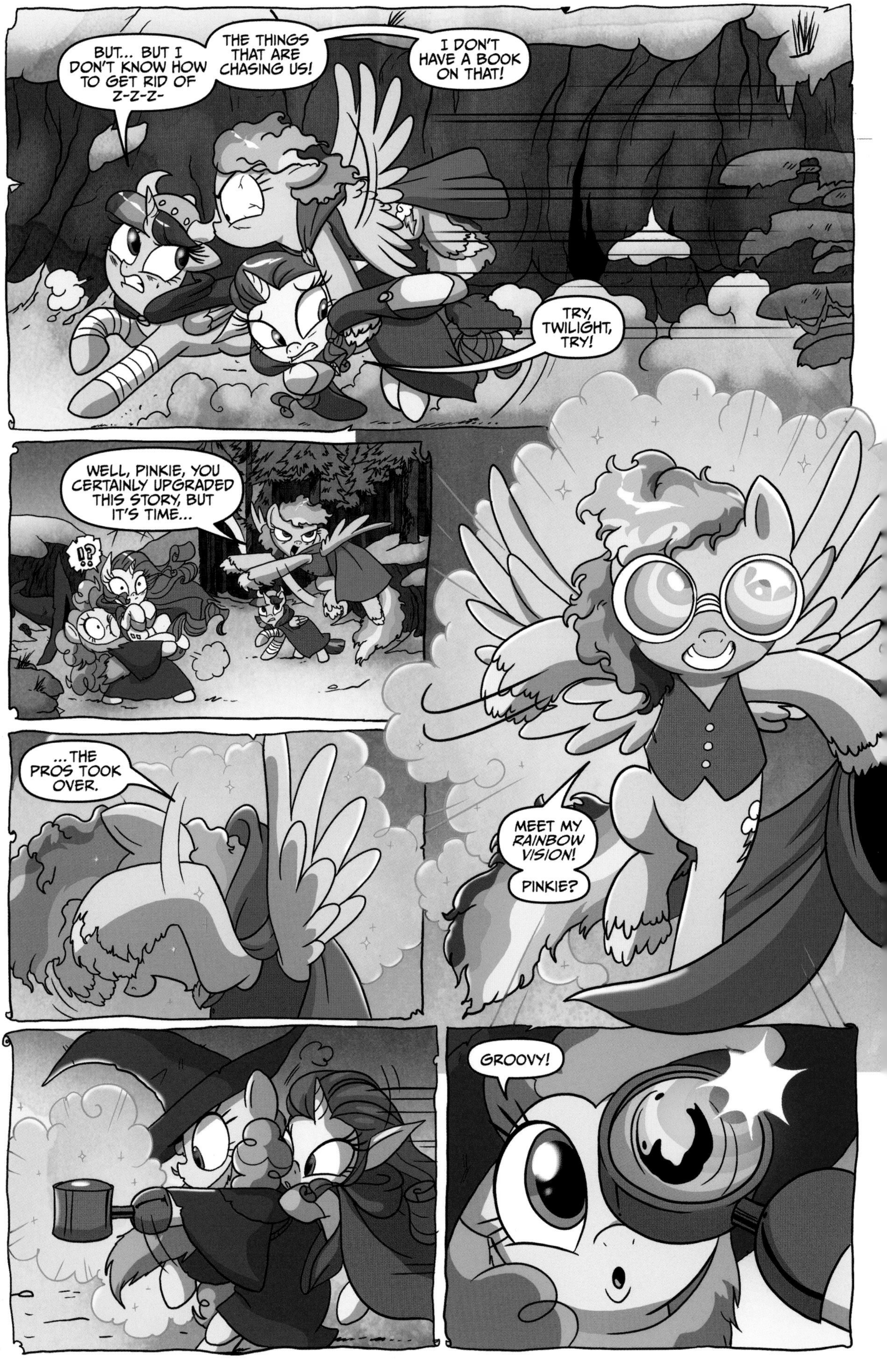
BUT... BUT I DON'T KNOW HOW TO GET RID OF Z-Z-Z-
THE THINGS THAT ARE CHASING US!
I DON'T HAVE A BOOK ON THAT!
TRY, TWILIGHT, TRY!
WELL, PINKIE, YOU CERTAINLY UPGRADED THIS STORY, BUT IT'S TIME...
!?
...THE PROS TOOK OVER.
MEET MY RAINBOW VISION!
PINKIE?
GROOVY!

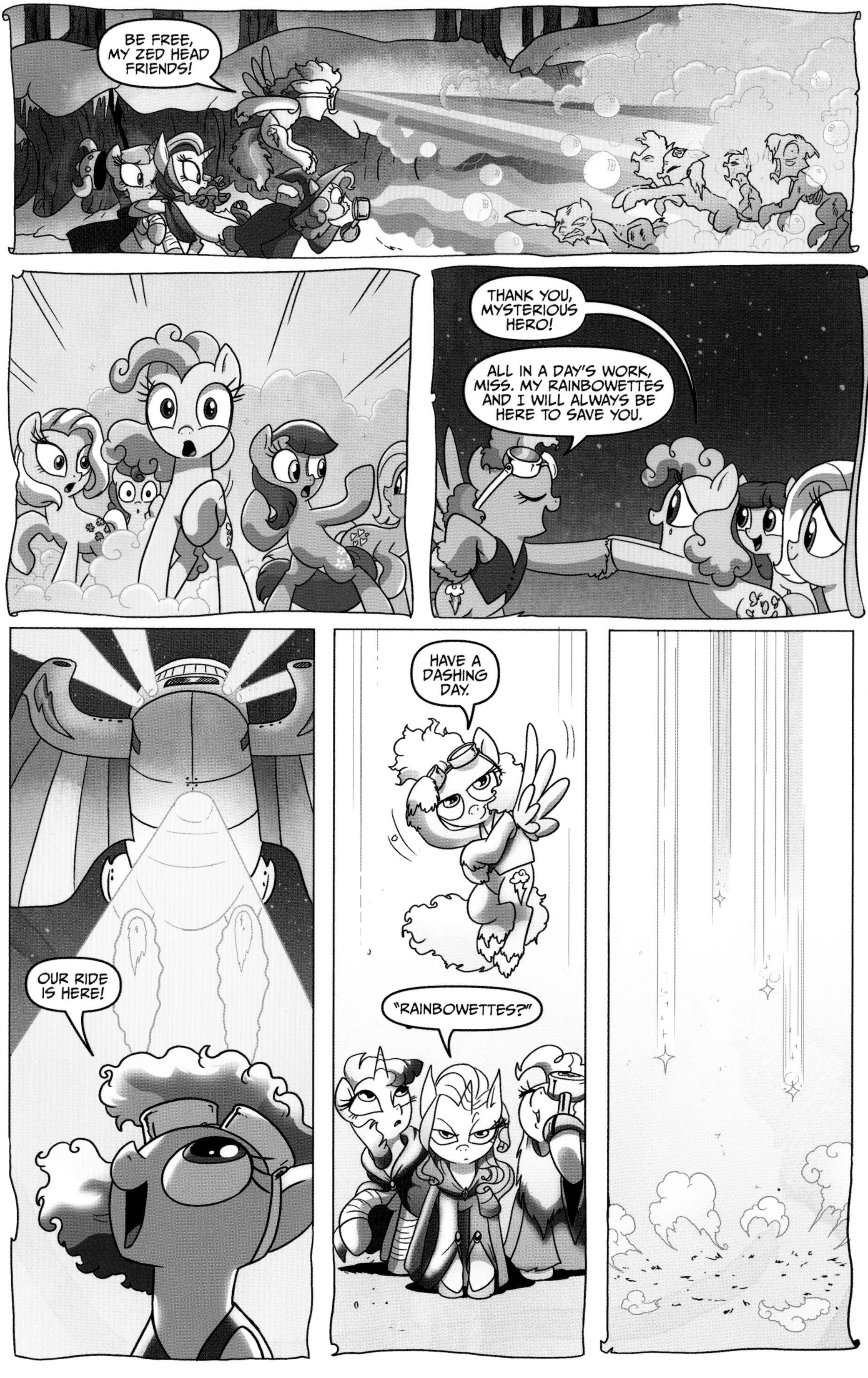
BE FREE, MY ZED HEAD FRIENDS!
THANK YOU, MYSTERIOUS HERO!
ALL IN A DAY'S WORK, MISS. MY RAINBOWETTES AND I WILL ALWAYS BE HERE TO SAVE YOU.
OUR RIDE IS HERE!
HAVE A DASHING DAY.
"RAINBOWETTES?"

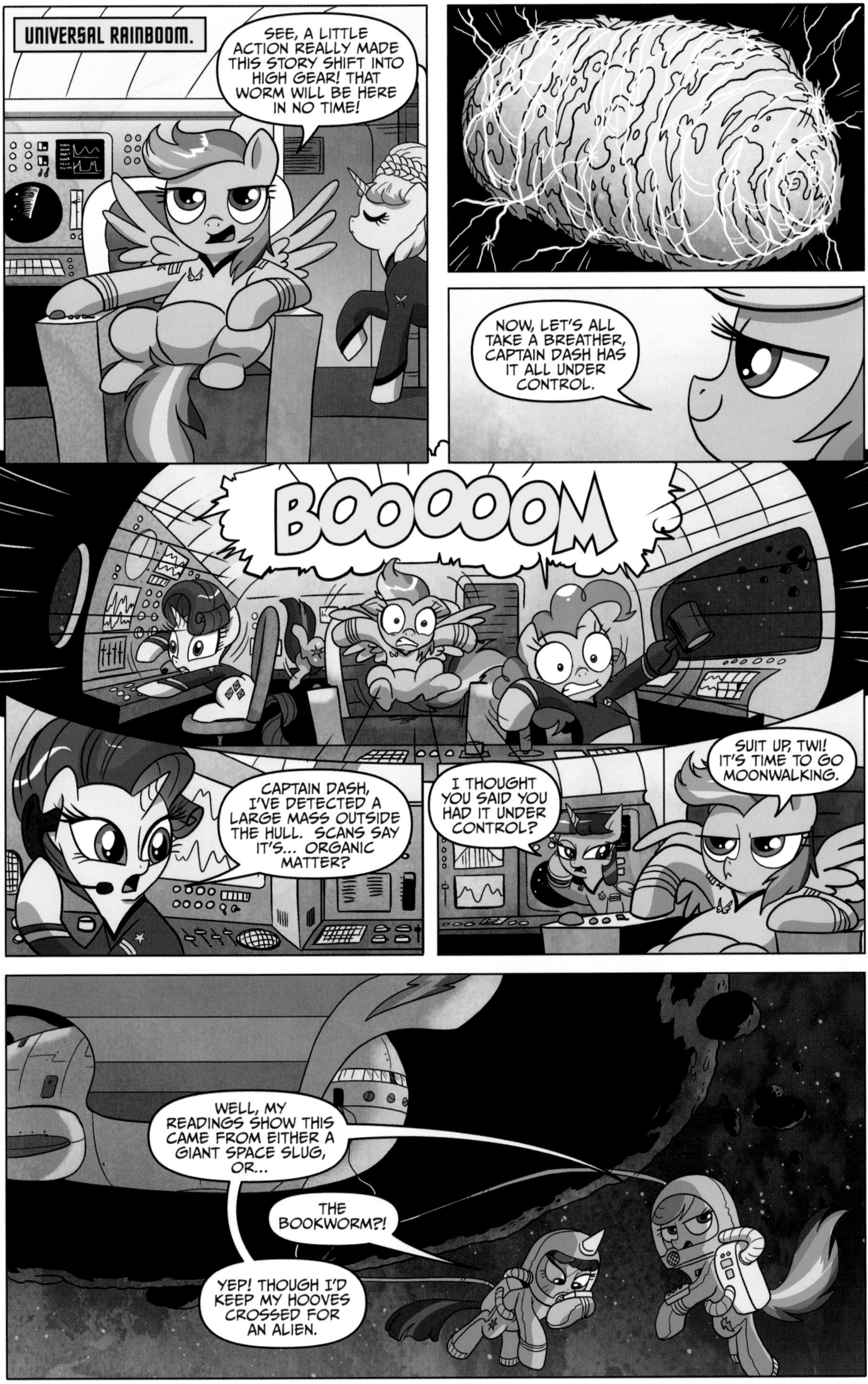
UNIVERSAL RAINBOOM.
SEE, A LITTLE ACTION REALLY MADE THIS STORY SHIFT INTO HIGH GEAR! THAT WORM WILL BE HERE IN NO TIME!
NOW, LET'S ALL TAKE A BREATHER, CAPTAIN DASH HAS IT ALL UNDER CONTROL.
BOOOOOM
CAPTAIN DASH, I'VE DETECTED A LARGE MASS OUTSIDE THE HULL. SCANS SAY IT'S... ORGANIC MATTER?
I THOUGHT YOU SAID YOU HAD IT UNDER CONTROL?
SUIT UP, TWI! IT'S TIME TO GO MOONWALKING.
WELL, MY READINGS SHOW THIS CAME FROM EITHER A GIANT SPACE SLUG, OR...
THE BOOKWORM?!
YEP! THOUGH I'D KEEP MY HOOVES CROSSED FOR AN ALIEN.

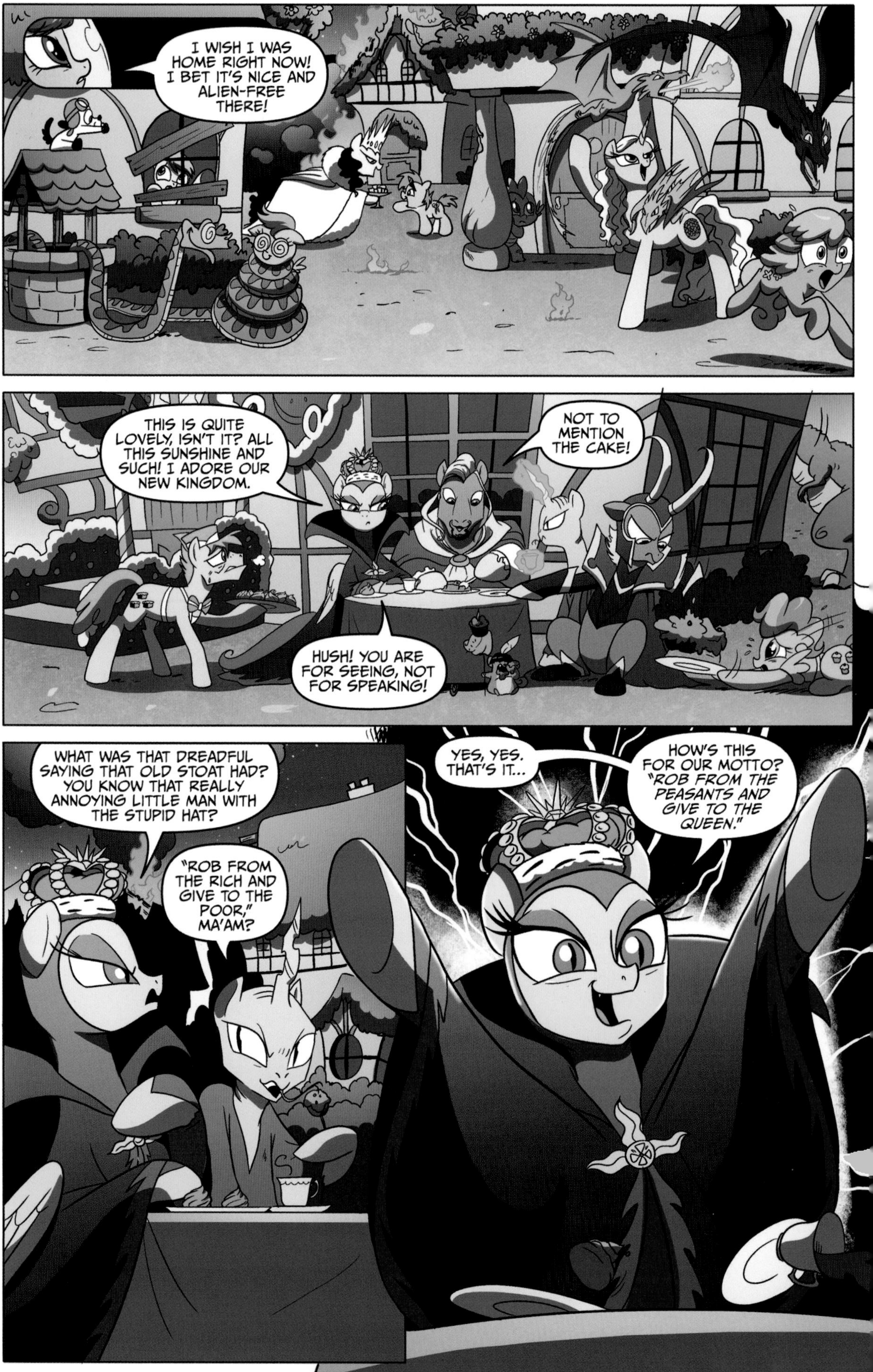
I WISH I WAS HOME RIGHT NOW! I BET IT'S NICE AND ALIEN-FREE THERE!
THIS IS QUITE LOVELY, ISN'T IT? ALL THIS SUNSHINE AND SUCH! I ADORE OUR NEW KINGDOM.
NOT TO MENTION THE CAKE!
HUSH! YOU ARE FOR SEEING, NOT FOR SPEAKING!
WHAT WAS THAT DREADFUL SAYING THAT OLD STOAT HAD? YOU KNOW THAT REALLY ANNOYING LITTLE MAN WITH THE STUPID HAT?
"ROB FROM THE RICH AND GIVE TO THE POOR," MA'AM?
YES, YES. THAT'S IT...
HOW'S THIS FOR OUR MOTTO? "ROB FROM THE PEASANTS AND GIVE TO THE QUEEN."

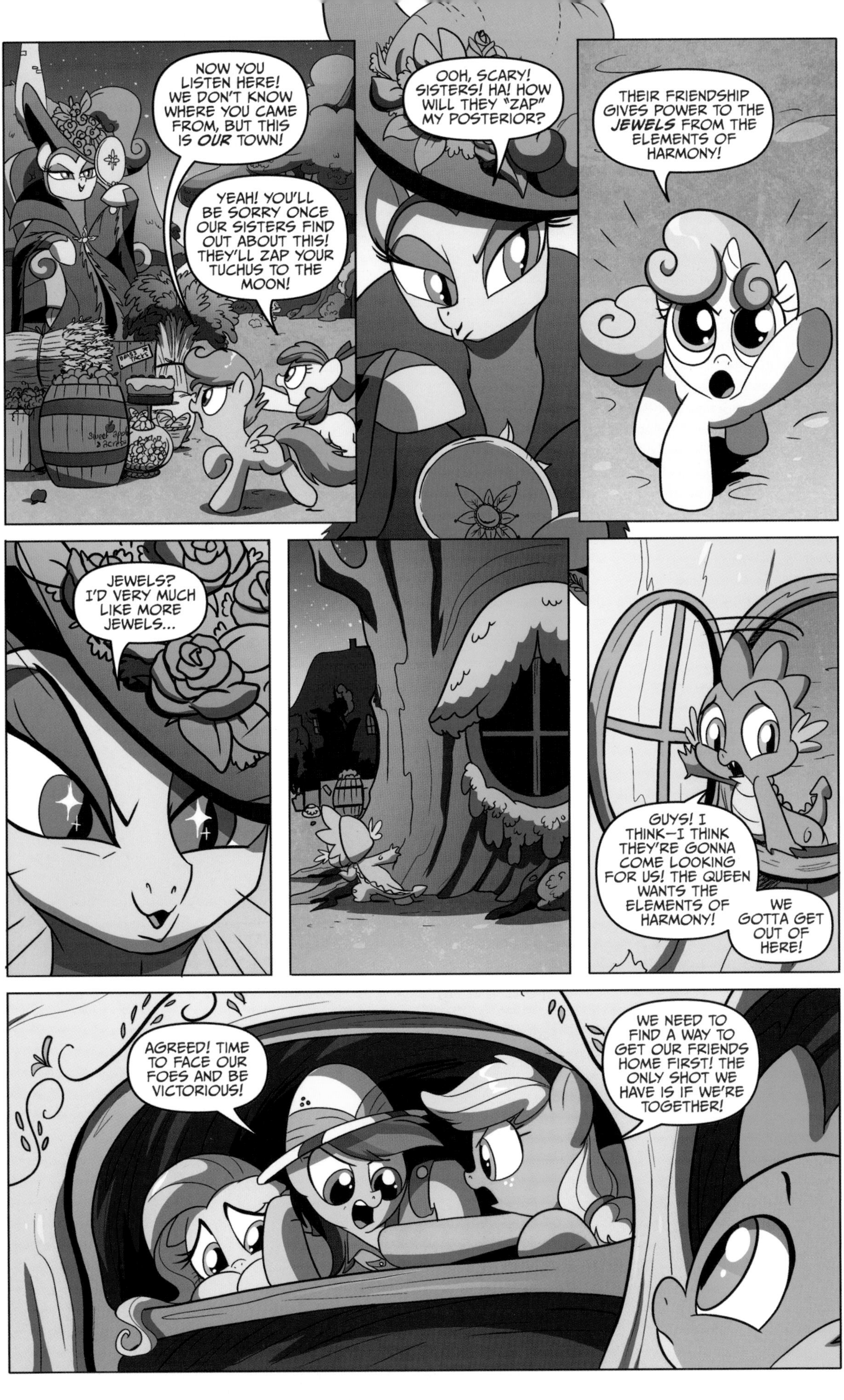

NOW YOU LISTEN HERE! WE DON'T KNOW WHERE YOU CAME FROM, BUT THIS IS *OUR* TOWN!
YEAH! YOU'LL BE SORRY ONCE OUR SISTERS FIND OUT ABOUT THIS! THEY'LL ZAP YOUR TUCHUS TO THE MOON!
OOH, SCARY! SISTERS! HA! HOW WILL THEY "ZAP" MY POSTERIOR?
THEIR FRIENDSHIP GIVES POWER TO THE *JEWELS* FROM THE ELEMENTS OF HARMONY!
JEWELS? I'D VERY MUCH LIKE MORE JEWELS...
GUYS! I THINK—I THINK THEY'RE GONNA COME LOOKING FOR US! THE QUEEN WANTS THE ELEMENTS OF HARMONY!
WE GOTTA GET OUT OF HERE!
AGREED! TIME TO FACE OUR FOES AND BE VICTORIOUS!
WE NEED TO FIND A WAY TO GET OUR FRIENDS HOME FIRST! THE ONLY SHOT WE HAVE IS IF WE'RE TOGETHER!

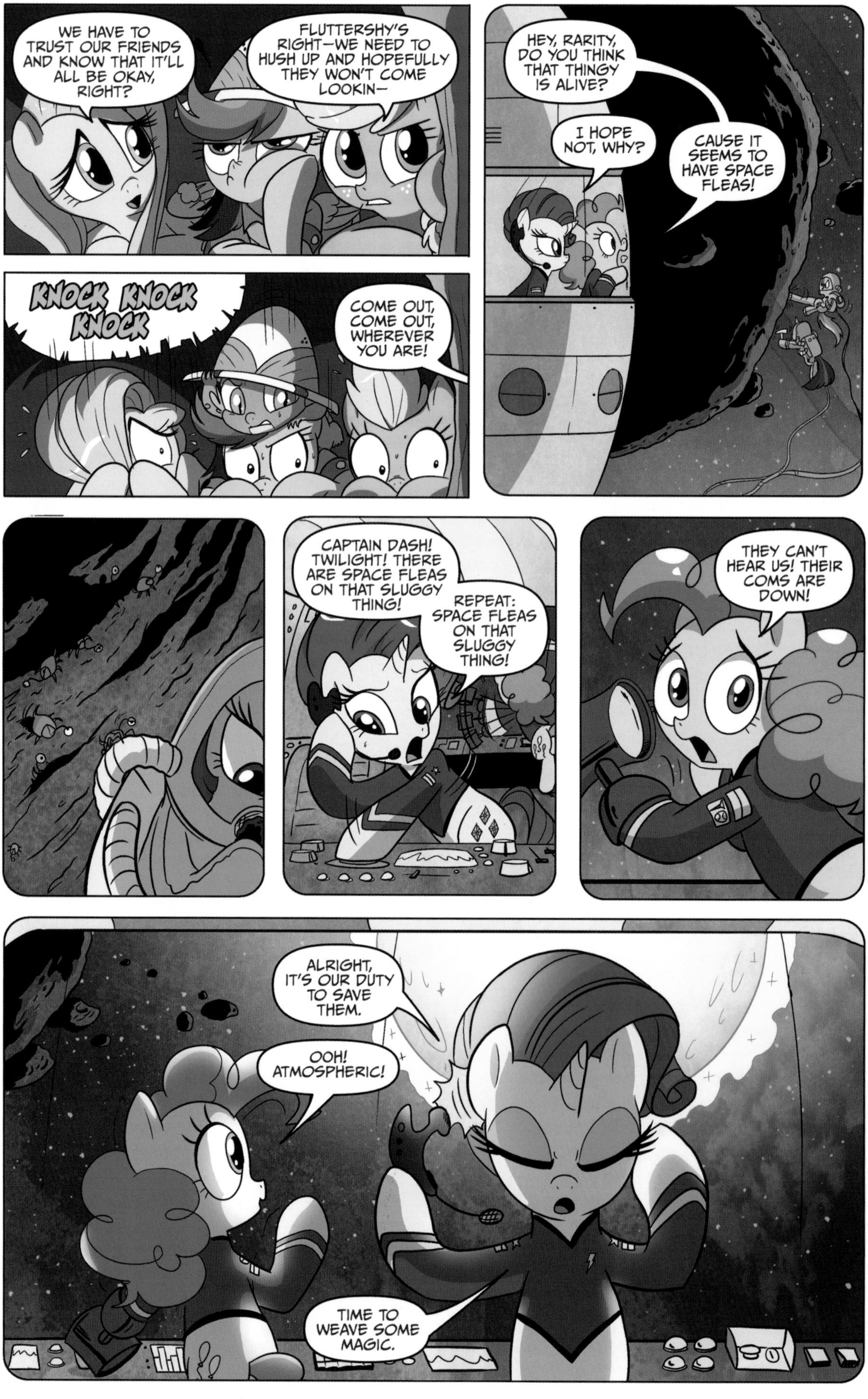
WE HAVE TO TRUST OUR FRIENDS AND KNOW THAT IT'LL ALL BE OKAY, RIGHT?
FLUTTERSHY'S RIGHT—WE NEED TO HUSH UP AND HOPEFULLY THEY WON'T COME LOOKIN—
KNOCK KNOCK KNOCK
COME OUT, COME OUT, WHEREVER YOU ARE!
HEY, RARITY, DO YOU THINK THAT THINGY IS ALIVE?
I HOPE NOT, WHY?
CAUSE IT SEEMS TO HAVE SPACE FLEAS!
CAPTAIN DASH! TWILIGHT! THERE ARE SPACE FLEAS ON THAT SLUGGY THING!
REPEAT: SPACE FLEAS ON THAT SLUGGY THING!
THEY CAN'T HEAR US! THEIR COMS ARE DOWN!
ALRIGHT, IT'S OUR DUTY TO SAVE THEM.
OOH! ATMOSPHERIC!
TIME TO WEAVE SOME MAGIC.

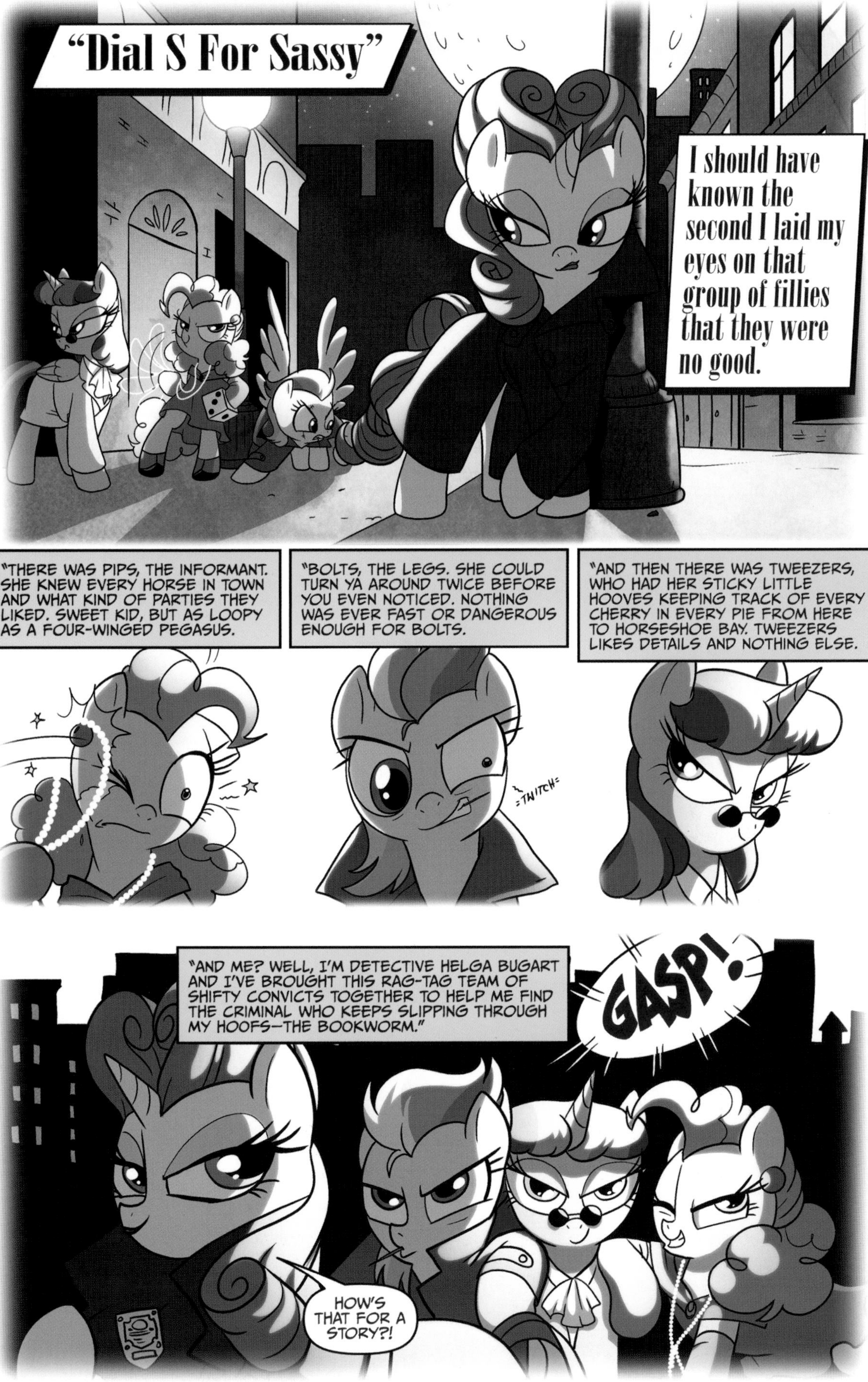
"Dial S For Sassy"
I should have known the second I laid my eyes on that group of fillies that they were no good.
"THERE WAS PIPS, THE INFORMANT. SHE KNEW EVERY HORSE IN TOWN AND WHAT KIND OF PARTIES THEY LIKED. SWEET KID, BUT AS LOOPY AS A FOUR-WINGED PEGASUS.
"BOLTS, THE LEGS. SHE COULD TURN YA AROUND TWICE BEFORE YOU EVEN NOTICED. NOTHING WAS EVER FAST OR DANGEROUS ENOUGH FOR BOLTS.
TWITCH
"AND THEN THERE WAS TWEEZERS, WHO HAD HER STICKY LITTLE HOOVES KEEPING TRACK OF EVERY CHERRY IN EVERY PIE FROM HERE TO HORSESHOE BAY. TWEEZERS LIKES DETAILS AND NOTHING ELSE.
"AND ME? WELL, I'M DETECTIVE HELGA BUGART AND I'VE BROUGHT THIS RAG-TAG TEAM OF SHIFTY CONVICTS TOGETHER TO HELP ME FIND THE CRIMINAL WHO KEEPS SLIPPING THROUGH MY HOOFS—THE BOOKWORM."
GASP!
HOW'S THAT FOR A STORY?!

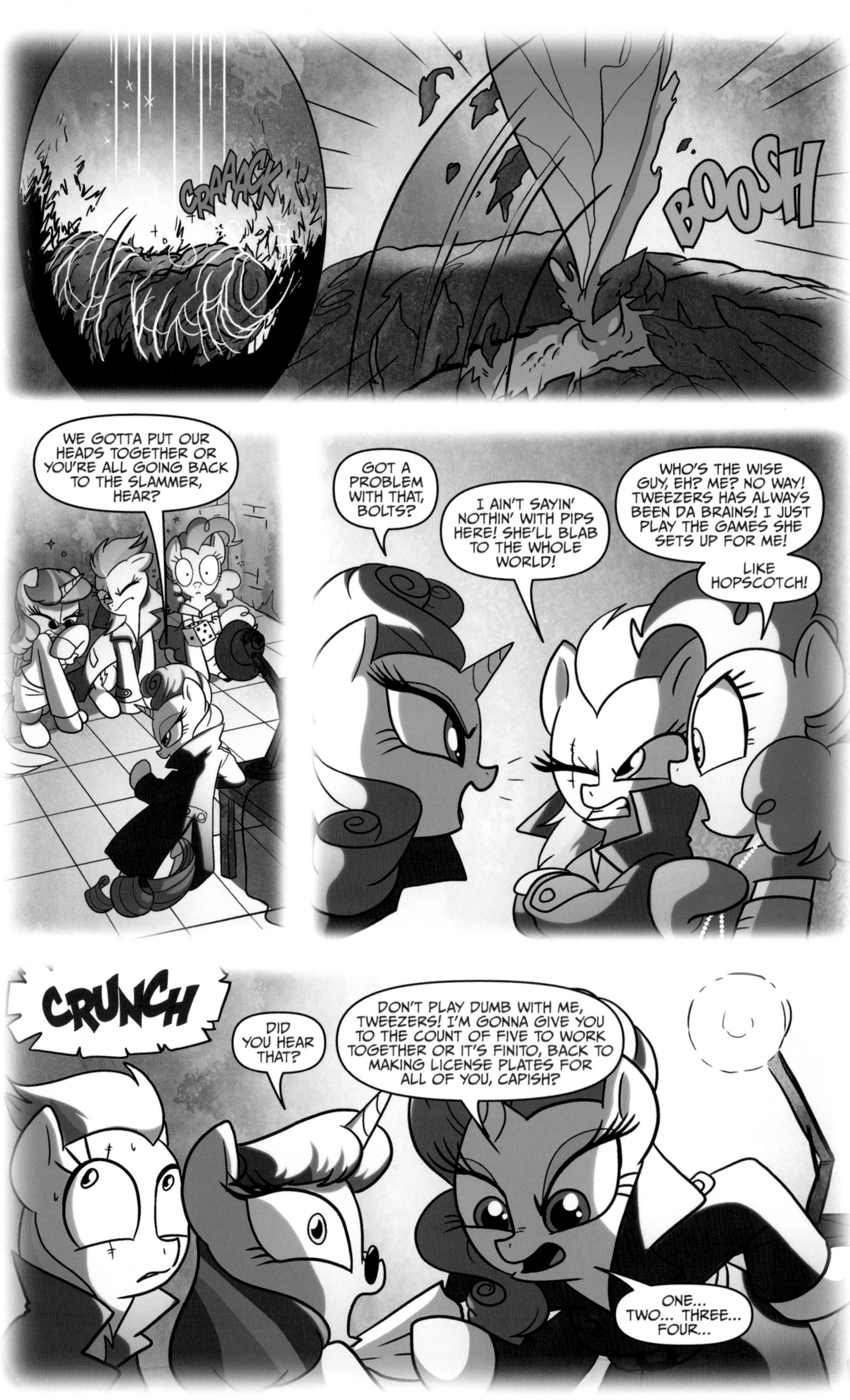
CRAAACK
BOOSH
WE GOTTA PUT OUR HEADS TOGETHER OR YOU'RE ALL GOING BACK TO THE SLAMMER, HEAR?
GOT A PROBLEM WITH THAT, BOLTS?
I AIN'T SAYIN' NOTHIN' WITH PIPS HERE! SHE'LL BLAB TO THE WHOLE WORLD!
WHO'S THE WISE GUY, EH? ME? NO WAY! TWEEZERS HAS ALWAYS BEEN DA BRAINS! I JUST PLAY THE GAMES SHE SETS UP FOR ME!
LIKE HOPSCOTCH!
CRUNCH
DID YOU HEAR THAT?
DON'T PLAY DUMB WITH ME, TWEEZERS! I'M GONNA GIVE YOU TO THE COUNT OF FIVE TO WORK TOGETHER OR IT'S FINITO, BACK TO MAKING LICENSE PLATES FOR ALL OF YOU, CAPISH?
ONE... TWO... THREE... FOUR...

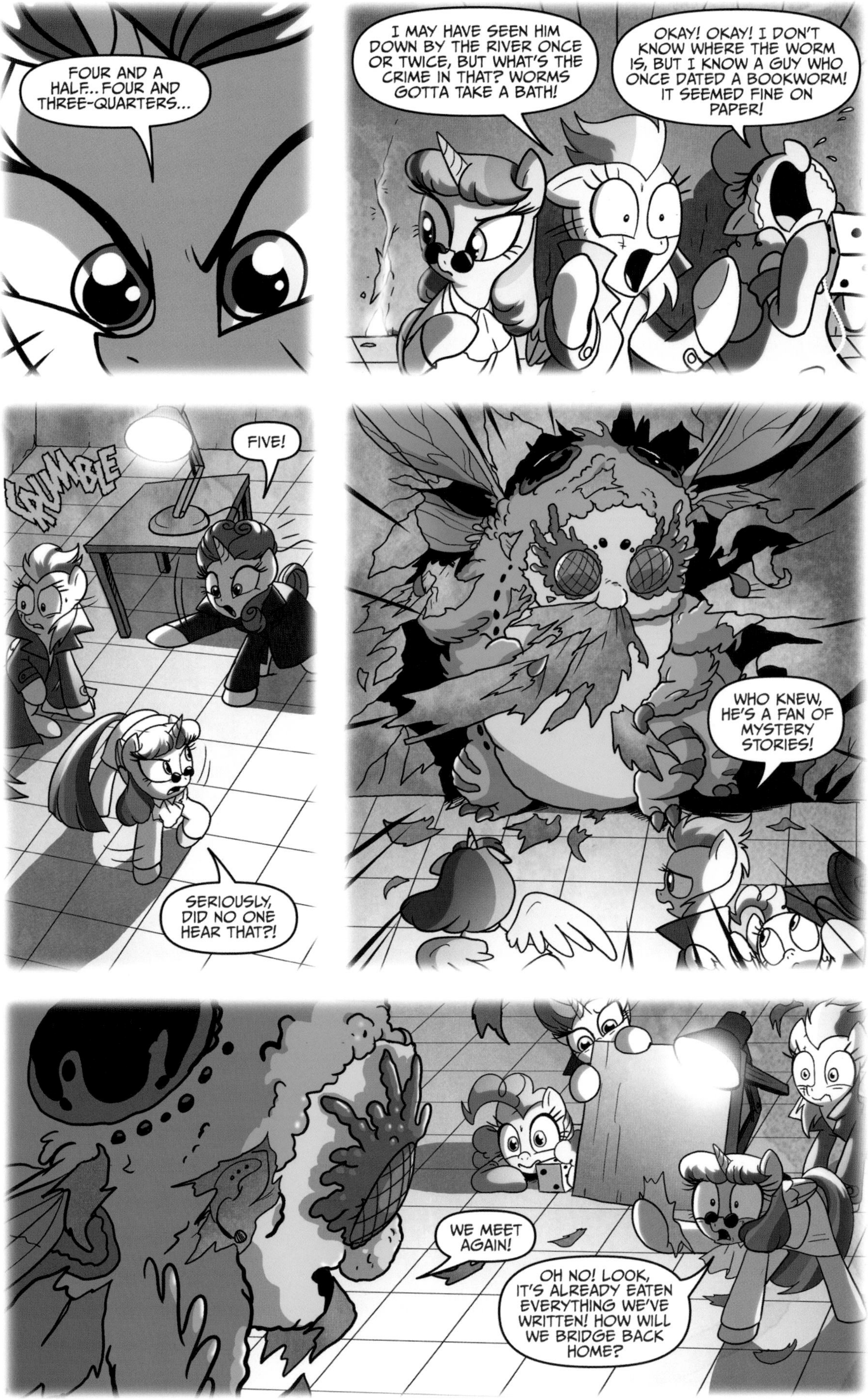
FOUR AND A HALF...FOUR AND THREE-QUARTERS...
I MAY HAVE SEEN HIM DOWN BY THE RIVER ONCE OR TWICE, BUT WHAT'S THE CRIME IN THAT? WORMS GOTTA TAKE A BATH!
OKAY! OKAY! I DON'T KNOW WHERE THE WORM IS, BUT I KNOW A GUY WHO ONCE DATED A BOOKWORM! IT SEEMED FINE ON PAPER!
RUMBLE
FIVE!
SERIOUSLY, DID NO ONE HEAR THAT?!
WHO KNEW, HE'S A FAN OF MYSTERY STORIES!
WE MEET AGAIN!
OH NO! LOOK, IT'S ALREADY EATEN EVERYTHING WE'VE WRITTEN! HOW WILL WE BRIDGE BACK HOME?

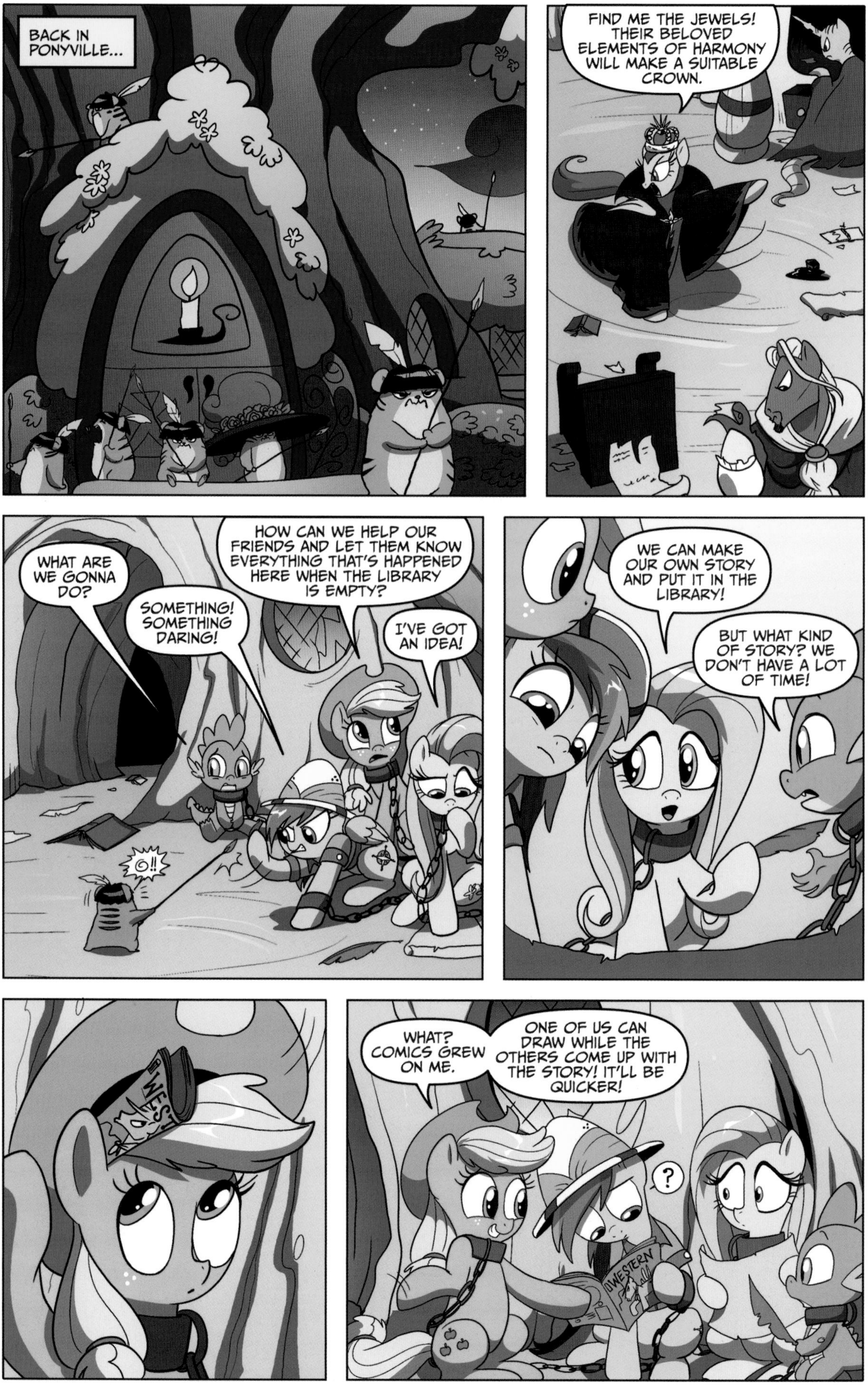
BACK IN PONYVILLE...
FIND ME THE JEWELS! THEIR BELOVED ELEMENTS OF HARMONY WILL MAKE A SUITABLE CROWN.
WHAT ARE WE GONNA DO?
SOMETHING! SOMETHING DARING!
HOW CAN WE HELP OUR FRIENDS AND LET THEM KNOW EVERYTHING THAT'S HAPPENED HERE WHEN THE LIBRARY IS EMPTY?
I'VE GOT AN IDEA!
G!!
WE CAN MAKE OUR OWN STORY AND PUT IT IN THE LIBRARY!
BUT WHAT KIND OF STORY? WE DON'T HAVE A LOT OF TIME!
WEST
WHAT? COMICS GREW ON ME.
ONE OF US CAN DRAW WHILE THE OTHERS COME UP WITH THE STORY! IT'LL BE QUICKER!
?
WESTERN

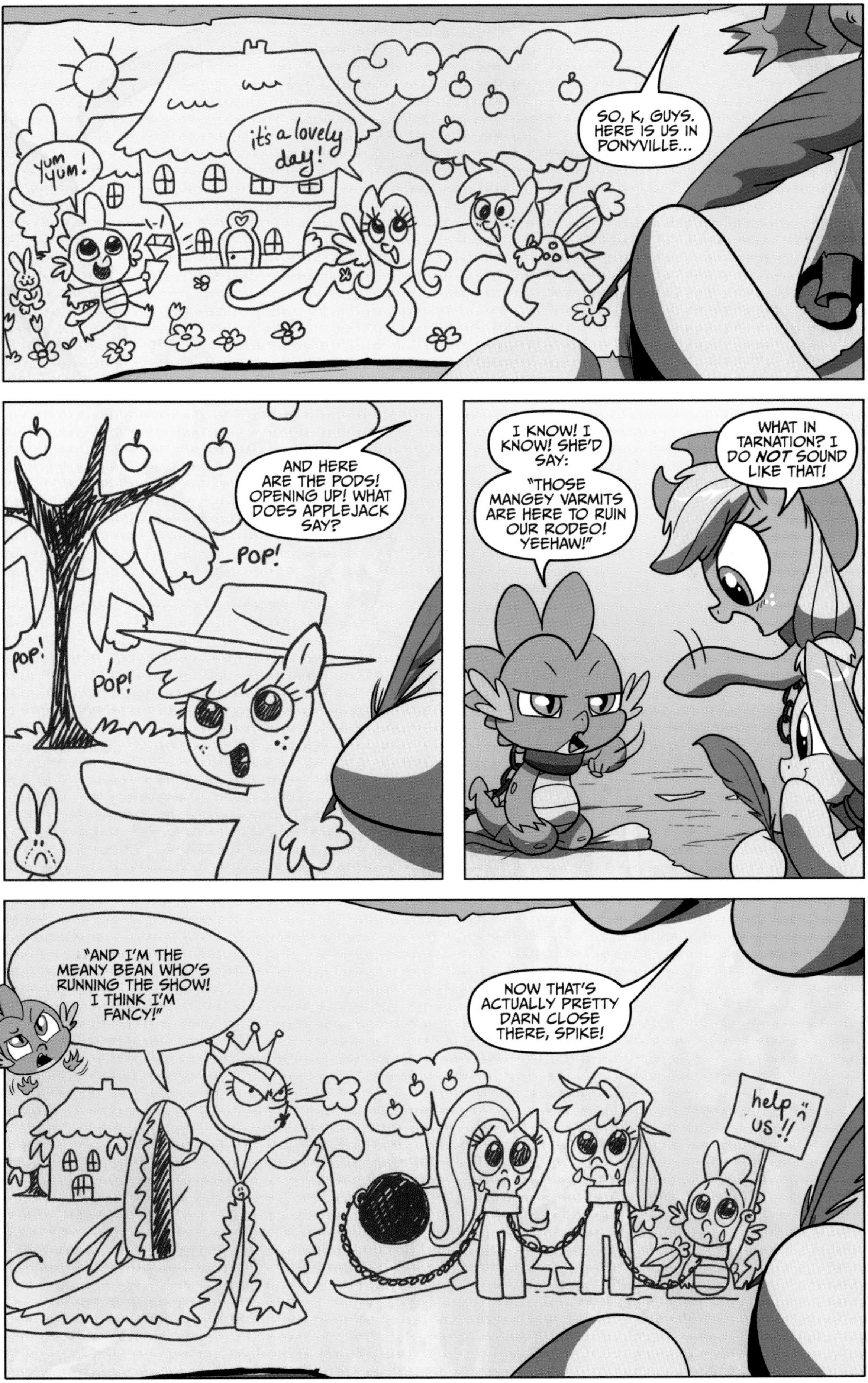

yum yum!
it's a lovely day!
SO, K, GUYS. HERE IS US IN PONYVILLE...
AND HERE ARE THE PODS! OPENING UP! WHAT DOES APPLEJACK SAY?
POP!
POP!
POP!
I KNOW! I KNOW! SHE'D SAY: "THOSE MANGEY VARMITS ARE HERE TO RUIN OUR RODEO! YEEHAW!"
WHAT IN TARNATION? I DO NOT SOUND LIKE THAT!
"AND I'M THE MEANY BEAN WHO'S RUNNING THE SHOW! I THINK I'M FANCY!"
NOW THAT'S ACTUALLY PRETTY DARN CLOSE THERE, SPIKE!
help us!!

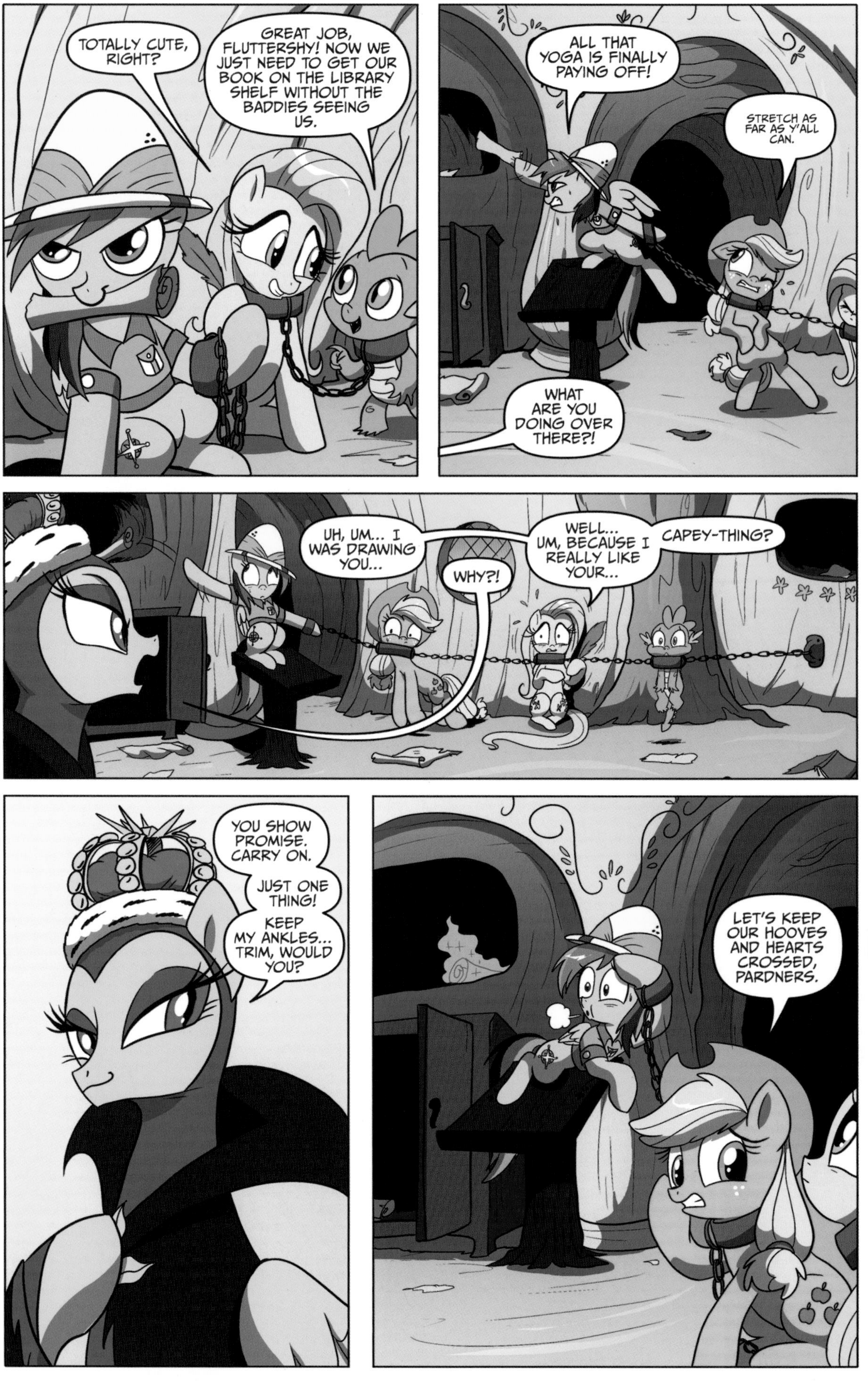

TOTALLY CUTE, RIGHT?
GREAT JOB, FLUTTERSHY! NOW WE JUST NEED TO GET OUR BOOK ON THE LIBRARY SHELF WITHOUT THE BADDIES SEEING US.
ALL THAT YOGA IS FINALLY PAYING OFF!
STRETCH AS FAR AS Y'ALL CAN.
WHAT ARE YOU DOING OVER THERE?!
UH, UM... I WAS DRAWING YOU...
WHY?!
WELL... UM, BECAUSE I REALLY LIKE YOUR...
CAPEY-THING?
YOU SHOW PROMISE. CARRY ON.
JUST ONE THING!
KEEP MY ANKLES... TRIM, WOULD YOU?
LET'S KEEP OUR HOOVES AND HEARTS CROSSED, PARDNERS.

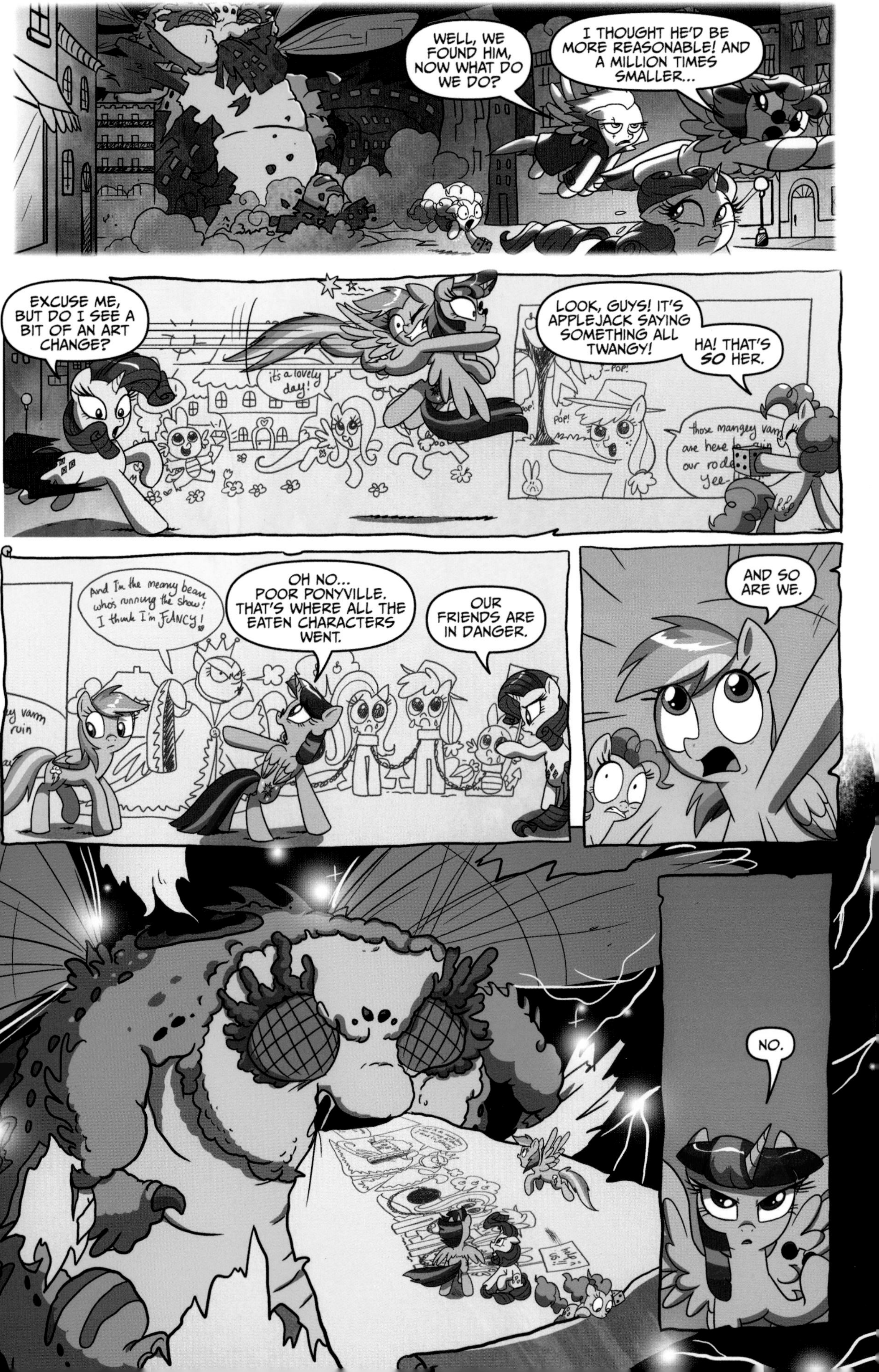
WELL, WE FOUND HIM, NOW WHAT DO WE DO?
I THOUGHT HE'D BE MORE REASONABLE! AND A MILLION TIMES SMALLER...
EXCUSE ME, BUT DO I SEE A BIT OF AN ART CHANGE?
it's a lovely day!
LOOK, GUYS! IT'S APPLEJACK SAYING SOMETHING ALL TWANGY!
POP!
POP!
POP!
HA! THAT'S SO HER.
those mangey varm
And I'm the meany bean who's running the show! I think I'm FANCY!
OH NO... POOR PONYVILLE. THAT'S WHERE ALL THE EATEN CHARACTERS WENT.
OUR FRIENDS ARE IN DANGER.
AND SO ARE WE.
NO.

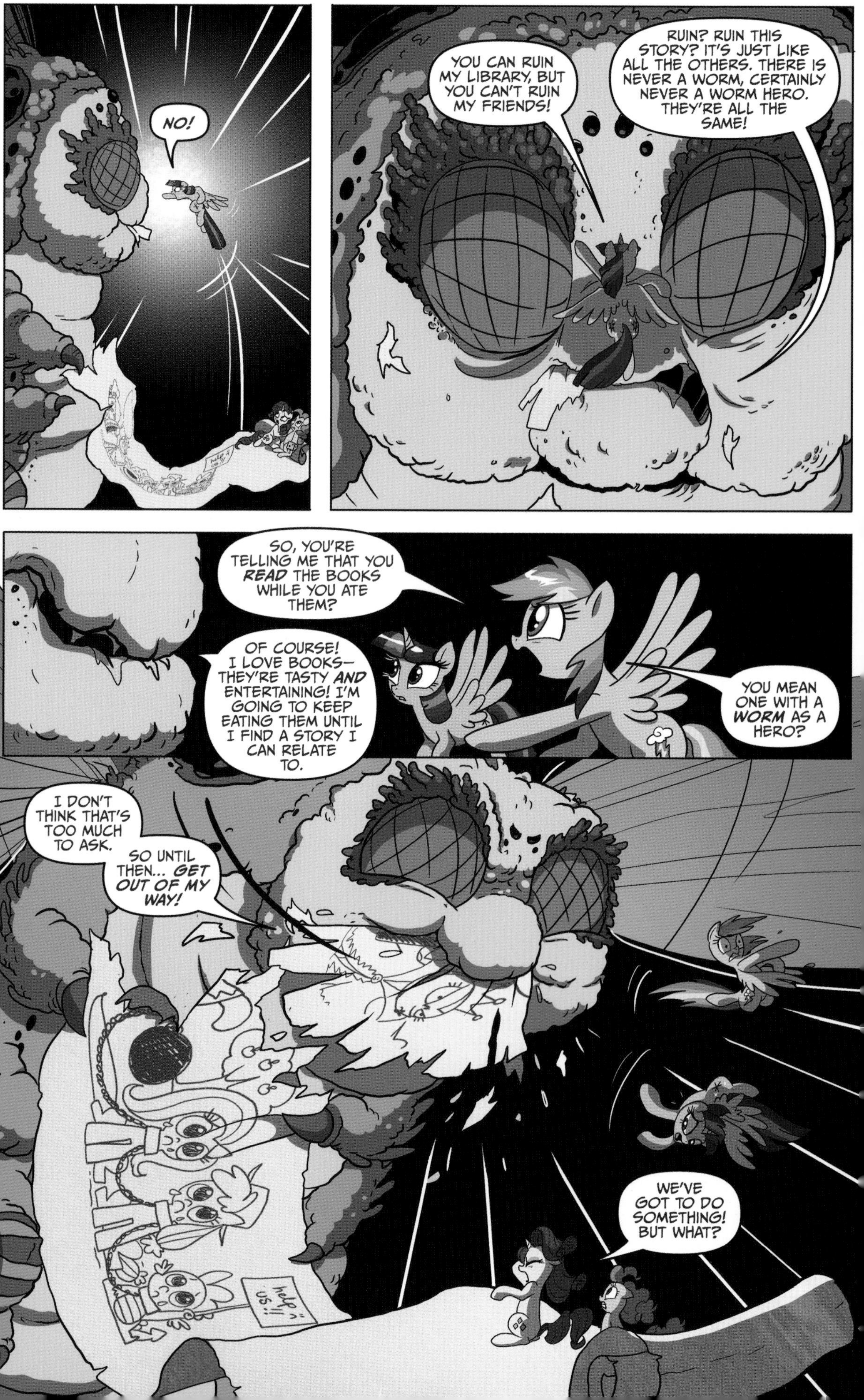
NO!
YOU CAN RUIN MY LIBRARY, BUT YOU CAN'T RUIN MY FRIENDS!
RUIN? RUIN THIS STORY? IT'S JUST LIKE ALL THE OTHERS. THERE IS NEVER A WORM, CERTAINLY NEVER A WORM HERO. THEY'RE ALL THE SAME!
SO, YOU'RE TELLING ME THAT YOU *READ* THE BOOKS WHILE YOU ATE THEM?
OF COURSE! I LOVE BOOKS— THEY'RE TASTY *AND* ENTERTAINING! I'M GOING TO KEEP EATING THEM UNTIL I FIND A STORY I CAN RELATE TO.
YOU MEAN ONE WITH A *WORM* AS A HERO?
I DON'T THINK THAT'S TOO MUCH TO ASK.
SO UNTIL THEN... *GET OUT OF MY WAY!*
WE'VE GOT TO DO SOMETHING! BUT WHAT?
help us!!

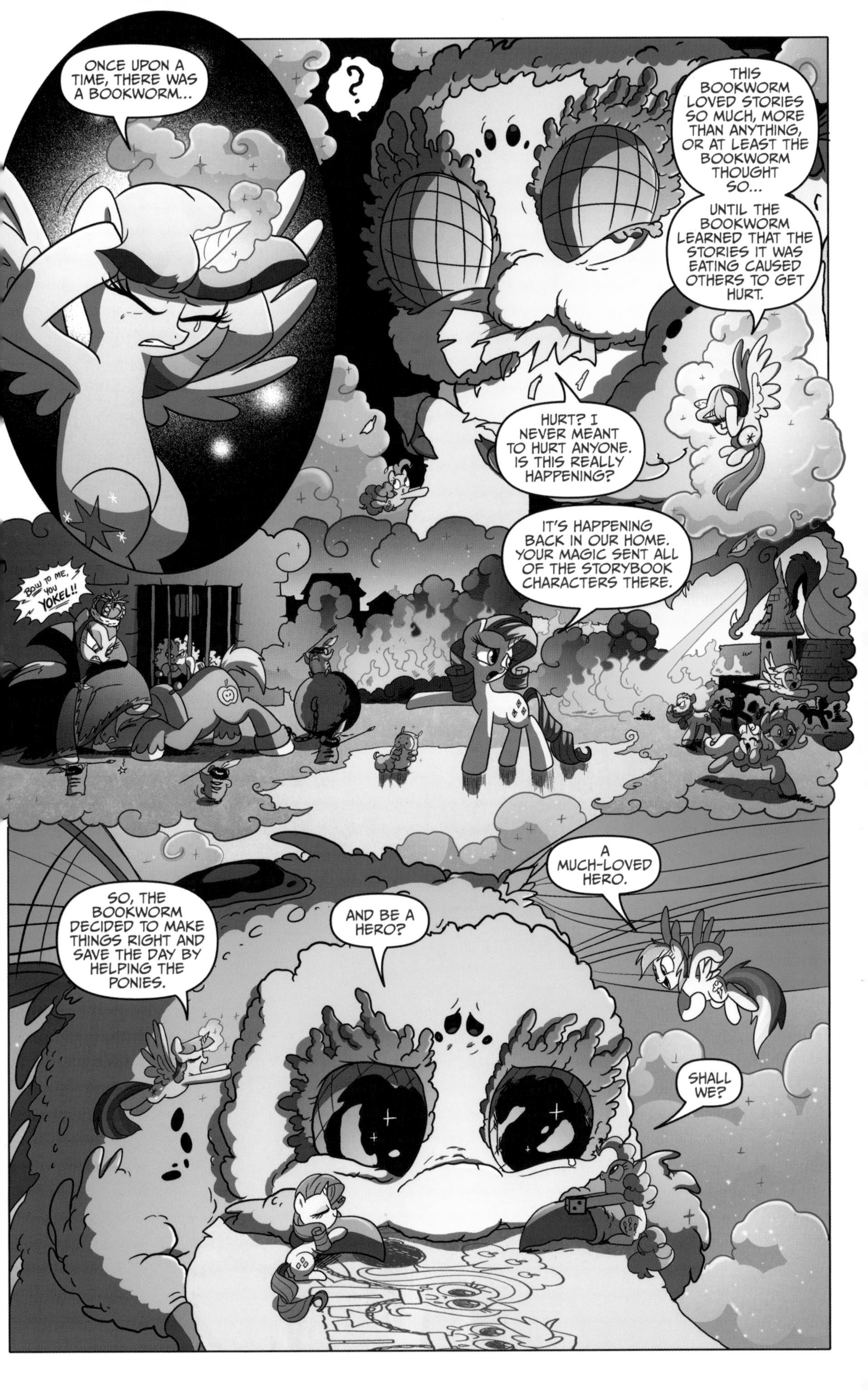
ONCE UPON A TIME, THERE WAS A BOOKWORM...
?
THIS BOOKWORM LOVED STORIES SO MUCH, MORE THAN ANYTHING, OR AT LEAST THE BOOKWORM THOUGHT SO...
UNTIL THE BOOKWORM LEARNED THAT THE STORIES IT WAS EATING CAUSED OTHERS TO GET HURT.
HURT? I NEVER MEANT TO HURT ANYONE. IS THIS REALLY HAPPENING?
IT'S HAPPENING BACK IN OUR HOME. YOUR MAGIC SENT ALL OF THE STORYBOOK CHARACTERS THERE.
BOW TO ME, YOU YOKEL!!
SO, THE BOOKWORM DECIDED TO MAKE THINGS RIGHT AND SAVE THE DAY BY HELPING THE PONIES.
AND BE A HERO?
A MUCH-LOVED HERO.
SHALL WE?

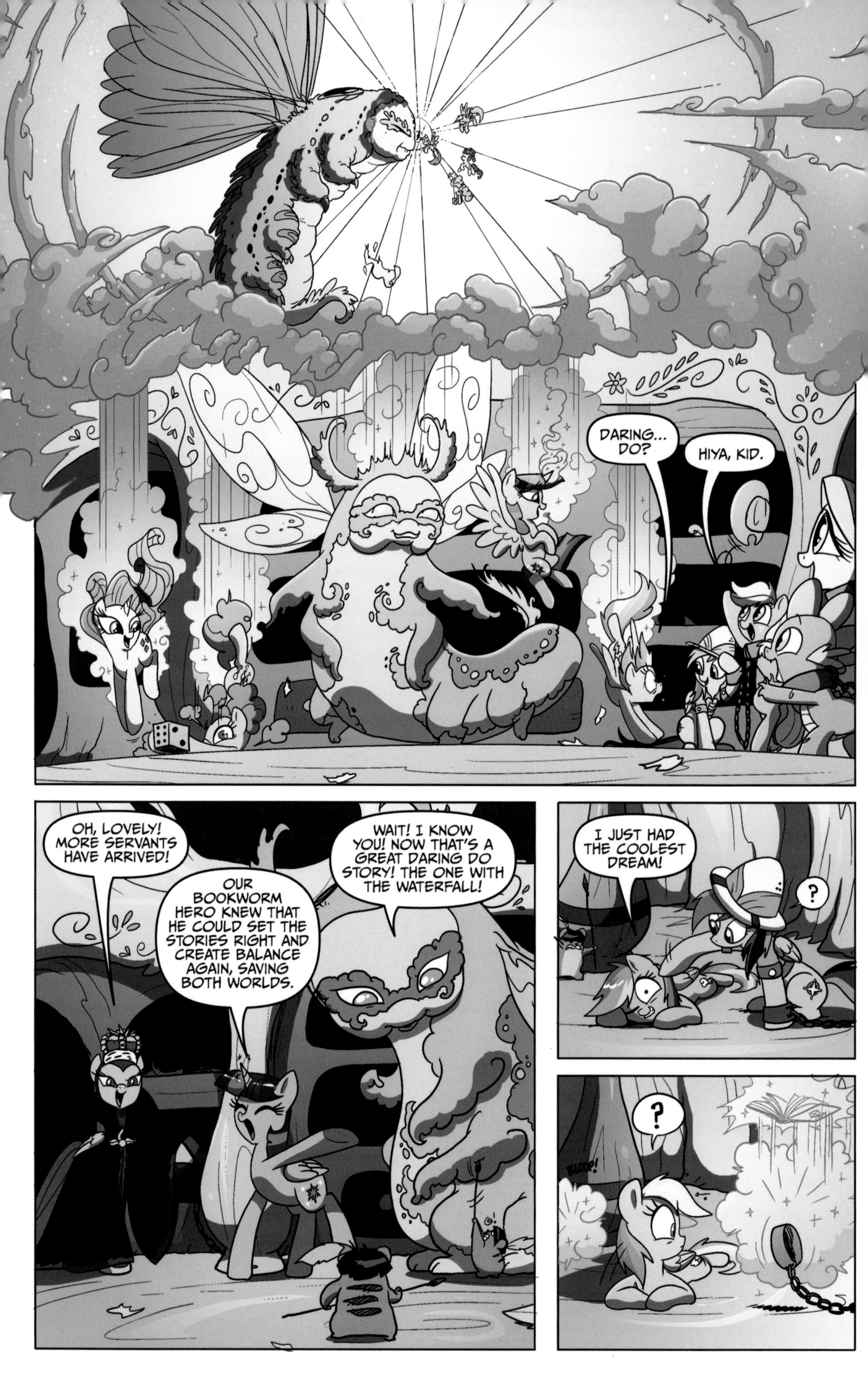
DARING... DO?
HIYA, KID.
OH, LOVELY! MORE SERVANTS HAVE ARRIVED!
OUR BOOKWORM HERO KNEW THAT HE COULD SET THE STORIES RIGHT AND CREATE BALANCE AGAIN, SAVING BOTH WORLDS.
WAIT! I KNOW YOU! NOW THAT'S A GREAT DARING DO STORY! THE ONE WITH THE WATERFALL!
I JUST HAD THE COOLEST DREAM!
?
?
BLOOP!

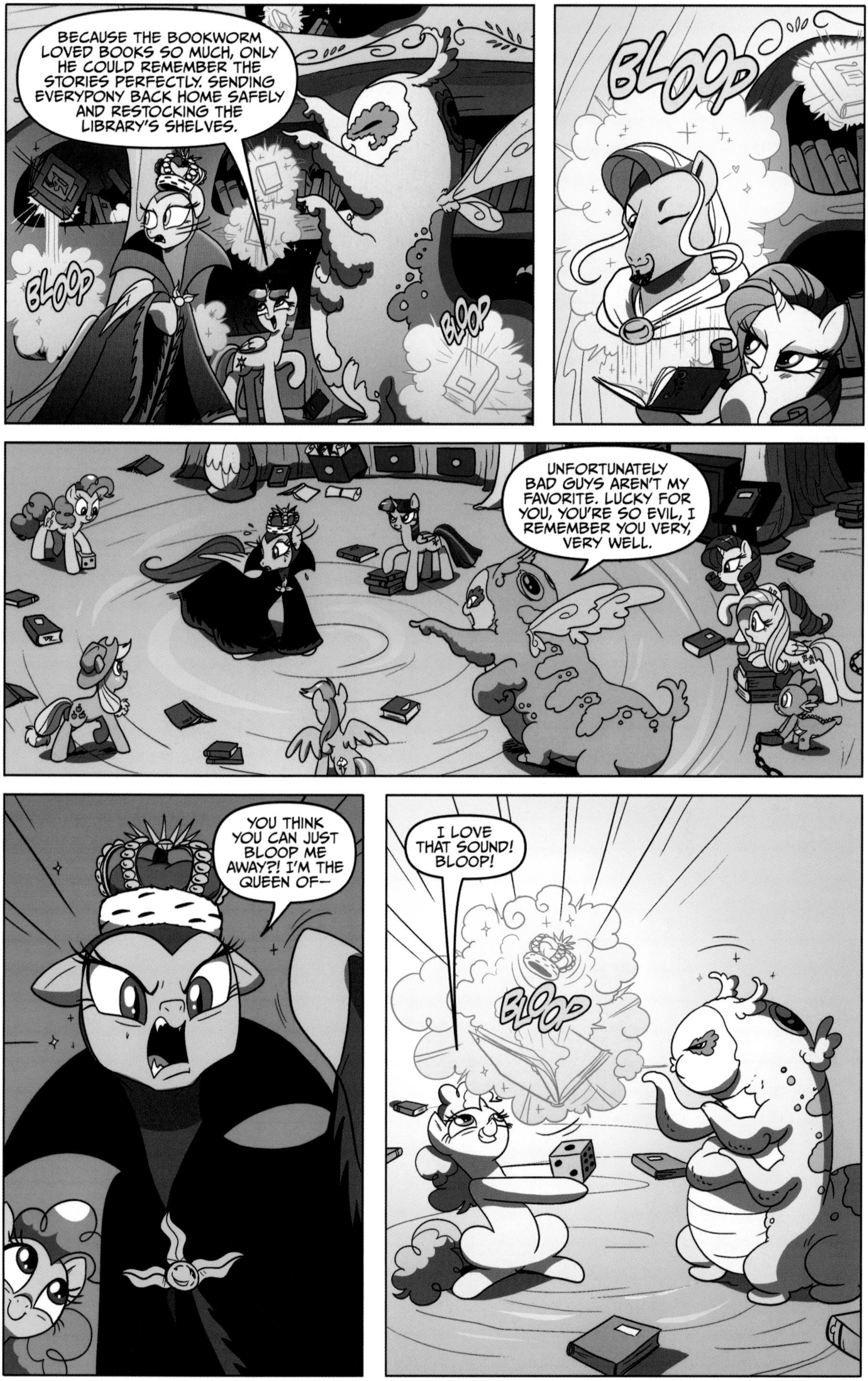
BECAUSE THE BOOKWORM LOVED BOOKS SO MUCH, ONLY HE COULD REMEMBER THE STORIES PERFECTLY. SENDING EVERYPONY BACK HOME SAFELY AND RESTOCKING THE LIBRARY'S SHELVES.
BLOOP
BLOOP
BLOOP
UNFORTUNATELY BAD GUYS AREN'T MY FAVORITE. LUCKY FOR YOU, YOU'RE SO EVIL, I REMEMBER YOU VERY, VERY WELL.
YOU THINK YOU CAN JUST BLOOP ME AWAY?! I'M THE QUEEN OF—
I LOVE THAT SOUND! BLOOP!
BLOOP

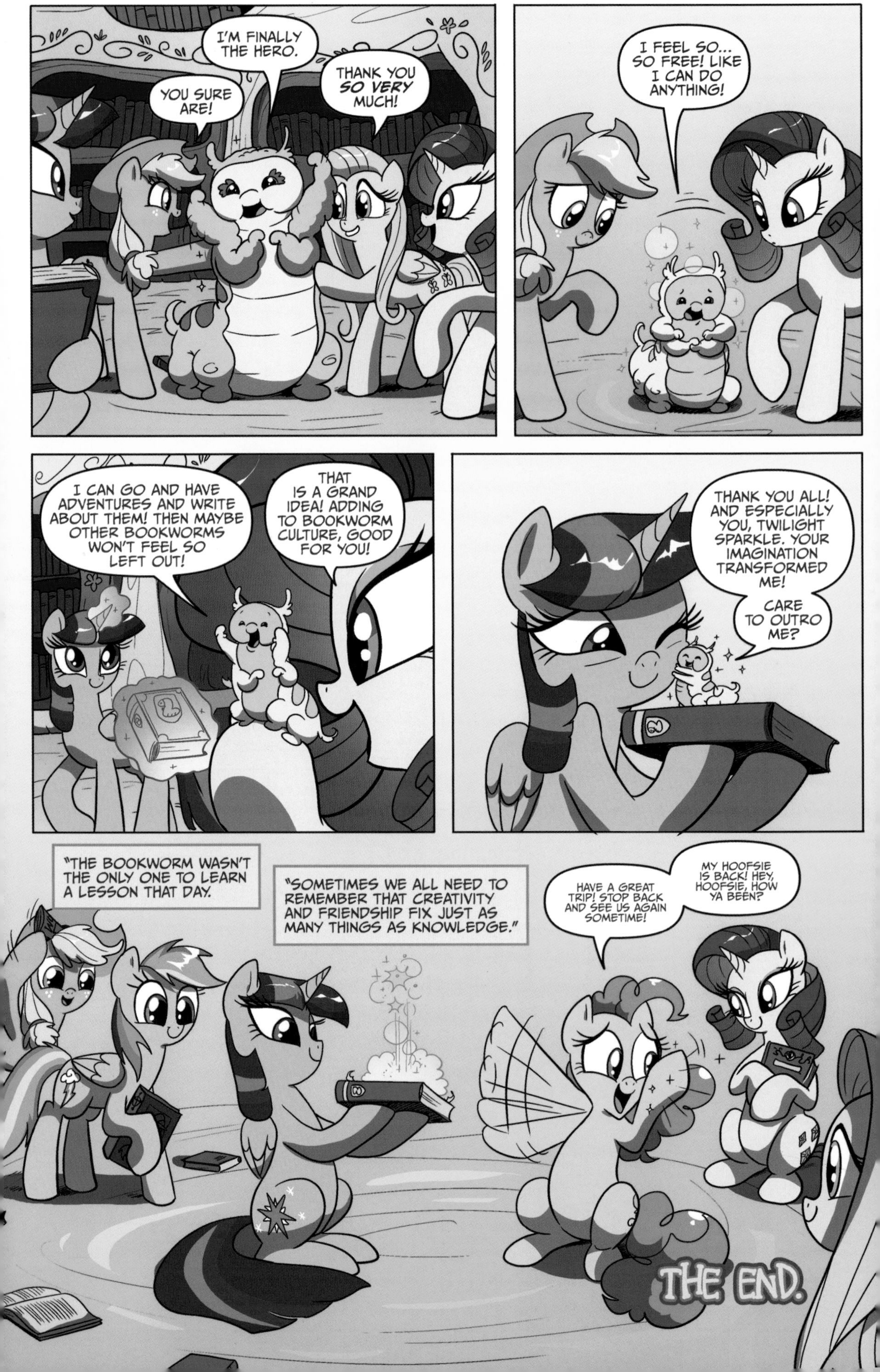
I'M FINALLY THE HERO.
YOU SURE ARE!
THANK YOU *SO VERY* MUCH!
I FEEL SO... SO FREE! LIKE I CAN DO ANYTHING!
I CAN GO AND HAVE ADVENTURES AND WRITE ABOUT THEM! THEN MAYBE OTHER BOOKWORMS WON'T FEEL SO LEFT OUT!
THAT IS A GRAND IDEA! ADDING TO BOOKWORM CULTURE, GOOD FOR YOU!
THANK YOU ALL! AND ESPECIALLY YOU, TWILIGHT SPARKLE. YOUR IMAGINATION TRANSFORMED ME!
CARE TO OUTRO ME?
"THE BOOKWORM WASN'T THE ONLY ONE TO LEARN A LESSON THAT DAY.
"SOMETIMES WE ALL NEED TO REMEMBER THAT CREATIVITY AND FRIENDSHIP FIX JUST AS MANY THINGS AS KNOWLEDGE."
HAVE A GREAT TRIP! STOP BACK AND SEE US AGAIN SOMETIME!
MY HOOFSIE IS BACK! HEY, HOOFSIE, HOW YA BEEN?
THE END.

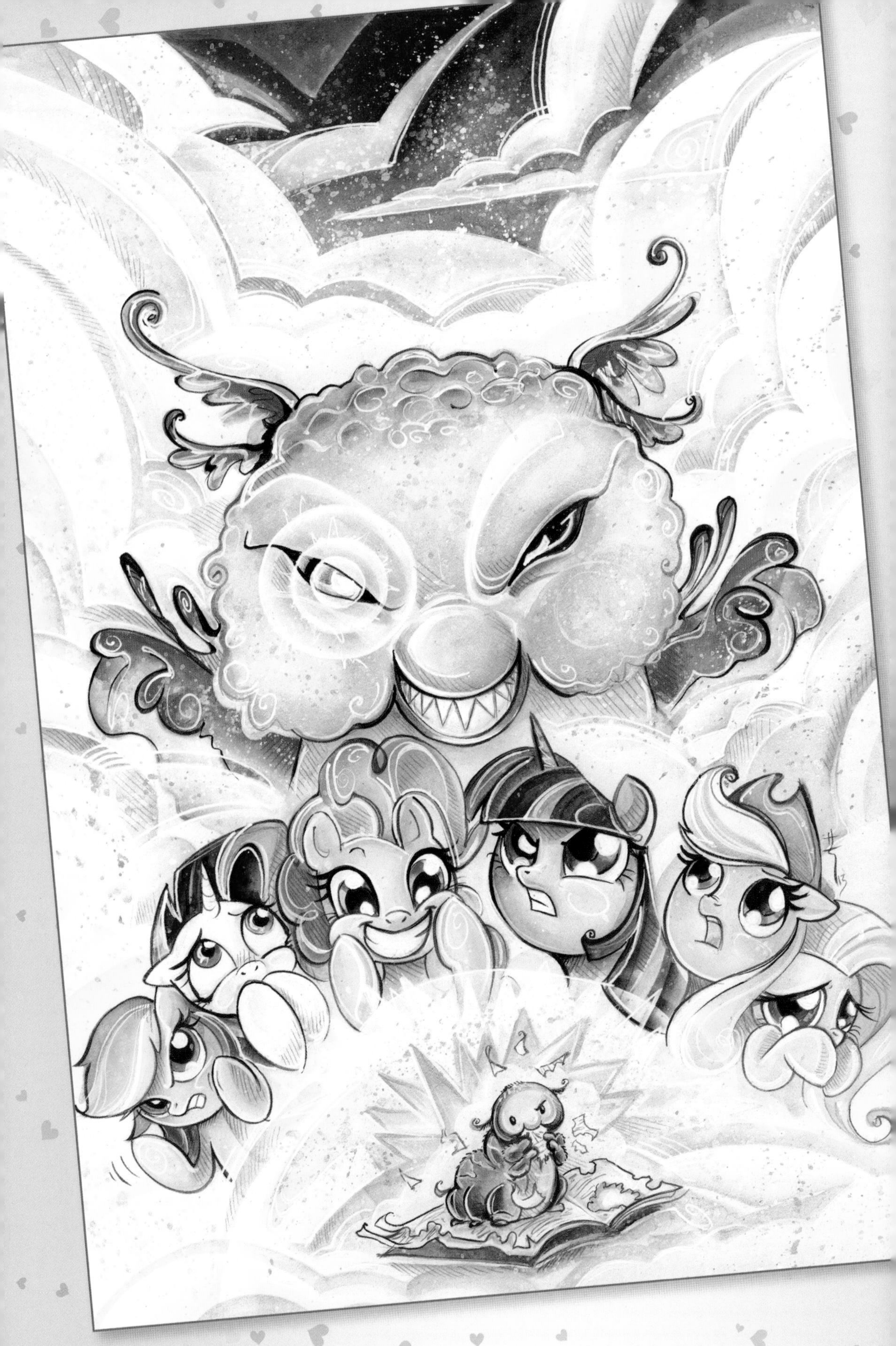

art BY Sara Richard

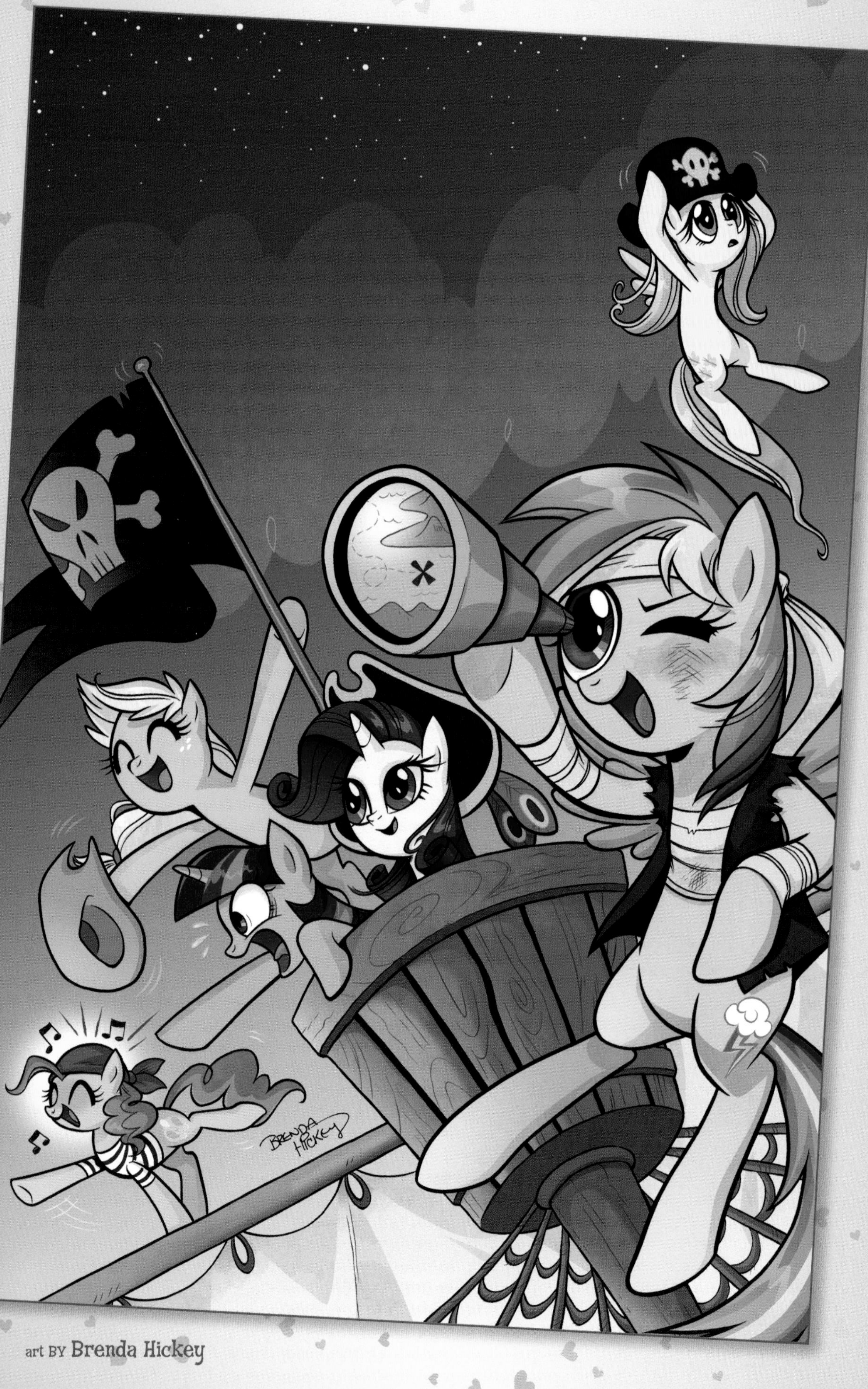
BRENDA HICKEY

art BY Brenda Hickey

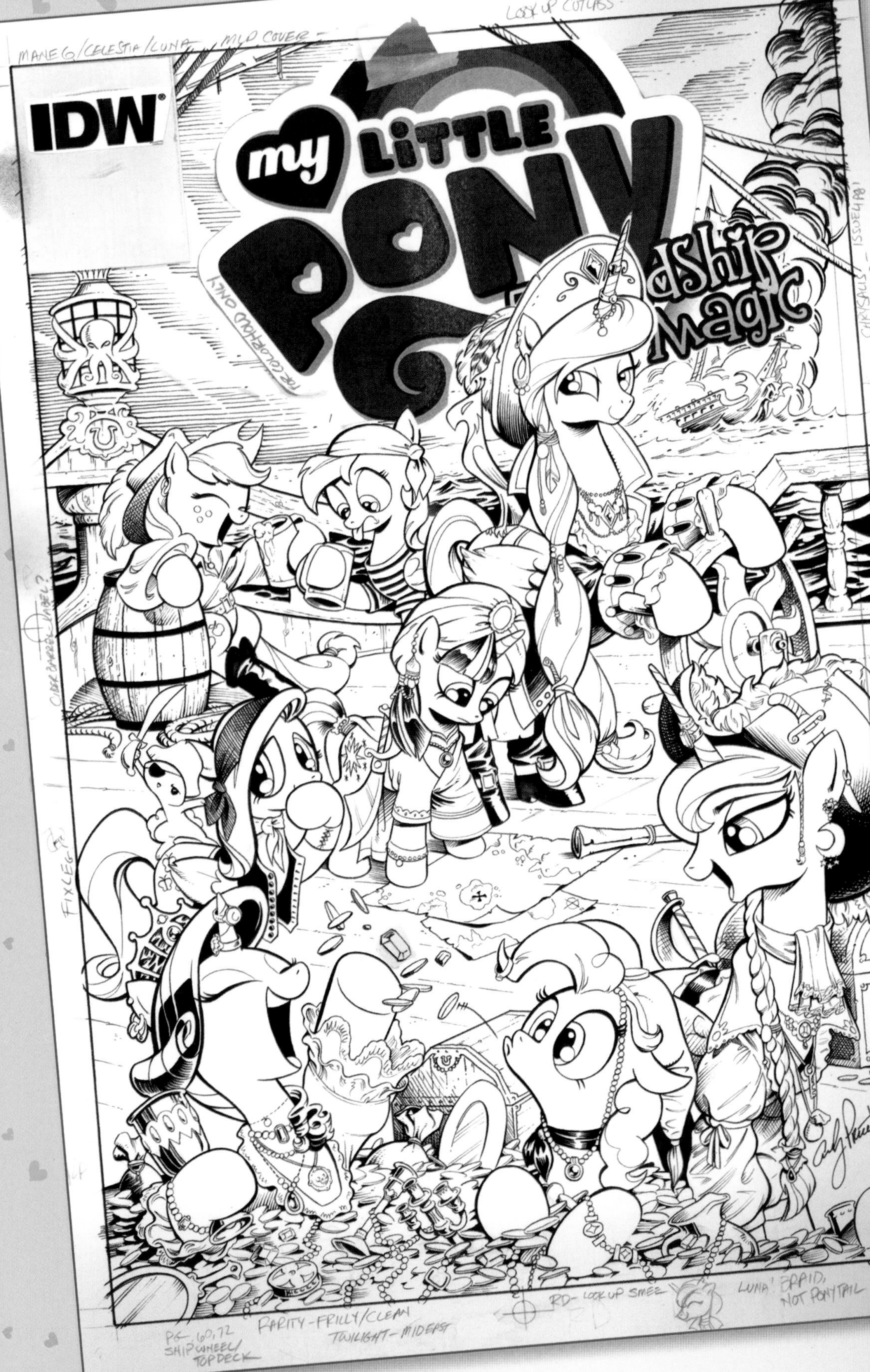

IDW
my LITTLE PONY
LOOK UP CUTLASS -
RD- LOOK UP SMEE
LUNA! BRAID, NOT PONYTAIL
RARITY-FRILLY/CLEAN

art BY Andy Price

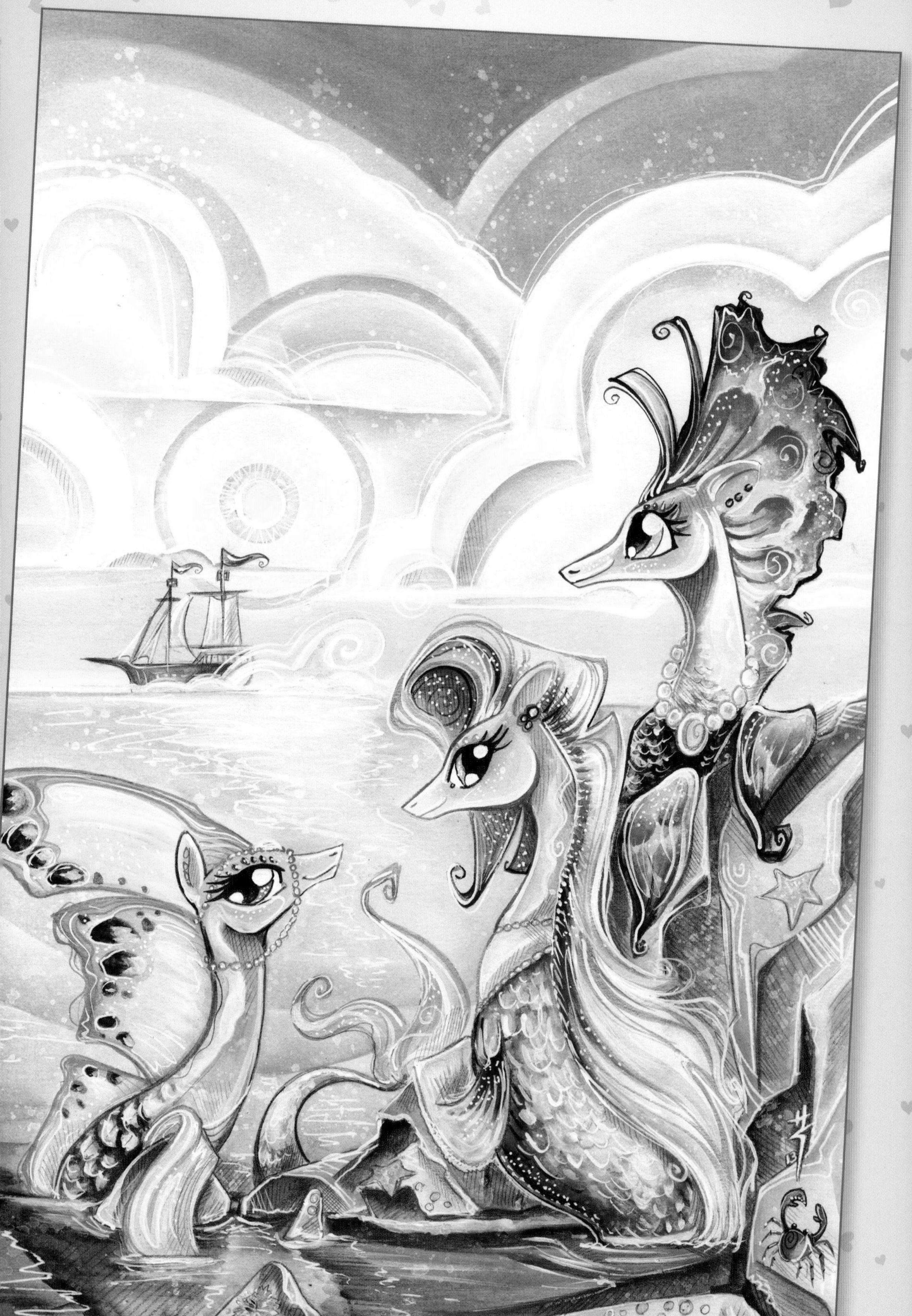

art BY Sara Richard

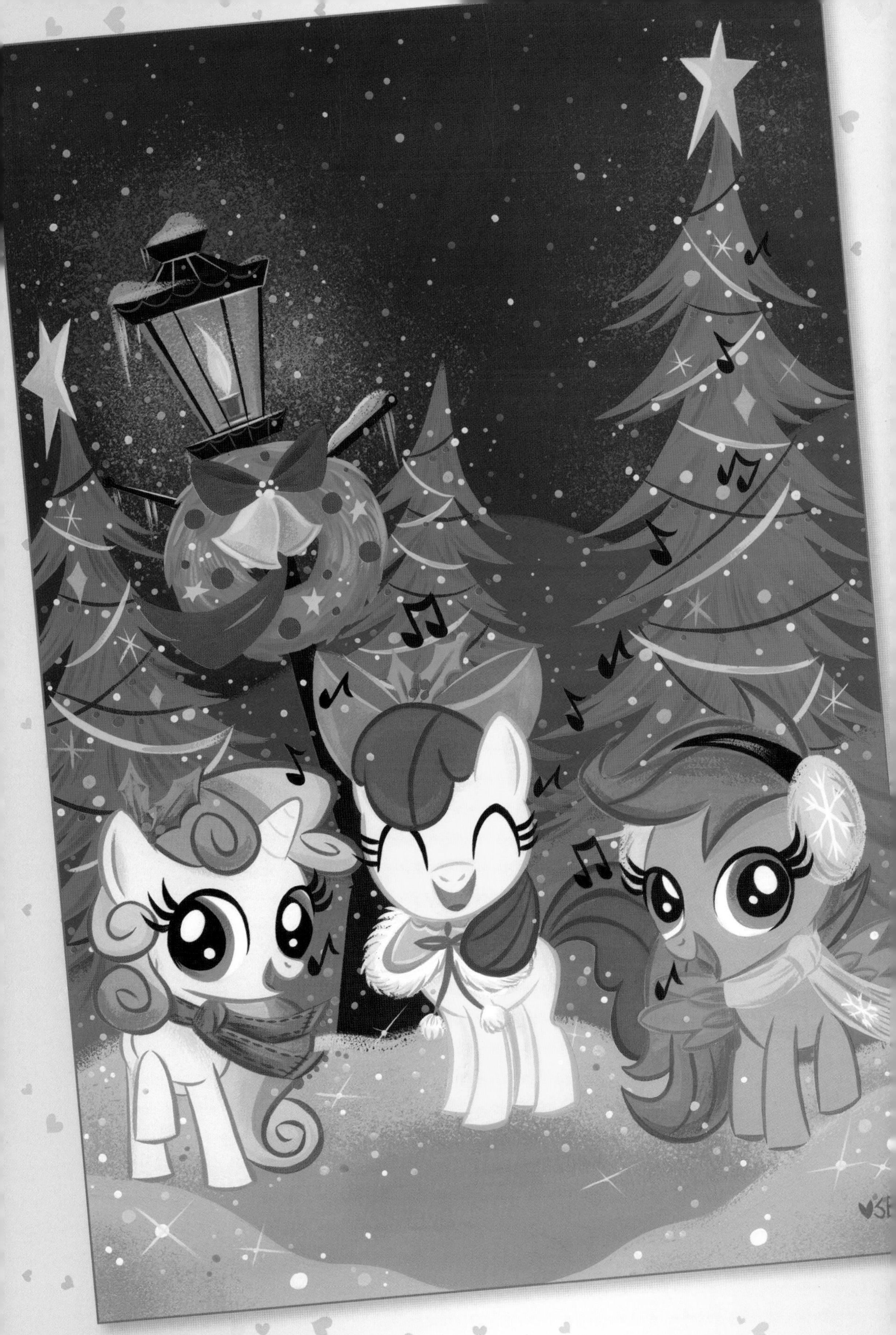

art BY Stephanie Buscema

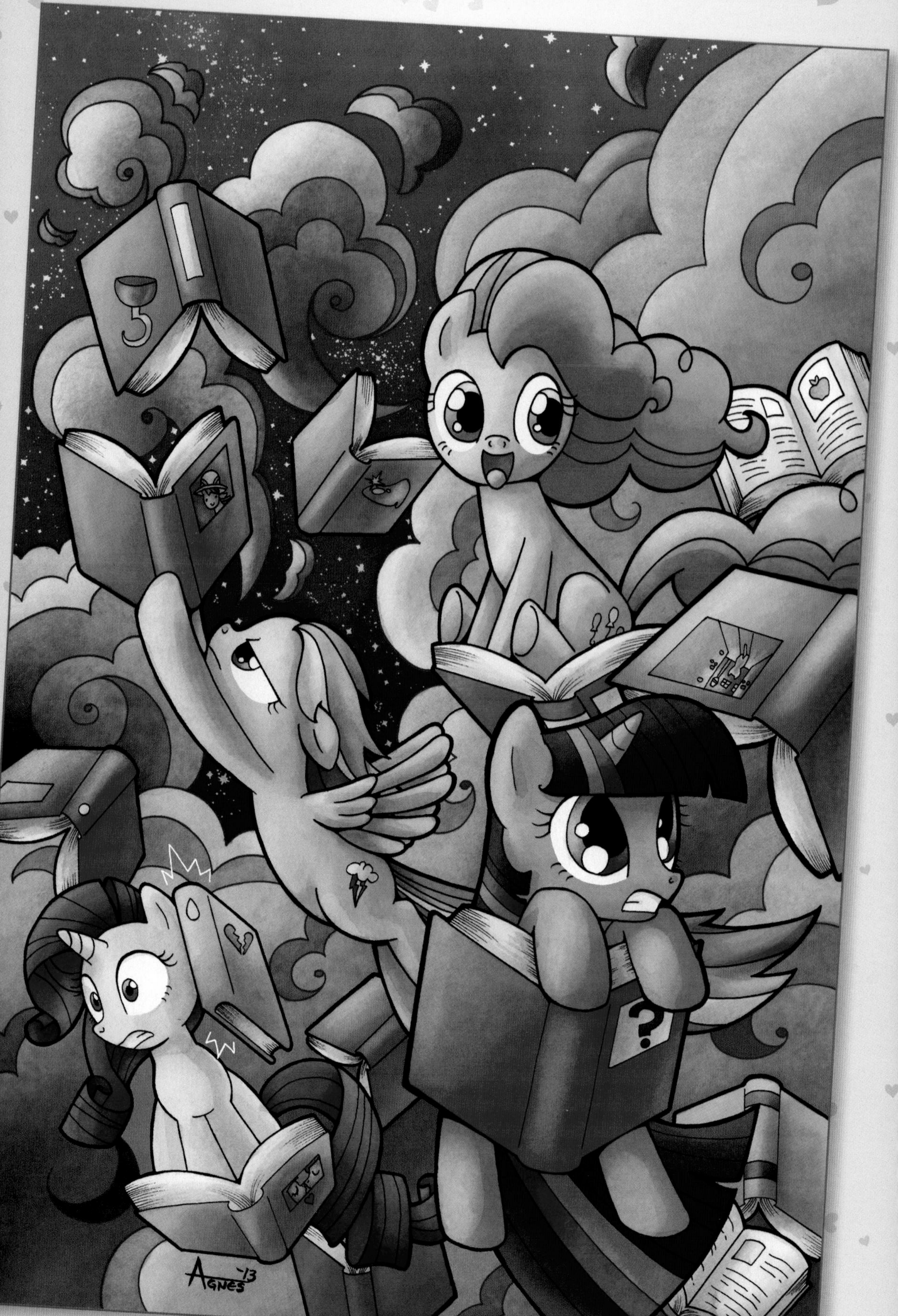
Agnes '13

art BY Agnes Garbowska

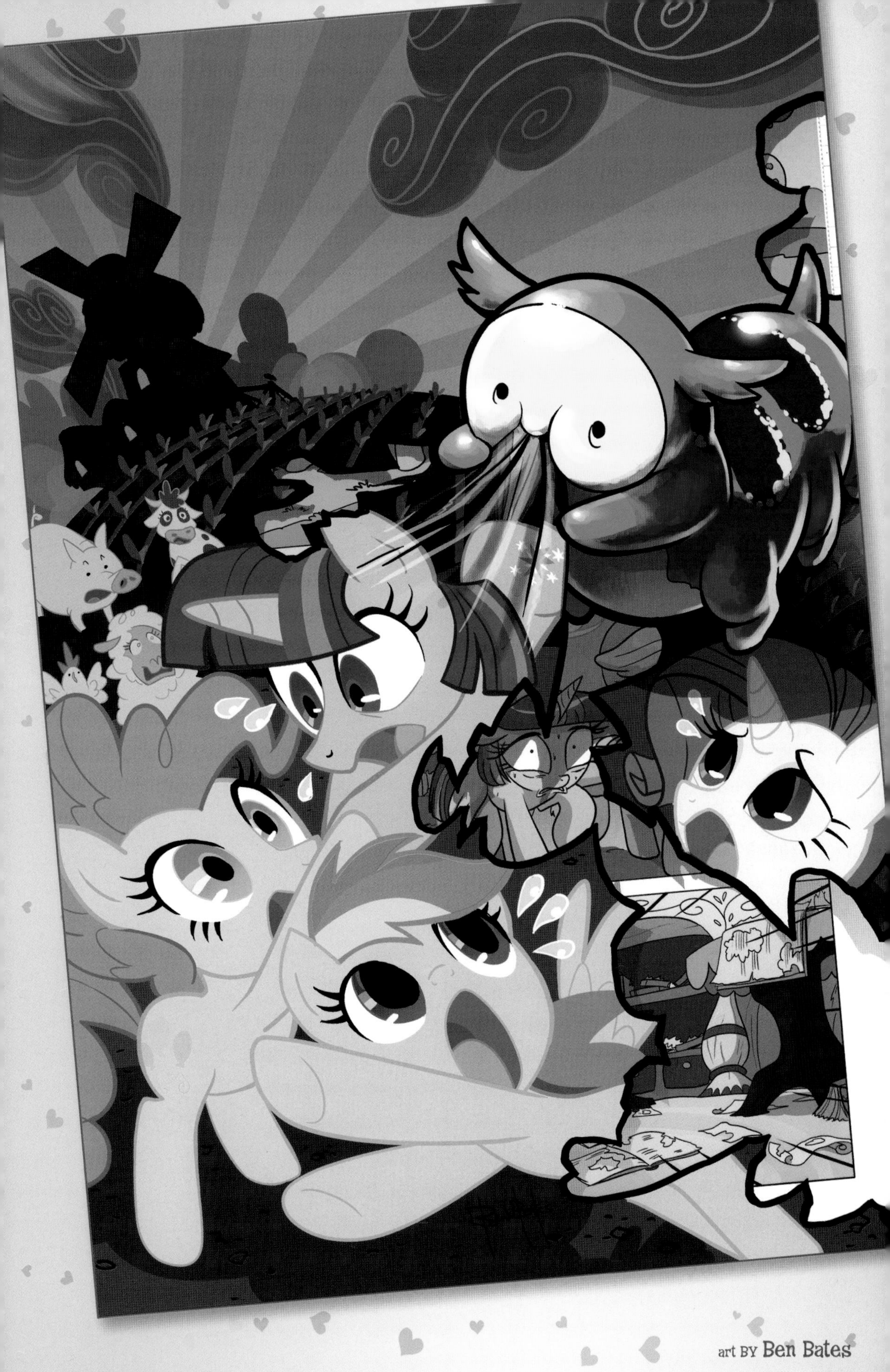

art BY Ben Bates

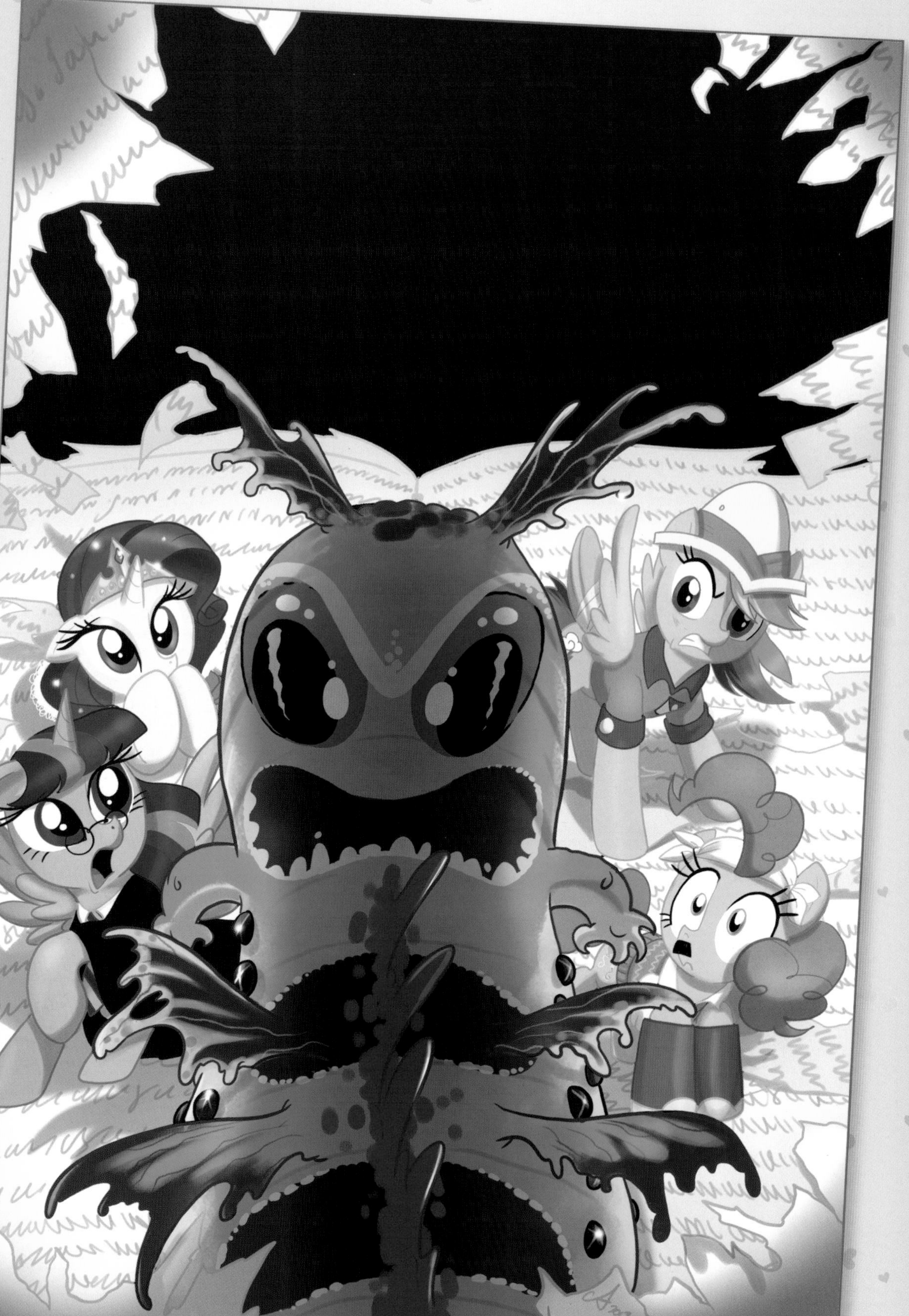

art BY Amy Mebberson

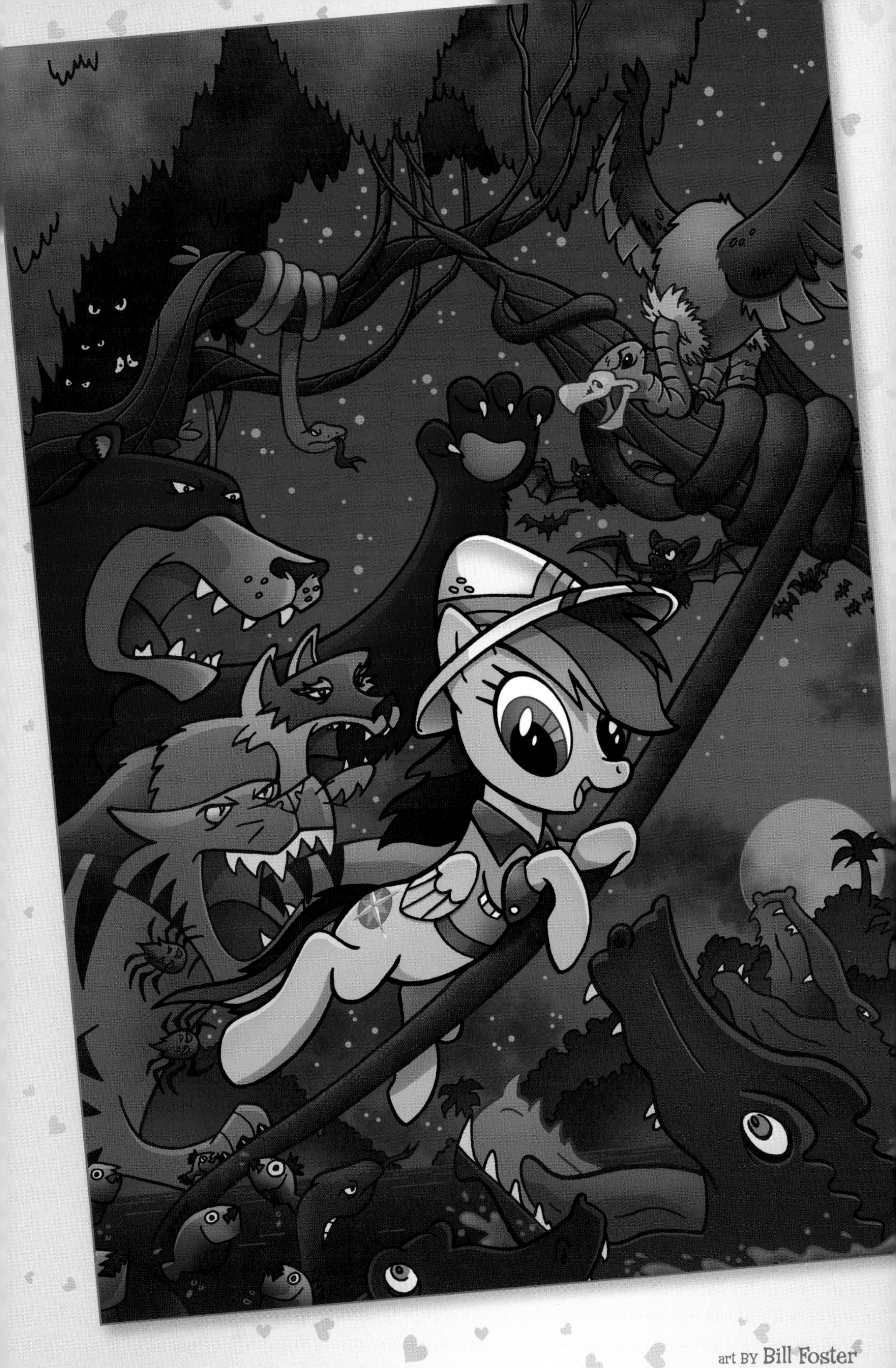

art BY Bill Foster